The Divine Comedy:
Selected Cantos

La divina commedia:
Canti scelti

The Divine Comedy: Selected Cantos

La divina commedia: Canti scelti

A Dual-Language Book

DANTE ALIGHIERI

Edited and Translated by
STANLEY APPELBAUM

DOVER PUBLICATIONS, INC.
Mineola, New York

Bibliographical Note

This Dover edition, first published in 2000, includes the full Italian text of 33 cantos from *La divina commedia* (reprinted from a standard edition), accompanied by a new English translation by Stanley Appelbaum, who also made the selection and wrote the Introduction, notes, and summaries of all omitted cantos.

Library of Congress Cataloging-in-Publication Data

Dante Alighieri, 1265–1321.
    [Divina commedia. English & Italian. Selections]
    The divine comedy : selected cantos = La divina commedia : canti scelti : a dual language book / Dante Alighieri ; edited and translated by Stanley Appelbaum.
       p. cm.
    ISBN 0-486-41127-3
    1. Dante Alighieri, 1265–1321—Translations into English. I. Title: Divina commedia : canti scelti. II. Appelbaum, Stanley. III. Title.

PQ4315.15 .A67 2000
851'.1—dc21
                                      99-056403

Manufactured in the United States of America
Dover Publications, Inc., 31 East 2nd Street, Mineola, N.Y. 11501

Contents

Paradiso / Paradise

INTRODUCTION

Dante's Life and Times

Dante's earthly existence is so scantily documented that even brief biographical sketches must be based on stray statements in his own writings and unverifiable reports by contemporaries and near-contemporaries. Stripping away the accumulation of obvious legends and unwarranted assumptions, the main facts appear to be as follows:

Dante (the name is a short form of Durante) Alighieri was born in Florence in late May of 1265. The family was technically noble—an ancestor had been knighted during the Second Crusade, more than a hundred years earlier—but the poet's father did not hold a high, or even highly respectable, position in society. Florence, like other cities of central and northern Italy at the time, was an independent city-state, similar to ancient Athens. These cities—in Dante's day, increasingly tending to change over from free "communes" into noblemen's possessions (*signorie*)—fought one another, leagued with one another, conquered one another, and set up shifting spheres of influence over one another. The papal domain, centering on Rome, divided these cities geographically from the south of Italy, which kept changing masters in Dante's lifetime: from the Hohenstaufen dynasty of Holy Roman Emperors, to the house of Anjou (Charles I of Anjou was a brother of the sainted French king Louis IX), then partially (the island of Sicily) to the kingdom of Aragon.

In 1277 Dante was betrothed to Gemma Donati, whom he later married. She was a distant cousin of Forese Donati, who was apparently to become a partner in Dante's carousals of the 1290s, and of Forese's brother, Corso Donati, who, as head of the "Black" faction of the Florentine Guelfs, was to become a political nemesis of the "White" Dante. (The entire era falls beneath the shadow of the opposition between Guelfs and Ghibellines.) Originating as 12th-century rival parties in Germany—Welf and Waiblingen—contending for the imperial throne, these parties, when later transferred to Italy, stood for other principles. Basically speaking—there were many nuances, especially because Italian politicians often used party affiliations as covers for family feuds and personal vendettas—the Ghibellines favored a strong presence of the emperor in Italy, whereas the Guelfs opposed this and sided with the popes. From Dante's infancy on, the Ghibellines were in permanent exile from Florence, but the local Guelfs subsequently divided into the above-mentioned factions.

It is clear from Dante's writings that he had a good education, but the details are disputed. Evidently, he enjoyed at least the mentorship of the older poet Brunetto Latini, whose *Tesoretto* ("Little Treasure") was a model for the *Divina Commedia* as an allegorical journey-poem, even suggesting specific details.

In 1289 Dante, who had already begun to write poetry, probably participated in two of his city's military actions: in June, the battle of Campaldino, with the city of Arezzo as adversary, and, in August, the capture of the Pisan fortress of Caprona. The 1290s seem to have been years of either a madcap existence, or of private philosophical studies, or both. They certainly were years of political endeavor.

In 1295, merely as a technical prerequisite for political service, Dante joined a professional guild, that of the doctors and apothecaries. In the next few years, he filled several minor offices, until he became one of the high magistrates called *priori* for the period June 15–August 15 of 1300 (the year of his fictional journey in the *Commedia*). One of the accomplishments of his group of *priori* was the brief banishment of peace-disturbing politicos of every persuasion, including Dante's own friend Guido Cavalcanti, a leading light of the *dolce stil novo* school of poetry that Dante brought to its peak.

In October of 1301, not knowing he would never again set foot in Florence, Dante was sent to Rome as one of three Florentine ambassadors to Pope Boniface VIII. Meanwhile, the duplicitous pope sent the high-born military adventurer Charles de Valois to Florence to "regulate" local affairs. Charles favored the Black faction, allowing them to achieve a very successful coup d'état. In 1302, Dante, in absentia, was charged with embezzlement and other crimes, fined, and banished for two years; before the year was over, his sentence was changed to death. After a couple of bungled White attempts to regain

Florence, Dante fell afoul of his fellow exiles, and became "a party of one."

During the remainder of his life he lived as a more or less honored guest at the courts of various north Italian lords, of course continuing to write all the while. In 1304, Dante found himself at Verona, where his host was Bartolommeo della Scala, and at Treviso. In 1306, he was a guest of the Malaspina family in Lunigiana. Hope of a sort flared up again when Emperor Henry VII came to Italy in 1311 to be crowned in Rome (his immediate predecessors had neglected to follow this precedent of Charlemagne's)—until Henry died of disease in 1313 without having accomplished anything for himself or for Dante (by putting pressure on the papacy to alter the Florentine viewpoint).

Later in 1313, Dante accepted the Veronese hospitality of perhaps his most distinguished patron, Cangrande della Scala, younger brother of the deceased Bartolommeo. In 1319, Dante moved to his final temporary haven, Ravenna. In 1320, he visited Verona to deliver a lecture on scientific geography. In 1321, after a diplomatic journey to Venice on his host's behalf, Dante died in Ravenna in mid-September, perhaps of malaria.

Works Other Than the *Commedia*

Mention of Dante's writings has been separated here from the sketch of his life because of the great difficulty of dating most of them. The towering reputation of the *Commedia* has led to the frequent designation of his other works as "minor," but some of them, especially the *Rime* and the *Vita nova*, are in fact great, and would have secured him a high reputation even if he had written nothing else.

The *Rime* ("Verses"), or *Canzoniere* ("Songbook"), is a posthumous collection of all the lyric poetry that Dante wrote between ca. 1285 and ca. 1306. His earlier poems are representative of the *dolce stil novo*, the specifically Florentine descendant of Provençal troubadour poetry and that of the earlier 13th-century Sicilian and Bolognese "schools." *Dolce stil novo* is characterized technically by great smoothness and euphony, while its content is a glorification of the beloved woman, who is etherealized until practically angelicized. Reflections of this style are to be found in the *Commedia*, particularly in the episodes dealing with Francesca (*Hell*, Canto V) and Matelda (*Purgatory*, Canto XXVIII). Many of Dante's later lyrics are much more dense with meaning and philosophical concepts.

The *Vita nova* (or *nuova*; meaning "New Life," but also "Youth") was written about 1292. In it Dante assembled a number of his *dolce stil novo* lyrics, connecting them with a limpid prose narrative that can be called a spiritual or mystic autobiography. Here he speaks of his overpowering love for a woman named Beatrice ("she who makes blessed"), whom he first met when he was nine, and she somewhat younger, and then again when he was eighteen. (One of Dante's sons later reported that this was Bice Portinari, who was married ca. 1287 and died in 1290, presumably in childbirth.) Even some of the soberest Dantologists seem to accept these meetings at ages nine and eighteen as gospel truth, but the frequency of references, in both the *Vita nova* and the *Commedia*, to the numbers three, nine, and their multiples in connection with Beatrice casts suspicion on the strict historical accuracy of these statements. At any rate, in the *Vita*, Dante reports Beatrice's death and his subsequent moral disorientation, ending with a promise to write a further work greater than any other ever dedicated to a mortal woman.

The *Convivio* ("Banquet"), probably written in the middle of the first decade of the 14th century, was left incomplete. In it, Dante intended to offer a philosophical "banquet" or "symposium" of poems and commentaries, choosing several of his later, more complex lyrics, and displaying vast amounts of erudition in extremely long prose explanations.

The Latin work *De vulgari eloquentia* ("On Literature in the Vernacular") was begun at about the same time as the *Convivio* and also was left incomplete. It is an important "defense" of fine writing in Italian (instead of in the international Latin of the scholarly community of Europe). Among the topics pregnant with significance for the *Commedia* and subsequent Italian literature are an evaluation of the suitability of various Italian dialects as a national standard, favoring Tuscan, and an enumeration of various levels of meaning in high-level literary works, including the allegorical, the practical-moral, and the spiritual.

The Latin work *Monarchia*, completed by 1313 and associated with Henry VII's stay in Italy, is Dante's major political statement. The institutions of the papacy and the Holy Roman Empire, he declares, are two separate and equally necessary bulwarks of Christian European life, and should not encroach on one another, let alone try to gain supremacy. Emperors who have neglected Italy, and popes who have amassed temporal power, are equally to blame for the catastrophic state of affairs Dante sees around him. These are basic, constantly recurring, themes in the *Commedia*.

Thirteen Latin epistles to various persons are dated between 1304 and 1316. The authenticity of the most fascinating ones has been called in question, including the letter to Cangrande della Scala concerning the plan of, and the levels of meaning in, the *Commedia*.

Two Latin eclogues, written about 1320, are truly of minor importance, while the Latin lecture that Dante delivered in Verona in 1320, the *Quaestio de aqua et terra* ("Question of the Water and Land"), is connected with the now peculiar-sounding geographical concepts of the *Commedia*.

The *Divina Commedia*

The *Commedia*, not only Dante's masterpiece but undeniably one of the greatest works of world literature, is a summation of all of Dante's skill and thought. It combines elements of various ancient and medieval literary genres: the vision (perhaps in a dream), the otherworld journey, the allegory, the encyclopedia of arts and sciences, the religious and political plaidoyer, and the very personal autobiography.

The dating of it is fraught with controversy. Some scholars believe it was begun even before Dante's exile. It was probably complete by the time Dante arrived in Ravenna. Throughout the poem, Dante maintains the fiction that his journey is taking place in the spring of 1300. All later events that he records are cast in the form of prophecies made to him by departed souls; the latest such event seems to date to 1313.

The year of the fictional journey, 1300, was important for Dante politically, but it was also a jubilee year in Rome, proclaimed by Boniface VIII. Dante's trip to the afterlife takes place in late March or early April, and lasts several days—perhaps from Good Friday to the middle of Easter week.

In every aspect of the work, Dante makes use of significant or "perfect" numbers, especially three and its multiples, in honor of the Trinity. Each of the three main parts (*cantiche*)—Hell, Purgatory, and *Paradise*—is divided into 33 "chapters" called cantos ("songs"), *Hell* being provided with an additional initial canto that can be seen as an introduction to the whole work; this makes a grand total of 100 cantos. (The cantos vary in length from 115 to 160 lines, the most frequently occurring line counts being 136 and 142.) There are many other large and small principles of organization; for example, Dante makes a major programmatic statement in the sixth canto of each *cantica*; many cantos contain formal repetitive patterns of phraseology and versification; each *cantica* ends with the word *stelle* ("stars").

The adjective *divina* was first officially attached to the title of the work in a Venetian printed edition of 1555, but Dante himself called it a *commedia*. As opposed to a *tragedia* (stage use is not implied), which ends in a bad situation and ought to employ only the most elevated language, his *commedia* ends most happily and employs many levels of speech. The scatology and highjinks of *Hell* are no longer to be found in the next two *cantiche,* but humor never disappears totally (in Canto XXI of *Purgatory,* Dante "blows Vergil's cover" by grinning broadly when Statius praises his poetic predecessor, unaware that he is addressing him), and, even in Paradise, Dante's feisty ancestor Cacciaguida can make the homespun statement, "Let them scratch where they itch!"

The translation and summaries in this dual-language edition trace the topography of Dante's three otherworldly regions in great detail. However, a few introductory words may be in order.

Hell is a funnel-shaped cavity, narrowing as it descends, located beneath the site of Jerusalem, which is the center of the surface of the northern hemisphere of the earth, the hemisphere that contains all the human inhabitants and virtually all the dry land. After a vestibule, or Ante-Hell, peopled by the souls of the listless, one must cross the Acheron to arrive at the first five circles, hugging the rim of the cavity: Limbo and the circles containing damned souls who were "incontinent" in various ways (the fifth circle is the swamp of Styx). Then comes the wall enclosing the City of Dis, and, next, the sixth circle (heretics). The seventh circle, that of the violent, is subdivided into three concentric rings, the first of which is the burning river Phlegethon. A steep bank leads down to the eighth circle, that of the fraudulent, which contains ten separate moats connected by transverse bridges. Moving down the well of giants, one arrives at the frozen lake of Cocytus, the four-zoned ninth circle of traitors, in the extremely narrow center of which is huge Lucifer himself and the three men he personally punishes. This is the center of the earth, and a dark cavern leads one ultimately to the earth's surface opposite Jerusalem, the southern hemisphere, in which only the mountainous island of Purgatory protrudes above the sea.

On that island, beyond the beach, the lowest part of the mountain-side, Ante-Purgatory, houses four groups of variously negligent (or murdered) but repentant souls. The gate to Purgatory proper is guarded by an angel who marks Dante's forehead with seven P's (for seven sins) that must be erased along the way, so that he, too, though still alive, is "purged" in readiness for Paradise. After that gate, the mountain has seven terraces around its perimeter, which are connected by steep rock-cut flights of stairs, each with its angel. The faults of those residing on the first three terraces may be summed up as love of an improper object; of those on the fourth, insufficiently vigorous love; of those on the fifth through seventh, excessively vigorous love. On top of the whole mountain is the earthly paradise once given to Adam and Eve.

The scheme of Paradise is a Christianized version of the pre-Copernican, Ptolemaic universe: the earth is at the center, unmoving, while nine concentric spheres move around it: the heavens of the seven "planets" (moon, Mercury, Venus, sun, Mars, Jupiter, Saturn; each housing appropriate souls), the heaven of the fixed stars, and the Primum Mobile (First Mover). Above that is the Empyrean, with its "rose" of saints and, at the very top, nine orders of angels circling the Trinity.

The poetic line (verse) used in the *Commedia* is the *endecasillabo* (eleven-syllable line), in which there is no necessarily regular alternation of strong and weak syllables, but which nevertheless frequently resembles English iambic pentameter with a "feminine" ending (the last two syllables are necessarily strong and weak, respectively). Occasionally there is a "masculine" ending (on a strong syllable), so that the line has only ten syllables; or a succession of two weak syllables after the last strong one, so that there are twelve in all. In counting the Italian syllables, it should be remembered that, *most* of the time, a vowel at the end of a word is read as if forming one composite sound with a vowel at the beginning of the word following (within the same line):

$$
\begin{array}{ccccccccccc}
1 & 2 & 3 & 4 & 5 & 6 & 7 & 8 & 9 & 10 & 11
\end{array}
$$

Ah quanto a dir qual era è cosa dura
STRONG WEAK

In further honor of the Trinity, the rhyme scheme is *terza rima* (if not invented by Dante, certainly it was here given its first important use): ABA BCB CDC DED, etc., beginning anew with each canto. On very rare occasions, to create a special effect, a single word (e.g., *Cristo* or *vidi*) is used three times in place of rhyming words. There are other technical variations.

Considering the time of writing, readers with some proficiency in the language will find that Dante's Italian is amazingly "current" and understandable—especially when a comparison is made with the much huger gap between medieval and modern forms of, say, English, German, and French. (The *Commedia* is fifty years earlier than *Sir Gawain and the Green Knight,* for instance!) Naturally, semantic and morphological changes (too numerous to list in a brief introduction) have taken place, but these are not daunting, and all should become clear when the reader compares the original text with the facing translation.

The language is basically Tuscan—more specifically, Florentine—but, when necessary (and especially to meet the grueling demands of his rhyme scheme), Dante does not hesitate to borrow word forms from other literary Italian dialects of the 13th century, such as Sicilian and Bolognese. Difficulties in Dante are not due to his language, but to his love of involved periphrasis, and to the inability of most modern readers to recognize many references to people and events that would have been immediately recognizable to his informed contemporaries. (In one passage he says that he made a point of mentioning famous people only!)

The greatness of the *Commedia* was soon perceived, and there are numerous early manuscript copies, some with remarkable illuminated illustrations. (Other important illustrators through the centuries have included Botticelli, Blake, and Doré. Countless musical works have also been based on the *Commedia.*) In the course of time there have been innumerable Italian editions and commentaries, and for some time "Dantology" has been a veritable industry in Italy—and rightly so. Although Dante occupies a pinnacle in world literature, he is particularly significant within the purely Italian context: he was the single most important consolidator of the national standard language (Italian fully separated itself from Latin only in the 10th century, and really did not possess a literature of world-class merit before Saint Francis and the lyric poets early in the 13th), supplying a foundation for much, if not all, that was to come.

This Dual-Language Edition

This volume contains, in Italian and in a new English translation, just under a full third of the entire work: 33 cantos out of the 100 (13 from the 34 of *Hell,* and ten each from the 33 each of *Purgatory* and

Paradise). Each canto included is complete; thus, not only do we provide the unbroken "building blocks" of the poem, but in each case the rhyme scheme is complete, and famous passages appear meaningfully within their exact context.

The cantos selected, in addition to the essential first three, which set the stage for the entire work and for *Hell* in particular, include those featuring Dante's four most celebrated interlocutors (Francesca, Farinata, Ulysses, and Ugolino) and those containing his most famous sustained passages (on the servitude of Italy, on the pains of exile, . . .), as well as cantos that discuss the arts of literature and painting, and a number of striking cantos that are representative of their respective *cantiche* (grisliness and burlesque black humor in *Hell,* a highly philosophical disquisition typical of the many such in *Purgatory,* and the stunningly beautiful final cantos of *Paradise*).

For the 67 cantos not translated *in extenso,* summaries have been provided in the proper places, to provide continuity. Although these summaries are necessarily brief, they go beyond a mere indication of the characters and events. They clearly identify the particular circle of Hell (and subdivisions), terrace of Purgatory, or heaven of Paradise that Dante is in, with the nature of their respective residents. They indicate the progression of time, so important to the poet. They enunciate the basic principles—theological, scientific, or otherwise—contained in many cantos; and they even supply such details as the progressive pattern of hymns sung at the different levels of Purgatory. Thus, readers will have a full introductory presentation of the work.

The Italian text adopted here is an extremely reliable one, with the advantage of up-to-date word spacing and punctuation. The translation (for which reference was made to three 20th-century commented editions of the Italian text and two fairly literal 19th-century English translations) is unlike any other known to this translator (but there have been so many that it was impossible even to glance at all!). There have been English prose and verse translations. Among those in verse, some have been in blank verse of varying line lengths, but with no attempt to make the English lines match the Italian in number (and, thus, in content), while others have attempted varying rhyme schemes (in English, always more of a glaring tour de force than in Italian, and almost axiomatically necessitating a further departure in meaning). The literal translation for this dual-language edition is strictly line-for-line (when not clause-for-clause); where differences in syntax precluded this, the sense is usually redistributed between two lines only, and very rarely among three.

The diction is modern American English, formal but (it is hoped) not too stiff (an occasional obsolescent conjunction or adverb, such as "lest" or "therefrom," was used to clarify the complicated syntax as succinctly as possible). Every attempt was made to avoid ambiguity (a curse of the 19th-century translations). Once in a while, an explanatory word, implicit though not actually present in the Italian, was added to clarify a situation quickly without a plethora of footnotes.

Nevertheless, there are new footnotes as well: more than five hundred of them (numbered afresh for each canto). It must be emphasized that these notes are intentionally brief and simple (to keep the pages uncluttered); their primary purpose is to give the reader unfamiliar with Dante—right on the same page—just enough information to keep on reading intelligently without being brought to a halt by difficulties in the text. Many of the notes identify the people Dante meets or hears about; others give the "key" to his often involved periphrases (he may take two or three lines merely to connote "the sun" or "the moon"). Yet others supply specialized historical or other data as deemed necessary (the reader is expected to have a general knowledge of history, geography, Christianity, etc., or access to at least a one-volume reference book). Once in a while, a note will point out an allegorical interpretation of a person or event, where the reader probably would miss an important point otherwise; but there is never any real analysis. A handful of notes supply variant readings of the Italian text based on different manuscript traditions (along with the corresponding modifications of the translation); while a very few report alternative interpretations of given words, phrases, or passages (such examples could have been multiplied considerably).

The Divine Comedy: Selected Cantos

La divina commedia: Canti scelti

INFERNO

Canto I

Nel mezzo del cammin di nostra vita
  mi ritrovai per una selva oscura
  chè la diritta via era smarrita.
Ah quanto a dir qual era è cosa dura
  esta selva selvaggia e aspra e forte
  che nel pensier rinova la paura!
Tant'è amara che poco è più morte;
  ma per trattar del ben ch'io vi trovai,
  dirò dell'altre cose ch'i' v'ho scorte.
Io non so ben ridir com'io v'entrai,
  tant'era pieno di sonno a quel punto
  che la verace via abbandonai.
Ma poi ch'i' fui al piè d'un colle giunto,
  là dove terminava quella valle
  che m'avea di paura il cor compunto,
guardai in alto, e vidi le sue spalle
  vestite già de' raggi del pianeta
  che mena dritto altrui per ogni calle.
Allor fu la paura un poco queta
  che nel lago del cor m'era durata
  la notte ch'i' passai con tanta pièta.
E come quei che con lena affannata
  uscito fuor del pelago alla riva
  si volge all'acqua perigliosa e guata,
così l'animo mio, ch'ancor fuggiva,
  si volse a retro a rimirar lo passo
  che non lasciò già mai persona viva.

HELL

Canto I

Midway in our life's journey[1]
  I found I was[2] in a dark forest,
  for I had strayed from the straight path.
Oh, how hard a thing it is to tell what it was like,
  this wild, rough forest, difficult to traverse,
  the thought of which brings back my fear!
It is so bitter that death is little less so;
  but, to discourse on the benefits I found there,
  I shall speak of the other things I perceived in it.
I cannot well report how I entered it,
  so full of slumber was I at that moment
  when I forsook the true way.
But after I had arrived at the foot of a hill
  that formed the end of that valley
  which had pierced my heart with fear,
I looked upward and saw the higher slopes
  already mantled in the rays of the planet[3]
  that guides one straight along every road.
Then that fear was somewhat calmed
  which had remained in the pool of my heart
  all that night I had spent in such anguish.
And like a man who, with panting breath,
  having stepped forth out of the sea onto the shore,
  turns back toward the perilous waters and gazes,
thus my mind, which was still fleeing,
  turned back to look upon the passage[4]
  that had never released a living person.

---

1. That is, at age 35, taking 70 as a normal life span.   2. Or: "I came to my senses."
3. The sun.   4. The forest.

3

Poi ch'èi posato un poco il corpo lasso,
   ripresi via per la spiaggia diserta,
   sì che 'l piè fermo sempre era 'l più basso.
Ed ecco, quasi al cominciar dell'erta,
   una lonza leggiera e presta molto,
   che di pel maculato era coverta;
e non mi si partìa d'innanzi al volto,
   anzi impediva tanto il mio cammino,
   ch'i' fui per ritornar più volte volto.
Temp'era dal principio del mattino,
   e 'l sol montava 'n su con quelle stelle
   ch'eran con lui quando l'amor divino
mosse di prima quelle cose belle;
   sì ch'a bene sperar m'era cagione
   di quella fera alla gaetta pelle
l'ora del tempo e la dolce stagione;
   ma non sì che paura non mi desse
   la vista che m'apparve d'un leone.
Questi parea che contra me venesse
   con la test'alta e con rabbiosa fame,
   sì che parea che l'aere ne temesse.
Ed una lupa, che di tutte brame
   sembiava carca nella sua magrezza,
   e molte genti fè già viver grame,
questa mi porse tanto di gravezza
   con la paura ch'uscìa di sua vista,
   ch'io perdei la speranza dell'altezza.
E qual è quei che volontieri acquista,
   e giugne 'l tempo che perder lo face,
   che 'n tutt'i suoi pensier piange e s'attrista;
tal mi fece la bestia sanza pace,
   che, venendomi incontro, a poco a poco
   mi ripigneva là dove 'l sol tace.
Mentre ch'i' ruvinava in basso loco,
   dinanzi alli occhi mi si fu offerto
   chi per lungo silenzio parea fioco.

After I had rested my weary body a little,
  I resumed my journey along the deserted rising ground,
  in such a way that the foot with a firm hold was always the lower one.
And behold, almost at the beginning of the rise,
  a nimble and very swift leopard,
  which was covered with spotted fur;[5]
and it did not depart from before my face;
  rather, it so obstructed my path
  that I turned to go back several times.
The hour was very early in the morning,
  and the sun was climbing upward in the company of those stars
  which were with it when Divine Love
first set those beautiful objects in motion;[6]
  so that the time of day and the mild season
  gave me cause to entertain optimistic hopes
about that beast with the speckled coat;
  but not so much so that I failed to take fright
  at the sight of a lion that appeared before me.
It seemed to be coming at me
  with its head held high and with a ravenous hunger,
  so that the very air seemed to be afraid of it.
And a she-wolf, which, emaciated as she was,
  seemed laden down with every sort of passion,
  and had already made many people live in melancholy,
aroused so much distress in me
  through the horror that issued from the sight of her
  that I lost all hopes of gaining the heights.
And like a man who is fond of acquiring possessions,
  and, when the time comes that causes him to lose them,
  weeps and is saddened in all his thoughts,
thus was I affected by the animal devoid of peace,
  which, coming at me, little by little
  was urging me back to the place where the sun is absent.
While I was plunging down into the depths,
  there appeared before my eyes
  one who, through long silence, appeared feeble.[7]

---

5. The three beasts obviously refer to three sins or moral shortcomings of Dante's, but the specific interpretations are hotly disputed.   6. It is late March or early April; the sun is in Aries; it was believed that the world was created in the springtime.   7. Vergil represents human reason, which becomes feeble through neglect and lack of use.

Quando vidi costui nel gran diserto,
  «Miserere di me» gridai a lui,
  «qual che tu sii, od ombra od omo certo!»
Rispuosemi: «Non omo, omo già fui,
  e li parenti miei furon lombardi,
  mantovani per patrïa ambedui.
Nacqui sub Julio, ancor che fosse tardi,
  e vissi a Roma sotto 'l buono Augusto
  al tempo delli dei falsi e bugiardi.
Poeta fui, e cantai di quel giusto
  figliuol d'Anchise che venne da Troia,
  poi che 'l superbo Ilïòn fu combusto.
Ma tu perchè ritorni a tanta noia?
  perchè non sali il dilettoso monte
  ch'è principio e cagion di tutta gioia?»
«Or se' tu quel Virgilio e quella fonte
  che spandi di parlar sì largo fiume?»
  rispuos'io lui con vergognosa fronte.
«O delli altri poeti onore e lume,
  vagliami 'l lungo studio e 'l grande amore
  che m'ha fatto cercar lo tuo volume.
Tu se' lo mio maestro e 'l mio autore;
  tu se' solo colui da cu' io tolsi
  lo bello stilo che m'ha fatto onore.
Vedi la bestia per cu' io mi volsi:
  aiutami da lei, famoso saggio,
  ch'ella mi fa tremar le vene e i polsi.»
«A te convien tenere altro vïaggio»
  rispuose poi che lagrimar mi vide,
  «se vuo' campar d'esto loco selvaggio:
chè questa bestia, per la qual tu gride,
  non lascia altrui passar per la sua via,
  ma tanto lo 'mpedisce che l'uccide;
e ha natura sì malvagia e ria,
  che mai non empie la bramosa voglia,
  e dopo 'l pasto ha più fame che pria.
Molti son li animali a cui s'ammoglia,
  e più saranno ancora, infin che 'l Veltro

When I saw him in the great wasteland,
  I called to him, "Take pity on me,
  whoever you are, departed spirit or living man!"
He answered me: "I am no man, I once was a man,
  and my parents were from northern Italy,
  both natives of Mantua.
I was born when Julius Caesar ruled, though this was late in his reign,
  and I lived in Rome under good Augustus
  in the time of the false and lying gods.
I was a poet, and I sang about that righteous
  son of Anchises[8] who came from Troy
  after haughty Ilium was burned.
But why are you returning to such distress?
  Why do you not climb the delightful mountain
  that is the beginning and cause of all joy?"
"Now, are you that famous Vergil, that fountain
  which gushes forth so rich a stream of language?"
  I answered him with a shamefaced brow.
"O honor and light of all other poets,
  may I derive benefit from the long study and great love
  that made me meditate upon your writings!
You are my teacher and my authority;
  you alone are the man from whom I acquired
  the elegant style that has won me honor.
See the beast that was the cause of my turning back:
  keep me against her, famous sage,
  for she makes my veins and arteries tremble."
"You must undertake a different journey,"
  he replied after seeing me shed tears,
  "if you wish to escape from this wild spot:
for this beast, on account of which you are lamenting,
  allows no man to pass her way,
  but obstructs him until she kills him;
and her nature is so malevolent and evil
  that she never satisfies her lustful cravings,
  and, after her meal, is hungrier than before.
Many are the animals with which she mates,
  and there will be more to come, until the Hound[9]

---

8. The son of Anchises is Aeneas, hero of the *Aeneid,* Vergil's major poem. 9. This messianic hero has been variously identified, often as Dante's Veronese host Cangrande della Scala.

verrà, che la farà morir con doglia.
Questi non ciberà terra nè peltro,
    ma sapïenza, amore e virtute,
    e sua nazion sarà tra feltro e feltro.
Di quella umile Italia fia salute
    per cui morì la vergine Cammilla,
    Eurialo e Turno e Niso di ferute.
Questi la caccerà per ogni villa,
    fin che l'avrà rimessa nello 'nferno,
    là onde invidia prima dipartilla.
Ond'io per lo tuo me' penso e discerno
    che tu mi segui, e io sarò tua guida,
    e trarrotti di qui per luogo etterno,
ove udirai le disperate strida,
    vedrai li antichi spiriti dolenti,
    che la seconda morte ciascun grida;
e vederai color che son contenti
    nel foco, perchè speran di venire
    quando che sia alle beate genti.
Alle qua' poi se tu vorrai salire,
    anima fia a ciò più di me degna:
    con lei ti lascerò nel mio partire;
chè quello imperador che là su regna,
    perch'io fu' ribellante alla sua legge,
    non vuol che 'n sua città per me si vegna.
In tutte parti impera e quivi regge;
    quivi è la sua città e l'alto seggio:
    oh felice colui cu' ivi elegge!»
E io a lui: «Poeta, io ti richeggio
    per quello Dio che tu non conoscesti,
    acciò ch'io fugga questo male e peggio,
che tu mi meni là dove or dicesti,
    sì ch'io veggia la porta di san Pietro
    e color cui tu fai cotanto mesti.»
Allor si mosse, e io li tenni retro.

arrives that will make her die in grief.
He will not feed on lands or coin,
  but on wisdom, love, and valor,
  and he will be born between poor cloths of felt.[10]
He will be the salvation of that humble Italy
  for whom the virgin Camilla,
  Euryalus, Turnus, and Nisus died of their wounds.[11]
He will hunt her down through every city
  until he puts her back into Hell,
  from which the Devil's envy first let her loose.
Therefore, for your own good, I think and judge
  that you should follow me; I shall be your guide
  and I shall draw you away from here through an everlasting place
where you will hear the screams of despair
  and see the ancient sorrowing spirits,
  each of whom laments his second death;
next, you will see those who are contented
  in the midst of their fire because they have hopes of arriving
  among the blessed people whenever their time comes.
Then, if you wish to ascend to the last-named,
  there will be a soul worthier of that than I am:
  I shall leave you with her when I depart;
for that Emperor who reigns up there,
  because I was a rebel to His law,
  does not wish people to enter His city through my agency.[12]
He is supreme master everywhere, but His particular realm is there;
  there lies His city and His lofty throne:
  Oh, happy the man He chooses for abiding there!"
And I said to him: "Poet, I beseech you,
  for the sake of that God you did not know,
  so that I may escape from this evil and worse,
lead me to the places you mentioned,
  so I can see Saint Peter's gate
  and those who you say are so unhappy."
Then he set forth and I kept behind him.

---

10. This intentionally enigmatic line has been endlessly discussed; if Feltro is printed with a capital *F* both times, the reference may be to localities governed by Cangrande.   11. All four are characters in the *Aeneid.*   12. Or: "does not wish me to enter His city."

Canto II

Lo giorno se n'andava, e l'aere bruno
  togliea li animai che sono in terra
  dalle fatiche loro; e io sol uno
m'apparecchiava a sostener la guerra
  sì del cammino e sì della pietate,
  che ritrarrà la mente che non erra.
O muse, o alto ingegno, or m'aiutate;
  o mente che scrivesti ciò ch'io vidi,
  qui si parrà la tua nobilitate.
Io cominciai: «Poeta che mi guidi,
  guarda la mia virtù s' ell'è possente,
  prima ch'all'alto passo tu mi fidi.
Tu dici che di Silvïo il parente,
  corruttibile ancora, ad immortale
  secolo andò, e fu sensibilmente.
Però, se l'avversario d'ogni male
  cortese i fu, pensando l'alto effetto
  ch'uscir dovea di lui e 'l chi e 'l quale,
non pare indegno ad omo d'intelletto;
  ch'e' fu dell'alma Roma e di suo impero
  nell'empireo ciel per padre eletto:
la quale e 'l quale, a voler dir lo vero,
  fu stabilita per lo loco santo
  u' siede il successor del maggior Piero.
Per questa andata onde li dai tu vanto,
  intese cose che furon cagione
  di sua vittoria e del papale ammanto.
Andovvi poi lo Vas d'elezïone,
  per recarne conforto a quella fede
  ch'è principio alla via di salvazione.
Ma io perchè venirvi? o chi 'l concede?
  Io non Enëa, io non Paulo sono:
  me degno a ciò nè io nè altri crede.

Canto II

Day was departing, and the dusky air
    was releasing the animals that exist on earth
    from their labors; and I alone
was preparing to undergo the war
    of both the physical and moral strain of the journey,
    which my unerring memory will report.
O Muses, O lofty intellect, aid me now;
    O my mind, which wrote down what I saw,
    here your nobility will be made manifest.
I began: "Poet, you that guide me,
    look upon my strength, whether it is sufficient,
    before you entrust me to the lofty road ahead.
You state that the father of Sylvius,[1]
    while still in the flesh, traveled
    to the immortal life, and lingered there in the body.
Yet, if the Enemy of all evil[2]
    was benevolent toward him, in view of the exalted outcome[3]
    that he would give rise to, and who and what he was,
no reasonable man would find that unjust;
    for he was chosen in the Empyrean[4] as the father
    of noble Rome and its empire:
both of which, truth to tell,
    were fixed upon as the holy site
    where the successor of the greatest Peter has his seat.
On this visit with which you credit him,
    he learned matters that became the reason
    for his victory and the papal robes.
Later, the Chosen Vessel[5] went there
    to bring us encouragement toward that faith
    which is the beginning of the way to salvation.
But why should *I* go there? And who grants it?
    I am not Aeneas, I am not Paul:
    neither I nor anyone else believes I am worthy to do so.

---

1. Aeneas, who visits the lower world in Book VI of the *Aeneid*.   2. God.   3. The founding of Rome, later to be the papal see and the coronation city of the Holy Roman Emperors, Dante's ideal twin world powers.   4. The highest heaven, where God is enthroned.   5. Saint Paul, who mentions a journey to the next world in 2 Corinthians 12.

Per che, se del venire io m'abbandono,
   temo che la venuta non sia folle:
   se' savio; intendi me' ch'i' non ragiono.»
E qual è quei che disvuol ciò che volle
   e per novi pensier cangia proposta,
   sì che dal cominciar tutto si tolle,
tal mi fec'io in quella oscura costa,
   perchè, pensando, consumai la 'mpresa
   che fu nel cominciar cotanto tosta.
«S'i' ho ben la parola tua intesa»
   rispuose del magnanimo quell'ombra,
   «l'anima tua è da viltate offesa;
la qual molte fïate l'omo ingombra
   sì che d'onrata impresa lo rivolve,
   come falso veder bestia quand'ombra.
Da questa tema acciò che tu ti solve,
   dirotti perch'io venni e quel ch'io 'ntesi
   nel primo punto che di te mi dolve.
Io era tra color che son sospesi,
   e donna mi chiamò beata e bella,
   tal che di comandare io la richiesi.
Lucevan li occhi suoi più che la stella;
   e cominciommi a dir soave e piana,
   con angelica voce, in sua favella:
'O anima cortese mantovana,
   di cui la fama ancor nel mondo dura,
   e durerà quanto 'l mondo lontana,
l'amico mio, e non della ventura,
   nella diserta piaggia è impedito
   sì nel cammin, che volt'è per paura;
e temo che non sia già sì smarrito,
   ch'io mi sia tardi al soccorso levata,
   per quel ch'i' ho di lui nel cielo udito.
Or movi, e con la tua parola ornata
   e con ciò c'ha mestieri al suo campare
   l'aiuta, sì ch'i' ne sia consolata.
I' son Beatrice che ti faccio andare;
   vegno del loco ove tornar disio;

So that, if I readily assent to the journey,
    I fear it may be an act of folly:
    you are wise; your understanding surpasses my words."
And, like a man who no longer wishes what he wished before,
    and changes his mind because of second thoughts,
    so that he withdraws totally from his undertaking,
that is how I acted on that dark slope,
    because, by reflecting, I canceled the enterprise
    that had been so speedily accepted at the outset.
"If I have understood your words correctly,"
    replied that shade of the noble-minded man,
    "your soul is oppressed by faintheartedness;
many a time that so encumbers a man
    that it makes him desist from an honorable undertaking,
    just as an animal shies when it mistakes what it sees.
In order for you to free yourself of this fear,
    I shall tell you why I came and what I heard
    at the first moment when I felt sorry for you.
I was among those who are dangling[6]
    when a blessed, beautiful lady called me,
    such a one that I asked her to command me.
Her eyes were gleaming more brightly than a star;[7]
    and she began speaking to me in soft, low tones,
    with an angel's voice, in her parlance:
'O courteous Mantuan soul,
    whose fame still endures in the world,
    and will endure as long as the world continues,
a friend of mine, but not of fortune's,
    on the deserted slope is so impeded
    in his travel that he has turned back out of fear;
and I am afraid he has already gone so far astray
    that I arose too late to help him,
    according to what I have heard about him in heaven.
Now go and, with your eloquent speech
    and with all that is needful for his rescue,
    aid him, so that I may be comforted with regard to him.
I who send you am Beatrice;
    I have come from a place to which I long to return;

---

6. Those in Limbo, neither in Hell nor Paradise. 7. Or: "more brightly than Venus."

amor mi mosse, che mi fa parlare.
Quando sarò dinanzi al signor mio,
  di te mi loderò sovente a lui.'
  Tacette allora, e poi comincia' io:
'O donna di virtù, sola per cui
  l'umana spezie eccede ogni contento
  di quel ciel c'ha minor li cerchi sui,
tanto m'aggrada il tuo comandamento,
  che l'ubidir, se già fosse, m'è tardi;
  più non t'è uo' ch'aprirmi il tuo talento.
Ma dimmi la cagion che non ti guardi
  dello scender qua giuso in questo centro
  dell'ampio loco ove tornar tu ardi.'
'Da che tu vuo' saper cotanto a dentro,
  dirotti brievemente' mi rispose,
  'perch'io non temo di venir qua entro.
Temer si dee di sole quelle cose
  c'hanno potenza di fare altrui male;
  dell'altre no, chè non son paurose.
Io son fatta da Dio, sua mercè, tale,
  che la vostra miseria non mi tange,
  nè fiamma d'esto incendio non m'assale.
Donna è gentil nel ciel che si compiange
  di questo impedimento ov'io ti mando,
  sì che duro giudicio là su frange.
Questa chiese Lucia in suo dimando
  e disse:—Or ha bisogno il tuo fedele
  di te, ed io a te lo raccomando—.
Lucia, nimica di ciascun crudele,
  si mosse, e venne al loco dov'i' era,
  che mi sedea con l'antica Rachele.
Disse:—Beatrice, loda di Dio vera,
  chè non soccorri quei che t'amò tanto,
  ch'uscì per te della volgare schiera?
non odi tu la pièta del suo pianto?
  non vedi tu la morte che 'l combatte
  su la fiumana ove 'l mar non ha vanto?—.

love, which makes me speak, bestirred me.
When I return and face my Master
    I shall often speak highly of you to Him.'
    Then she fell silent, and I began next:
'O virtuous lady, through whom alone
    the human race surpasses all else contained
    in that heaven whose revolutions are smallest,[8]
I am so pleased by your command
    that my obedience would be too late even if it had already taken place;
    you need only disclose your wishes to me.
But tell me why you do not hesitate
    to descend to this lowly region
    from the vast place to which you are eager to return.'
'Seeing that you wish to know in such depth,
    I shall tell you briefly,' she replied,
    'why I do not fear to enter here.
One should fear only those things
    which have the power of doing one harm,
    but not any other things, for they are not frightening.
I was created by God such, thanks to Him,
    that your wretchedness does not affect me,
    nor do the flames of this fire assail me.
There is a noble lady[9] in heaven who feels compassion
    regarding that obstacle I am sending you to overcome,
    so that she is infringing the severe laws up above.
She summoned Saint Lucy to her
    and said: "Now your devotee has need
    of you, and I commend him to you."
Lucy, an enemy to all cruelty,
    departed and came to the place where I was,
    seated alongside the matriarch Rachel.
She said: "Beatrice, God's true praise,
    why are you not aiding the man who loved you so,
    the one who, for your sake, stood out from the common herd?
Do you not hear the anguish of his weeping?
    Do you not see the death that combats him
    on the river so mighty that the sea cannot compare with it?"

---

8. The heaven of the moon, and thus the earth, which is contained within it.
9. The Blessed Virgin, or Prevenient Grace. Saint Lucy, mentioned three lines later, represents Illuminating Grace.

Al mondo non fur mai persone ratte
a far lor pro o a fuggir lor danno,
com'io, dopo cotai parole fatte,
venni qua giù del mio beato scanno,
fidandomi nel tuo parlare onesto,
ch'onora te e quei ch'udito l'hanno.'
Poscia che m'ebbe ragionato questo,
li occhi lucenti lacrimando volse;
per che mi fece del venir più presto;
e venni a te così com'ella volse;
d'innanzi a quella fiera ti levai
che del bel monte il corto andar ti tolse.
Dunque che è? perchè, perchè restai?
perchè tanta viltà nel cuore allette?
perchè ardire e franchezza non hai?
poscia che tai tre donne benedette
curan di te ne la corte del cielo,
e 'l mio parlar tanto ben t'impromette?»
Quali i fioretti, dal notturno gelo
chinati e chiusi, poi che 'l sol li 'mbianca
si drizzan tutti aperti in loro stelo,
tal mi fec'io di mia virtute stanca,
e tanto buono ardire al cor mi corse,
ch'i' cominciai come persona franca:
«Oh pietosa colei che mi soccorse!
e te cortese ch'ubidisti tosto
alle vere parole che ti porse!
Tu m'hai con disiderio il cor disposto
sì al venir con le parole tue,
ch'i' son tornato nel primo proposto.
Or va, ch'un sol volere è d'ambedue:
tu duca, tu segnore, e tu maestro.»
Così li dissi; e poi che mosso fue,
intrai per lo cammino alto e silvestro.

Canto III

PER ME SI VA NELLA CITTÀ DOLENTE,
PER ME SI VA NELL'ETTERNO DOLORE,
PER ME SI VA TRA LA PERDUTA GENTE.

There have never been people in the world so swift
  to secure their welfare or to shun their harm
  than I was after such words were spoken;
I descended here from my blessed seat,
  entrusting myself to your noble speech,
  which honors you and those who have heard it.'
After she had explained all this to me,
  she turned aside her gleaming eyes and wept;
  by doing so she made me more eager to come,
and I came to you as she desired;
  I saved you from that beast
  that cut off your direct path to the beautiful mountain.
And so, what is happening? Why, why do you hang back?
  Why do you lodge such cowardice in your heart?
  Why do you lack boldness and free spirits,
when three such blessed ladies
  are concerned about you in the court of heaven
  and my words promise you so much good?"
As little flowers, bowed and closed
  by nighttime chill, once the sun whitens them
  straighten themselves on their stalks and open fully,
just so I overcame the weariness of my will,
  and so much beneficial boldness flowed into my heart
  that I began to say, like a man set free:
"Oh, how merciful is she who came to my aid!
  And how noble are you who immediately obeyed
  the true words she spoke to you!
You have so disposed my heart to making the journey,
  and ardently, with your words
  that I have returned to my earlier intention.
Proceed now, for we both have one desire:
  you are my guide, my commander, and my instructor."
  Thus I spoke to him; and after he set out
I entered upon the difficult, rugged path.

Canto III

"THROUGH ME ONE PASSES INTO THE CITY OF GRIEF,
  THROUGH ME ONE PASSES INTO ETERNAL SORROW,
  THROUGH ME ONE PASSES AMONG THE LOST PEOPLE.

GIUSTIZIA MOSSE IL MIO ALTO FATTORE:
  FECEMI LA DIVINA POTESTATE,
  LA SOMMA SAPÏENZA E 'L PRIMO AMORE.
DINANZI A ME NON FUOR COSE CREATE
  SE NON ETTERNE, E IO ETTERNA DURO.
  LASCIATE OGNI SPERANZA, VOI CH'ENTRATE.
Queste parole di colore oscuro
  vid'ïo scritte al sommo d'una porta;
  per ch'io: «Maestro, il senso lor m'è duro.»
Ed elli a me, come persona accorta:
  «Qui si convien lasciare ogni sospetto;
  ogni viltà convien che qui sia morta.
Noi siam venuti al loco ov'io t'ho detto
  che tu vedrai le genti dolorose
  c'hanno perduto il ben dell'intelletto.»
E poi che la sua mano alla mia pose
  con lieto volto, ond'io mi confortai,
  mi mise dentro alle segrete cose.
Quivi sospiri, pianti e alti guai
  risonavan per l'aere sanza stelle,
  per ch'io al cominciar ne lagrimai.
Diverse lingue, orribili favelle,
  parole di dolore, accenti d'ira,
  voci alte e fioche, e suon di man con elle
facevano un tumulto, il qual s'aggira
  sempre in quell'aura sanza tempo tinta,
  come la rena quando turbo spira.
E io ch'avea d'error la testa cinta,
  dissi: «Maestro, che è quel ch'i' odo?
  e che gent'è che par nel duol sì vinta?»
Ed elli a me: «Questo misero modo
  tengon l'anime triste di coloro
  che visser sanza infamia e sanza lode.
Mischiate sono a quel cattivo coro
  delli angeli che non furon ribelli
  nè fur fedeli a Dio, ma per sè foro.

JUSTICE ACTIVATED MY LOFTY MAKER:
   I WAS MADE BY DIVINE POWER,
   HIGHEST WISDOM, AND PRIMAL LOVE.[1]
BEFORE ME THERE WERE NO THINGS CREATED
   SAVE ETERNAL ONES,[2] AND I ENDURE ETERNALLY.
   ABANDON ALL HOPE, YOU THAT ENTER."
These words in a dark color
   I saw written at the top of a gate;
   so that I said: "Master, their meaning is hard for me."
And he replied, like a discerning person:
   "Here one must set aside all hesitation;
   here all faintheartedness must be quelled.
We have come to the place where I told you
   you would see the sorrowful folk
   who have lost the mind's highest good."[3]
And, after placing his hand in mine
   with a cheerful expression that comforted me,
   he led me into the secret realm.
Here sighs, laments, and loud wails
   resounded through the starless air,
   so that at first they made me weep.
Various tongues, horrible languages,
   sorrowful words, wrathful tones,
   voices loud and feeble, and the slapping of hands along with them,
created an uproar, which circulates
   always in that dark air which gives no indication of time,
   as sand does when a whirlwind blows.
And I, whose head was garlanded by doubts,
   said: "Master, what is this I hear?
   And what folk is this that seems so overcome by woe?"
And he replied: "This wretched existence
   is the lot of the unhappy souls of those
   who lived without incurring either disgrace or praise.[4]
They are intermingled with that worthless band
   of angels who were neither rebellious
   nor faithful to God, but stood apart.

1. That is (in sequence), the Father, the Son, and the Holy Spirit. 2. Hell was created in response to the revolt of the bad angels, which occurred before anything perishable had been created. 3. That is, the contemplation of Truth, or God. 4. These are people who were "lukewarm" in life, too sluggish to take sides on important issues, even though they were not actively evil.

Caccianli i ciel per non esser men belli,
  nè lo profondo inferno li riceve,
  ch'alcuna gloria i rei avrebber d'elli.»
E io: «Maestro, che è tanto greve
  a lor, che lamentar li far sì forte?»
Rispuose: «Dicerolti molto breve.
Questi non hanno speranza di morte,
  e la lor cieca vita è tanto bassa,
  che 'nvidïosi son d'ogni altra sorte.
Fama di loro il mondo esser non lassa;
  misericordia e giustizia li sdegna:
  non ragioniam di lor, ma guarda e passa.»
E io, che riguardai, vidi una insegna
  che girando correva tanto ratta,
  che d'ogni posa mi parea indegna;
e dietro le venìa sì lunga tratta
  di gente, ch'io non averei creduto
  che morte tanta n'avesse disfatta.
Poscia ch'io v'ebbi alcun riconosciuto,
  vidi e conobbi l'ombra di colui
  che fece per viltà il gran rifiuto.
Incontanente intesi e certo fui
  che questa era la setta de' cattivi,
  a Dio spiacenti ed a' nemici sui.
Questi sciaurati, che mai non fur vivi,
  erano ignudi, stimolati molto
  da mosconi e da vespe ch'eran ivi.
Elle rigavan lor di sangue il volto,
  che, mischiato di lagrime, ai lor piedi
  da fastidiosi vermi era ricolto.
E poi ch'a riguardare oltre mi diedi,
  vidi genti alla riva d'un gran fiume:
  per ch'io dissi: «Maestro, or mi concedi
ch'i' sappia quali sono, e qual costume
  le fa di trapassar parer sì pronte,
  com'io discerno per lo fioco lume.»

The heavens expel them so as not to be less beautiful,
   nor will the depths of Hell accept them,
   lest the damned be able to boast of their presence."
I said: "Master, what is so burdensome
   to them that makes them lament so greatly?"
   He answered: "I shall tell you very briefly.
These people have no hope of dying,
   and their blind life is so lowly
   that they are envious of any other fate.
The world does not allow them to be remembered;
   mercy and justice scorn them:
   let us not discuss them; merely gaze and pass on."
And I, looking again, saw a banner
   moving in a circle so swiftly
   that it seemed disdainful of any halt;[5]
and behind it came such a long train
   of people, that I would not have believed
   that death had undone so many.
After I recognized some of them,
   I saw and identified the shade of the man
   who through cowardice made the great refusal.[6]
At once I understood and was certain
   that this was the group of wretches
   who were displeasing both to God and to His enemies.
These miserable creatures, who were never really alive,
   were naked and were constantly stung
   by blowflies and wasps which were there.
The wasps covered their faces with rivulets of blood,
   which, mingled with tears, at their feet
   was gathered by disgusting worms.
And after I spent further time looking,
   I saw people on the bank of a wide river:
   so that I said: "Master, now grant me
to know of what sort they are, and what kind of existence
   makes them seem so eager to cross over,
   as far as I can make out in this weak light."

---

5. Or: "it seemed never to come to rest, because it was unworthy of being planted."
6. Most commentators take this to be Pope Celestine V, who reigned for only five months in 1294 before abdicating, and thus permitting the election of Dante's nemesis, Boniface VIII.

Ed elli a me: «Le cose ti fier conte
   quando noi fermerem li nostri passi
   su la trista riviera d'Acheronte.»
Allor con li occhi vergognosi e bassi,
   temendo no 'l mio dir li fosse grave,
   infino al fiume del parlar mi trassi.
Ed ecco verso noi venir per nave
   un vecchio, bianco per antico pelo,
   gridando: «Guai a voi, anime prave!
Non isperate mai veder lo cielo:
   i' vegno per menarvi all'altra riva
   nelle tenebre etterne, in caldo e 'n gelo.
E tu che se' costì, anima viva,
   pàrtiti da cotesti che son morti.»
   Ma poi che vide ch'io non mi partiva,
disse: «Per altra via, per altri porti
   verrai a piaggia, non qui, per passare:
   più lieve legno convien che ti porti.»
E 'l duca lui: «Caron, non ti crucciare:
   vuolsi così colà dove si puote
   ciò che si vuole, e più non dimandare.»
Quinci fuor quete le lanose gote
   al nocchier della livida palude,
   che 'ntorno alli occhi avea di fiamme rote.
Ma quell'anime, ch'eran lasse e nude,
   cangiar colore e dibattìeno i denti,
   ratto che 'nteser le parole crude:
bestemmiavano Dio e lor parenti,
   l'umana spezie e 'l luogo e 'l tempo e 'l seme
   di lor semenza e di lor nascimenti.
Poi si raccolser tutte quante inseme,
   forte piangendo, alla riva malvagia
   ch'attende ciascun uom che Dio non teme.
Caron dimonio, con occhi di bragia,
   loro accennando, tutti li raccoglie;
   batte col remo qualunque s'adagia.
Come d'autunno si levan le foglie
   l'una appresso dell'altra, fin che 'l ramo
   vede alla terra tutte le sue spoglie,

And he replied: "These things will be made known to you
  when we bring our steps to a halt
  on the sad banks of the Acheron."
Then, with my eyes shame-filled and downcast,
  fearing lest my words were annoying to him,
  I abstained from speaking till we reached the river.
And behold, coming toward us in a boat,
  an old man, white-haired from age,
  shouting: "Woe to you, wicked souls!
Do not expect ever to see the sky again:
  I come to take you to the other bank
  amid the eternal darkness, the heat, and the cold.
And you over there, the living soul,
  move away from these who are dead."
  But when he saw that I was not moving away,
he said: "By another route, via other ports
  you will come ashore to proceed on your way, not here,
  it is a lighter vessel that must bear you."[7]
And my guide said to him: "Charon, do not get angry:
  it is thus wished in the place where whatever is wished
  is possible, so ask no more questions."
Thereupon the hairy cheeks of the boatman
  of the colorless swamp grew still,
  while flames rotated around his eyes.
But those souls, who were weary and naked,
  changed color, and their teeth chattered,
  as soon as they understood his cruel words:
they cursed God and their parents,
  the human race, and the place, time, and origin
  of their lineage and birth.
Then they all gathered together,
  weeping loudly, on the malevolent banks
  that await every man who does not fear God.
The demon Charon, with eyes like live coals,
  signaling to them, assembled them all,
  beating any straggler with his oar.
Just as, in autumn, leaves detach
  one after another, until the bough
  sees all its lost riches on the ground,

---

7. This is a specific prediction of events occurring later in the poem.

similemente il mal seme d'Adamo
  gittansi di quel lito ad una ad una,
  per cenni come augel per suo richiamo.
Così sen vanno su per l'onda bruna,
  e avanti che sien di là discese,
  anche di qua nuova schiera s'auna.
«Figliuol mio,» disse 'l maestro cortese,
  «quelli che muoion nell'ira di Dio
  tutti convegnon qui d'ogni paese;
e pronti sono a trapassar lo rio,
  chè la divina giustizia li sprona,
  sì che la tema si volve in disio.
Quinci non passa mai anima bona;
  e però, se Caron di te si lagna,
  ben puoi sapere omai che 'l suo dir sona.»
Finito questo, la buia campagna
  tremò sì forte, che dello spavento
  la mente di sudore ancor mi bagna.
La terra lagrimosa diede vento,
  che balenò una luce vermiglia
  la qual mi vinse ciascun sentimento;
e caddi come l'uom che 'l sonno piglia.

[SUMMARY OF CANTO IV: When a thunderclap awakens Dante, he is on the
other side of the Acheron, on the brink of the abyss of Hell. Vergil leads him
down to the first of the circles that ring the abyss, Limbo (or, Limbus), where
he himself resides. This is the eternal home of the unbaptized: children who
died before receiving that rite, or worthy pagans who lived before the coming of Christ. They undergo no physical torment, but continually sigh because they can never see God. At the Harrowing of Hell, Jesus released the

---

Canto V

Così discesi del cerchio primaio
  giù nel secondo, che men luogo cinghia,
  e tanto più dolor, che punge a guaio.

in like manner did the evil descendants of Adam
    cast themselves from that bank one by one,
    obeying signals like a bird responding to the fowler's lure.[8]
Thus they depart upon the brown waters,
    and even before they disembark on the other side,
    a new group assembles over here.
"My son," said my courteous master,
    "those who die in the wrath of God
    all gather here from every country;
and they are eager to cross the river
    because divine justice spurs them on,
    so that their fear is transformed into longing.
Here no good soul ever passes;
    and therefore, if Charon complained about your presence,
    you can now be well aware of what his words signify."[9]
When he had said this, the dark countryside
    trembled so strongly that the memory
    of the fright still bathes me in sweat.
The tear-soaked soil produced a wind
    from which flashed a vermilion light
    that overpowered all my senses,
and I fell like a man overcome by sleep.

---

biblical patriarchs from this circle. In a hemisphere of light piercing the general gloom, the travelers are greeted by the Greek poet Homer and the Latin poets Horace, Ovid, and Lucan, who accept Dante as their equal. On the grounds of a "noble castle," Dante meets various heroes of ancient Roman history and legend, as well as the great Greek and Roman philosophers, moralists, and scholars. Then Vergil leads him on into the darkness again.]

Canto V

Thus I descended from the first circle
    down to the second, which encloses a smaller area
    but all the more suffering, which stimulates lamenting.

---

8. Or: "like a falcon, returning to the falconer when called back."   9. The gist is: Dante will be able to reach the higher realms of the afterlife (and eventually gain salvation).

Stavvi Minòs orribilmente, e ringhia:
  essamina le colpe nell'entrata;
  giudica e manda secondo ch'avvinghia.
Dico che quando l'anima mal nata
  li vien dinanzi, tutta si confessa;
  e quel conoscitor delle peccata
vede qual luogo d'inferno è da essa;
  cignesi con la coda tante volte
  quantunque gradi vuol che giù sia messa.
Sempre dinanzi a lui ne stanno molte:
  vanno a vicenda ciascuna al giudizio;
  dicono e odono, e poi son giù volte.
«O tu che vieni al doloroso ospizio,»
  disse Minòs a me quando mi vide,
  lasciando l'atto di cotanto offizio,
«guarda com'entri e di cui tu ti fide:
  non t'inganni l'ampiezza dell'entrare!...»
  E 'l duca mio a lui: «Perchè pur gride?
Non impedir lo suo fatale andare:
  vuolsi così colà dove si puote
  ciò che si vuole, e più non dimandare.»
Ora incomincian le dolenti note
  a farmisi sentire; or son venuto
  là dove molto pianto mi percuote.
Io venni in luogo d'ogni luce muto,
  che mugghia come fa mar per tempesta,
  se da contrari venti è combattuto.
La bufera infernal, che mai non resta,
  mena li spirti con la sua rapina:
  voltando e percotendo li molesta.
Quando giungon davanti alla ruina,
  quivi le strida, il compianto, il lamento;
  bestemmian quivi la virtù divina.
Intesi ch'a così fatto tormento
  enno dannati i peccator carnali,
  che la ragion sommettono al talento.

There Minos[1] stands in a horrible form, snarling:
   at the entrance he examines each soul's wrongdoing;
   then passes judgment and sends them down, by the way he enlaces himself.
I mean that, when the soul that was born for its own hurt
   comes before him, it makes a full confession;
   and that connoisseur of sin
sees what part of Hell it merits;
   he wraps his tail around himself as many times
   as the number of the circle to which he wants to send it.
Many souls are always standing before him;
   each one appears for judgment in its turn;
   they speak, they hear their fate, and then are whirled away downward.
"O you that have come to the doleful dwelling,"
   Minos said to me when he saw me,
   interrupting the performance of such an important duty,
"take care how you enter and to whom you entrust yourself:
   let not the spaciousness of the entrance deceive you! . . ."
   And my guide said to him: "Why are you shouting, too?
Do not obstruct his destined journey:
   it is thus wished in the place where whatever is wished
   is possible, so ask no more questions."
Now the sorrowing tones begin
   to be audible to me; now I have arrived
   where much weeping shakes me.
I came to a place bereft of all light,
   which bellows like the sea in a storm
   when it is combated by winds from different directions.
The hellish tempest, which never ceases,
   carries the spirits along on its ravaging blast:
   spinning them and shaking them, it causes them distress.
When they arrive in front of the precipice,[2]
   here are the screams, the mourning, the lament;
   here they curse the divine power.
I understood that to torment of this sort
   those are condemned who sin through lust,
   subordinating their reasoning powers to their desires.

---

1. A legendary king of ancient Crete who became a judge in the Greco-Roman Hades.   2. Probably one of the landslides caused by the earthquake at the time of the Harrowing of Hell.

E come li stornei ne portan l'ali
  nel freddo tempo a schiera larga e piena,
  così quel fiato li spiriti mali
di qua, di là, di giù, di su lì mena;
  nulla speranza li conforta mai,
  non che di posa, ma di minor pena.
E come i gru van cantando lor lai,
  faccendo in aere di sè lunga riga,
  così vidi venir, traendo guai,
ombre portate dalla detta briga:
  per ch'i' dissi: «Maestro, chi son quelle
  genti che l'aura nera sì gastiga?»
«La prima di color di cui novelle
  tu vuo' saper» mi disse quelli allotta,
  «fu imperadrice di molte favelle.
A vizio di lussuria fu sì rotta,
  che libito fè licito in sua legge
  per tòrre il biasmo in che era condotta.
Ell'è Semiramìs, di cui si legge
  che succedette a Nino e fu sua sposa:
  tenne la terra che 'l Soldan corregge.
L'altra è colei che s'ancise amorosa,
  e ruppe fede al cener di Sicheo;
  poi è Cleopatràs lussurïosa.
Elena vedi, per cui tanto reo
  tempo si volse, e vedi il grande Achille,
  che con amore al fine combattèo.
Vedi Parìs, Tristano»; e più di mille
  ombre mostrommi, e nominommi, a dito
  ch'amor di nostra vita dipartille.
Poscia ch'io ebbi il mio dottore udito
  nomar le donne antiche e' cavalieri,
  pietà mi giunse, e fui quasi smarrito.
I' cominciai: «Poeta, volontieri
  parlerei a quei due che 'nsieme vanno,
  e paion sì al vento esser leggieri.»

And, just as the wings of starlings carry them off
  in the cold season in a wide, dense flock,
  so did that wind toss the evil spirits there
this way and that, up and down;
  no hope ever consoles them,
  neither of rest, nor even a slackening of their punishment.
And, just as cranes go chanting their lamentations,
  forming a long line in the sky,
  so did I see coming, and uttering wails,
shades carried by the above-mentioned strife of winds:
  so that I said: "Master, who are those
  people whom the dark air punishes so?"
"The first of those about whom you wish
  to be informed," he said to me then,
  "was empress over peoples speaking many languages.
She was so given over to the vice of lust
  that in her laws she made what she desired permissible,
  in order to remove the blame her actions had incurred.
She is Semiramis,[3] of whom we read
  that she followed Nimus on the throne and was his wife:
  she ruled the land that the Sultan now governs.
The second one is the woman[4] who killed herself for love,
  and broke her faith to the ashes of Sichaeus;
  the next one is the lascivious Cleopatra.
Here you see Helen, on whose account so many years
  were evilly spent, and you see the great Achilles,
  who battled with love to the very end.[5]
You see Paris, Tristan"; and more than a thousand
  shades he pointed out to me, naming them,
  whom love had severed from our life.
After I had heard my instructor
  name the ladies and knights of olden days,
  compassion seized me, and I nearly lost my senses.
I began: "Poet, gladly
  would I speak with those two who are proceeding together
  and seem to be so weightless in the wind."

---

3. A legendary incestuous empress of Assyria.   4. Dido, queen of Carthage, widow
of the Tyrian Sichaeus; she had an unfortunate love affair with the hero of Vergil's
Aeneid.   5. In poems later than the *Iliad,* Achilles is credited with several amours, including one with the Trojan princess Polyxena just before his death.

Ed elli a me: «Vedrai quando saranno
   più presso a noi; e tu allor li priega
   per quello amor che i mena, ed ei verranno.»
Sì tosto come il vento a noi li piega,
   mossi la voce: «O anime affannate,
   venite a noi parlar, s'altri nol niega!»
Quali colombe, dal disio chiamate,
   con l'ali alzate e ferme al dolce nido
   vegnon per l'aere dal voler portate;
cotali uscir della schiera ov'è Dido,
   a noi venendo per l'aere maligno,
   sì forte fu l'affettüoso grido.
«O animal grazïoso e benigno
   che visitando vai per l'aere perso
   noi che tignemmo il mondo di sanguigno,
se fosse amico il re dell'universo,
   noi pregheremmo lui della tua pace,
   poi c'hai pietà del nostro mal perverso.
Di quel che udire e che parlar vi piace,
   noi udiremo e parleremo a vui,
   mentre che 'l vento, come fa, ci tace.
Siede la terra dove nata fui
   su la marina dove 'l Po discende
   per aver pace co' seguaci sui.
Amor, ch'al cor gentil ratto s'apprende,
   prese costui della bella persona
   che mi fu tolta; e 'l modo ancor m'offende.
Amor, ch'a nullo amato amar perdona,
   mi prese del costui piacer sì forte,
   che, come vedi, ancor non m'abbandona.
Amor condusse noi ad una morte:
   Caina attende chi a vita ci spense.»
   Queste parole da lor ci fur porte.

And he replied: "You shall see when they are
   closer to us; and then entreat them
   in the name of that love which leads them, and they will come."
As soon as the wind turned them toward us,
   I gave voice: "O troubled souls,
   come speak with us, unless Someone[6] forbids it!"
Like doves which, summoned by desire,
   return to their sweet nest on raised, motionless wings,
   borne through the air by their wishes,
so did they leave the group that included Dido,
   coming to us through the unhealthy air,
   so powerful was my affectionate call.
"O gracious and benevolent living being,
   you that come through the dark purple air to visit
   us who tinged the world blood-red,
if the King of the Universe were our friend,
   we would pray to Him to give you peace,
   because you take pity on our severe misfortune.
Concerning that which it pleases you two to hear and say,
   we shall listen and speak to you,
   while the wind dies down in this place as it now does.
The land where I was born[7] is located
   on the coast to which the Po descends
   to gain peace from its pursuing tributaries.
Love, which is quickly kindled in a noble heart,
   infatuated this man with the beautiful body
   that was taken from me; and the manner of it still does me injury.[8]
Love, which exempts no person loved from loving in return,
   infatuated me so strongly with this man's attractions
   that, as you see, it has not yet left me.
Love led the two of us to a single death:
   Caina[9] awaits the one who deprived us of life."
   These words were uttered by them to us.

---

6. God.   7. Ravenna. The speaker is Francesca of Rimini, daughter of Da Polenta, the lord of Ravenna; she married Gianciotto Malatesta, son of the lord of Rimini. She fell in love with her husband's brother Paolo (who had held a public office in Florence), and Gianciotto killed them both; this occurred when Dante was about twenty.   8. Because she was given no time to make her peace with God and thus gain salvation.   9. The section of the lowest circle of Hell that is reserved for those who betrayed their kindred.

Quand'io intesi quell'anime offense,
  china' il viso, e tanto il tenni basso,
  fin che 'l poeta mi disse: «Che pense?»
Quando rispuosi, cominciai: «Oh lasso,
  quanti dolci pensier, quanto disio
  menò costoro al doloroso passo!»
Poi mi rivolsi a loro e parla' io,
  e cominciai: «Francesca, i tuoi martìri
  a lacrimar mi fanno tristo e pio.
Ma dimmi: al tempo de' dolci sospiri,
  a che e come concedette amore
  che conosceste i dubbiosi disiri?»
E quella a me: «Nessun maggior dolore
  che ricordarsi del tempo felice
  nella miseria; e ciò sa 'l tuo dottore.
Ma s'a conoscer la prima radice
  del nostro amor tu hai cotanto affetto,
  dirò come colui che piange e dice.
Noi leggiavamo un giorno per diletto
  di Lancialotto come amor lo strinse:
  soli eravamo e sanza alcun sospetto.
Per più fïate li occhi ci sospinse
  quella lettura, e scolorocci il viso;
  ma solo un punto fu quel che ci vinse.
Quando leggemmo il disïato riso
  esser baciato da cotanto amante,
  questi, che mai da me non fia diviso,
la bocca mi baciò tutto tremante.
  Galeotto fu il libro e chi lo scrisse:
  quel giorno più non vi leggemmo avante.»
Mentre che l'uno spirto questo disse,
  l'altro piangea, sì che di pietade
  io venni men così com'io morisse;
e caddi come corpo morto cade.

When I understood how those souls had been injured,
   I bowed my head and kept it down until
   the poet said to me: "What are you thinking?"
On replying, I began: "Alas,
   how many sweet thoughts, how much desire
   led these people to their painful doom!"
Then I turned to them and spoke,
   beginning: "Francesca, your sufferings
   make me sad and compassionate to the point of tears.
But tell me: in the season of sweet sighs,
   by what sign, and how, did love grant you
   the recognition of your undeclared[10] desires?"
And she replied: "There is no greater sorrow
   than to recall happy times
   in the midst of misery; and your instructor knows this.
But if you have such a great longing to know
   the earliest root of our love,
   I shall tell you, as one who speaks and weeps.
One day, for amusement, we were reading
   of how love embraced Lancelot:
   we were alone and free from all misgivings.
Several times that reading
   made our eyes meet and our faces grow pale;
   but it was only a single moment that conquered us.
When we read of how the longed-for lips
   were kissed by a lover of such worth,
   this man, who shall never be separated from me,
kissed me full on the mouth, all a-tremble.
   Our Gallehault[11] was the book and its author:
   that day we read on no further."
While the one spirit was saying this,
   the other wept, so that out of compassion
   I fainted as if I were dying;
and I fell as a dead body falls.

---

10. Or: "dangerous." 11. The knight who introduced Lancelot to the intimacy of Queen Guinevere, wife of King Arthur. Later on, *galeotto* as a common noun became an Italian term for pander, but it had not yet been so degraded in Dante's time.

[SUMMARY OF CANTO VI: When Dante awakens, he is already in the third circle, where dirty rain, snow, and hail constantly beat down on those who were gluttons in life. They lie prostrate and are guarded and tormented by the three-headed monster Cerberus, who lets the two journeyers pass after Vergil throws earth into his maws. A single sufferer sits up; as a fellow Florentine, named Ciacco ("swine"), he informs Dante of the political events that will occur in Florence in the next three years (culminating in the victory of the Black faction of the Guelf party); tells him he will come across certain other Florentines in lower circles of Hell; and states that Florence's troubles are due to pride, envy, and avarice. Asked by Dante whether the suffering in Hell will increase or diminish after the Last Judgment, Vergil replies that it will increase because the sinners will be that much more "perfect" and will thus feel more pain. Reaching the point for further descent, they come upon the demon Plutus.

SUMMARY OF CANTO VII: Plutus challenges the newcomers, but is felled by a rebuke from Vergil. Now in the fourth circle, Dante sees two lines of sinners pushing weights, each line constantly moving alongside the other from opposite directions. These sinners, who strike and insult each other, were spendthrifts and misers; some of the avaricious were once Church prelates. Fortune, which does not allow men to keep what they amass, is, Vergil explains, a divine agency carrying out God's will. By this time it is after midnight, and the journeyers reach the far side of the fourth circle and descend to the fifth, where the wrathful stand naked in the bog called Styx, fighting and maiming one another. Below the surface are the souls of the sullen, or

Canto X

Ora sen va per un secreto calle,
    tra 'l muro de la terra e li martìri,
    lo mio maestro, e io dopo le spalle.
«O virtù somma, che per li empi giri
    mi volvi» cominciai, «com'a te piace,
    parlami, e sodisfammi a'miei disiri.
La gente che per li sepolcri giace
    potrebbesi veder? già son levati
    tutt'i coperchi, e nessun guardia face.»
Ed elli a me: «Tutti saran serrati
    quando di Iosafàt qui torneranno
    coi corpi che là su hanno lasciati.
Suo cimitero da questa parte hanno

melancholy-slothful. Walking around the bog, Dante and Vergil arrive at a tower.

SUMMARY OF CANTO VIII: Atop the tower they see two flames, exchanging signals with another flame far off. The boatman of the Styx, who brings the wrathful to their permanent locations, is Phlegyas. As the travelers are rowed across, the spirit of Filippo Argenti, a wrathful Florentine, bobs up from the swamp and embraces Dante, who is anything but compassionate; he is glad when Argenti is attacked by fellow sinners and submerged again. Now Dante and Vergil, leaving the first few circles of Hell, which contain those who sinned because of passion or character flaws, approach the City of Dis, which houses truly malevolent or perverted souls. The pinnacles of its buildings glow red from the flames below. At the gates, the journeyers are halted by a multitude of fallen angels, who threaten to deprive Dante of Vergil's company. Vergil parleys with them, but they shut the gates.

SUMMARY OF CANTO IX: Even Vergil is apprehensive now: he has not descended so deeply into Hell since ancient times, and aid that he was expecting is not yet on hand. The three ancient Greek Furies appear and threaten to turn Dante to stone with the head of Medusa, but he shields his eyes. Suddenly a heavenly angel arrives on the wind, rebukes the insolent demons who had shut the gates, and compels them to allow the two poets to enter. Now in the sixth circle, they see a wide plain filled with tombs with upraised lids. The tombs are surrounded by flames, and sighs issue from them. The souls within them are those of heretics.]

Canto X

Now along a hidden path
    between the city wall and the torments
    my master proceeds, and I behind him.
"O lofty power, you that through the evil circles
    lead me in a winding path," I began, "as it pleases you
    speak to me, and content my wishes.
Would it be possible to see the people who lie
    in these tombs? All the lids
    are already raised, and no one stands guard."
And he replied: "They will all be enclosed
    when they return here from Jehoshaphat[1]
    with the bodies they left up on earth.
In this place are buried

---

1. The venue of the Last Judgment.

con Epicuro tutt'i suoi seguaci,
che l'anima col corpo morta fanno.
Però alla dimanda che mi faci
quinc'entro satisfatto sarà tosto,
e al disio ancor che tu mi taci.»
E io: «Buon duca, non tegno riposto
a te mio cuor se non per dicer poco,
e tu m'hai non pur mo a ciò disposto.»
«O Tosco che per la città del foco
vivo ten vai così parlando onesto,
piacciati di restare in questo loco.
La tua loquela ti fa manifesto
di quella nobil patrïa natio
alla qual forse fui troppo molesto.»
Subitamente questo suono uscìo
d'una dell'arche; però m'accostai,
temendo, un poco più al duca mio.
Ed el mi disse: «Volgiti: che fai?
Vedi là Farinata che s'è dritto:
dalla cintola in su tutto 'l vedrai.»
Io avea già il mio viso nel suo fitto;
ed el s'ergea col petto e con la fronte
com'avesse l'inferno in gran dispitto.
E l'animose man del duca e pronte
mi pinser tra le sepulture a lui,
dicendo: «Le parole tue sien conte.»
Com'io al piè della sua tomba fui,
guardommi un poco, e poi, quasi sdegnoso,
mi dimandò: «Chi fuor li maggior tui?»
Io ch'era d'ubidir disideroso,
non lil celai, ma tutto lil'apersi;
ond'ei levò le ciglia un poco in soso,
poi disse: «Fieramente furo avversi
a me e a miei primi e a mia parte,
sì che per due fïate li dispersi.»

Epicurus and all his followers,
who declare that the soul dies with the body.
But the question you put to me
will soon be answered right here,
and the wish you conceal from me[2] will be granted as well."
I said: "Kindly guide, I keep my heart
hidden from you solely to avoid asking too many questions,
and it is not merely now that you have warned me to that effect."
"O Tuscan, you that through the city of fire
are thus proceeding alive, speaking politely,
may it please you to linger in this place.
Your speech makes it plain that you are
a native of that noble homeland[3]
to which I was perhaps too burdensome."
These words issued suddenly
from one of the tombs; so that, in fear,
I moved a little closer to my guide.
And he said to me: "Turn around. What are you doing?
See Farinata[4] there, who has raised himself:
you will see him completely from the waist up."
I had already fastened my eyes on his;
and he straightened up his chest and his brow
as if he held Hell in great contempt.
And my guide's encouraging and ready hands
pushed me toward him among the burials,
while he said: "Let your words be few."[5]
When I was at the foot of his tomb,
he looked at me a while, and then, as if scornful,
asked me: "Who were your ancestors?"
I, who was eager to obey,
did not conceal their names, but revealed them fully;
whereupon he raised his eyebrows somewhat,
then said: "They were fiercely opposed
to me, my forebears, and my party,
so that I drove them out twice."

---

2. Probably the desire to meet Farinata.   3. Florence.   4. Farinata degli Uberti,
head of Florence's Ghibelline party in the years just preceding Dante's birth. He exiled the Guelfs (including Dante's family) twice; later his own party was definitively
exiled, in 1266. The Guelfs remained bitterly opposed to their return.   5. Or: "mod-
erate, fitting."

«S'ei fur cacciati, ei tornar d'ogni parte»
  rispuosi lui «l'una e l'altra fiata;
    ma i vostri non appreser ben quell'arte.»
Allor surse alla vista scoperchiata
  un'ombra lungo questa infino al mento:
    credo che s'era in ginocchie levata.
Dintorno mi guardò, come talento
  avesse di veder s'altri era meco;
    e poi che il sospecciar fu tutto spento,
piangendo disse: «Se per questo cieco
  carcere vai per altezza d'ingegno,
    mio figlio ov'è? perchè non è ei teco?»
E io a lui: «Da me stesso non vegno:
  colui ch'attende là, per qui mi mena,
    forse cui Guido vostro ebbe a disdegno.»
Le sue parole e 'l modo della pena
  m'avean di costui già letto il nome;
    però fu la risposta così piena.
Di subito drizzato gridò: «Come
  dicesti? elli ebbe? non viv'elli ancora?
    non fiere li occhi suoi il dolce lome?»
Quando s'accorse d'alcuna dimora
  ch'io facea dinanzi alla risposta,
    supin ricadde e più non parve fora.
Ma quell'altro magnanimo a cui posta
  restato m'era, non mutò aspetto,
    nè mosse collo, nè piegò sua costa;
e sè continuando al primo detto,
  «S'elli han quell'arte» disse «male appresa,
    ciò mi tormenta più che questo letto.
Ma non cinquanta volte fia raccesa
  la faccia della donna che qui regge,
    che tu saprai quanto quell'arte pesa.

"If they were expelled, they returned from all sides,"
  I replied, "one time and the other;
  but your[6] people did not learn that art very well."[7]
At that moment, in the uncovered opening
  a shade arose next to that one, visible down to the chin;
  I believe it had risen to its knees.
It looked around me, as if it desired
  to see whether anyone else was with me;
  after its hopes were all disappointed,
it said, weeping: "If you journey through this pitch-dark
  prison because of the loftiness of your intellect,
  where is my son? Why is he not with you?"
And I replied: "I do not come alone:
  the man who is waiting there is guiding me here
  toward one whom your[8] Guido perhaps disdained."[9]
His words and the nature of his punishment
  had already given me his name;
  that is why my answer was so complete.
Raising himself up suddenly, he shouted: "What
  did you say? He 'disdained'? Is he no longer living?
  Does the sweet light no longer strike his eyes?"
When he noticed that I was making
  a slight delay before responding,
  he fell flat on his back again and was no longer to be seen outside.
But that other large-souled man, at whose request
  I had tarried, did not change his expression,
  bow his head, or lower his body;
taking up the end of our earlier conversation,
  he said: "if they failed to learn that art well,
  that tortures me more than this resting place does.
But the face of the lady who governs here[10]
  will not be reillumined fifty times
  before you yourself learn how sorrowful that art is.

---

6. In addressing Farinata, Dante uses forms of *voi*, the polite, respectful, "you." He does this with only a handful of people in the whole poem.   7. They never returned. 8. Again, the polite "your."   9. The second spirit in Cavalcante de' Cavalcanti, father of Guido Cavalcanti, a major poet and a great friend of Dante's. This line is difficult and has been interpreted, and even repunctuated, in various ways.   10. The goddess of the underworld, Proserpina or Hecate, identified with the moon; thus, before fifty months pass, Dante will be definitively exiled.

E se tu mai nel dolce mondo regge,
    dimmi: perchè quel popolo è sì empio
    incontr'a' miei in ciascuna sua legge?»
Ond'io a lui: «Lo strazio e 'l grande scempio
    che fece l'Arbia colorata in rosso,
    tali orazion fa far nel nostro tempio.»
Poi ch'ebbe sospirato e 'l capo scosso,
    «A ciò non fu' io sol» disse, «nè certo
    sanza cagion con li altri sarei mosso.
Ma fu' io solo, là dove sofferto
    fu per ciascun di torre via Fiorenza,
    colui che la difesi a viso aperto.»
«Deh, se reposi mai vostra semenza»
    prega' io lui, «solvetemi quel nodo
    che qui ha inviluppata mia sentenza.
El par che vio veggiate, se ben odo,
    dinanzi quel che 'l tempo seco adduce,
    e nel presente tenete altro modo.»
«Noi veggiam, come quei c'ha mala luce,
    le cose» disse «che ne son lontano;
    cotanto ancor ne splende il sommo duce.
Quando s'appressano o son, tutto è vano
    nostro intelletto; e s'altri non ci apporta,
    nulla sapem di vostro stato umano.
Però comprender puoi che tutta morta
    fia nostra conoscenza da quel punto
    che del futuro fia chiusa la porta.»
Allor, come di mia colpa compunto,
    dissi: «Or direte dunque a quel caduto
    che 'l suo nato è co' vivi ancor congiunto;
e s'i' fui, dianzi, alla risposta muto,
    fate i saper che 'l feci che pensava
    già nell'error che m'avete soluto.»
E già il maestro mio mi richiamava;
    per ch'i' pregai lo spirto più avaccio
    che mi dicesse chi con lu' istava.
Dissemi: «Qui con più di mille giaccio:
    qua dentro è 'l secondo Federico,
    e 'l Cardinale; e delli altri mi taccio.»

And—so may you return to the sweet world!—
   tell me why your citizens are so cruel
   to my family in each of their laws?"
I replied: "The massacre and the great slaughter
   that tinged the waters of the Arbia[11] red
   is the reason we make such prayers in our church."
After sighing and shaking his head,
   he said: "I was not the only one behind that, nor indeed
   would I have gone along with the rest without a reason.
But I *was* the only one, when it was agreed upon
   by everybody to wipe out Florence,
   who defended the city publicly."
"Please—so may your descendants find peace some day!—"
   I entreated him, "untie that knot for me
   which has now impeded my thinking.
It seems that, if I hear correctly, you dead people see
   in advance that which time is to bring with it,
   whereas for things present it is otherwise with you."
"We see, like those with poor sight,"
   he said, "the things that are distant from us;
   that much light we still receive from our Highest Ruler.
When things draw near or actually occur, our mind
   is totally useless; and, if others do not bring us word,
   we know nothing about your current human condition.
Therefore you can comprehend that our consciousness
   will be totally extinct from the moment
   when the gate to the future will be shut."[12]
Then, feeling remorse for my fault,
   I said: "Now please tell that man who fell back
   that his son is still among the living;
and if, earlier, I failed to reply,
   let him know that I did so because my thoughts
   were already in the confusion that you have clarified."
And my master was already calling me back;
   so that I asked the spirit more hastily
   to tell me who else was with him.
He said: "I lie here with more than a thousand:
   in here are Frederick the Second[13]
   and the cardinal;[14] about the rest I am silent."

---

11. A river near Siena where the Ghibellines overcame the Guelfs in 1260 (battle of Montaperti).   12. On Judgment Day.   13. The free-thinking Holy Roman Emperor of the early 13th century.   14. Ottaviano degli Ubaldini, a Ghibelline who "sold his soul" for his party.

Indi s'ascose; ed io inver l'antico
  poeta volsi i passi, ripensando
  a quel parlar che mi parea nemico.
Elli si mosse; e poi, così andando,
  mi disse: «Perchè se' tu sì smarrito?»
  E io li sodisfeci al suo dimando.
«La mente tua conservi quel ch'udito
  hai contra te» mi comandò quel saggio.
«E ora attendi qui» e drizzò 'l dito:
«quando sarai dinanzi al dolce raggio
  di quella il cui bell'occhio tutto vede,
  da lei saprai di tua vita il vïaggio.»
Appresso volse a man sinistra il piede:
  lasciammo il muro e gimmo inver lo mezzo
  per un sentier ch'a una valle fiede
che 'nfin là su facea spiacer suo lezzo.

[SUMMARY OF CANTO XI: Dante and Vergil briefly take cover from the stench behind the monument of the 5th-century Pope Anastasius II, said to be heretical. Vergil explains that three circles remain, those of the more grievous sinners. Circle Seven, for the violent, contains three divisions: for those violent against other men, against themselves, and against God and nature. The remaining circles are for frauds and traitors. The sinners seen earlier were merely "incontinent," not "malicious" or "bestial." There is a special discussion about the sin of usury. It is now about two hours before sunrise, and the travelers must descend a steep precipice.

SUMMARY OF CANTO XII: The entry to the rugged gorge is guarded by the Cretan Minotaur, who gnaws himself in rage, but yields to Vergil's command. This was one of the precipices created by the earthquake at the Harrowing of Hell. The first division of the seventh circle is a boiling river of blood in which those violent against others are immersed to different allotted extents. Among the centaurs who patrol the banks, shooting arrows at any soul that rises unduly high, are Nessus, who caused the death of Hercules, and Chiron, tutor of Achilles. Nessus carries Dante on his back as they ford the river. In the stream Dante sees various tyrants of ancient Greco-Roman and medieval Italian history, the assassin of an English royal, and contemporary Italian highwaymen.

SUMMARY OF CANTO XIII: The second division of the seventh circle is a forest of stunted trees; harpies feed upon their discolored leaves. Dante, seeming to hear voices, breaks off a small branch, and the tree bleeds and laments. This is the punishment of suicides. This particular tree contains the soul of Pier delle Vigne, chancellor to Emperor Frederick II (see note 13 to Canto

Thereupon he hid himself; and I toward the ancient
   poet turned my steps, thinking again
   about that prophecy which seemed hostile to me.
He set out; then, proceeding thus,
   he said to me: "Why are you in such a stupor?"
   And I answered his question.
"Let your mind store up that which
   you have heard to your harm," that sage commanded me.
   "And now pay attention," and he raised his finger:
"When you are face to face with the gentle beams
   of that lady whose beautiful eyes see all,
   you will learn the course of your life from her."
Next, he turned his feet to the left:
   we departed from the wall and headed for the center
   along a trail that strikes into a valley
that made its unpleasant stench felt all the way up there.

X); he killed himself after falling into disfavor because of envious people.
Dante asks him how the souls of suicides become such trees, and whether
they will ever rejoin their bodies. The double reply: such a soul, after being
assigned to the forest by Minos (see Canto V), sprouts wherever it lands; on
Judgment Day, these souls will obtain their bodies, but, because they themselves destroyed them, the bodies will not clothe them again, but will hang
forever on the thorny trees. Now two naked souls are pursued in Dante's direction by hounds, who rend them. One is Lano of Siena, the other Jacomo
da Sant'Andrea of Padua, both of whom courted death through profligacy. A
bush tattered in the encounter states that it came from Florence, which is
fated always to be torn by warring factions because it abandoned its ancient
patron Mars for Saint John the Baptist, and Mars is vengeful.

SUMMARY OF CANTO XIV: Dante returns the scattered leaves to the dam-
aged bush. He and Vergil then enter the innermost ring of the seventh circle, a sandy desert peopled by naked souls, some supine, some seated in a
crouch, some roaming. Falling flakes of fire heat the sand and burn the souls.
One disdainful recumbent spirit is Capaneus, a Greek warrior who defied
the gods. He and the other supine souls were blasphemers, "violent against
God"; those crouching were usurers, "violent against human industry"; those
roaming were sodomites, "violent against nature." Edging along away from
the hot sand, Dante is led to Phlegethon, a red, boiling stream issuing from
the forest; its banks and edges are of stone. The source of all the bodies of
water in Hell is the tears falling from the statue of an old man within Mount
Ida on Crete. Dante will see the river Cocytus later, but will not see the river
Lethe until he is in Purgatory. As he now proceeds, he must walk on the safe
stone ledges bordering Phlegethon.]

Canto XV

Ora cen porta l'un de' duri margini;
   e 'l fummo del ruscel di sopra aduggia,
   sì che dal foco salva l'acqua e li argini.
Quale i Fiamminghi tra Guizzante e Bruggia,
   temendo il fiotto che 'nver lor s'avventa,
   fanno lo schermo perchè 'l mar si fuggia;
e quale i Padovan lungo la Brenta,
   per difender lor ville e lor castelli,
   anzi che Chiarentana il caldo senta;
a tale imagine eran fatti quelli,
   tutto che nè sì alti nè sì grossi,
   qual che si fosse, lo maestro felli.
Già eravam dalla selva rimossi
   tanto, ch'i' non avrei visto dov'era,
   perch'io in dietro rivolto mi fossi,
quando incontrammo d'anime una schiera
   che venìan lungo l'argine, e ciascuna
   ci riguardava come suol da sera
guardare uno altro sotto nuova luna;
   e sì ver noi aguzzavan le ciglia
   come 'l vecchio sartor fa nella cruna.
Così adocchiato da cotal famiglia,
   fui conosciuto da un, che mi prese
   per lo lembo e gridò: «Qual maraviglia!»
E io, quando 'l suo braccio a me distese,
   ficca' li li occhi per lo cotto aspetto,
   sì che 'l viso abbruciato non difese
la conoscenza sua al mio intelletto;
   e chinando la mano alla sua faccia,
   rispuosi: «Siete voi qui, ser Brunetto?»
E quelli: «O figliuol mio, non ti dispiaccia
   se Brunetto Latino un poco teco
   ritorna in dietro e lascia andar la traccia.»

Canto XV

Now our path runs along one of the stony edges;
    and the smoke from the stream forms a cloud above,
    so that it shields the water and the embankments from the falling fire.
Just as the Flemings between Wissant[1] and Bruges,
    fearing the flood that hurls itself at them,
    build dikes so that the ocean will flee;
and as the Paduans erect levees along the river Brenta
    to protect their towns and fortresses
    before the Carinzia region feels the heat;[2]
in such guise those embankments were made,
    although their builder, whoever he was,
    did not make them so high or thick.
We were already so far distant from the forest
    that I would not have seen where it was
    even had I turned around to look,
when we came upon a band of souls
    who were coming along the embankment, each one of them
    looking at us as one man is wont to look
at another in the evening when the moon is new;
    and they were peering at us with difficulty,
    as an aged tailor does at the eye of his needle.
Thus observed by such a group,
    I was recognized by one, who took me
    by the hem of my garment and shouted: "What a wonder!"
And I, when he stretched out his arm to me,
    fixed my eyes on his burnt features,
    so that the scorching of his face did not prevent
my mind from recognizing him;
    and, bending my hand toward his face,
    I replied: "Are *you*[3] here, Master Brunetto?"
And he said: "O my son, do not be displeased
    if for a while Brunetto Latini[4] turns back
    with you and lets his group pass by."

---

1. A town near Calais. 2. Before the spring snowmelt on the mountains of
Carinzia swells the Brenta. 3. *Voi* is the respectful "you." 4. Latini was a major
Florentine intellectual of the 13th century, author of the (French-language) encyclo-
pedic work *Li livres dou trésor* ("The Treasure") and an allegorical didactic poem in
Italian, *Il tesoretto* ("The Little Treasure"), that was a direct influence on Dante's
Comedy. He was a mentor to the young Dante.

I' dissi lui: «Quanto posso, ven preco;
 e se volete che con voi m'asseggia,
 faròl, se piace a costui che vo seco.»
«O figliuol,» disse, «qual di questa greggia
 s'arresta punto, giace poi cent'anni
 sanz'arrostarsi quando 'l foco il feggia.
Però va oltre: i' ti verrò a' panni;
 e poi rigiugnerò la mia masnada,
 che va piangendo i suoi etterni danni.»
I' non osava scender della strada
 per andar par di lui; ma 'l capo chino
 tenea com'uom che reverente vada.
El cominciò: «Qual fortuna o destino
 anzi l'ultimo dì qua giù ti mena?
 e chi è questi che mostra 'l cammino?»
«Là su di sopra, in la vita serena»
 rispuos'io lui, «mi smarri' in una valle,
 avanti che l'età mia fosse piena.
Pur ier mattina le volsi le spalle:
 questi m'apparve, tornand'io in quella,
 e reducemi a ca per questo calle.»
Ed elli a me: «Se tu segui tua stella,
 non puoi fallire a glorïoso porto,
 se ben m'accorsi nella vita bella;
e s'io non fossi sì per tempo morto,
 veggendo il cielo a te così benigno,
 dato t'avrei all'opera conforto.
Ma quello ingrato popolo maligno
 che discese di Fiesole ab antico,
 e tiene ancor del monte e del macigno,
ti si farà, per tuo ben far, nemico:
 ed è ragion, chè tra li lazzi sorbi
 si disconvien fruttar lo dolce fico.
Vecchia fama nel mondo li chiama orbi;
 gent'è avara, invidiosa e superba:
 dai lor costumi fa che tu ti forbi.

I said to him: "I beg you all I can to do so;
    and if you want me to sit down with you,
    I will, if it pleases the one I am traveling with."
"O son," he said, "anyone from this herd
    that halts for just a moment must later lie a hundred years
    without protecting himself when the fire strikes him.
Therefore, proceed: I shall walk along near you;
    and then I shall rejoin my company,
    which continues to lament its eternal pains."
I did not dare to step down from the path
    to walk next to him; but I kept my head
    lowered like a man expressing reverence.
He began: "What fortune or destiny
    leads you down here before your last day?
    And who is this that shows you the way?"
"Up above, in the brightness of life,"
    I replied, "I lost my way in a valley,
    before my life span was complete.
Just yesterday morning I turned my back on it:
    this man appeared as I was returning to it,
    and is leading me back home[5] by this path."
He said to me: "If you follow your star,
    you cannot fail to reach a glorious haven,
    if I observed things well while still enjoying the beauty of life;
and if I had not died so early,[6]
    on seeing that heaven was so well-intentioned toward you
    I would have encouraged you in your literary career.
But that ungrateful, malicious folk
    which came down from Fiesole in ancient days,[7]
    and still has the characteristics of mountain and rock,
will make itself your enemy because of your correct dealings:
    and rightly so, because among sour sorb trees
    it is not fitting for sweet figs to bear fruit.
An old saying in the world calls them blind;[8]
    they are a greedy, envious, and prideful people:
    see that you cleanse yourself of their ways.

---

5. That is, toward heaven. 6. The point is not that Latini died young, but that
Dante was still young (thirty or under) when the older man died. 7. Florence (the
"folk" in question) is said to have been founded in the 1st century B.C. by hill dwellers
from nearby Fiesole, made to resettle there, and by a number of (more respectable)
settlers from Rome itself. 8. There are numerous explanations of this saying.

La tua fortuna tanto onor ti serba,
    che l'una parte e l'altra avranno fame
    di te; ma lungi fia dal becco l'erba.
Faccian le bestie fiesolane strame
    di lor medesme, e non tocchin la pianta,
    s'alcuna surge ancora in lor letame
in cui riviva la sementa santa
    di que' Roman che vi rimaser quando
    fu fatto il nido di malizia tanta.»
«Se fosse tutto pieno il mio dimando»
    rispuosi lui, «voi non sareste ancora
    dell'umana natura posto in bando;
che 'n la mente m'è fitta, e or m'accora,
    la cara e buona imagine paterna
    di voi quando nel mondo ad ora ad ora
m'insegnavate come l'uom s'etterna:
    e quant'io l'abbia in grado, mentr'io vivo
    convien che nella mia lingua si scerna.
Ciò che narrate di mio corso scrivo,
    e serbolo a chiosar con altro testo
    a donna che saprà, s'a lei arrivo.
Tanto vogl'io che vi sia manifesto,
    pur che mia coscïenza non mi garra,
    che alla Fortuna, come vuol, son presto.
Non è nuova alli orecchi miei tal arra:
    però giri Fortuna la sua rota
    come le piace, e 'l villan la sua marra.»
Lo mio maestro allora in su la gota
    destra si volse in dietro, e riguardommi;
    poi disse: «Bene ascolta chi la nota.»
Nè per tanto di men parlando vommi
    con ser Brunetto, e dimando chi sono
    li suoi compagni più noti e più sommi.
Ed elli a me: «Saper d'alcuno è bono;
    delli altri fia laudabile tacerci,
    che 'l tempo sarìa corto a tanto sòno.
In somma sappi che tutti fur cherci
    e litterati grandi e di gran fama,

Your fortune has so much honor in store for you
    that both parties[9] will be hungry
    to have you; but the grass will be far from the goat.
Let the animals from Fiesole make fodder
    of one another; let them not touch the plant,
    if one still sprouts amid their manure,
in which there lives again the holy seed
    of those Romans who remained there when
    the nest of such malevolence was founded."[10]
"If my wishes were fully granted,"
    I replied, "you would not yet be
    exiled from human existence;
for I retain planted in my mind—and it saddens me now—
    the dear, kind paternal image
    of you when, in life, from time to time
you used to teach me how a man immortalizes his name:
    and, as long as I live, it is fitting for my tongue
    to make known just how grateful I am for it.
That which you tell of the course of my life, I am writing down
    and saving it to be interpreted, along with other remarks,
    by the lady who will know how, if I reach her.
I want this only to be clear to you:
    that, provided my conscience does not give me pangs,
    I am ready to face Fortune, whatever she wishes.
Such a foretaste is not new to my ears:
    and so, let Fortune spin her wheel
    however she likes, and the peasant wield his mattock."
Now my master turned around
    to the right and looked at me,
    then said: "He who takes heed is a good listener."
That interruption does not keep me from continuing to talk
    with Master Brunetto, and I ask him who are
    his most famous and distinguished companions.
He replied: "It is a good thing to learn about some of them;
    about the rest it will be praiseworthy to be silent,
    because time would be scant for such a long account.
In short, you should know that they were all ecclesiastics
    and great, very celebrated writers,

---

9. The White and the Black factions of the Guelfs.   10. Thus, Dante considered
himself to be a descendant of those early Florentines who came from Rome.

d'un peccato medesmo al mondo lerci.
Priscian sen va con quella turba grama,
  e Francesco d'Accorso; anche vedervi,
  s'avessi avuto di tal tigna brama,
colui potéi che dal servo de' servi
  fu trasmutato d'Arno in Bacchiglione,
  dove lasciò li mal protesi nervi.
Di più direi; ma 'l venire e 'l sermone
  più lungo esser non può, però ch'i' veggio
  là surger novo fummo del sabbione.
Gente vien con la quale esser non deggio:
  sieti raccomandato il mio Tesoro
  nel qual io vivo ancora, e più non cheggio.»
Poi si rivolse, e parve di coloro
  che corrono a Verona il drappo verde
  per la campagna; e parve di costoro
quelli che vince, non colui che perde.

[SUMMARY OF CANTO XVI: Amid the other homosexuals perpetually walking under the rain of fire, Dante meets three more prominent 13th-century
Florentines, who ask him whether what they have heard recently about the
decline of their city is true. He confirms their worst fears, blaming the city's
troubles on rapacity and the influx and rise of new families that do not value

---

Canto XVII

«Ecco la fiera con la coda aguzza,
  che passa i monti, e rompe i muri e l'armi;
  ecco colei che tutto 'l mondo appuzza!»
Sì cominciò lo mio duca a parlarmi;
  e accennolle che venisse a proda
  vicino al fin de' passeggiati marmi.
E quella sozza imagine di froda
  sen venne, ed arrivò la testa e 'l busto,
  ma 'n su la riva non trasse la coda.

sullied in life by one and the same sin.[11]
Priscian[12] walks here in that dismal throng,
   and Francesco d'Accorso;[13] you could also see there,
   had you had the desire for such ringworm,
the man who, by order of 'the servant of the servants,'
   was transferred from the Arno to the Bacchiglione,[14]
   where he laid down his evilly stretched sinews.
I would tell you about others, but my accompanying you and my speaking
   may not go on any longer, because I see
   new smoke arising from the sand over there.
People are coming with whom I must not consort:
   let me commend my *Treasure* to you,
   in which I still live, and I ask no more."
Then he turned, and seemed like one of those
   who race on foot at Verona for the prize of green cloth
   through the countryside; and, from among them, he seemed
like the winner, not the loser.

---

traditional ways. Dante and Vergil now reach the point where the river
plunges down a cliff into the next lower circle. Vergil asks Dante to give him
the cord with which his waist was girded; he then throws it into the abyss,
from which a strange monster flies up.]

Canto XVII

"Here is the beast with the pointed tail,
   which passes over mountains and breaks through walls and weapons;
   here is the one that infects the whole world!"
Thus my guide began to address me;
   and he made a sign to the beast to land
   near the end of the stone slabs we had walked on.
And that foul image of fraud
   arrived, and placed its head and torso on the bank,
   but did not draw up its tail onto it.

---

11. Homosexuality.   12. A Latin grammarian of the 6th century A.D.   13. Or:
Accursio; a prominent law professor.   14. "Servant of the servants of God" is a title of
the popes. This specific pope was Boniface VIII, whom Dante hated. The man transferred was the bishop Andrea Mozzi (or: di Mozzi; de' Mozzi). The transfer was from
Florence (on the Arno) to Vicenza (on the Bacchiglione).

La faccia sua era faccia d'uom giusto,
  tanto benigna avea di fuor la pelle,
  e d'un serpente tutto l'altro fusto;
due branche avea pilose infin l'ascelle;
  lo dosso e 'l petto e ambedue le coste
  dipinti avea di nodi e di rotelle:
con più color, sommesse e sopraposte
  non fer mai drappi Tartari nè Turchi,
  nè fuor tai tele per Aragne imposte.
Come tal volta stanno a riva i burchi,
  che parte sono in acqua e parte in terra,
  e come là tra li Tedeschi lurchi
lo bivero s'assetta a far sua guerra,
  così la fiera pessima si stava
  su l'orlo che, di pietra, il sabbion serra.
Nel vano tutta sua coda guizzava,
  torcendo in su la venenosa forca
  ch'a guisa di scorpion la punta armava.
Lo duca disse: «Or convien che si torca
  la nostra via un poco insino a quella
  bestia malvagia che colà si corca.»
Però scendemmo alla destra mammella,
  e diece passi femmo in su lo stremo,
  per ben cessar la rena e la fiammella.
E quando noi a lei venuti semo,
  poco più oltre veggio in su la rena
  gente seder propinqua al luogo scemo.
Quivi 'l maestro «Acciò che tutta piena
  esperïenza d'esto giron porti»
  mi disse, «va, e vedi la lor mena.
Li tuoi ragionamenti sian là corti:
  mentre che torni, parlerò con questa,
  che ne conceda i suoi omeri forti.»
Così ancor su per la strema testa
  di quel settimo cerchio tutto solo
  andai, dove sedea la gente mesta.

Its face was the face of an honest man,
  so benevolent was its complexion outwardly,
  but all the rest of its body was that of a serpent.
It had two clawed arms hairy to the armpits;
  its back, chest, and both sides
  were ornamented with knots and circles:
Neither Tartars nor Turks ever made fabrics
  with more colors, in woof and warp,
  nor was such a web set up by Arachne[1] on her loom.
Just as, at times, skiffs lie by the shore
  partly in the water and partly on land,
  and just as, yonder among the gluttonous Germans,
the beaver prepares to make its war,[2]
  thus that most evil beast clung
  to the rim of stone that encloses the sand.
Its entire tail was twitching in the void,
  twisting upward the poisonous fork
  that armed its tip like a scorpion's.
My guide said: "Now we must inflect
  our way somewhat until we reach that
  malevolent animal which lies over there."
Therefore we went down to the right-hand rounding of the cliff,
  and walked ten paces along the brink,
  in order to avoid the sand and the flakes of fire.
And when we have reached the beast,
  I see a little farther ahead on the sand
  people seated near the abyss.
Here my master said to me: "So that
  your experience of this ring will be complete,
  go and look at their mode of existence.
Let your conversations there be brief:
  until you return I shall be speaking to that beast,
  asking it to lend us its strong shoulders."
Thus again along the outermost edge
  of that seventh circle I proceeded
  all alone to where the sorrowful people were seated.

---

1. The skilled weaver who challenged the goddess Minerva (Athene) to a contest
and was changed into a spider.   2. The beaver was said to "make war" on its prey—
that is, catch fish—by immersing itself partially: dipping its tail and stirring up the
water with it.

Per li occhi fora scoppiava lor duolo;
  di qua, di là soccorrìen con le mani
  quando a' vapori, e quando al caldo suolo:
non altrimenti fan di state i cani
  or col ceffo, or col piè, quando son morsi
  o da pulsi o da mosche o da tafani.
Poi che nel viso a certi li occhi porsi,
  ne' quali il doloroso foco casca,
  non ne conobbi alcun; ma io m'accorsi
che dal collo a ciascun pendea una tasca
  ch'avea certo colore e certo segno,
  e quindi par che 'l loro occhio si pasca.
E com'io riguardando tra lor vegno,
  in una borsa gialla vidi azzurro
  che d'un leone avea faccia e contegno.
Poi, procedendo di mio sguardo il curro,
  vidine un'altra come sangue rossa,
  mostrando un'oca bianca più che burro.
E un che d'una scrofa azzurra e grossa
  segnato avea lo suo sacchetto bianco,
  mi disse: «Che fai tu in questa fossa?
Or te ne va; e perchè se' vivo anco,
  sappi che 'l mio vicin Vitalïano
  sederà qui dal mio sinistro fianco.
Con questi fiorentin son padovano:
  spesse fïate m'intronan li orecchi
  gridando: 'Vegna il cavalier sovrano,
che recherà la tasca coi tre becchi!'»
  Qui distorse la bocca e di fuor trasse
  la lingua come bue che 'l naso lecchi.
E io, temendo no 'l più star crucciasse
  lui che di poco star m'avea 'mmonito,
  torna'mi in dietro dall'anime lasse.
Trova' il duca mio ch'era salito
  già su la groppa del fiero animale,
  e disse a me: «Or sie forte e ardito.

Their grief broke forth from their eyes;
   on this side and that they were defending themselves with their hands
   now from the fiery air, now from the hot ground:
no otherwise do dogs do in the summer
   now with their muzzles, now with their paws, when they are bitten
   by fleas, flies, or gadflies.
After I directed my eyes at the faces of some
   of those on whom the painful fire falls,
   I failed to recognize any; but I noticed
that from each one's neck hung a moneybag
   that had a certain color and a certain coat-of-arms,
   and thereupon their eyes seem to feed.
And, as I walk among them observing,
   I saw on a yellow purse a blue figure
   that had the head and the bearing of a lion.[3]
Then, as the course of my gaze proceeded,
   I saw another bag red as blood
   displaying a goose whiter than butter.
And one man, whose white pouch
   was adorned with a fat blue sow,
   said to me: "What are you doing in this moat?
Go away now; and because you are still alive,
   know that my townsman Vitaliano[4]
   will some day sit here at my left side.
Along with these Florentines I am a Paduan:
   many a time they deafen my ears
   shouting: 'Let that supreme knight come
who will bear the bag with three he-goats!'"[5]
   Then he twisted his mouth and stuck out
   his tongue, like an ox licking its muzzle.
And, fearing lest my lingering further might vex
   the one who had instructed me to tarry only briefly,
   I turned back and left the weary souls.
I found that my guide had already
   mounted on the haunch of the fierce animal;
   he said to me: "Now be strong and bold.

---

3. This was the coat-of-arms of the Gianfigliazzi family of Florence. The next two coats-of-arms described are those of the Ubbriachi family of Florence and the Scrovegni family of Padua. 4. Vitaliano del Dente of Padua. 5. Giovanni di Buiamonte of Florence, "supreme" among all these usurers; he had been given the title of Cavaliere.

Omai si scende per sì fatte scale:
  monta dinanzi, ch'i' voglio esser mezzo,
  sì che la coda non possa far male.»
Qual è colui che sì presso ha 'l riprezzo
  della quartana, c'ha già l'unghie smorte,
  e triema tutto pur guardando il rezzo,
tal divenn'io alle parole porte;
  ma vergogna mi fè le sue minacce,
  che innanzi a buon segnor fa servo forte.
I' m'assettai in su quelle spallacce:
  sì volli dir, ma la voce non venne
  com'io credetti: «Fa che tu m'abbracce.»
Ma esso, ch'altra volta mi sovenne
  ad altro forse, tosto ch'io montai
  con le braccia m'avvinse e mi sostenne;
e disse: «Gerïon, moviti omai:
  le rote larghe, e lo scender sia poco:
  pensa la nova soma che tu hai.»
Come la navicella esce di loco
  in dietro in dietro, sì quindi si tolse;
  e poi ch'al tutto si sentì a gioco,
là 'v'era il petto, la coda rivolse,
  e quella tesa, come anguilla, mosse,
  e con le branche l'aere a sè raccolse.
Maggior paura non credo che fosse
  quando Fetòn abbandonò li freni,
  per che 'l ciel, come pare ancor, si cosse;
nè quando Icaro misero le reni
  sentì spennar per la scaldata cera,
  gridando il padre a lui 'Mala via tieni!',
che fu la mia, quando vidi ch'i' era
  nell'aere d'ogni parte, e vidi spenta
  ogni veduta fuor che della fera.
Ella sen va notando lenta lenta:
  rota e discende, ma non me n'accorgo
  se non che al viso e di sotto mi venta.

We are now to descend by a staircase of this nature:
>   get on in front, for I want to be in the middle,
>   so that the tail cannot harm you."
Like a man who is so close to feeling the horrible chills
>   of quartan fever that his fingernails are already pale,
>   and he shakes all over if he merely looks at a shady place,
thus I became on hearing the words he spoke;
>   but his admonitions filled me with shame,
>   which in the presence of a good master makes a servant strong.
I settled down on that awful back:
>   I wanted to say—but my voice failed to come
>   the way I expected: "Be sure to put your arms around me!"
But my guide, who had come to my aid at other times
>   in other straits, as soon as I had mounted
>   wrapped me in his arms and kept me steady,
saying: "Geryon, now move:
>   let your gyrations be wide, and your descent gentle:
>   keep in mind the new kind of burden that you bear."
As a boat leaves the shore
>   backwards, thus did he take off from there;
>   and, once he felt himself completely at large,
he turned his tail where his chest had been
>   and moved that tail, outstretched like an eel,
>   and drew the air toward himself with his paws.
I do not believe there was greater fear
>   when Phaethon[6] let go the reins,
>   thereby burning the sky (and it still shows),[7]
or when unhappy Icarus[8] felt
>   his back losing its feathers because the wax had been heated,
>   while his father shouted to him: "You are keeping the wrong course!"
than mine was when I saw that I was
>   in mid-air on all sides, and I saw the sight
>   of all else other than the beast extinguished.
He goes floating down extremely slowly:
>   he descends in circles, but I am not aware of it,
>   except that a wind blows in my face and below me.

---

6. Son of the sun god, who borrowed his father's chariot and drove it too recklessly, causing a cosmic conflagration.   7. The visible aftereffect of the burning is the Milky Way.   8. On escaping from the labyrinth in Crete that he himself had built, Daedalus made wings, held on with wax, for himself and his son Icarus, but the boy flew too close to the sun and fell to earth when the wax melted.

Io sentìa già dalla man destra il gorgo
   far sotto noi un orribile scroscio,
   per che con li occhi 'n giù la testa sporgo.
Allor fu' io più timido allo scoscio,
   però ch'i' vidi fuochi e senti' pianti;
   ond'io tremando tutto mi raccoscio.
E vidi poi, chè nol vedea davanti,
   lo scendere e 'l girar per li gran mali
   che s'appressavan da diversi canti.
Come 'l falcon ch'è stato assai su l'ali,
   che sanza veder logoro o uccello
   fa dire al falconiere 'Ohmè, tu cali!',
discende lasso onde si move snello,
   per cento rote, e da lunge si pone
   dal suo maestro, disdegnoso e fello;
così ne puose al fondo Gerïone
   al piè al piè della stagliata rocca
   e, discarcate le nostre persone,
si dileguò come da corda cocca.

[SUMMARY OF CANTO XVIII: The eighth circle, called Malabolge ("evil pouches"), is a round space sloping sharply downward to a central well-like shaft that plunges down to the ninth circle. The steep sides of this eighth circle are furrowed by ten successive moats, for various punishments, which are bridged over by several rocky ridges. In the first moat, two lines of sinners pass each other in opposite directions, all whipped by horned demons. In one group is Venedico de' Caccianemici of Bologna, who acted as a pander for his sister. In the other is the ancient Greek hero Jason, who seduced the princesses Hypsipyle and Medea. In the second moat, flatterers are immersed in human excrement; among them is Alessio de' Interminelli of Lucca.

SUMMARY OF CANTO XIX: The third moat of the eighth circle is riddled with man-size holes, like those in the perimeter of the baptistery font in Florence, one of which Dante says he once broke to save a drowning person. In the holes in the moat, sinners are placed head downward with only their feet and ankles protruding; flames, of an intensity varying with their guilt, play along their soles. These were simonists, men of the Church who used their position for unlawful gain. Vergil leads Dante down into the moat, where he meets ex-Pope Nicholas III (reigned 1277–1280), who thinks

I already heard the rapids to our right
    making a horrible roar beneath us,
    and so I stick out my head, eyes downward.
Then I was more fearful of loosening my thigh hold,
    because I saw fires and heard laments;
    so that, trembling all over, I tighten my thighs.
And then I saw—for I did not see it earlier—
    our descent and circling amid the great torments
    that were coming nearer from various directions.
Like a falcon that has been too long on the wing
    and, without seeing its lure or its prey,
    makes the falconer say "Alas, you are coming down!"
and descends in weariness to the place from which it rose briskly,
    making a hundred circles, and alights far
    from its owner, indignant and vexed;
thus did Geryon set us down at the bottom
    at the very foot of the jagged cliff,
    and, freed from the burden of our bodies,
vanished like an arrow-notch shot from a bowstring.

Dante is Boniface VIII (1294–1303), who is to replace him in that posture so
that he, Nicholas, can join the earlier simoniac popes who are farther underground, below his head. Boniface, in turn, will be replaced by Clement V
(1303–1314), who moved the papal see to Avignon and served the French
throne more faithfully than he served the Church. Nicholas himself had
taken bribes (or misused tithes) to foster a conspiracy against the Angevins
in southern Italy. Dante delivers a harsh diatribe against simonists, to Vergil's
satisfaction. Vergil then carries him out of the third moat and over to the
fourth.

SUMMARY OF CANTO XX: In the fourth moat of the eighth circle is a procession of people whose heads have been twisted entirely around, so that
they must walk backwards. These are augurs and soothsayers who defied
God by prying into the secrets of the future. Dante weeps and is chided by
Vergil for sorrowing at God's just judgment. Among the throng of ancients
and moderns is the Theban seer Tiresias; his daughter Manto (of whom
Vergil now relates how she roamed the world before settling on the site
where his native city, Mantua, was later founded and named after her); and
a variety of more recent occultists, astrologers, and witches. The moon is now
setting, and Vergil urges haste.]

Canto XXI

Così di ponte in ponte, altro parlando
　che la mia comedìa cantar non cura,
　venimmo; e tenavamo il colmo, quando
restammo per veder l'altra fessura
　di Malebolge e li altri pianti vani;
　e vidila mirabil-mente oscura.
Quale nell'arzanà de' Viniziani
　bolle l'inverno la tenace pece
　a rimpalmare i legni lor non sani,
chè navicar non ponno; in quella vece
　chi fa suo legno novo e chi ristoppa
　le coste a quel che più vïaggi fece;
chi ribatte da proda e chi da poppa;
　altri fa remi e altri volge sarte;
　chi terzeruolo e artimon rintoppa—;
tal, non per foco, ma per divin'arte,
　bollìa là giuso una pegola spessa,
　che 'nviscava la ripa d'ogni parte.
I' vedea lei, ma non vedea in essa
　mai che le bolle che 'l bollor levava,
　e gonfiar tutta, e riseder compressa.
Mentr'io là giù fisamente mirava,
　lo duca mio, dicendo 'Guarda, guarda!',
　mi trasse a sè del loco dov'io stava.
Allor mi volsi come l'om cui tarda
　di veder quel che li convien fuggire
　e cui paura subita sgagliarda,
che, per veder, non indugia 'l partire;
　e vidi dietro a noi un diavol nero
　correndo su per lo scoglio venire.
Ahi quant'elli era nell'aspetto fero!
　e quanto mi parea nell'atto acerbo,
　con l'ali aperte e sovra i piè leggero!
L'omero suo, ch'era aguto e superbo,
　carcava un peccator con ambo l'anche,
　e quei tenea de' piè ghermito il nerbo.

Canto XXI

Thus from bridge to bridge, discussing other matters,
    Which my *Comedy* is not concerned to sing of,
        we proceeded; and we were at the top of a bridge when
we halted to look at the next moat
    of Malebolge and the next vain laments;
        and I saw that it was wondrously dark.
Just as, in the shipyard of the Venetians,
    sticky pitch boils in winter
        to be smeared again onto their damaged ships
because they cannot sail, and, instead of sailing,
    one man repairs his ship and another caulks
        the sides of a ship that has made many voyages;
one man hammers at the bow and another at the stern;
    another makes oars and another twists rigging;
        and yet another patches the foresail and the mainsail:
in like manner, heated not by fire but by a divine art,
    there was boiling down there a thick pitch,
        which coated the banks on every side.
I saw it, but could not make out within it
    anything but the bubbles that the boiling raised,
        while the whole river of pitch swelled and then subsided to a level.
As I was staring fixedly down there,
    my guide, saying "Take care, take care!,"
        drew me to his side from the place where I was standing.
Then I turned, like one who longs
    to see that which he ought to flee
        and is disheartened by sudden fear,
so that, much as he would like to look, he does not delay his departure;
    and I saw behind us a black devil
        running toward us along the rocky ridge.
Oh, how fierce he looked,
    and how cruel he seemed in his behavior,
        with open wings and nimble of foot!
His shoulder, which was sharp and raised,
    was burdened by a sinner, with both hips slung over,
        and the demon was gripping him by his insteps.[1]

---

1. Dante had reported in Canto V that sinners were automatically whisked to their eternal stations after being judged by Minos; here, devils go to fetch them, following the folk tradition.

Del nostro ponte disse: «O Malebranche,
  ecco un delli anzïan di santa Zita!
Mettetel sotto, ch'i' torno per anche
a quella terra ch'i' ho ben fornita:
  ogn'uom v'è barratier, fuor che Bonturo;
  del no per li denar vi si fa ita.»
Là giù il buttò, e per lo scoglio duro
  si volse; e mai non fu mastino sciolto
  con tanta fretta a seguitar lo furo.
Quel s'attuffò, e tornò su convolto;
  ma i demon che del ponte avean coperchio,
  gridar: «Qui non ha luogo il Santo Volto:
qui si nuota altrimenti che nel Serchio!
  Però, se tu non vuo' di nostri graffi,
  non far sopra la pegola soverchio.»
Poi l'addentar con più di cento raffi,
  disser: «Coverto convien che qui balli,
  sì che, se puoi, nascosamente accaffi.»
Non altrimenti i cuoci a' lor vassalli
  fanno attuffare in mezzo la caldaia
  la carne con li uncin, perchè non galli.
Lo buon maestro «Acciò che non si paia
  che tu ci sia» mi disse, «giù t'acquatta
  dopo uno scheggio, ch'alcun schermo t'aia;
e per nulla offension che mi sia fatta,
  non temer tu, ch'i' ho le cose conte,
  e altra volta fui a tal baratta.»
Poscia passò di là dal co del ponte;
  e com'el giunse in su la ripa sesta,
  mestier li fu d'aver sicura fronte.
Con quel furore e con quella tempesta
  ch'escono i cani a dosso al poverello
  che di subito chiede ove s'arresta,

From the bridge we were on, he called: "O Malebranche,[2]
  here is one of Saint Zita's magistrates![3]
  Put him under the pitch, while I go back for more
to that city where I laid in a good supply:
  every man there is a grafter, except Bonturo;[4]
  for the sake of money, 'no' becomes 'yes'[5] there."
He threw him down, and along the hard ridge
  he turned back, and never was an unleashed mastiff
  so swift to pursue a thief.
The man plunged in and bobbed up again all covered in pitch;
  but the demons who had the bridge as a covering overhead
  shouted: "Here we do not display the Holy Countenance:[6]
swimming here is different than in the Serchio![7]
  And so, if you do not want any of our scratching,
  do not show yourself above the surface of the pitch."
Then they tore into him with more than a hundred hooks,
  saying: "Here you must do your dancing under cover,
  so that you may rake in the money secretly, if you can."
In just such a way, cooks make their scullions
  dip the meat into the middle of the cauldron
  with hooks to keep it from floating.
My good master said to me: "So that it is not evident
  that you are here, squat down
  behind a block of stone, to give yourself some protection;
and, no matter what insult is offered to me,
  have no fear, because these matters are familiar to me,
  and I have already been in such a wrangle."
Then he passed beyond the head of the bridge;
  and, when he arrived on the sixth bank,
  he needed to display firm coolness.
With the fury and the racket
  with which dogs run out to attack a beggar
  who unexpectly halts to ask alms from where he stands,

---

2. "Evil Paws," the general name for the demons in the fifth moat of the eighth circle.   3. Zita was a popular saint of Lucca.   4. Meant ironically: Bonturo Dati was the
biggest grafter in town.   5. The word for "yes" in the Italian text is *ita*, which is actually Latin (used in official documents at the time).   6. A very old crucifix, blackened
with age, venerated in Lucca.   7. Lucca's river.

usciron quei di sotto al ponticello,
  e porser contra lui tutt'i runcigli;
  ma el gridò: «Nessun di voi sia fello!
Innanzi che l'uncin vostro mi pigli,
  traggasi avante l'un di voi che m'oda,
  e poi d'arruncigliarmi si consigli.»
Tutti gridaron: «Vada Malacoda!»;
  per ch'un si mosse—e li altri stetter fermi—
  e venne a lui dicendo: «Che li approda?»
«Credi tu, Malacoda, qui vedermi
  esser venuto» disse 'l mio maestro
  «sicuro già da tutti vostri schermi,
sanza voler divino e fato destro?
  Lascian'andar, chè nel cielo è voluto
  ch'i' mostri altrui questo cammin silvestro.»
Allor li fu l'orgoglio sì caduto,
  che si lasciò cascar l'uncino a' piedi,
  e disse alli altri: «Omai non sia feruto.»
E 'l duca mio a me: «O tu che siedi
  tra li scheggion del ponte quatto quatto,
  sicuramente omai a me tu riedi.»
Per ch'io mi mossi, ed a lui venni ratto;
  e i diavoli si fecer tutti avanti,
  sì ch'io temetti ch'ei tenesser patto:
così vid'ïo già temer li fanti
  ch'uscivan patteggiatti di Caprona,
  veggendo sè tra nemici cotanti.
I' m'accostai con tutta la persona
  lungo 'l mio duca, e non torceva li occhi
  dalla sembianza lor ch'era non bona.
Ei chinavan li raffi e «Vuo' che 'l tocchi»
  diceva l'un con l'altro «in sul groppone?»
  E rispondìen: «Sì, fa che lile accocchi!»
Ma quel demonio che tenea sermone
  col duca mio, si volse tutto presto,
  e disse: «Posa, posa, Scarmiglione!»

those demons sallied out from under the bridge
  and pointed all their hooks at him;
  but he shouted: "Let none of you be cruel!
Before your hooks touch me,
  let one of you come forward to hear me out,
  and then you can decide about lacerating me."
They all shouted: "Let Malacoda[8] go!"
  And so one moved forward, while the rest stood still,
  and came to him, saying: "What good will it do him?"
"Malacoda, do you think you would see me
  have come this far," my master said,
  "already fortified against all your obstacles,
were it not for the divine will and fate's favor?
  Allow us to proceed, for it is desired in heaven
  that I show another man this rugged path."
Then the demon's pride fell so far
  that he let the hook drop at his feet,
  and said to the others: "Now let him not be wounded."
And my guide said to me: "You that sit
  squatting among the blocks on the bridge,
  now return to me without fear."
And so I stirred myself and came to him swiftly;
  and the devils all moved forward,
  so that I doubted whether they would keep their agreement:
similarly I once saw the fear of the foot-soldiers
  who were leaving Caprona under safe-conduct,
  when they saw themselves in the midst of so many enemies.[9]
With my whole body I moved close
  to my guide and never detached my eyes
  from the devils, whose appearance promised no good.
They were pointing their hooks and saying to one another:
  "Do you want me to hit him on the back?"
  And they were replying: "Yes, let him have it!"
But that demon who had taken an oath
  with my guide turned very rapidly
  and said, "Relax, relax, Scarmiglione!"[10]

8. "Evil Tail." Many of these devils' names appear to be humorous deformations of actual family names of Dante's time. 9. After the Florentines, in alliance with Lucca, captured the Pisan fort Caprona in 1289; Dante evidently participated. 10. "Disheveled" or "Disarranger."

Poi disse a noi: «Più oltre andar per questo
    iscoglio non si può, però che giace
    tutto spezzato al fondo l'arco sesto.
E se l'andare avante pur vi piace,
    andatevene su per questa grotta;
    presso è un altro scoglio che via face.
Ier, più oltre cinqu'ore che quest'otta,
    mille dugento con sessanta sei
    anni compiè che qui la via fu rotta.
Io mando verso là di questi miei
    a reguardar s'alcun se ne sciorina:
    gite con lor, che non saranno rei.»
«Tra'ti avante, Alichino, e Calcabrina,»
    cominciò elli a dire, «e tu, Cagnazzo;
    e Barbariccia guidi la decina.
Libicocco vegn'oltre e Draghignazzo,
    Cirïatto sannuto e Graffiacane
    e Farfarello e Rubicante pazzo.
Cercate intorno le boglienti pane:
    costor sian salvi infino all'altro scheggio
    che tutto intero va sopra le tane.»
«Ohmè, maestro, che è quel ch'i' veggio?»
    diss'io. «Deh, sanza scorta andianci soli,
    se tu sa' ir; ch'i' per me non la cheggio.
Se tu se' sì accorto come suoli,
    non vedi tu ch'e' digrignan li denti,
    e con le ciglia ne minaccian duoli?»
Ed elli a me: «Non vo' che tu paventi:
    lasciali digrignar pur a lor senno,
    ch'e' fanno ciò per li lessi dolenti.»
Per l'argine sinistro volta dienno;
    ma prima avea ciascun la lingua stretta
    coi denti verso lor duca per cenno;
ed elli avea del cul fatto trombetta.

Then he said to us: "It is impossible to proceed further
   along this ridge, because the sixth arch
   lies at the bottom, all in pieces.
And so, if you still wish to move onward,
   make your way via this slope;
   nearby is another ridge that forms a path.[11]
Yesterday, five hours later than the present time,
   made one thousand two hundred and sixty-six
   years since the path was destroyed.[12]
I am sending some of my men that way
   to check whether any sinner is hanging himself out to dry:
   go with them, for they will not be malicious."
"Step forward, Alichino and Calcabrina,"[13]
   he began saying, "and you, Cagnazzo;[14]
   and let Barbariccia[15] lead the company of ten.
Let Libicocco come, too, and Draghignazzo,
   tusked Ciriatto and Graffiacane[16]
   and Farfarello[17] and crazy Rubicante.[18]
Search all around the boiling birdlime:
   let these two be safe until the next ridge
   that is intact and crosses over the dens."
"Alas, master, what is this I see?"
   I said. "Please, let us leave alone without an escort,
   if you know the way, because I myself do not ask for any.
If you are as alert as you usually are,
   do you not see that they are gnashing their teeth,
   and threatening harm to us with their eyebrows?"
And he replied: "I want you to have no fear:
   let them gnash as much as they like,
   because they are doing it for the benefit of the boiling sufferers."
Along the left slope we made a turn;
   but previously each one had stuck out his tongue
   toward their leader as a sign of readiness, pressing it with his teeth,
and their leader had made a trumpet of his behind.

---

11. This later proves to be a lie: all the bridges over the sixth moat are down.
12. When Christ harrowed Hell. 13. Calcabrina may mean "Frost Treader."
14. "Vicious Dog." 15. "Curly Beard." 16. "Dog Scratcher." 17. "Coltsfoot" (a
plant), a popular name for devils in folklore. 18. Probably means "Ruddy."

[SUMMARY OF CANTO XXII: As Dante, Vergil, and the ten demons proceed, grafters keep bobbing up out of the pitch. One who lingers too long is hauled up and tortured. Several decades earlier he was in the service of Thibault, king of Navarre. He describes some of his neighbors in the pitch, originally from Sardinia. While the unruly demons squabble, this sinner manages to escape. Then two of the demons have a fight. Both of them fall into the pitch themselves, and have to be fished out by their companions.

SUMMARY OF CANTO XXIII: Dante is afraid that the demons' latest problems will make them even more vicious, and that they will forget their promise of immunity. When an attack is really imminent, Vergil takes Dante in his arms and slides on his back down the steep slope to the sixth moat of

Canto XXIV

In quella parte del giovanetto anno
    che 'l sole i crin sotto l'Aquario tempra
    e già le notti al mezzo dì sen vanno,
quando la brina in su la terra assempra
    l'imagine di sua sorella bianca,
    ma poco dura alla sua penna tempra;
lo villanello a cui la roba manca,
    si leva, e guarda, e vede la campagna
    biancheggiar tutta; ond'ei si batte l'anca,
ritorna in casa, e qua e là si lagna,
    come 'l tapin che non sa che si faccia;
    poi riede, e la speranza ringavagna,
veggendo il mondo aver cangiata faccia
    in poco d'ora, e prende suo vincastro,
    e fuor le pecorelle a pascer caccia.
Così mi fece sbigottir lo mastro
    quand'io li vidi sì turbar la fronte,
    e così tosto al mal giunse lo 'mpiastro;
chè, come noi venimmo al guasto ponte,
    lo duca a me si volse con quel piglio
    dolce ch'io vidi prima a piè del monte.
Le braccia aperse, dopo alcun consiglio
    eletto seco riguardando prima
    ben la ruina, e diedemi di piglio.

the eighth circle, where the demons of the fifth moat have no power. Now they see, walking in a circle, people who are wearing monastic robes and cowls gilded on the outside, but made of lead, so that the sinners—the hypocrites—are heavily burdened. Dante speaks with two of them, friars from Bologna. Next, Dante sees Caiaphas, the high priest who advised putting Jesus to death. He, and the other members of his council, lie naked on the path, where the lead-robed sinners must walk on them. One of the friars now reveals the earlier lie of the demons: only by scrambling up among the ruins of a bridge can Dante and Vergil regain a safe path onward. They depart. Vergil's expression is angry and perturbed because of the deception.]

Canto XXIV

In that part of the young year
　　when the sun moderates its rays in Aquarius,[1]
　　and the nights are returning to half of a full day,[2]
when the hoarfrost on the ground copies
　　the image of its white sister,[3]
　　but its quill does not long retain its sharpness,[4]
the peasant, who is short of provisions,
　　gets up, looks around outdoors, and sees the countryside
　　all white; so that he slaps himself on the hip,
returns to his house, and complains on all sides,
　　like a wretch who does not know what to do;
　　then he goes out again, and recovers hope,
seeing that the world has changed its appearance
　　in a short while, and takes up his crook,
　　and drives his sheep out to graze.
Thus did my master cause me alarm
　　when I saw him furrow his brow that way,
　　and just as quickly did the poultice arrive for the wound;
because, when we came to the ruined bridge,
　　my guide turned to me with that gentle
　　look which I first saw at the foot of the mountain.[5]
He opened his arms; after taking some counsel
　　with himself, he first studied
　　the wreckage well, then took hold of me.

---

1. January–February.　2. Or: "are departing to the southern hemisphere," growing longer there but shorter in our (Dante's) climes.　3. Snow.　4. It does not coat the ground long.　5. In Canto I.

E come quei ch'adopera ed estima,
   che sempre par che 'nnanzi si proveggia,
   così, levando me su ver la cima
d'un ronchione, avvisava un'altra scheggia
   dicendo: «Sovra quella poi t'aggrappa;
   ma tenta pria s'è tal ch'ella ti reggia.»
Non era via da vestito di cappa,
   chè noi a pena, ei lieve e io sospinto,
   potavam su montar di chiappa in chiappa;
e se non fosse che da quel precinto
   più che dall'altro era la costa corta,
   non so di lui, ma io sarei ben vinto.
Ma perchè Malebolge inver la porta
   del bassissimo pozzo tutta pende,
   lo sito di ciascuna valle porta
che l'una costa surge e l'altra scende:
   noi pur venimmo al fine in su la punta
   onde l'ultima pietra si scoscende.
La lena m'era del polmon sì munta
   quand'io fui su, ch'i' non potea più oltre,
   anzi m'assisi nella prima giunta.
«Omai convien che tu così ti spoltre»
   disse 'l maestro; «chè, seggendo in piuma,
   in fama non si vien, nè sotto coltre;
sanza la qual chi sua vita consuma,
   cotal vestigio in terra di sè lascia,
   qual fummo in aere ed in acqua la schiuma.
E però leva su: vinci l'ambascia
   con l'animo che vince ogni battaglia,
   se col suo grave corpo non s'accascia.
Più lunga scala convien che si saglia;
   non basta dal costoro esser partito:
   se tu m'intendi, or fa sì che ti vaglia.»
Leva'mi allor, mostrandomi fornito
   meglio di lena ch'i' non mi sentìa,
   e dissi: «Va, ch'i' son forte e ardito.»
Su per lo scoglio prendemmo la via,
   ch'era ronchioso, stretto e malagevole,
   ed erto più assai che quel di pria.

And, like a man who calculates while he acts,
    who always seems to take the needful preliminary measures,
    just so, lifting me up toward the top
of a rocky spur, he indicated another rock splinter,
    saying: "Now catch hold of that one;
    but first test it to see whether it is strong enough to support you."
That was no path for someone dressed in a leaden cloak,
    because, he moving lightly and I being pushed forward, we were barely able
    to climb from one projecting rock to another;
and if it had not been the case that from that embankment
    the descent was shorter than from the preceding one,
    I do not know about him, but *I* would surely have been overcome.
But, because all of Malebolge inclines downward
    toward the entrance to the lowest pit,
    the layout of each moat requires
that one side is higher and the other lower:
    well, we came to the end at the point
    where the final stone is broken away.
The breath was so milked out of my lungs
    when I got up there that I could go no farther,
    but sat down as soon as we arrived.
"Now you must shake off your laziness,"
    my master said, "because no one achieves fame
    by sitting on down or lying beneath blankets;
and whoever uses up his life without fame
    leaves the same traces behind him on earth
    as smoke does in the air, or foam in water.
And so, arise: overcome your breathlessness
    with the strong mind that wins every battle
    if it does not slump along with its heavy body.
We still need to climb a longer staircase;[6]
    it is not enough that we leave these sinners behind:
    if you understand me, now act as if it counted!"
Then I arose, exhibiting a greater
    supply of breath than I really felt I had,
    and I said: "Proceed, for I am strong and bold."
We made our way up along the ridge,
    which was spurred, narrow, and hard to negotiate,
    and much higher than the one before.

---

6. In Purgatory.

Parlando andava per non parer fievole;
   onde una voce uscì dell'altro fosso,
   a parole formar disconvenevole.
Non so che disse, ancor che sovra 'l dosso
   fossi dell'arco già che varca quivi:
   ma chi parlava ad ire parea mosso.
Io era volto in giù, ma li occhi vivi
   non poteano ire al fondo per lo scuro;
   per ch'io: «Maestro, fa che tu arrivi
dall'altro cinghio e dismontiam lo muro;
   chè, com'i' odo quinci e non intendo,
   così giù veggio e neente affiguro.»
«Altra risposta» disse «non ti rendo
   se non lo far; chè la dimanda onesta
   si de' seguir con l'opera tacendo.»
Noi discendemmo il ponte dalla testa
   dove s'aggiugne con l'ottava ripa,
   e poi mi fu la bolgia manifesta;
e vidivi entro terribile stipa
   di serpenti, e di sì diversa mena
   che la memoria il sangue ancor mi scipa.
Più non si vanti Libia con sua rena;
   chè se chelidri, iaculi e faree
   produce, e cencri con anfisibena,
nè tante pestilenzie nè sì ree
   mostrò già mai con tutta l'Etïopia
   nè con ciò che di sopra al Mar Rosso èe.
Tra questa cruda e tristissima copia
   correan genti nude e spaventate,
   sanza sperar pertugio o elitropia:
con serpi le man dietro avean legate;
   quelle ficcavan per le ren la coda
   e il capo, ed eran dinanzi aggroppate.
Ed ecco a un ch'era da nostra proda,
   s'avventò un serpente che 'l trafisse
   là dove 'l collo alle spalle s'annoda.

I spoke as I went in order not to appear weak;
   whereupon from the next moat there issued a voice
   unadapted to forming words.
I do not know what it said, even though I was already
   atop the arch that crossed over in that place:
   but it seemed as if the speaker were in motion.
I was looking down, but my eyes—those of a living man—
   were unable to reach the bottom for the darkness;
   so that I said: "Master, please come
to the next embankment and let us descend the wall;
   because, just as I hear things here and fail to understand,
   in the same way I look down and can make out nothing."
"No other reply," he said, "do I give you
   than to do as you ask; because an honorable request
   should be followed by actions without words."
We descended from the bridge at the end
   where it joins up with the eighth embankment,
   and then the moat was clearly visible to me;
and in it I saw a frightful accumulation
   of serpents, and of so many different sorts
   that the memory of it still curdles my blood.
Let not Libya with its sands boast of more;
   because if it produces *chelydri, jaculi,* and *phareae,*
   and *cenchres* along with *amphisbaenae,*[7]
never did it display so many or such evil
   pestilences along with all of Ethiopia
   or the lands that lie next to the Red Sea.
In the midst of this cruel and most unpleasant multitude
   naked, frightened people were running,
   with no hope of a hiding place or a heliotrope:[8]
they had their hands tied behind them with serpents,
   which were thrusting their tails and heads
   through the men's loins, and were knotted in front.
And behold, upon one man who was near our bank
   a serpent hurled itself, piercing him
   where the neck is joined to the back.

---

7. All these serpents are mentioned by Lucan in his poem *Pharsalia.* 8. A stone
that renders its bearer invisible (and is an antidote to venom?).

Nè *o* sì tosto mai nè *i* si scrisse,
  com'el s'accese ed arse, e cener tutto
  convenne che cascando divenisse;
e poi che fu a terra sì distrutto,
  la polver si raccolse per sè stessa,
  e 'n quel medesmo ritornò di butto:
così per li gran savi si confessa
  che la fenice more e poi rinasce,
  quando al cinquecentesimo anno appressa:
erba nè biada in sua vita non pasce,
  ma sol d'incenso lacrime e d'amomo,
  e nardo e mirra son l'ultime fasce.
E qual è quel che cade, e non sa como,
  per forza di demon ch'a terra il tira,
  o d'altra oppilazion che lega l'omo,
quando si leva, che 'ntorno si mira
  tutto smarrito della grande angoscia
  ch'elli ha sofferta, e guardando sospira;
tal era il peccator levato poscia.
  Oh potenza di Dio, quant'è severa,
  che cotai colpi per vendetta croscia!
Lo duca il domandò poi chi ello era;
  per ch'ei rispuose: «Io piovvi di Toscana,
  poco tempo è, in questa gola fera.
Vita bestial mi piacque e non umana,
  sè come a mul ch'i' fui; son Vanni Fucci
  bestia, e Pistoia mi fu degna tana.»
E io al duca: «Dilli che non mucci,
  e domanda che colpa qua giù 'l pinse;
  ch'io 'l vidi uomo di sangue e di crucci.»
E 'l peccator, che 'ntese, non s'infinse,
  ma drizzò verso me l'animo e 'l volto,
  e di trista vergogna si dipinse;
poi disse: «Più mi duol che tu m'hai colto
  nella miseria dove tu mi vedi,
  che quando fui dell'altra vita tolto.
Io non posso negar quel che tu chiedi:
  in giù son messo tanto perch'io fui
  ladro alla sagrestia de' belli arredi,

Never was an *o* or an *i* written as quickly
    as that man caught fire and burned, and had to
    turn completely into ash as he fell;
and after he had reached the ground thus disintegrated,
    the ashes assembled of their own accord,
    and immediately formed the same man again:
in like manner it is reported by the great poets
    that the phoenix dies and is then reborn
    when it approaches its five hundredth year:
in its lifetime it feeds neither on grass nor on grain,
    but only on drops of incense and balsam,
    and nard and myrrh are its final windingsheet.
And like the man who falls,[9] and does not know why,
    through the force of a demon that pulls him to the ground,
    or from another obstruction that binds a man,
and who, when he stands up, gazes all around,
    totally bewildered by the great anguish
    he has suffered, and as he looks he sighs;
in the same state was that sinner when he stood up afterward.
    Oh, the power of God, how severe it is
    that it pelts down such blows in retribution!
My guide then asked him who he was;
    and so he replied: "Not long ago
    I rained down from Tuscany into this wild gorge.
A bestial life pleased me, not a human one,
    as befitting the mule[10] that I was; I am Vanni Fucci
    the animal, and Pistoia was a worthy lair for me."
And I said to my guide: "Tell him not to make a getaway,
    and ask him what crime propelled him down here;
    because I knew him to be a man of blood and anger."
And the sinner, who heard this, put on no false front,
    but directed his mind and face toward me,
    displaying wretched shame;
then he said: "I am more grieved that you have caught me
    in the unhappy state in which you see me
    than I was when I was snatched away from the other life.
I cannot refuse to tell you what you request:
    I have been placed in such a low circle because I was
    a thief of the beautiful ornaments in the sacristy,[11]

---

9. An epileptic.   10. Illegitimate child.   11. In the Pistoia cathedral.

e falsamente già fu apposto altrui.
    Ma perchè di tal vista tu non godi,
    se mai sarai di fuor da' luoghi bui,
apri li orecchi al mio annunzio, e odi:
    Pistoia in pria de' Neri si dimagra:
    poi Fiorenza rinova gente e modi.
Tragge Marte vapor di Val di Magra
    ch'è di torbidi nuvoli involuto;
    e con tempesta impetüosa e agra
sovra Campo Picen fia combattuto;
    ond'ei repente spezzerà la nebbia,
    sì ch'ogni Bianco ne sarà feruto.
E detto l'ho perchè doler ti debbia!»

[SUMMARY OF CANTO XXV: Vanni Fucci now makes an obscene gesture to
God, and serpents coil around him. Then he is pursued by Cacus, a monster
killed by Hercules for cattle rustling (Cacus is here described as a centaur).
Continuing his sojourn among the thieves in the seventh moat of the eighth
circle, Dante meets five Florentines. Around one of them a snake wraps

---

Canto XXVI

Godi, Fiorenza, poi che se' sì grande,
    che per mare e per terra batti l'ali,
    e per lo 'nferno tuo nome si spande!
Tra li ladron trovai cinque cotali
    tuoi cittadini onde mi ven vergogna,
    e tu in grande orranza non ne sali.
Ma se presso al mattin del ver si sogna,
    tu sentirai di qua da picciol tempo
    di quel che Prato, non ch'altri, t'agogna.
E se già fosse, non saria per tempo:
    così foss'ei, da che pur esser dee!
    chè più mi graverà, com più m'attempo.

and someone else was falsely accused.
    But, in order that you may take no joy in such a sight,
    if you ever emerge from the dark places,
open your ears to my prediction, and listen:
    first Pistoia will be thinned of its Blacks:
    then Florence will have new people and government.
Mars is bringing lightning from Valdimagra
    that is enveloped in dense clouds;
    and with an impetuous, fierce storm
there will be combat on Campo Piceno;
    so that the lightning will suddenly pierce the mist
    and every White will be struck by it.[12]
And I have told you this so that it may hurt you!"

---

itself until the two are merged into an unheard-of monster. A second man, bitten by another snake, exchanges shapes with his assailant. (The two attacking snakes are actually two of the Florentines in a temporary guise; the fifth Florentine remains human throughout the proceedings.)]

Canto XXVI

Rejoice, Florence, because you are so great
    that you beat your wings on land and sea,
    and your name is spread in Hell!
Among the thieves I found five such
    who were our citizens—from which I derive shame
    and you do not come off with much prestige.
But, if dreams that occur toward morning tell the truth,
    only a short time from now you will feel
    what Prato, let alone others, wishes for you.[1]
And if it were already so, it would not be too soon:
    let it be so, since it must happen anyway!
    For it will grieve me all the more, the older I get.

---

12. The Black faction of the Guelf party was expelled from Pistoia in 1301, but the Blacks took over in Florence later that year. In 1302, the "lightning from Valdimagra" (Moroello Malaspina of Lunigiana in the Valdimagra, who was to be Dante's host in 1306) won a battle against the Whites (Dante's faction) on the Campo Piceno just outside Pistoia. There are other interpretations of this prophecy-after-the-fact.   1. The town of Prato was under Florence's thumb, and duly resentful.

Noi ci partimmo, e su per le scalee
 che n'avean fatte i borni a scender pria,
 rimontò 'l duca mio e trasse mee;
e proseguendo la solinga via,
 tra le schegge e tra' rocchi dello scoglio
 lo piè sanza la man non si spedìa.
Allor mi dolsi, e ora mi ridoglio
 quando drizzo la mente a ciò ch'io vidi,
 e più lo 'ngegno affreno ch'i' non soglio,
perchè non corra che virtù nol guidi;
 sì che, se stella bona o miglior cosa
 m'ha dato 'l ben, ch'io stessi nol m'invidi.
Quante il villan ch'al poggio si riposa,
 nel tempo che colui che 'l mondo schiara
 la faccia sua a noi tien meno ascosa,
come la mosca cede a la zanzara,
 vede lucciole giù per la vallea,
 forse colà dov'e' vendemmia ed ara;
di tante fiamme tutta risplendea
 l'ottava bolgia, sì com'io m'accorsi
 tosto che fui là 've 'l fondo parea.
E qual colui che si vengiò con li orsi
 vide 'l carro d'Elia al dipartire,
 quando i cavalli al cielo erti levorsi,
che nol potea sì con li occhi seguire,
 ch'el vedesse altro che la fiamma sola,
 sì come nuvoletta, in su salire;
tal si move ciascuna per la gola
 del fosso, chè nessuna mostra il furto,
 e ogni fiamma un peccatore invola.
Io stava sovra 'l ponte a veder surto,
 sì che s'io non avessi un ronchion preso,
 caduto sarei giù sanz'esser urto.
E 'l duca, che mi vide tanto atteso,
 disse: «Dentro dai fuochi son li spirti;
 ciascun si fascia di quel ch'elli è inceso».
«Maestro mio,» rispuos'io, «per udirti
 son io più certo; ma già m'era avviso
 che così fosse, e già voleva dirti:

We took our leave and, up along the stairs
    that the projecting rocks had formed for us when we came down earlier,
    my guide ascended again, drawing me with him;
and, as we pursued our lonely way,
    among the splinters and crags of the ridge,
    our feet could not go forward without the help of our hands.
Then I sorrowed, and I sorrow again now
    when I turn my memory back to what I saw,
    and I rein my mind in more than I am wont to do,
lest it race ahead where virtue does not guide it;
    so that, if a lucky star or something better[2]
    has given me that asset, I may not begrudge it to myself.[3]
When a peasant reposes on a hill
    in the season when the star that illuminates the world
    has its face least hidden from us,[4]
at the time when flies give way to mosquitos,[5]
    as many fireflies as he sees down in the valley,
    perhaps in the place where he picks his grapes and plows;
with just so many flames the eighth moat
    was all resplendent, as I observed
    as soon as I reached a point from which the bottom was visible.
And, just as the man who avenged himself with bears[6]
    saw Elijah's chariot as it departed,
    when the horses raised themselves up toward heaven,
so that he could not follow them with his eyes in such a way
    that he could make out anything but just the flame
    rising upward like a little cloud;
in like manner each flame moves through the gorge
    of the moat, for none of them reveals what it has stolen,
    and each flame steals a sinner from sight.
I was standing on the bridge, leaning over as I watched,
    so that, if I had not taken hold of a rocky spur,
    I would have fallen down without being pushed.
And my guide, who saw me so absorbed,
    said: "Inside the fires are spirits:
    each one is shrouded by that which burns him within."
"My master," I replied, "through listening to you
    I am more convinced; but I had already assumed
    that that was the case, and I already wanted to ask you:

---

2. Divine grace.   3. That is, lose it by misusing it.   4. In the summer.   5. In the evening.   6. The prophet Elisha; bears killed urchins who had mocked him.

chi è in quel foco che vien sì diviso
    di sopra, che par surger della pira
    dov'Eteòcle col fratel fu miso?»
Rispuose a me: «Là dentro si martira
    Ulisse e Dïomede, e così inseme
    alla vendetta vanno come all'ira;
e dentro dalla lor fiamma si geme
    l'agguato del caval che fè la porta
    onde uscì de' Romani il gentil seme.
Piangevisi entro l'arte per che, morta,
    Deïdamìa ancor si duol d'Achille,
    e del Palladio pena vi si porta.»
«S'ei posson dentro da quelle faville
    parlar» diss'io, «maestro, assai ten priego
    e ripriego, che il priego vaglia mille,
che non mi facci dell'attender niego
    fin che la fiamma cornuta qua vegna:
    vedi che del disio ver lei mi piego!»
Ed elli a me: «La tua preghiera è degna
    di molta loda, e io però l'accetto;
    ma fa che la tua lingua si sostegna.
Lascia parlare a me, ch'i' ho concetto
    ciò che tu vuoi; ch'ei sarebbero schivi,
    perchè fuor greci, forse del tuo detto.»
Poi che la fiamma fu venuta quivi
    dove parve al mio duca tempo e loco,
    in questa forma lui parlare audivi:
«O voi che siete due dentro ad un foco,
    s'io meritai di voi mentre ch'io vissi,
    s'io meritai di voi assai o poco
quando nel mondo li alti versi scrissi,
    non vi movete; ma l'un di voi dica

Who is in that fire which is so divided
    on top that it seems to arise from the pyre
    on which Eteocles was placed along with his brother?"[7]
He answered: "There within are tormented
    Ulysses and Diomedes, and thus together
    they go to their retribution the way they went to their acts of rage;
and inside their flame they groan for
    the ambush of the horse that created the gate
    from which the noble seed of the Romans issued.[8]
Inside there, they weep for the ruse by which, even after death,
    Deidamia still grieves for Achilles,[9]
    and they bear the penalty for the Palladium."[10]
"If within those sparks they can
    speak," I said, "master, I heartily entreat you
    again and again, and let my entreaty count for a thousand,
that you do not refuse me permission to wait
    until the horned flame arrives here:
    you see that I am bending toward it in my desire!"
And he replied: "Your entreaty is worthy
    of much praise, and so I grant it;
    but see to it that your tongue restrains itself.
Let me do the talking, because I have understood
    what you have in mind; for they would be shy,
    perhaps, of your speech because they were Greeks."[11]
After the flame had approached to the extent
    that my guide considered it the right time and place,
    I heard him speak in these terms:
"O you two that are enclosed in one fire,
    if I gained credit with you while I lived,
    if I gained much or little credit with you
when back in the world I wrote the lofty verses,
    do not stir; but let one of you tell

---

7. Eteocles and Polynices, sons of Oedipus, killed each other fighting for mastery
over Thebes; when they were cremated, even their ashes formed two separate heaps.
8. The Trojan Horse, devised by Ulysses (Odysseus), led to the destruction of Troy,
from which Aeneas escaped to the west, where his descendants founded Rome.   9.
To save him from death in the Trojan War, Achilles' mother dressed him as a girl and
hid him on the island of Scyros, where the princess Deidamia fell in love with him;
Ulysses and Diomedes discovered his identity and took him away.   10. Ulysses and
Diomedes stole this statue, which gave the Trojans divine protection.   11. A puzzling
line with many interpretations; perhaps they would dislike Dante because of his (alleged) Roman, and thus Trojan, ancestry.

dove per lui perduto a morir gissi.
Lo maggior corno della fiamma antica
    cominciò a crollarsi mormorando
    pur come quella cui vento affatica;
indi la cima qua e là menando,
    come fosse la lingua che parlasse,
    gittò voce di fuori, e disse: «Quando
mi diparti' da Circe, che sottrasse
    me più d'un anno là presso a Gaeta,
    prima che sì Enea la nomasse,
nè dolcezza di figlio, nè la pièta
    del vecchio padre, nè 'l debito amore
    lo qual dovea Penelopè far lieta,
vincer poter dentro da me l'ardore
    ch'i' ebbi a divenir del mondo esperto,
    e delli vizi umani e del valore;
ma misi me per l'alto mare aperto
    sol con un legno e con quella compagna
    picciola dalla qual non fui diserto.
L'un lito e l'altro vidi infin la Spagna,
    fin nel Morrocco, e l'isola de Sardi,
    e l'altre che quel mare intorno bagna.
Io e' compagni eravam vecchi e tardi
    quando venimmo a quella foce stretta
    dov'Ercule segnò li suoi riguardi,
acciò che l'uom più oltre non si metta:
    dalla man destra mi lasciai Sibilia,
    dall'altra già m'avea lasciata Setta.
'O frati,' dissi, 'che per cento milia
    perigli siete giunti all'occidente,
    a questa tanto picciola vigilia
de' nostri sensi ch'è del rimanente,
    non vogliate negar l'esperïenza,
    di retro al sol, del mondo sanza gente.
Considerate la vostra semenza:
    fatti non foste a viver come bruti,
    ma per seguir virtute e canoscenza.'

where he happened to die without the knowledge of others."
The taller horn of the ancient flame
   began to shake with a murmur
   just like one that is buffeted by the wind;
then, moving its summit to and fro,
   as if that were its tongue speaking,
   it emitted a voice, which said: "When
I left Circe,[12] who held me in retreat
   over a year close to Gaeta
   before Aeneas gave it that name,
neither affection for my son nor duty
   to my aged father, nor the due love
   that should have made Penelope[13] happy,
were able to subdue within me the eagerness
   I felt to become acquainted with the world,
   and with human vices and goodness;
but I set out on the open high seas
   alone with one vessel and with those few companions
   by whom I was never abandoned.
I beheld both shores[14] all the way to Spain,
   up to Morocco, and the island of the Sardinians,
   and the others which that sea bathes all around.
I and my companions were already old and slow-moving
   when we arrived at that narrow strait
   where Hercules marked his boundaries,[15]
so that man might proceed no further:
   on the right, I left Seville behind me;
   on the other side, I had already left Ceuta behind.
'O brothers,' I said, 'you that through a hundred thousand
   perils have come to the west,
   in this all-too-brief wakefulness
of our senses that remains to us,
   do not be willing to forgo the experience
   of the uninhabited world,[16] as we follow the sun.
Reflect on your ancestry:
   you were not born to live like brute animals,
   but to pursue moral perfection and knowledge.'

---

12. A sorceress who detained Ulysses during his voyage home after the Trojan War; this reference tells the reader that the speaker is Ulysses.   13. Wife of Ulysses.   14. Of the Mediterranean.   15. The Pillars of Hercules (Strait of Gibraltar).   16. The southern hemisphere, consisting entirely of ocean in Dante's frame of reference.

Li miei compagni fec'io sì aguti,
  con questa orazion picciola, al cammino,
  che a pena poscia li avrei ritenuti;
e volta nostra poppa nel mattino,
  dei remi facemmo ali al folle volo,
  sempre acquistando dal lato mancino.
Tutte le stelle già dall'altro polo
  vedea la notte, e 'l nostro tanto basso,
  che non surgea fuor del marin suolo.
Cinque volte racceso e tante casso
  lo lume era di sotto dalla luna,
  poi che 'ntrati eravam nell'alto passo,
quando n'apparve una montagna, bruna
  per la distanza, e parvemi alta tanto
  quanto veduta non aveva alcuna.
Noi ci allegrammo, e tosto tornò in pianto;
  chè della nova terra un turbo nacque,
  e percosse del legno il primo canto.
Tre volte il fè girar con tutte l'acque:
  alla quarta levar la poppa in suso
  e la prora ire in giù, com'altrui piacque,
infin che 'l mar fu sopra noi richiuso.»

[SUMMARY OF CANTO XXVII: Dante, still in the eighth moat of the eighth circle, where the sinners who gave evil counsel in life are punished by being enveloped in flames, is now addressed by a man from Romagna, who asks for recent news from home. Dante replies with a catalogue of current catastrophes. The questioner is Count Guido of Montefeltro, who gave Pope Boniface VIII (Dante's *bête noire*) advice on how to reduce the Colonna family's stronghold in the hill town of Palestrina. When Guido died, Saint Francis tried to save his soul because Guido had become a Franciscan monk, but the "black cherub" sent to take his soul to Hell won out on a theological technicality, gleefully spouting to Guido the (now famous) line: "Maybe you weren't aware that I was a logician!" Dante and Vergil now proceed toward the ninth moat, where the sowers of discord are punished.

SUMMARY OF CANTO XXVIII: The former schismatics and scandalmongers in the ninth moat are mangled, mutilated, or split open in various fashions. Dante is addressed by Mohammed, who was erroneously considered at the time as the leader of a Christian schism; Mohammed sends a warning to a

I made my companions so fanatical
  to make the journey, with this brief speech,
  that afterwords I would barely have been able to hold them back;
and, turning our stern toward the east,
  we made wings of our oars in our mad flight,
  continually bearing left.
Already we saw at night all the stars
  of the southern hemisphere, and we saw our own pole star so low
  that it did not rise beyond the level of the sea.
Five times the sublunary light
  had been rekindled and just as often extinguished[17]
  since we had entered into our difficult passage,
when a mountain[18] appeared to us, murky
  because of the distance, and it seemed to me higher
  than any other I had ever seen.
We rejoiced, but our joy soon turned to tears;
  because from the new-found land a whirlwind sprang up
  and struck the nearer end of the vessel.
Three times it made it spin around along with all the waters:
  at the fourth onslaught it made the stern rise
  and the prow descend, as it pleased Someone,[19]
until the sea had closed over us again."

still-living schismatic in northwestern Italy. Dante then meets some recent Italian sowers of strife, as well as Curio, the Roman said to have advised Julius Caesar to cross the Rubicon, thus touching off the long civil wars. Finally a spirit appears that is swinging its severed head by the hair like a lantern; this is the war-loving late-12th-century troubadour Bertran de Born (later celebrated by Ezra Pound), alleged to have encouraged Crown Prince Henry of England to revolt against his father, Henry II.

SUMMARY OF CANTO XXIX: It is now early afternoon, and Vergil urges haste. Dante is disappointed not to have seen his father's unruly cousin Geri del Bello; Vergil tells Dante that Geri *was* there, gesturing threateningly at Dante, presumably because his murder had not yet been avenged. In the tenth and last moat of the eighth circle, falsifiers of all kinds are smitten with a variety of noisome diseases. Two men seen scratching their itching scabs are Griffolino of Arezzo, who obtained money by promising he could teach someone to fly, and in revenge was burned as an alchemist; and Capocchio of Siena (perhaps a native Florentine), another alchemist who was burned.]

17. That is, five months had passed.   18. No doubt, the mountain of Purgatory.
19. God.

Canto XXX

Nel tempo che Iunone era crucciata
    per Semelè contra 'l sangue tebano,
    come mostrò una e altra fiata,
Atamante divenne tanto insano,
    che veggendo la moglie con due figli
    andar carcata da ciascuna mano,
gridò: «Tendiam le reti, sì ch'io pigli
    la leonessa e' leoncini al varco»;
    e poi distese i dispietati artigli,
prendendo l'un ch'avea nome Learco,
    e rotollo e percosselo ad un sasso;
    e quella s'annegò con l'altro carco.
E quando la fortuna volse in basso
    l'altezza de' Troian che tutto ardiva,
    si che 'nsieme col regno il re fu casso,
Ecuba trista, misera e cattiva,
    poscia che vide Polissena morta,
    e del suo Polidoro in su la riva
del mar si fu la dolorosa accorta,
    forsennata latrò sì come cane;
    tanto il dolor le fè la mente torta.
Ma nè di Tebe furie nè troiane
    si vider mai in alcun tanto crude,
    non punger bestie, non che membra umane,
quant'io vidi due ombre smorte e nude,
    che mordendo correvan di quel modo
    che 'l porco quando del porcil si schiude.
L'una giunse a Capocchio, ed in sul nodo
    del collo l'assannò, sì che, tirando,
    grattar li fece il ventre al fondo sodo.
E l'Aretin, che rimase, tremando,

Canto XXX

At the time when Juno was angry
    at the people of Thebes because of Semele,[1]
    as she demonstrated time after time,
Athamas became so insane
    that, seeing his wife go burdened
    with two children, one on each arm,
he shouted: "Let us spread the nets, so I can capture
    the lioness and her cubs as they pass by!"
And then he stretched out his pitiless talons,
seizing the one child whose name was Learchus,
    whirled him and dashed him against a rock;
    and his wife drowned herself with her other burden.[2]
And when fortune turned to such a low point
    the greatness of the Trojans, which had dared everything,
    so that, together with the kingdom, the king was annihilated,
unhappy, wretched, captive Hecuba,
    upon seeing Polyxena dead,
    and in her grief catching sight
of her Polydorus on the seashore,
    lost her wits and barked like a dog;
    so greatly did sorrow twist her mind.[3]
But neither the furies of Thebes nor those of Troy
    were ever seen to be so cruel to anyone,
    while goading beasts, not to speak of human bodies,
as they were when I saw them goading two pale, naked shades
    who were running around and biting the way
    a hog does when released from its sty.
One of them came up to Capocchio, and gored him
    in the nape of the neck, so that, pulling him,
    he made him scrape his belly against the hard ground.
And the man from Arezzo,[4] who remained there trembling,

---

1. Juno (Hera) was angry because Jupiter (Zeus) had committed adultery with the Theban lady Semele. 2. Athamas, ruler of Thebes, was married to Semele's sister Ino. Juno drove him mad in the way Dante tells. 3. When Troy fell, its queen, Hecuba, who had already lost numerous children in the war, now lost the two mentioned, and went mad. 4. Griffolino, introduced in the preceding canto, as was Capocchio.

mi disse: «Quel folletto è Gianni Schicchi,
   e va rabbioso altrui così conciando.»
«Oh!» diss'io lui, «se l'altro non ti ficchi
   li denti a dosso, non ti sia fatica
   a dir chi è pria che di qui si spicchi.»
Ed elli a me: «Quell'è l'anima antica
   di Mirra scellerata, che divenne
   al padre fuor del dritto amore amica.
Questa a peccar con esso così venne,
   falsificando sè in altrui forma,
   come l'altro che là sen va, sostenne,
per guadagnar la donna della torma,
   falsificare in sè Buoso Donati,
   testando e dando al testamento norma.»
E poi che i due rabbiosi fuor passati
   sovra cu' io avea l'occhio tenuto
   rivolsilo a guardar li altri mal nati.
Io vidi un, fatto a guisa di lëuto,
   pur ch'elli avesse avuta l'anguinaia
   tronca dall'altro che l'uomo ha forcuto.
La grave idropesì, che sì dispaia
   le membra con l'omor che mal converte,
   che 'l viso non risponde alla ventraia,
faceva lui tener le labbra aperte
   come l'etico fa, che per la sete
   l'un verso il mento e l'altro in su rinverte.
«O voi che sanz'alcuna pena sete,
   e non so io perchè, nel mondo gramo,»
   diss'elli a noi, «guardate e attendete
alla miseria del maestro Adamo:
   io ebbi vivo assai di quel ch'i' volli,
   e ora, lasso!, un gocciol d'acqua bramo.
Li ruscelletti che de' verdi colli

said to me: "That goblin is Gianni Schicchi,[5]
and he goes about rabidly mutilating people that way."
"Oh," I said to him, "so may that second goblin not plant
    its teeth in you!—let it not be wearisome to you
    to tell me who it is before it dashes away from here."
And he replied: "That is the ancient soul
    of evil Myrrha,[6] who became
    a lover to her father beyond the limits of proper love.
She came to sin with him,
    belying herself in the guise of another,
    just as that first goblin, who is there departing, dared,
in order to win the queen of the herd,
    to impersonate Buoso Donati,
    making a will and having it notarized."
And after the two mad beings, on whom
    I had kept my eyes, had passed from view,
    I turned back to look at the others who were born for evil.
I saw one who was shaped like a lute,
    or would have been if he had had his groin
    amputated of man's two forking appendages.[7]
His serious case of dropsy, which so disproportions
    the body with the fluids it digests improperly
    that the face does not correspond to the paunch,
made him keep his lips open
    the way a consumptive does, who from thirst
    curls one of them toward the chin and the other one upward.
"O you that are without any penalty,
    and I do not know why, here in this dismal world,"
    he said to us, "observe and pay attention
to the misery of Master Adamo:
    while alive, I had plenty of whatever I wanted,
    and now, alas, I crave for a drop of water.
The brooks that from the green hills

---

5. A Florentine of the Cavalcanti clan, hired by the family of Buoso Donati—who had willed the fortune to the Church—to impersonate Buoso on his deathbed and dictate a new will in favor of the family. Gianni's "cut" was the "queen of the herd," a very fine mare or she-mule. This passage was the inspiration for the clever libretto to Puccini's *Gianni Schicchi*.   6. A princess of ancient Cyprus; for her crime she was metamorphosed into the myrrh tree.   7. His small head and big belly would have resembled a lute exactly, except that he had legs.

del Casentin discendon giuso in Arno,
faccendo i lor canali freddi e molli,
sempre mi stanno innanzi, e non indarno,
chè l'imagine lor vie più m'asciuga
che 'l male ond'io nel volto mi discarno.
La rigida giustizia che mi fruga
tragge cagion del loco ov'io peccai
a metter più li miei sospiri in fuga.
Ivi è Romena, là dov'io falsai
La lega suggellata del Batista;
per ch'io il corpo su arso lasciai.
Ma s'io vedessi qui l'anima trista
di Guido o d'Alessandro o di lor frate,
per Fonte Branda non darei la vista.
Dentro c'è l'una già, se l'arrabbiate
ombre che vanno intorno dicon vero;
ma che mi val, c'ho membra legate?
s'io fossi pur di tanto ancor leggero
ch'i' potessi in cent'anni andare un'oncia,
io sarei messo già per lo sentero,
cercando lui tra questa gente sconcia,
con tutto ch'ella volge undici miglia,
e men d'un mezzo di traverso non ci ha.
Io son per lor tra sì fatta famiglia:
e' m'indussero a batter li fiorini
ch'avevan tre carati di mondiglia.»
E io a lui: «Chi son li due tapini
che fumman come man bagnate 'l verno,
giacendo stretti a' tuoi destri confini?»
«Qui li trovai — e poi volta non dierno — »
rispuose, «quando piovvi in questo greppo,
e non credo che dieno in sempiterno.
L'una è la falsa ch'accusò Giuseppo;
l'altr'è il falso Sinon greco da Troia:
per febbre aguta gittan tanto leppo.»

of the Casentino[8] run down into the Arno,
  making their channels cool and soft,
are always before my eyes, and not for nothing,
  because their image makes me drier
  than the disease that makes my face grown thin.
The severe justice that torments me
  takes its occasion from the place where I sinned
  to send my sighs flying faster.
There lies Romena,[9] where I falsified
  the alloy that is minted with the image of the Baptist;[10]
  for which I left my body up there burned.
But if I could see down here the wretched soul
  of Guido, Alessandro, or their brother,[11]
  I would not trade that sight for Fonte Branda.[12]
One of them[13] is already in here, if the rabid
  shades who go about speak the truth;
  but what good is that to me if my limbs are bound?
If I were only so much lighter
  that I could walk an inch in a hundred years,
  I would already have set out on the trail,
seeking him out among these misshapen people,
  even though the moat is eleven miles around
  and is no less than half a mile across.
Because of them, I am one of a family like this:
  they induced me to coin the florins
  that contained three carats of base metal."
I said to him: "Who are those two wretches
  who are reeking like wet hands in wintertime,
  and are lying up against your right-hand boundaries?"
"I found them there, and they have not turned since,"
  he answered, "when I rained down into this chasm,
  and I do not believe they will ever turn for all eternity.
One is the lying woman who accused Joseph;[14]
  the other is the lying Greek Sinon from Troy:[15]
  severe fever makes them give off such a great stench."

---

8. Uplands where the headwaters of the river Arno are located.   9. A castle in the Casentino district.   10. The gold florin, the internationally accepted coinage of Florence.   11. The Counts of Romena.   12. A spring near Romena.   13. Guido, the only one of the brothers who died before 1300, the date Dante assigns to his journey. 14. Potiphar's wife, in Genesis.   15. Pretending to be a renegade from the Greek camp, Sinon persuaded the Trojans to accept the wooden horse within their walls.

E l'un di lor, che si recò a noia
forse d'esser nomato sì oscuro,
col pugno li percosse l'epa croia.
Quella sonò come fosse un tamburo;
e mastro Adamo li percosse il volto
col braccio suo, che non parve men duro,
dicendo a lui: «Ancor che mi sia tolto
lo muover per le membra che son gravi,
ho io il braccio a tal mestiere sciolto.»
Ond'ei rispuose: «Quando tu andavi
al fuoco, non l'avei tu così presto:
ma sì e più l'avei quando coniavi.»
E l'idropico: «Tu di' ver di questo:
ma tu non fosti sì ver testimonio
là 've del ver fosti a Troia richesto.»
«s'io dissi falso, e tu falsasti il conio»
disse Sinone; «e son qui per un fallo,
e tu per più ch'alcun altro demonio!»
«Ricorditi, spergiuro, del cavallo»
rispuose quel ch'avea infiata l'epa;
«e sieti reo che tutto il mondo sallo!»
«E te sia rea la sete onde ti crepa»
disse 'l greco «la lingua, e l'acqua marcia
che 'l ventre innanzi li occhi sì t'assiepa!»
Allora il monetier: «Così si squarcia
la bocca tua per tuo mal come sòle;
chè s'i' ho sete ed umor mi rinfarcia,
tu hai l'arsura e 'l capo che ti dole;
e per leccar lo specchio di Narcisso,
non vorresti a 'nvitar molte parole.»
Ad ascoltarli er'io del tutto fisso,
quando 'l maestro mi disse: «Or pur mira!
che per poco che teco non mi risso.»
Quand'io 'l senti' a me parlar con ira,
volsimi verso lui con tal vergogna,
ch'ancor per la memoria mi si gira.
Qual è colui che suo dannaggio sogna,
che sognando desidera sognare,

And one of them, who took it ill,
  perhaps, that he was described so dishonorably,
  hit him with his fist on his vile, hard belly.
The belly resounded like a drum;
  and Master Adamo hit the other's face
  with his arm, which seemed no less hard,
saying to him: "Although I have lost
  the power to move because my body is heavy,
  my arm is free for such a necessity."
Whereupon the other countered: "When you were on the way
  to be burned, you did not have it so handy,
  but you did, and even more so, when you were coining."
The dropsical man said: "In this you speak the truth:
  but you were not so truthful a witness
  when you were asked to tell the truth in Troy."
"If I told a lie—well, you falsified the coinage!"
  said Sinon, "and I am here for one crime,
  whereas you are here for more than any other demon!"
"Perjurer, remember the horse,"
  replied the man with the swollen belly;
  "and may it be bitter to you that the whole world knows it!"
"And may you find bitter," the Greek said, "the thirst
  from which your tongue is cracking, and the putrid water
  that makes your stomach such a high fence in front of your eyes!"
Then the coiner said: "In the same way, your mouth
  is chapped from your disease as it usually is;
  for, if I am thirsty and stuffed with fluids,
you have your fever and your aching head;
  and, if you could lick Narcissus's mirror,[16]
  you would not wait for many words of invitation."
I was completely absorbed in listening to them,
  when my master said to me: "Just keep on looking!
  It would not take much for me to quarrel with you."
When I heard him address me in anger,
  I turned toward him in such great shame
  that it still spins around in my memory.
Like a man who dreams that he meets some harm
  and, in his dream, wishes he is only dreaming,

---

16. "Narcissus's mirror" is water: the Greek youth fell in love with his own image reflected in a spring.

sì quel ch'è, come non fosse, agogna,
tal mi fec'io, non possendo parlare,
  che disïava scusarmi, e scusava
  me tuttavia, e nol mi credea fare.
«Maggior difetto men vergogna lava»
  disse 'l maestro, «che 'l tuo non è stato;
  però d'ogne trestizia ti disgrava:
e fa ragion ch'io ti sia sempre a lato,
  se più avvien che fortuna t'accoglia
  dove sien genti in simigliante piato;
chè voler ciò udire è bassa voglia.»

[SUMMARY OF CANTO XXXI: Leaving the eighth circle, Dante hears a loud
horn blast and thinks he sees towers looming through the murk. They are
really rebellious giants, from the Bible and Greek mythology, who encircle
the round opening of the shaft that plunges into the ninth, and last, circle.
They emerge, from the waist up, from inside the perimeter of the shaft. First
is Nimrod, who caused the confusion of languages when the tower of Babel
was being built (he is not a giant in the Bible); it is he who blew the horn.
Then the travelers see the ancient Greek giant Ephialtes, who warred against
the gods. At Vergil's request, the third giant, Antaeus, who was killed by
Hercules, picks up the two journeyers, stoops down, and places them safely
at the bottom of the shaft.

Canto XXXIII

La bocca sollevò dal fiero pasto
  quel peccator, forbendola a' capelli
  del capo ch'elli avea di retro guasto.
Poi cominciò: «Tu vuo' ch'io rinovelli
  disperato dolor che 'l cor mi preme
  già pur pensando, pria ch'io ne favelli.
Ma se le mie parole esser dien seme
  che frutti infamia al traditor ch'i' rodo,
  parlare e lacrimar vedrai inseme.
Io non so chi tu se' nè per che modo
  venuto se' qua giù; ma fiorentino
  mi sembri veramente quand'io t'odo.

so that he hopes that what is happening is not really so,
just so did I become, unable to speak,
    desiring to make my excuses, continuing
    to make my excuses,[17] but not believing I was doing so.[18]
"Less shame than that washes away a greater fault,"
    my master said, "than yours was;
    and so, unburden yourself of all sadness:
and keep in mind that I am always beside you,
    if it occurs again that fortune takes you
    where people are engaged in a similar squabble;
for the desire to listen to such things is a base desire."

SUMMARY OF CANTO XXXII: The ninth circle is reserved for traitors of various types; they are trapped in a frozen lake with only their heads emerging.
In the first division, called Caina after the first fratricide, traitors to kindred
are punished; here Dante meets some figures from recent Italian history. In
the next division, named Antenora after a legendary betrayer of Troy, traitors
to their country are located; here Dante soundly reviles and manhandles
Bocca degli Abati, who was deemed responsible for the crushing defeat of
the Florentine Guelfs at Montaperti (see Canto X, note 11). Other 13th-
century Italians are in the same group. Now Dante finds two sinners frozen
in a single hole, one gnawing the other's skull. Dante asks the vicious spirit
to identify himself.]

Canto XXXIII

That sinner raised his mouth
    from his savage meal, wiping it on the hair
    of the head that he had mangled in back.
Then he began: "You want me to refresh
    a desperate sorrow that oppresses my heart
    when I merely think of it, even before I speak of it.
But if my words are to be a seed
    bringing the fruit of infamy to the traitor whom I gnaw,
    you will see me speaking and weeping at the same time.
I do not know who you are or how
    you have come down here; but a Florentine
    you truly seem to me when I listen to you.

---

17. By blushing.   18. Because he was not doing so with words.

Tu dei saper ch'i' fui conte Ugolino,
  e questi è l'arcivescovo Ruggieri:
  or ti dirò perch'i son tal vicino.
Che per l'effetto de' suo' mai pensieri,
  fidandomi di lui, io fosse preso
  e poscia morto, dir non è mestieri;
però quel che non puoi avere inteso,
  ciò è come la morte mia fu cruda,
  udirai, e saprai s'e' m'ha offeso.
Breve pertugio dentro dalla muda
  la qual per me ha il titol della fame,
  e 'n che conviene ancor ch'altrui si chiuda,
m'avea mostrato per lo suo forame
  più lune già, quand'io feci 'l mal sonno
  che del futuro mi squarciò 'l velame.
Questi pareva a me maestro e donno,
  cacciando il lupo e' lupicini al monte
  per che i Pisan veder Lucca non ponno.
Con cagne magre, studiose e conte
  Gualandi con Sismondi e con Lanfranchi
  s'avea messi dinanzi dalla fronte.
In picciol corso mi parìeno stanchi
  lo padre e' figli, e con l'agute scane
  mi parea lor veder fender li fianchi.
Quando fui desto innanzi la dimane,
  pianger senti' fra 'l sonno i miei figliuoli
  ch'eran con meco, e domandar del pane.
Ben se' crudel, se tu già non ti duoli
  pensando ciò che 'l mio cor s'annunziava;
  e se non piangi, di che pianger suoli?
Già eran desti, e l'ora s'appressava
  che 'l cibo ne solea essere addotto,
  e per suo sogno ciascun dubitava;

You should know that I was Count Ugolino,
    and this man is Archbishop Ruggieri:[1]
    now I shall tell you why I am a neighbor of this sort.
That as a result of his evil plans
    I was captured while trusting in him
    and then killed, there is no need to tell;
and so, that which you cannot have learned—
    that is, how cruel my death was—
    you will hear, and you will know whether he injured me.
A small hole inside the mew[2]
    which in memory of me is called the "hunger tower,"
    and in which it is fitting for still others to be imprisoned,
had showed me through its opening
    several moons already, when I slept the baleful sleep
    that rent the veil of the future for me.
I dreamed this man was master and lord of the hunt,
    pursuing a wolf and its cubs on the mountain
    that prevents the Pisans from seeing Lucca.[3]
Along with thin, eager, trained hounds
    he had put Gualandi, Sismondi, and Lanfranchi[4]
    in the forefront of the chase.
Before long the father and the sons
    appeared to be tired, and by sharp fangs
    I dreamed I saw their flanks ripped open.
When I awoke, before morning,[5]
    I heard my sons,[6] who were with me,
    crying in their sleep and asking for bread.
You are really cruel if you do not already grieve
    thinking of what my heart foretold to me;
    and if you are not weeping, what usually makes you weep?
They were now awake, and the hour was approaching
    when food was normally brought to us,
    and each of us was in doubt because of his dream;

---

1. In a diplomatic ploy, Ugolino della Gherardesca handed over some Pisan strongholds to the inimical Florence and Lucca, and was accused of treason. Archbishop
Ruggieri degli Ubaldini of Pisa invited him back from exile and treacherously imprisoned him. Ugolino died in 1289.   2. A loft in which birds of prey were kept while
molting.   3. Mount San Giuliano.   4. Families allied with the archbishop.   5. A
dream at that time of day was believed to be a true prophecy.   6. Dante portrays four
young sons, but Ugolino was really imprisoned with two sons and two grandsons; his
sons were already mature men.

e io senti' chiavar l'uscio di sotto
     all'orribile torre; ond'io guardai
     nel viso a'mie' figliuoi sanza far motto.
Io non piangea, sì dentro impetrai:
     piangevan elli; e Anselmuccio mio
     disse: 'Tu guardi sì, padre! che hai?'
Perciò non lacrimai nè rispuos'io
     tutto quel giorno nè la notte appresso,
     infin che l'altro sol nel mondo uscìo.
Come un poco di raggio si fu messo
     nel doloroso carcere, e io scorsi
     per quattro visi il mio aspetto stesso,
ambo le man per lo dolor mi morsi;
     ed ei, pensando ch'i' 'l fessi per voglia
     di manicar, di subito levorsi
e disser: 'Padre, assai ci fia men doglia
     se tu mangi di noi: tu ne vestisti
     queste misere carni, e tu le spoglia'.
Queta'mi allor per non farli più tristi;
     lo dì e l'altro stemmo tutti muti;
     ahi dura terra, perchè non t'apristi?
Poscia che fummo al quarto dì venuti,
     Gaddo mi si gettò disteso a' piedi,
     dicendo: 'Padre mio, chè non m'aiuti?'
Quivi morì; e come tu mi vedi,
     vid'io cascar li tre ad uno ad uno
     tra 'l quinto dì e 'l sesto; ond'io mi diedi,
già cieco, a brancolar sovra ciascuno,
     e due dì li chiamai, poi che fur morti:
     poscia, più che 'l dolor, potè 'l digiuno.»
Quand'ebbe detto ciò, con li occhi torti
     riprese 'l teschio misero co' denti,
     che furo all'osso, come d'un can, forti.
Ahi Pisa, vituperio delle genti
     del bel paese là dove 'l sì sona,
     poi che i vicini a te punir son lenti,
muovasi la Capraia e la Gorgona,

and I heard the door at the foot of the horrible tower
  being nailed shut; so that I looked
  my sons in the face without uttering a word.
I was not weeping, because I had turned to stone inside:
  they *were* weeping; and my Anselmuccio
  said: 'The way you stare, father! What is wrong?'
Nevertheless I neither wept nor answered
  all that day and the following night,
  until the next sun rose over the world.
When a small sunbeam entered
  the sorrowful prison, and I observed
  my own expression on their four faces,
I bit my two hands in my grief;
  and they, thinking that I did so out of a desire
  to eat, suddenly arose
and said: 'Father, it will be much less grievous to us
  if you eat of us: you clothed us
  in this miserable flesh, and now divest us of it.'
Then I calmed myself to avoid making them sadder;
  that day and the next we remained completely silent;
  ah, hard earth, why did you not open?
After we had arrived at the fourth day,
  Gaddo threw himself full length at my feet,
  saying: 'Father, why do you not help me?'
There he died; and, just as you see me,
  I saw the other three drop one by one
  between the fifth day and the sixth; whereupon I began,
already blinded, to grope over each one,
  and I called upon them for two days after they had died:
  later, my hunger surpassed my sorrow."
When he had said that, with distorted eyes
  he once more seized the wretched skull with his teeth,
  which bit as strongly into bone as a dog's.
Ah, Pisa, disgrace of the peoples
  of that beautiful country where they say *sì*,[7]
  since your neighbors are slow to punish you,
may Capraia and Gorgona[8] move from their places

---

7. Dante, and others, designated some nations by their words for "yes": *sì* for Italy, *oïl* for northern France, and *oc* for southern France (Languedoc).   8. Islands offshore from Pisa.

e faccian siepe ad Arno in su la foce,
sì ch'elli annieghi in te ogni persona!
Chè se 'l conte Ugolino aveva voce
d'aver tradita te delle castella,
non dovei tu i figliuoi porre a tal croce.
Innocenti facea l'età novella,
novella Tebe, Uguiccione e 'l Brigata
e li altri due che 'l canto suso appella.
Noi passammo oltre, là 've la gelata
ruvidamente un'altra gente fascia,
non volta in giù, ma tutta riversata.
Lo pianto stesso lì pianger non lascia,
e 'l duol che truova in su li occhi rintoppo,
si volge in entro a far crescer l'ambascia;
chè le lagrime prime fanno groppo,
e sì come visiere di cristallo,
rïempion sotto 'l ciglio tutto il coppo.
E avvegna che sì come d'un callo,
per la freddura ciascun sentimento
cessato avesse del mio viso stallo,
già mi parea sentire alquanto vento:
per ch'io: «Maestro mio, questo chi move?
non è qua giù ogne vapore spento?»
Ed elli a me: «Avaccio sarai dove
di ciò ti farà l'occhio la risposta,
veggendo la cagion che 'l fiato piove.»
E un de' tristi della fredda crosta
gridò a noi: «O anime crudeli,
tanto che dato v'è l'ultima posta,
levatemi dal viso i duri veli,
sì ch'ïo sfoghi 'l duol che 'l cor m'impregna,
un poco, pria che 'l pianto si raggeli.»
Per ch'io a lui: «Se vuo' ch'i' ti sovvegna,
dimmi chi se', e s'io non ti disbrigo,
al fondo della ghiaccia ir mi convegna.»
Rispuose adunque: «I' son frate Alberigo;
io son quel dalle frutta del mal orto,

and block up the Arno at its mouth,
   so that it drowns every person in you!
For, if Count Ugolino was reputed
   to have betrayed you with the strongholds,
   you should still not have tortured his sons that way.
Their youth made innocents,
   you modern Thebes,[9] of Uguiccione and Brigata
   and the other two whom my song names earlier.
We proceeded on our way to where the ice
   roughly swathes another class of people,
   who keep their faces not looking down,[10] but completely upturned.
There, their very weeping prevents them from weeping,
   and the sorrow that finds no outlet at their eyes
   is turned inward to increase their anguish;
for their very first tears form a lump of ice,
   and, like a crystal visor,
   fill the entire eye cavity below the brow.
And, even though, as if from a callus,
   because of the cold all trace of sensation
   had departed from my face,
I already seemed to feel a little breeze:
   so that I said: "Master, who is setting this in motion?
   Is not all air movement extinguished down here?"
And he replied: "Soon you will be where
   your own eyes will give you the answer to that,
   when they see the cause of the exhalation."
And one of the wretches in the cold crust
   shouted to us: "O cruel souls,
   so much so that you are assigned to the lowest region,
lift the tough veils from my face
   so I can vent the sorrow that fills my heart,
   for just a while before my tears freeze over."
So that I replied: "If you want me to help you,
   tell me who you are, and if I fail to disencumber you,
   let me be sent to the very bottom of this ice."
So he replied: "I am Brother Alberigo;
   I am the one known for the fruit from the evil orchard,

---

9. The ancient Greek city where so much violence occurred. 10. As in Caina, the
first division of the ninth circle.

che qui riprendo dattero per figo.»
«Oh!» diss'io lui, «or se' tu ancor morto?»
Ed elli a me: «Come 'l mio corpo stea
nel mondo su, nulla scïenza porto.
Cotal vantaggio ha questa Tolomea,
che spesse volte l'anima ci cade
innanzi ch'Atropòs mossa le dea.
E perchè tu più volontier mi rade
le 'nvetriate lacrime dal vólto,
sappie che tosto che l'anima trade
come fec'io, il corpo suo l' è tolto
da un demonio, che poscia il governa
mentre che 'l tempo suo tutto sia vòlto.
Ella ruina in sì fatta cisterna;
e forse pare ancor lo corpo suso
dell'ombra che di qua dietro mi verna.
Tu 'l dei saper, se tu vien pur mo giuso:
elli è ser Branca d'Oria, e son più anni
poscia passati ch'el fu sì racchiuso.»
«Io credo» diss'io lui «che tu m'inganni;
chè Branca d'Oria non morì unquanche,
e mangia e bee e dorme e veste panni.»
«Nel fosso su» diss'el «de' Malebranche,
là dove bolle la tenace pece,
non era giunto ancor Michel Zanche,
che questi lasciò il diavolo in sua vece
nel corpo suo, ed un suo prossimano
che 'l tradimento insieme con lui fece.
Ma distendi oggimai in qua la mano;
aprimi li occhi.» E io non lil' apersi;
e cortesia fu lui esser villano.
Ahi Genovesi, uomini diversi
d'ogne costume e pien d'ogni magagna,
perchè non siete voi del mondo spersi?

and here I am repaid in dates for figs."[11]
"Oh," I said, "are you already dead?"
He answered: "What my body is doing
  in the world above, I have no idea.
This Tolomea[12] has the advantage
  that often a soul lands here
  before Atropos[13] sends it on its way.
And, so that you may more willingly scrape away
  the glassy tears from my face,
  know that, as soon as a soul betrays
as I did, its body is taken over
  by a demon, who rules it thereafter
  until its life span is completed.
The soul plunges into this well;
  and perhaps the body of the shade wintering
  behind me here is still visible up above.
You ought to know, if you have just now come down here:
  he is Sir Branca d'Oria,[14] and several years
  have gone by since he was locked in as you see him."
"I believe," I said, "that you are deceiving me,
  for Branca d'Oria has not yet died,
  but eats and drinks and sleeps and wears clothes."
"In the moat of Malebranche up above," he said,
  "where the sticky pitch boils,
  Michele Zanche had not yet arrived
when this man left a devil in his stead
  in his body, as did one of his relatives
  who committed the betrayal together with him.
But now stretch out your hand to me;
  open my eyes." But I did not open them for him;
  and it was courtesy[15] to be rude to him.
Oh, Genoese, men alien
  to all civilized ways, and full of every blemish,
  why have you not been driven from the world?

---

11. Doubly repaid: dates were more rare and expensive than figs. Alberigo de'
Manfredi had his guest killed at the fruit course of a banquet.   12. The division of the
ninth circle in which Dante is now located; the sinners there betrayed their guests. The
name is derived from some ancient traitor named Ptolemy.   13. The ancient Greek
Fate whose task it was to cut the thread of an individual's life.   14. Or Doria, a
Genoese nobleman who murdered his father-in-law, Michele Zanche, whose own soul
is in the eighth moat of the eighth circle.   15. That is, compliance with God's design.

Chè col peggiore spirto di Romagna
  trovai di voi un tal, che per sua opra
  in anima in Cocito già si bagna,
ed in corpo par vivo ancor di sopra.

Canto XXXIV

«*Vexilla regis prodeunt inferni*
  verso di noi; però dinanzi mira»
  disse 'l maestro mio «se tu 'l discerni.»
Come quando una grossa nebbia spira,
  o quando l'emisperio nostro annotta,
  par di lungi un molin che 'l vento gira,
veder mi parve un tal dificio allotta;
  poi per lo vento mi ristrinsi retro
  al duca mio; chè non li era altra grotta.
Già era, e con paura il metto in metro,
  là dove l'ombre tutte eran coperte,
  e transparìen come festuca in vetro.
Altre sono a giacere; altre stanno erte,
  quella col capo e quella con le piante;
  altra, com'arco, il volto a' piè rinverte.
Quando noi fummo fatti tanto avante,
  ch'al mio maestro piacque di mostrarmi
  la creatura ch'ebbe il bel sembiante,
d'innanzi mi si tolse e fè restarmi,
  «Ecco Dite» dicendo, «ed ecco il loco
  ove convien che di fortezza t'armi.»
Com'io divenni allor gelato e fioco,
  nol dimandar, lettor, ch'i' non lo scrivo,
  però ch'ogni parlar sarebbe poco.
Io non mori', e non rimasi vivo:
  pensa oggimai per te, s'hai fior d'ingegno,
  qual io divenni, d'uno e d'altro privo.

For, alongside the worst spirit from Romagna,[16]
   I found a countryman of yours[17] so evil that, through his deed,
   his soul is already bathing in Cocytus,[18]
while up on earth he still seems alive and in his body.

Canto XXXIV

"*Vexilla regis prodeunt inferni*[1]
   toward us; and so look in front of you,"
   my master said, "to see if you can make him out."
Just as, when a thick fog is blowing,
   or when night falls in our hemisphere,
   a mill turned by the wind is seen far off,
I seemed to see such a mechanism at that time;
   then, because of the wind, I shrunk behind
   my guide, for there was no other shelter against it.
I was already, and with fear I put it into meter,
   where the departed shades were totally covered over,
   showing through the ice like straws seen through glass.
Some of them are recumbent, others are erect,
   one with head upward and another with soles upward;
   yet others bend their faces to their feet like bows.
When we had advanced so far forward
   that my master was pleased to show me
   the creature that was once so beautiful,[2]
he moved away from in front of me and made me stand still,
   saying: "There is Dis,[3] and there is the place
   where you must arm yourself with strength."
How cold and weak I then became,
   do not ask, reader, for I shall not write it,
   because anything I might say would be inadequate.
I did not die, and I did not stay alive:
   now imagine on your own, if you have even a little intelligence,
   in what a state I was, bereft of one and the other.[4]

---

16. Alberigo.   17. Branca.   18. The frozen lake.   1. "The banners of the king of Hell are advancing." Dante added the fourth Latin word, *inferni* ("of Hell"), to the first line of a famous 6th-century hymn by Venantius Fortunatus.   2. Lucifer was a bright angel before his fall.   3. A Roman designation of the ruler of the underworld; later in the canto, the same demon is called Lucifer and Beelzebub.   4. Life and death.

Lo 'mperador del doloroso regno
   da mezzo il petto uscìa fuor della ghiaccia;
   e più con un gigante io mi convegno,
che giganti non fan con le sue braccia:
   vedi oggimai quant'esser dee quel tutto
   ch'a così fatta parte si confaccia.
S'el fu sì bello com'elli è or brutto,
   e contra 'l suo fattore alzò le ciglia,
   ben dee da lui procedere ogni lutto.
Oh quanto parve a me gran maraviglia
   quand'io vidi tre facce alla sua testa!
   L'una dinanzi, e quella era vermiglia;
l'altr'eran due, che s'aggiugnìeno a questa
   sovresso 'l mezzo di ciascuna spalla,
   e sè giugnìeno al luogo della cresta:
e la destra parea tra bianca e gialla;
   la sinistra a vedere era tal, quali
   vegnon di là onde 'l Nilo s'avvalla.
Sotto ciascuna uscivan due grand'ali,
   quanto si convenìa a tanto uccello:
   vele di mar non vid'io mai cotali.
Non avean penne, ma di vispistrello
   era lor modo; e quelle svolazzava,
   sì che tre venti si movean da ello:
quindi Cocito tutto s'aggelava.
   Con sei occhi piangea, e per tre menti
   gocciava 'l pianto e sanguinosa bava.
Da ogni bocca dirompea co' denti
   un peccatore, a guisa di maciulla,
   sì che tre ne facea così dolenti.
A quel dinanzi il mordere era nulla
   verso 'l graffiar, che tal volta la schiena
   rimanea della pelle tutta brulla.
«Quell'anima là su c'ha maggior pena»
   disse 'l maestro, «è Giuda Scarïotto,
   che 'l capo ha dentro e fuor le gambe mena.
Delli altri due c'hanno il capo di sotto,
   quel che pende dal nero ceffo è Bruto
   — vedi come si storce! e non fa motto! — ;

The emperor of the sorrowful realm
    emerged from the ice to the middle of his chest;
    and I am closer in size to a giant
than giants are to just his arms:
    now imagine how great the whole must be
    that corresponds to a part of such magnitude.
If he was once as beautiful as he now is ugly,
    and still raised his brows pridefully against his Maker,
    it is only just that all sorrow derives from him.
Oh, what a great marvel it seemed to me
    when I saw three faces on his head!
    One was in front, and that one was vermilion;
there were two others, which were added to that one
    above the middle of each shoulder,
    and they joined at the place of his crest:
the right-hand one seemed to be somewhere between white and yellow;
    the left-hand one was such to see as the people
    who come from where the Nile forms a valley.[5]
Below each face two wings emerged, as large
    as was suitable to such a large bird:
    I never saw ship's sails of so great a size.
They were not feathered, but like a bat's
    in nature: and he kept flapping them,
    so that three winds proceeded from him:
hence all of Cocytus was frozen over.
    With six eyes he wept, and down three chins
    dripped his tears and his bloody drool.
In each mouth he was breaking up with his teeth
    a sinner, as if with a fiber-dressing comb,
    so that he was giving three of them such pain.
For the man in front, the biting was nothing
    compared to the scratching, for at times his back
    was stripped of all its skin.
"That soul up there which endures the greatest penalty,"
    my master said, "is Judas Iscariot,
    who has his head inside and waves his legs outside.
Of the other two, whose heads are below,
    the one hanging from the black snout is Brutus—
    see how he writhes, and says not a word!—

---

5. The third face was as black as an Ethiopian's.

e l'altro è Cassio che par sì membruto.
Ma la notte risurge, e oramai
è da partir, chè tutto avem veduto.»
Com'a lui piacque, il collo li avvinghiai;
ed el prese di tempo e luogo poste;
e quando l'ali fuoro aperte assai,
appigliò sè alle vellute coste:
di vello in vello giù discese poscia
tra 'l folto pelo e le gelate croste.
Quando noi fummo là dove la coscia
si volge, a punto in sul grosso dell'anche,
lo duca, con fatica e con angoscia,
volse la testa ov'elli avea le zanche,
e aggrappossi al pel com'uom che sale,
sì che 'n inferno i' credea tornar anche.
«Attienti ben, chè per cotali scale»
disse 'l maestro, ansando com'uom lasso,
«conviensi dipartir da tanto male.»
Poi uscì fuor per lo foro d'un sasso,
e puose me in su l'orlo a sedere;
appresso porse a me l'accorto passo.
Io levai li occhi, e credetti vedere
Lucifero com'io l'avea lasciato;
e vidili le gambe in su tenere;
e s'io divenni allora travagliato,
la gente grossa il pensi, che non vede
qual è quel punto ch'io avea passato.
«Lèvati su» disse 'l maestro «in piede:
la via è lunga e 'l cammino è malvagio,
e già il sole a mezza terza riede.»
Non era camminata di palagio
là 'v'eravam, ma natural burella
ch'avea mal suolo e di lume disagio.
«Prima ch'io dell'abisso mi divella,
maestro mio», diss'io quando fui dritto,

and the other, who seems so sturdy of limb, is Cassius.[6]
But night is rising again, and it is now time
to depart, for we have seen everything."
As he wished, I hugged his neck;
and he calculated the time and place;
and when the wings were sufficiently open,
he took hold of the shaggy sides;
then, from tuft to tuft he descended
between the thick hair and the frozen crusts.
When we had reached the point where the thigh
begins to round, at the greatest thickness of the haunch,
my guide, tired and anguished,
turned his head in the direction of that monster's shanks,
and caught hold of the hair like a man who climbs,
so that I thought I was returning to Hell again.
"Hold on tight, for by such a staircase,"
said my master, panting like a weary man,
"we must leave behind such great evil."
Then he issued out through an opening in a rock,
and set me down on the rim to sit;
next, he directed his prudent steps toward me.
I raised my eyes, and thought I would see
Lucifer just as I had left him;
but I saw him with his legs upward;
and whether I became puzzled at that moment,
let ignorant people imagine, those who fail to see
what point it was that I had passed.
"Get up on your feet," my master said;
"the way is long and the road is rough,
and the sun is already reaching halfway to tierce again."[7]
It was no palatial hall,
the place where we were, but a natural cavern,
uneven underfoot and devoid of light.
"Before I tear myself away from the abyss,
master," I said after I stood up,

---

6. Dante associates the assassins of Julius Caesar with Judas as arch-traitors because, in his political creed, the Holy Roman Empire, which can theoretically be traced back to Caesar, was an equal partner with the papacy in governing the world.
7. Halfway between the ecclesiastical hour of prime (6:00 A.M.) and that of tierce (9 A.M.) would be 7:30 A.M.

«a trarmi d'erro un poco mi favella:
ov'è la ghiaccia? e questi com'è fitto
sì sottosopra? a come, in sì poc'ora,
da sera a mane ha fatto il sol tragitto?»
Ed elli a me: «Tu imagini ancora
d'esser di là dal centro, ov'io mi presi
al pel del vermo reo che 'l mondo fora.
Di là fosti cotanto quant'io scesi;
quand'io mi volsi, tu passasti 'l punto
al qual si traggon d'ogni parte i pesi.
E se' or sotto l'emisperio giunto
ch'è opposito a quel che la gran secca
coverchia, e sotto 'l cui colmo consunto
fu l'uom che nacque e visse sanza pecca:
tu hai i piedi in su picciola spera
che l'altra faccia fa della Giudecca.
Qui è da man, quando di là è sera:
e questi, che ne fè scala col pelo,
fitto è ancora sì come prim'era.
Da questa parte cadde giù dal cielo;
e la terra, che pria di qua si sporse,
per paura di lui fè del mar velo,
e venne all'emisperio nostro; e forse
per fuggir lui lasciò qui luogo voto
quella ch'appar di qua, e su ricorse.»
Luogo è là giù da Belzebù remoto
tanto quanto la tomba si distende,
che non per vista, ma per suono è noto
d'un ruscelletto che quivi discende
per la buca d'un sasso, ch'elli ha roso,
col corso ch'elli avvolge, e poco pende.

"tell me something to free me from bewilderment:
Where is the ice? And why is this monster embedded
    upside down this way? And how, in such a short time,
    did the sun travel from evening to morning?"
And he replied: "You still imagine
    you are on the far side of the center, where I took hold
    of the hair of that evil worm which bores through the world.
You were on that side all the while I was descending;
    when I turned around, you passed the point
    to which weights are attracted from all sides.[8]
And you have now arrived beneath the celestial hemisphere
    which is at the antipodes of the one which the great land mass
    covers, and below the zenith of which died
the Man who was born and lived without sin:[9]
    your feet are planted on a small disc
    that has its counterpart in Giudecca.[10]
Here it is morning when it is evening there:
    and this demon, whose hair served us as a ladder,
    is still embedded as he was before.
He fell headlong from heaven on this side of earth's center;
    and the land that formerly extended over here,
    through fear of him covered itself with ocean,
and moved to our northern hemisphere; and perhaps,
    as it fled from him, an empty space was left here[11]
    by the land that is visible in *this* hemisphere, when it thrust upward."[12]
There is a place down there as far distant from Beelzebub
    as his underground realm[13] extends;
    this place can be perceived not by sight, but by the sound
of a little brook[14] that runs down into it,
    through a cavity in a rock which it has eroded,
    with a winding course and a gentle incline.

---

8. The center of the earth, the center of gravity.   9. Jesus died in Jerusalem, the
midpoint (in Dante's view) of the earth's surface in the northern hemisphere. The
northern hemisphere was thought to contain all the earth's dry land, except for the
mountain of Purgatory, at the antipodes from Jerusalem.   10. Giudecca, named for
Judas, is the fourth and last division of the ninth circle, where Lucifer is located.
11. Presumably, the cavern.   12. The "land that is visible in *this* hemisphere" is the
mountain of Purgatory.   13. There are other interpretations of *tomba*, entailing different views about the passageway that Dante and Vergil follow.   14. Probably the
runoff from the river Lethe (see *Purgatory*, Canto XXVIII).

Lo duca e io per quel cammino ascoso
   intrammo a ritornar nel chiaro mondo;
   e sanza cura aver d'alcun riposo
salimmo su, el primo e io secondo,
   tanto ch'i' vidi delle cose belle
   che porta 'l ciel, per un pertugio tondo;
e quindi uscimmo a riveder le stelle.

My guide and I, along that hidden path,
    entered onto our return to the world of brightness;
    and, not concerned with taking any rest,
we ascended, he first and I second,
    until I saw some of the beautiful things
    that heaven bears, through a circular opening;
and from there we emerged to see the stars again.

PURGATORIO

Canto I

Per correr migliori acque alza le vele
  omai la navicella del mio ingegno,
  che lascia dietro a sè mar sì crudele;
e canterò di quel secondo regno
  dove l'umano spirito si purga
  e di salire al ciel diventa degno.
Ma qui la morta poesì resurga,
  o sante Muse, poi che vostro sono;
  e qui Calliopè alquanto surga,
seguitando il mio canto con quel sòno
  di cui le Piche misere sentiro
  lo colpo tal, che disperar perdono.
Dolce color d'orïental zaffiro,
  che s'accoglieva nel sereno aspetto
  del mezzo, puro insino al primo giro,
alli occhi miei ricominciò diletto,
  tosto ch'io usci' fuor dell'aura morta
  che m'avea contristati li occhi e 'l petto.
Lo bel pianeta che d'amar conforta
  faceva tutto rider l'orïente,
  velando i Pesci, ch'erano in sua scorta.
I' mi volsi a man destra, e puosi mente
  all'altro polo, e vidi quattro stelle

PURGATORY

Canto I

To travel better waters, the little boat
   of my intellect now hoists its sails,
   leaving behind a sea so cruel;
and I shall sing about that second realm,
   where the human spirit is purged
   and becomes worthy of ascending to heaven.
But here let my poetry, which dealt with death, return to life,
   O sacred Muses, since I belong to you,
   and here let Calliope[1] rise somewhat higher,
accompanying my song with that music
   the force of which the unhappy magpies
   felt so strongly that they despaired of pardon.[2]
The gentle color of oriental sapphire,
   which was gathering on the serene face
   of the atmosphere all the way to the horizon,
brought delight back to my eyes
   the moment that I emerged from the dead air
   that had saddened my eyes and my breast.
The beautiful planet that encourages us to love[3]
   was making all the east smile,
   dimming the Fishes, which were escorting it.[4]
I turned to the right, and set my mind
   on that other pole,[5] and I saw four stars[6]

---

1. The muse of epic poetry.   2. The presumptuous daughters of an ancient king of Thessaly challenged the Muses to a singing contest, and were turned into magpies. 3. Venus.   4. Venus is in Pisces; it is about an hour before daybreak.   5. The South Pole.   6. Representing the four cardinal virtues: prudence, justice, fortitude, temperance.

non viste mai fuor ch'alla prima gente.
Goder pareva il ciel di lor fiammelle:
   oh settentrïonal vedovo sito,
   poi che privato se' di mirar quelle!
Com'io da loro sguardo fui partito,
   un poco me volgendo all'altro polo,
   là onde il Carro già era sparito,
vidi presso di me un veglio solo,
   degno di tanta reverenza in vista,
   che più non dee a padre alcun figliuolo.
Lunga la barba e di pel bianco mista
   portava, a' suoi capelli simigliante,
   de' quai cadeva al petto doppia lista.
Li raggi delle quattro luci sante
   fregiavan sì la sua faccia di lume,
   ch'i' 'l vedea come 'l sol fosse davante.
«Chi siete voi che contro al cieco fiume
   fuggita avete la pregione etterna?»
   diss'el, movendo quelle oneste piume.
«Chi v'ha guidati, o che vi fu lucerna,
   uscendo fuor della profonda notte
   che sempre nera fa la valle inferna?
Son le leggi d'abisso così rotte?
   o è mutato in ciel novo consiglio,
   che, dannati, venite alle mie grotte?»
Lo duca mio allor mi diè di piglio,
   e con parole e con mani e con cenni
   reverenti mi fè le gambe e 'l ciglio.
Poscia rispuose lui: «Da me non venni:
   donna scese dal ciel, per li cui prieghi
   della mia compagnia costui sovvenni.
Ma da ch'è tuo voler che più si spieghi
   di nostra condizion com'ell'è vera,
   esser non puote il mio che a te si nieghi.
Questi non vide mai l'ultima sera;
   ma per la sua follia le fu sì presso,
   che molto poco tempo a volger era.

never before seen except by the first people.[7]
The sky seemed to rejoice in their little flames:
    oh, northern hemisphere, how bereft you are,
    since you are denied the sight of them!
When I had finished looking at them,
    turning a little toward the other pole,[8]
    where the Big Dipper had already disappeared,
I saw near me an old man standing alone,
    of an appearance deserving of such reverence
    that no son owes more to his father.
He bore a long beard that was partly white,
    similar to his hair,
    the two strands of which fell onto his chest.
The beams from the four holy stars
    adorned his face with light in such a way
    that, as I looked at him, the sun seemed to shine directly on him.
"Who are you two that, following the underground river,
    have escaped from the eternal prison?"
    he asked, moving that honorable beard.
"Who guided you, or what served you as a lantern,
    as you issued forth from the deep night
    that makes the valley of Hell perpetually black?
Are the laws of the abyss thus infringed?
    Or has a new decree been passed in heaven,
    that you, the damned, arrive at my cliffs?"
Then my guide took hold of me,
    and by means of words, hands, and signs
    made me bend my knees and head in reverence.
Then he replied: "I have not come on my own:
    a lady descended from heaven, at whose request
    I aided this man with my company.
But, since it is your wish that I explain further
    the truth about our status,
    it cannot be my wish to refuse you.
This man has never seen his final evening;
    but through his folly he was so close to it
    that very little time had yet to elapse.

---

7. By Adam and Eve; because Dante depicts the terrestrial paradise as located at the summit of the mountain of Purgatory.   8. The North Pole.

Sì com'io dissi, fui mandato ad esso
   per lui campare; e non li era altra via
   che questa per la quale i' mi son messo.
Mostrata ho lui tutta la gente ria;
   e ora intendo mostrar quelli spirti
   che purgan sè sotto la tua balìa.
Com'io l'ho tratto, sarìa lungo a dirti;
   dell'alto scende virtù che m'aiuta
   conducerlo a vederti e a udirti.
Or ti piaccia gradir la sua venuta:
   libertà va cercando, ch'è sì cara,
   come sa chi per lei vita rifiuta.
Tu 'l sai, che non ti fu per lei amara
   in Utica la morte, ove lasciasti
   la vesta ch'al gran dì sarà sì chiara.
Non son li editti etterni per noi guasti;
   chè questi vive, e Minòs me non lega;
   ma son del cerchio ove son li occhi casti
di Marzia tua, che 'n vista ancor ti priega,
   o santo petto, che per tua la tegni:
   per lo suo amore adunque a noi ti piega.
Lasciane andar per li tuoi sette regni:
   grazie riporterò di te a lei,
   se d'esser mentovato là giù degni.»
«Marzïa piacque tanto alli occhi miei
   mentre ch'i' fu' di là» diss'elli allora,
   «che quante grazie volse da me, fei.
Or che di là dal mal fiume dimora,
   più muover non mi può, per quella legge
   che fatta fu quando me n' usci' fora.
Ma se donna del ciel ti move e regge,
   come tu di', non c'è mestier lusinghe:
   bastisi ben che per lei mi richegge.
Va dunque, e fa che tu costui ricinghe
   d'un giunco schietto e che li lavi 'l viso,

As I said, I was sent to him
   to rescue him; and there was no other road for him
   than this one, on which I set out.
I have showed him all the evil folk;
   and now I intend to show him those spirits
   who are cleansing themselves under your governance.
How I have guided him would be long in the telling;
   a power descends from on high which helps me
   lead him to see and hear you.
Now may it please you to welcome his coming:
   he is seeking freedom, which is so dear,
   as that man knows who gives up his life for it.
You know this, since, for freedom, death
   was not bitter for you in Utica,[9] where you left behind
   the garment that will be so bright on the great day.[10]
The eternal edicts are not broken on our account,
   for this man is alive, and Minos does not bind me;
   rather, I am from the circle that contains the chaste eyes
of your Marcia,[11] who visibly still begs you,
   O holy heart, to consider her yours:
   for love of her, therefore, be indulgent to us.
Let us travel through your seven circles:
   I shall bring back thanks to her for your aid,
   if you deign to be mentioned down there."
"Marcia was so pleasing to my eyes
   all the while I was on earth," he then said,
   "that, as many favors as she asked of me, I did.
Now that she dwells on the far side of the evil river,[12]
   she can no longer influence me, in accordance with that law
   which was made when I emerged from there.[13]
But if a lady from heaven influences and supports you
   as you say, there is no need of flattery:
   let it suffice that you are making this request of me for her sake.
And so, go and see that you gird this man
   with a rush stalk shorn of its leaves,[14] and that you wash his face,

---

9. This word tells us that the old man is Marcus Porcius Cato, who killed himself for love of freedom after Julius Caesar conquered the city of Utica in North Africa in 46 B.C.   10. His body, which will shine on Judgment Day.   11. Cato's wife, seen by Dante in Canto IV of *Hell*.   12. Acheron.   13. Cato was liberated from Limbo when Christ harrowed Hell; it is forbidden for him to pity the damned.   14. Or: "free of nodes."

sì ch'ogni sucidume quindi stinghe;
  chè non si converrìa, l'occhio sorpriso
  d'alcuna nebbia, andar dinanzi al primo
  ministro, ch'è di quei di paradiso.
Questa isoletta intorno ad imo ad imo,
  là giù colà dove la batte l'onda,
  porta de' giunchi sovra 'l molle limo;
null'altra pianta che facesse fronda
  o indurasse, vi puote aver vita,
  però ch'alle percosse non seconda.
Poscia non sia di qua vostra reddita;
  lo sol vi mosterrà, che surge omai,
  prendere il monte a più lieve salita.»
Così sparì; e io su mi levai
  sanza parlare, e tutto mi ritrassi
  al duca mio, e li occhi a lui drizzai.
El cominciò: «Seguisci li miei passi:
  volgiànci in dietro, chè di qua dichina
  questa pianura a' suoi termini bassi.»
L'alba vinceva l'ora mattutina
  che fuggìa innanzi, sì che di lontano
  conobbi il tremolar della marina.
Noi andavam per lo solingo piano
  com'om che torna alla perduta strada,
  che 'nfino ad essa li pare ire invano.
Quando noi fummo là 've la rugiada
  pugna col sole, e, per essere in parte
  dove adorezza, poco si dirada,
ambo le mani in su l'erbetta sparte
  soavemente 'l mio maestro pose:
  ond'io, che fui accorto di sua arte,
porsi ver lui le guance lacrimose:
  ivi mi fece tutto discoverto
  quel color che l'inferno mi nascose.
Venimmo poi in sul lito diserto,
  che mai non vide navicar sue acque
  omo che di tornar sia poscia esperto.

so that you cleanse it of all filth;
for it would not be fitting, with eyes clouded
    by any mist, to go before the first
    angelic servant, since he is one of those from Paradise.
This little island, all around, at its base,
    where the waves beat it,
    bears rushes in its soft mud;
no other plant that produces foliage
    or hard bark can live there
    because it cannot yield pliantly to the gusts of wind.
Afterwards, let not your return be in this quarter;
    the sun, which is now rising, will show you
    how to attack the mountain by an easier ascent."
Thereupon he disappeared, and I stood up
    without speaking, and moved quite close
    to my guide, directing my eyes toward him.
He began: "Follow in my steps:
    let us turn back, because over here this plain
    slopes down to its lowest level."
Dawn was conquering the morning hour,[15]
    which was fleeing from it, so that in the distance
    I could discern the trembling light on the sea.
We were walking along the solitary plain
    like men who return to the road they have strayed from
    and, until they find it again, feel that their journey is in vain.
When we reached the spot where the dew
    fights with the sun and, because it is in a place
    where breezes blow, evaporates only slowly,
my master gently placed
    both his hands outspread on the grass:
    so that I, understanding his action,
extended my tear-stained cheeks to him:
    there he uncovered completely
    my complexion, which Hell had hidden.
Then we arrived on the deserted shore,
    whose waters were never seen to be navigated
    by any man who later experienced a return.

---

15. That is, the final hour of night. Some Italian editions have *ôra* (= *aura*) instead
of *ora*; thus: "was conquering the morning breeze."

Quivi mi cinse sì com'altrui piacque:
  oh maraviglia! chè qual elli scelse
  l'umile pianta, cotal si rinacque
subitamente là onde l'avelse.

[SUMMARY OF CANTO II: Dante now sees a red light coming his way over
the sea, with a patch of white on either side of it. It is a white-winged angel
in a bark, from which more than a hundred psalm-singing souls disembark
on the shore. Dante attempts to embrace one, but clutches only air. This soul
proves to be the Tuscan musician Casella, a friend of the poet's. With these
other souls of the recently deceased, he embarked at the mouth of the Tiber;
it is there that souls not slated for Hell are first mustered. Casella sings his
own setting of one of Dante's lyric poems. Then Cato appears and urges
everyone to start up the mountain.

SUMMARY OF CANTO III: Dante, seeing his own shadow but not Vergil's, is
afraid that he has been deserted, but his guide appears and reassures him,
adding that human reason, without Revelation, is inadequate to understand
such otherworldly phenomena as the physics of departed souls. Vergil cannot
find a path up the steep mountainside. Now the travelers are joined by a
group of souls who are local residents; they died in contumacy against the
Church (excommunicated), though they repented at the last moment, and
must remain where they are, outside Purgatory, thirty times the length of
their contumacy, unless the waiting period is reduced in answer to the
prayers of the living. Their spokesman is Manfred (died 1266), grandson of
Holy Roman Emperor Henry VI and natural son of Frederick II; Manfred,
king of Sicily, was killed after being conquered at Benevento by Charles of
Anjou, who fought on behalf of the pope.

Canto VI

Quando si parte il gioco della zara,
  colui che perde si riman dolente,
  repetendo le volte, e tristo impara:
con l'altrose ne va tutta la gente;
  qual va dinanzi, e qual di dietro il prende,
  e qual da lato li si reca a mente:
el non s'arresta, e questo e quello intende;
  a cui porge la man, più non fa pressa;
  e così dalla calca si difende.
Tal era io in quella turba spessa,
  volgendo a loro, e qua e là, la faccia,

Here he girded me as that man wished:
>oh, marvel! for, just as that humble plant
>was when he picked it, just so did it grow back
suddenly in the place from which he had torn it.

SUMMARY OF CANTO IV: The souls of the excommunicated show Dante and Vergil a narrow cleft through which they can begin their ascent. The climb is arduous. While they rest on a terrace that encircles the mountain, Vergil gives Dante a long lesson on the astronomical phenomena of the southern hemisphere; and he assures Dante that he will be less and less tired, the higher they climb. A nearby voice proves to be that of Belacqua, an old friend of the poet's, lazy but witty. He is one of a slothful group sojourning on that terrace: those who indolently delayed repenting until their deathbed, and who must now wait outside Purgatory for a time equal to the span of their earthly life (here, too, the prayers of the living can shorten the wait). It is now noon, and Vergil summons the poet onward.

SUMMARY OF CANTO V: As they continue, the travelers meet, on a slope, another group of souls who are surprised that Dante casts a shadow. These are people who were violently slain but (unlike Francesca, identified in note 7 to Canto V of *Hell*) still had enough time to repent. The three individual members of the group who converse with Dante, all of whom died toward the end of the 13th century, are: Jacopo del Cassero, who was murdered by a political opponent; Buonconte of Montefeltro, son of the Guido in Canto XXVII of *Hell* (like his father, Buonconte had an angel and a devil fight over his soul, but in his own case the angel won); and a woman called Pia, usually identified as Pia de' Tolomei of Siena, whose husband caused her death.]

Canto VI

When a dice game of hazard breaks up,
>the loser stays behind sadly,
>going over his throws and learning to his sorrow:
all the bystanders go off with the other man;
>one walks in front of him, another plucks at him behind,
>and yet another goes beside him, bidding for his attention:
the winner does not halt as he listens to this man and that;
>the one to whom he hands out money no longer crowds around him;
>and thus he protects himself from the throng.
Such was I in that dense gathering,
>turning my face to them, and to and fro,

e promettendo mi sciogliea da essa.
Quiv'era l'Aretin che dalle braccia
 fiere di Ghin di Tacco ebbe la morte,
 e l'altro ch'annegò correndo in caccia.
Quivi pregava con le mani sporte
 Federigo Novello, e quel da Pisa
 che fè parer lo buon Marzucco forte.
Vidi Conte Orso e l'anima divisa
 dal corpo suo per astio e per inveggia,
 com'e' dicea, non per colpa commisa;
Pier della Broccia dico; e qui proveggia,
 mentr'è di qua, la donna di Brabante,
 sì che però non sia di peggior greggia.
Come libero fui da tutte quante
 quell'ombre che pregar pur ch'altri prieghi,
 sì che s'avacci lor divenir sante,
io cominciai: «El par che tu mi nieghi,
 o luce mia, espresso in alcun testo
 che decreto del cielo orazion pieghi;
e questa gente prega pur di questo:
 sarebbe dunque loro speme vana,
 o non m'è 'l detto tuo ben manifesto?»
Ed elli a me: «La mia scrittura è piana;
 e la speranza di costor non falla,
 se ben si guarda con la mente sana;
chè cima di giudicio non s'avvalla
 perchè foco d'amor compia in un punto
 ciò che de' sodisfar chi qui si stalla;
e là dov'io fermai cotesto punto,
 non s'ammendava, per pregar, difetto,
 perchè 'l priego da Dio era disgiunto.
Veramente a così alto sospetto
 non ti fermar, se quella nol ti dice

and by means of promises[1] I tried to liberate myself from them.
On this side stood the man from Arezzo[2] who was killed
   by the fierce arms of Ghino di Tacco,
   and that other man who drowned while escaping pursuers.[3]
On that side, praying with outstretched hands,
   stood Federigo Novello[4] and the man from Pisa
   who made good Marzucco display his fortitude.[5]
I saw Count Orso[6] and the soul that was separated
   from his body through rancor and through envy,
   as he declared, and not for any crime he had committed:
I mean Pierre de la Brosse;[7] and let the lady of Brabant
   take measures while still here on earth
   lest on that account she join a flock worse than this one!
When I was quit of all
   those shades who were only praying to have others pray for them,
   so that their becoming holy might be hastened,
I began: "It seems to me that you deny,
   O my light, expressly in a passage of your poem
   that prayer can bend a decree of heaven;
whereas these people are praying for precisely that:
   is their hope therefore in vain,
   or is your declaration not fully clear to me?"
And he replied: "What I wrote is straightforward;
   but the hope of these people is not erroneous,
   if it is considered carefully with a sound mind;
for the summit of justice cannot be considered to lower itself
   if it allows the heat of love to accomplish in just a moment
   the satisfaction that those sojourning here must make;
and in the passage where I made that point,
   the fault could not be amended by prayer
   because that prayer was detached from the true God.[8]
Nevertheless, do not linger
   in such deep doubts, unless they are confirmed by that lady

---

1. Promises to tell their relatives to pray for them.   2. Benincasa da Laterina.
These six people who were murdered but died repentant are all figures of the late
13th century.   3. Guccio dei Tarlati.   4. A count of the Casentino district.   5. A
murdered son of one Marzucco, who, it is said, courageously forgave the offense.
6. Orso degli Alberti.   7. A chancellor of Philip III of France; the king's second wife,
Marie of Brabant, was blamed for Pierre's death.   8. Vergil's statement in the *Aeneid*
was made with reference to a pagan who lived long before Christ; the Christian dis-
pensation *does* allow prayer to shorten a stay in Purgatory.

che lume fia tra 'l vero e lo 'ntelletto:
Non so se 'ntendi; io dico di Beatrice:
    tu la vedrai di sopra, in su la vetta
    di questo monte, ridere e felice.»
E io: «Segnore, andiamo a maggior fretta,
    chè già non m'affatico come dianzi,
    e vedi omai che 'l poggio l'ombra getta.»
«Noi anderem con questo giorno innanzi»
    rispuose, «quanto più potremo omai;
    ma 'l fatto è d'altra forma che non stanzi.
Prima che sie là su, tornar vedrai
    colui che già si cuopre della costa,
    sì che' suoi raggi tu romper non fai.
Ma vedi là un'anima che posta
    sola soletta inverso noi riguarda:
    quella ne 'nsegnerà la via più tosta.»
Venimmo a lei: o anima lombarda,
    come ti stavi altera e disdegnosa
    e nel mover delli occhi onesta e tarda!
Ella non ci dicea alcuna cosa,
    ma lasciavane gir, solo sguardando
    a guisa di leon quando si posa.
Pur Virgilio si trasse a lei, pregando
    che ne mostrasse la miglior salita;
    e quella non rispuose al suo dimando,
ma di nostro paese e della vita
    c'inchiese; e 'l dolce duca incominciava
    «Mantova . . .», e l'ombra, tutta in sè romita,
surse ver lui del loco ove pria stava,
    dicendo: «O Mantovano, io son Sordello
    della tua terra!»; e l'un l'altro abbracciava.
Ahi serva Italia, di dolore ostello,
    nave senza nocchiere in gran tempesta,
    non donna di provincie, ma bordello!
Quell'anima gentil fu così presta,
    sol per lo dolce suon della sua terra,
    di fare al cittadin suo quivi festa;

who will be the light between the truth and human reason:
I do not know whether you understand; I am speaking of Beatrice;
   you will see her up above, atop the summit
   of this mountain, smiling and blissful."
I said: "My lord, let us proceed with greater haste,
   for I am now not as weary as before,
   and you see that the hill is already casting a shadow."
"We shall journey forward along with this day,"
   he replied, "as much as we still can;
   but the fact is different from what you imagine.
Before you arrive up there, you will see the return
   of that sun which is now being covered by the mountainside
   so that you no longer cause its rays to be intercepted.
But see over there a soul that, standing
   all alone, is looking our way:
   it will teach us the quickest path."
We came up to it: O Italian soul,
   how haughtily and disdainfully you stood,
   and with what a dignified and slow movement of the eyes!
It said nothing to us,
   but allowed us to proceed, merely watching us
   like a recumbent lion.
Vergil alone went up to it, asking it
   to show us the best place to ascend;
   and it did not respond to his question,
but of our country and life
   it inquired; and my gentle guide began:
   "Mantua . . . ," when the shade that had been totally self-absorbed
rose up toward him from the place where it stood before,
   saying: "O Mantuan, I am Sordello[9]
   from your land!" and they embraced each other.
Alas, slavish Italy, inn of sorrows,
   ship without steersman in a great tempest,
   not a mistress of provinces but a brothel!
That noble soul was so prompt,
   merely at the sweet name of its homeland,
   to welcome its fellow citizen here;

---

9. Sordello da Goito, a 13th-century troubadour who served at various Italian courts; his work was admired by Dante—and, later, by Robert Browning.

e ora in te non stanno sanza guerra
   li vivi tuoi, e l'un l'altro si rode
   di quei ch'un muro ed una fossa serra.
Cerca, misera, intorno dalle prode
   le tue marine, e poi ti guarda in seno,
   s'alcuna parte in te di pace gode.
Che val perchè ti racconciasse il freno
   Iustinïano se la sella è vota?
   Sanz'esso fora la vergogna meno.
Ahi gente che dovresti esser devota,
   e lasciar seder Cesare in la sella,
   se bene intendi ciò che Dio ti nota,
guarda come esta fiera è fatta fella
   per non esser corretta dalli sproni,
   poi che ponesti mano alla predella.
O Alberto tedesco ch'abbandoni
   costei ch'è fatta indomita e selvaggia,
   e dovresti inforcar li suoi arcioni,
giusto giudicio dalle stelle caggia
   sovra 'l tuo sangue, e sia novo e aperto
   tal che 'l tuo successor temenza n'aggia!
Ch'avete tu e 'l tuo padre sofferto,
   per cupidigia di costà distretti,
   che 'l giardin dello 'mperio sia diserto.
Vieni a veder Montecchi e Cappelletti,
   Monaldi e Filippeschi, uom sanza cura:
   color già tristi, e questi con sospetti!
Vien, crudel, vieni, e vedi la pressura
   de' tuoi gentili, e cura lor magagne;
   e vedrai Santafior com'è oscura!
Vieni a veder la tua Roma che piagne
   vedova sola, e dì e notte chiama:

and now your living inhabitants do not remain in you
   without warfare, and one gnaws the other
   although they are enclosed by a single wall and a single moat.
Unhappy land, look around your coasts
   at your maritime cities, and then look at your heartland,
   and see whether any of your regions enjoys peace.
What was the good of your bridle being repaired
   by Justinian[10] if the saddle is empty?
   If he had not done so, there would be less disgrace.
Alas, you folk that ought to be pious[11]
   and allow the emperor to occupy the saddle,
   if you understand clearly what God commands you to do,
see how refractory this animal has become
   from not being admonished by the spurs,
   ever since you placed your hands on the reins.
O German Albert,[12] you that abandon
   the horse that has become untamed and wild,
   whereas you ought to straddle its saddlebows,
may a just judgment fall from the stars
   upon your family, and may it be so unusual and public
   that your successor is frightened by it!
For you and your father, detained
   up north out of greed, have allowed
   the garden of the empire to be laid waste.
Come and see the Montecchi and the Cappelletti,[13]
   the Monaldi and the Filippeschi, O unconcerned man:
   the former already unhappy, and the latter fearing the worst!
Come, cruel man, come, and see the distress
   of your noble families, and cure their infirmities;
   and you will see how dark Santafiora[14] is!
Come and see your Rome, which weeps,
   a lonely widow, and calls by day and night:

---

10. The 6th-century emperor who codified the laws.   11. The clergy.   12. He became emperor in 1298, but, occupied with German affairs, did not visit Rome to be
crowned.   13. Dante names four noble families (some Guelf, some Ghibelline)
ruined by their mutual hostility. The Montecchi ("Montagues") and the Cappelletti
("Capulets") were really from different cities; Shakespeare's Italian sources may have
misinterpreted this line of Dante's and made them hostile neighbors in Verona.
14. A region that was under fire from the Sienese. Other editions read: "see how secure Santafiora is!"

«Cesare mio, perchè non m'accompagne?»
Vieni a veder la gente quanto s'ama!
e se nulla di noi pietà ti move,
a vergognar ti vien della tua fama.
E se licito m'è, o sommo Giove
che fosti in terra per noi crucifisso,
son li giusti occhi tuoi rivolti altrove?
O è preparazion che nell'abisso
del tuo consiglio fai per alcun bene
in tutto dell'accorger nostro scisso?
Chè le città d'Italia tutte piene
son di tiranni, e un Marcel diventa
ogni villan che parteggiando viene.
Fiorenza mia, ben puoi esser contenta
di questa digression che non ti tocca,
mercè del popol tuo che si argomenta.
Molti han giustizia in cuore, e tardi scocca
per non venir sanza consiglio all'arco;
ma il popol tuo l'ha in sommo della bocca.
Molti rifiutan lo comune incarco;
ma il popol tuo sollicito risponde
sanza chiamare e grida: «I' mi sobbarco!»
Or ti fa lieta, chè tu hai ben onde:
tu ricca, tu con pace, e tu con senno!
s'io dico ver, l'effetto nol nasconde.
Atene e Lacedemona, che fenno
l'antiche leggi e furon sì civili,
fecero al viver bene un picciol cenno
verso di te che fai tanto sottili
provedimenti, ch'a mezzo novembre
non giugne quel che tu d'ottobre fili.
Quante volte, del tempo che rimembre,
legge, moneta, officio e costume
hai tu mutato e rinovate membre!
E se ben ti ricordi e vedi lume,
vedrai te somigliante a quella inferma
che non può trovar posa in su le piume,
ma con dar volta suo dolore scherma.

"My emperor, why are you not here with me?"
Come and see how your people love one another!
    And if no compassion for us affects you,
    come and be ashamed for your reputation.
And if I may be permitted to say it, O supreme God,
    You that were crucified on earth for us,
    are Your just eyes directed elsewhere?
Or is this a preparation that, in the depths
    of Your wisdom, You are making for some benefit
    which is totally cut off from our perceptions?
For the cities of Italy are all full
    of tyrants, and any peasant
    who comes and joins a party becomes a Marcellus.[15]
My Florence,[16] you can be very satisfied
    with this digression, which does not affect you
    thanks to your citizens who strive for your welfare.
Many people have justice in their hearts, but the arrow flies slowly
    because it does not come to the bow without deliberation;
    whereas your citizens have justice on the tip of their tongue.
Many people refuse public office,
    but your citizens are committed and respond
    without being called, shouting: "I bend my back to the burden!"
Now rejoice, for you have sufficient cause:
    you are rich, you are peaceful, you are sensible!
    That I speak the truth, the results do not conceal.
Athens and Sparta, which made
    the laws of antiquity and were so civic-minded,
    gave us merely a tiny hint of proper behavior
compared to you, you that make such fine-spun
    decisions that what you spin in October
    does not last till the middle of November.
How many times, in the period you can recall,
    you have changed your laws, coinage, government,
    and ways, and renovated your body!
And if you remember correctly and see clearly,
    you will find that you resemble a sick woman
    who is unable to find rest on her featherbed,
but wards off her pain by constantly turning.

---

15. An ancient Roman who sided with Pompey against Caesar.   16. The passage
beginning here must be understood as bitterly ironic and sarcastic.

Canto VII

Poscia che l'accoglienze oneste e liete
  furo iterate tre e quattro volte,
  Sordel si trasse, e disse: «Voi, chi siete?»
«Anzi che a questo monte fosser volte
  l'anime degne di salire a Dio,
  fur l'ossa mie per Ottavian sepolte.
Io son Virgilio; e per null'altro rio
  lo ciel perdei che per non aver fè.»
  Così rispuose allora il duca mio.
Qual è colui che cosa innanzi a sè
  subita vede ond'e' si maraviglia,
  che crede e non, dicendo 'Ella è . . . non è . . .',
tal parve quelli; e poi chinò le ciglia,
  e umilmente ritornò ver lui,
  e abbracciòl là 've 'l minor s'appiglia.
«O gloria de' Latin» disse «per cui
  mostrò ciò che potea la lingua nostra,
  o pregio etterno del loco ond'io fui,
qual merito o qual grazia mi ti mostra?
  S'io son d'udir le tue parole degno,
  dimmi se vien d'inferno, e di qual chiostra.»
«Per tutt'i cerchi del dolente regno»
  rispuose lui «son io di qua venuto:
  virtù del ciel mi mosse, e con lei vegno.
Non per far, ma per non fare ho perduto
  a veder l'alto sol che tu disiri
  e che fu tardi per me conosciuto.
Luogo è là giù non tristo da martìri,
  ma di tenebre solo, ove i lamenti
  non suonan come guai, ma son sospiri.
Quivi sto io coi pargoli innocenti
  dai denti morsi della morte avante
  che fosser dall'umana colpa essenti;
quivi sto io con quei che le tre sante
  virtù non si vestiro, e sanza vizio

Canto VII

After the dignified and joyous greetings
   were repeated three and four times,
     Sordello stepped back and asked: "Who are you two?"
"Before the souls worthy to ascend to God
   were directed to this mountain,
     my bones were buried by Octavian.
I am Vergil; and for no other fault
   did I lose heaven than for not having the true faith."
     Thus did my guide then reply.
Like a man who sees an unexpected thing
   in front of him, so that he is amazed
     and does and does not believe it, saying: "It is . . . it is not so,"
such did Sordello appear; then he lowered his brows,
   and humbly turned back toward him,
     clasping him where an inferior takes hold.[1]
"O glory of the Latins," he said, "through whom
   our language demonstrated what it was capable of,
     O eternal honor of the place I came from,
what merit or what grace shows you to me?
   If I am worthy to hear your words,
     tell me if you are coming from Hell, and from which region."
"Through all the circles of the sorrowful kingdom,"
   he replied, "I have come to this place:
     a heavenly power bestirred me, and I come with its protection.
Not by commission, but by omission, I have lost
   the view of the lofty sun that you long for,
     and which was recognized by me too late.
There is a place down there which is not saddened by tortures,
   but merely by darkness, where our laments
     do not sound like wailing, but are sighs.
There I dwell along with the innocent babes
   who were bitten by the teeth of death before
     they were exempted from man's original sin;
there I dwell with those who did not clothe themselves
   with the three holy virtues, but, free from vice,

---

1. This has variously been taken to be: the knees, the chest, the thighs, the feet.

conobber l'altre e seguir tutte quante.
Ma se tu sai e puoi, alcuno indizio
da' noi per che venir possiam più tosto
là dove purgatorio ha dritto inizio.»
Rispuose: «Loco certo non c'è posto;
licito m'è andar suso ed intorno;
per quanto ir posso, a guida mi t'accosto.
Ma vedi già come dichina il giorno,
e andar su di notte non si puote;
però è bon pensar di bel soggiorno.
Anime sono a destra qua remote:
se mi consenti, io ti merrò ad esse,
e non sanza diletto ti fier note.»
«Com'è ciò?» fu risposto. «Chi volesse
salir di notte, fora elli impedito
d'altrui, o non sarrìa chè non potesse?»
E 'l buon Sordello in terra fregò 'l dito,
dicendo: «Vedi, sola questa riga
non varcheresti dopo il sol partito:
non però ch'altra cosa desse briga
che la notturna tenebra ad ir suso:
quella col non poder la voglia intriga.
Ben si porìa con lei tornare in giuso
e passeggiar la costa intorno errando,
mentre che l'orizonte il dì tien chiuso.»
Allora il mio segnor, quasi ammirando,
«Menane» disse «dunque là 've dici
ch'aver si può diletto dimorando.»
Poco allungati c'eravam di lici,
quand'io m'accorsi che 'l monte era scemo,
a guisa che i vallon li sceman quici.
«Colà» disse quell'ombra «n'anderemo
dove la costa face di sè grembo;
e quivi il novo giorno attenderemo.»
Tra erto e piano era un sentiero sghembo,
che ne condusse in fianco della lacca,

knew and abided by all the others.[2]
But if you know and are able, give us
    some indication of how we can arrive more quickly
    in the place where Purgatory has its real beginning."[3]
He replied: "A fixed place has not been assigned;
    I am allowed to go up and around;
    to the extent that I can, I will accompany you as a guide.
But see how day is already declining,
    and it is not possible to ascend by night;
    therefore it would be proper to think about a good resting place.
There are souls some distance from here at the right:
    if you permit me, I shall lead you to them,
    and they will be made known to you, not without your enjoyment."
"How is that?" came the reply. "If someone wanted
    to ascend by night, would he be hindered
    by any one else, or would he fail to climb through his own inability?"
And honorable Sordello marked the ground, rubbing it with his finger,
    and said: "See, not even this line
    could you cross after the sun's departure:
not because anything else created an obstacle
    to mounting upward, but only because of the darkness of night:
    that darkness entangles the will, and makes it powerless.
Nevertheless, in the dark, you could go back down again
    and wander all around the mountainside,
    all the while that the horizon shuts up the daylight."
Then my lord, as if in amazement,
    said: "Then take us where you say
    we can have enjoyment while we stay there."
We had not proceeded far from there
    when I noticed that the mountain was hollowed out
    in the way that gorges hollow them here on earth.
"Over yonder," said that shade, "we will go
    to the spot where the slope forms a basin;
    and there we shall await the coming day."
There was an oblique trail, neither too steep nor quite level,
    which led us alongside the depression

2. The virtuous pagans now in Limbo knew the cardinal virtues of prudence, justice, fortitude, and temperance, but were still unaware of the theological virtues of faith, hope, and charity. 3. Although already ascending the mountain where Purgatory is located, Dante is still on its outskirts, Ante-Purgatory.

là dove più ch'a mezzo muore il lembo.
  Oro e argento fine, cocco e biacca,
    indaco, legno lucido, sereno,
    fresco smeraldo in l'ora che si fiacca,
dall'erba e dalli fior dentr'a quel seno
    posti ciascun sarìa di color vinto,
    come dal suo maggiore è vinto il meno.
Non avea pur natura ivi dipinto,
    ma di soavità di mille odori
    vi facea uno incognito e indistinto.
'Salve, Regina' in sul verde e 'n su' fiori,
    quindi seder cantando anime vidi,
    che per la valle non parean di fori.
«Prima che 'l poco sole omai s'annidi»
    cominciò il Mantovan che ci avea volti,
    «tra costor non vogliate ch'io vi guidi.
Di questo balzo meglio li atti e' volti
    conoscerete voi di tutti quanti,
    che nella lama giù tra essi accolti.
Colui che più siede alto e fa sembianti
    d'aver negletto ciò che far dovea,
    e che non move bocca alli altrui canti,
Rodolfo imperador fu, che potea
    sanar le piaghe c'hanno Italia morta,
    sì che tardi per altro si ricrea.
L'altro che nella vista lui conforta,
    resse la terra dove l'acqua nasce
    che Molta in Albia, e Albia in mar ne porta:
Ottacchero ebbe nome, e nelle fasce
    fu meglio assai che Vincislao suo figlio
    barbuto, cui lussuria e ozio pasce.
E quel Nasetto che stretto a consiglio
    par con colui c'ha sì benigno aspetto,
    morì fuggendo e disfiorando il giglio:

to the place where the bank is more than half gone.
Gold and pure silver, cochineal and white lead,
  indigo—that bright, sky-blue wood—[4]
cool emerald at the moment when it is split,
would each be surpassed in color
  by the grass and flowers located in that hollow,
  just as the lesser is surpassed by the greater.
Nature had not only painted colors there,
  but from the sweetness of a thousand aromas
  had created there a single unknown and indistinguishable one.
There, on the green lawn and amid the flowers, I saw
  souls sitting and chanting the *Salve regina*;[5]
because of the valley they were not visible from outside.
"Before the little remaining sun returns to its nest,"
  began the Mantuan who had brought us around there,
  "do not ask me to guide you into these people's company.
From this crag you will better discern
  the actions and the faces of them all
  than you would if welcomed among them on the valley floor.
The man who is seated highest and gives the impression
  of having neglected his duty,[6]
  and who does not move his lips to the others' chant,
was the emperor Rudolph,[7] who had the power
  to heal the wounds that have killed Italy,
  which now cannot soon be revived by others.
The next man, who seems to be consoling him,
  governed the land where the waters spring
  which the Moldau carries to the Elbe, and the Elbe to the sea:
his name was Ottocar,[8] and even when in his swaddling clothes
  he was already much better than his son Wenceslaus is,
  bearded, for he feeds on lust and sloth.
And that Small-nose,[9] who seems joined in counsel
  with the man who has such a benign appearance,[10]
  died while escaping and deflowering the lily banner:

---

4. This line also has been interpreted as: "bright, clear amber"—and in other ways, as well.   5. "Hail, queen": the famous hymn to the Virgin.   6. All the residents in this valley are rulers who were so preoccupied with affairs of state that they neglected their loftier duties (or made their peace with God very late in life).   7. The first Hapsburg emperor (died 1298), the father of the Albert in the preceding canto. 8. Ottocar II, king of Bohemia (died 1278). His son was Wenceslaus IV (died 1305). 9. Philip III, the bold, of France (died 1285), defeated in war by Peter III of Aragon. 10. Henry the Fat of Navarre (died 1274).

guardate là come si batte il petto!
   L'altro vedete c'ha fatto alla guancia
   della sua palma, sospirando, letto.
Padre e suocero son del mal di Francia:
   sanno la vita sua viziata e lorda,
   e quindi viene il duol che sì li lancia.
Quel che par sì membruto e che s'accorda,
   cantando, con colui dal maschio naso,
   d'ogni valor portò cinta la corda;
e se re dopo lui fosse rimaso
   lo giovanetto che retro a lui siede,
   ben andava il valor di vaso in vaso,
che non si puote dir dell'altre rede;
   Iacomo e Federigo hanno i reami;
   del retaggio miglior nessun possiede.
Rade volte risurge per li rami
   l'umana probitate; e questo vole
   quei che la dà, perchè da lui si chiami.
Anche al Nasuto vanno mie parole
   non men ch'all'altro, Pier, che con lui canta,
   onde Puglia e Proenza già si dole.
Tant'è del seme suo minor la pianta,
   quanto più che Beatrice e Margherita,
   Costanza di marito ancor si vanta.
Vedete il re della semplice vita
   seder là solo, Arrigo d'Inghilterra;
   questi ha ne' rami suoi migliore uscita.
Quel che più basso tra costor s'atterra,
   guardando in suso, è Guiglielmo Marchese,
   per cui e Alessandria e la sua guerra
fa pianger Monferrato e Canavese.»

just see how he beats his breast!
Look at that other man[11] who, sighing, has made
of his palm a pillow for his cheek.
They are the father and father-in-law of the curse of France:[12]
they are aware of his vice-ridden, corrupt life,
and therefrom comes the grief that lances them so.
The man who seems so large of limb,[13] and attunes himself
in his chant to the one with the masculine nose,[14]
was girded with every good quality;
and if the young man[15] sitting behind him
had remained as his successor on the throne,
that virtue would have been transferred from vessel to vessel,
but the same cannot be said about his other heirs;
James and Frederick[16] possess the kingdoms;
neither one possesses any of the preferable inheritance.
Only seldom does human integrity rise from the trunk
into the branches; and so it is willed
by the One who bestows it, so that it may be recognized as His gift.
My words apply to Big-nose[17] also,
no less than to Peter,[18] who is singing with him,
for on his account Apulia and Provence are already suffering.[19]
The plant is inferior to its seed to the same degree
that Constance still boasts of her husband
more than Beatrice and Margaret do of theirs.[20]
Look at the king who led a simple life
seated over there alone, Henry of England;[21]
he has a better result in his branches.[22]
The man at the lowest ground level among them,
who is looking upward, is the marquess Guglielmo,
on whose account Alessandria, with its warfare,
makes Montferrat and Canavese weep."[23]

---

11. This is Henry of Navarre, again.   12. Philip and Henry were father and father-in-law, respectively, of Philip IV, the Fair, of France (died 1314), whom Dante loathed. 13. Peter III of Aragon (died 1285).   14. Charles I of Anjou, conqueror of Sicily in 1266 (died 1285).   15. One of the sons of Peter III.   16. Other heirs of Peter III, kings of Aragon and Sicily.   17. Charles I of Anjou.   18. Peter III of Aragon. 19. The realms of Charles's inferior son Charles II.   20. Charles II is as much inferior to his father as the husband of the princess Constance, Peter III, was superior to the elder Charles himself, who was the husband successively of the princesses Beatrice and Margaret.   21. Henry III (died 1272).   22. Edward I (died 1307). 23. Guglielmo, marquess of Montferrat and Canavese, was captured in 1292 and held prisoner in Alessandria, a city in Piedmont. His realms weep both because of this and because his son failed to avenge him.

[SUMMARY OF CANTO VIII: At sunset, the spirits in the valley sing the evening hymn *Te lucis ante terminum*. Two angels, dressed in green and with green wings, and carrying flaming swords, alight on the banks overlooking the valley. They have been sent by the Virgin to guard against a serpent. Dante, Vergil, and Sordello now enter the valley, and Dante is addressed by the Pisan judge Nino de' Visconti, who, after the shock of learning that Dante is alive (a shock that Sordello shares), asks the poet to remember him to his (Nino's)

Canto IX

La concubina di Titone antico
 già s'imbiancava al balco d'orïente,
 fuor delle braccia del suo dolce amico;
di gemme la sua fronte era lucente,
 poste in figura del freddo animale
 che con la coda percuote la gente;
e la notte de' passi con che sale
 fatti avea due nel loco ov'eravamo,
 e 'l terzo già chinava in giuso l'ale;
quand'io, che meco avea di quel d'Adamo,
 vinto dal sonno, in su l'erba inchinai
 là 've già tutti e cinque sedevamo.
Nell'ora che comincia i tristi lai
 la rondinella presso alla mattina,
 forse a memoria de' suo' primi guai,
e che la mente nostra, peregrina
 più dalla carne e men da' pensier presa,
 alle sue visïon quasi è divina,
in sogno mi parea veder sospesa
 un'aguglia nel ciel con penne d'oro,
 con l'ali aperte ed a calare intesa;
ed esser mi parea là dove foro

daughter. Now in the sky the four morning stars (the cardinal virtues) have been replaced by three others (the theological virtues). The serpent appears and is driven off by the angels, who then fly away. Dante now converses with Currado Malaspina, who asks about his home on earth. Dante has not been there, but assures him that his family is illustrious. Currado then predicts that in less than seven years Dante's opinion will be strikingly confirmed (in 1306 a cousin of the speaker was host to Dante in his exile).]

Canto IX

The concubine of ancient Tithonus[1]
   was already whitening on the balcony of the east,
   away from the arms of her sweet lover;
her brow was gleaming with gems
   arranged in the form of the cold animal
   that strikes people with its tail;[2]
and, of the steps it takes while ascending, night
   had taken two in the place where we were,
   and the third was already bending its wings downward;[3]
when I, who had the stuff of Adam with me,[4]
   overcome by sleep, lay down on the grass
   where all five of us[5] were already seated.
At the hour when the swallow
   begins its sad laments, near morning,
   perhaps because it recalls its original sorrows,[6]
and when our mind, wandering
   farther from the flesh and less occupied with thoughts,
   is almost prophetic in its visions,
I dreamed I saw an eagle
   hovering in the sky on golden pinions;
   its wings were spread and it was poised to swoop;
and I thought I was located where

---

1. This mythical "concubine" usually represents dawn (Dante may mean it was day-break back in Italy), but perhaps a better interpretation here is: moonrise (nocturnal "dawn").   2. The moon is in the constellation Scorpio.   3. Each "step" is an hour, and night was considered to begin at 6 P.M., so that it is now nearly nine (other interpretations make the "steps" longer, so that it really is almost daybreak).   4. I was alive and in my body.   5. Dante, Vergil, Sordello, Nino de' Visconti, and Currado Malaspina.   6. The swallow, in Greek mythology, was once a woman who suffered from family tragedies.

abbandonati i suoi da Ganimede,
 quando fu ratto al sommo consistoro.
Fra me pensava: «Forse questa fiede
 pur qui per uso, e forse d'altro loco
 disdegna di portarne suso in piede.»
Poi mi parea che, poi rotata un poco,
 terribil come folgor discendesse,
 e me rapisse suso infino al foco.
Ivi parea che ella e io ardesse;
 e sì lo 'ncendio imaginato cosse,
 che convenne che 'l sonno si rompesse.
Non altrimenti Achille si riscosse,
 li occhi svegliati rivolgendo in giro
 e non sappiendo là dove si fosse,
quando la madre da Chirone a Schiro
 trafuggò lui dormendo in le sue braccia,
 là onde poi li Greci il dipartiro;
che mi scoss'io, sì come dalla faccia
 mi fuggì 'l sonno, e diventa' ismorto,
 come fa l'uom che, spaventato, agghiaccia.
Da lato m'era solo il mio conforto,
 e 'l sole er'alto già più che due ore,
 e 'l viso m'era alla marina torto.
«Non aver tema» disse il mio segnore;
 «fatti sicur, chè noi semo a buon punto:
 non stringer, ma rallarga ogni vigore.
Tu se' omai al purgatorio giunto:
 vedi là il balzo che 'l chiude dintorno;
 vedi l'entrata là 've par disgiunto.
Dianzi, nell'alba che procede al giorno,
 quando l'anima tua dentro dormìa
 sovra li fiori ond'è là giù adorno,
venne una donna, e disse: 'I' son Lucia:
 lasciatemi pigliar costui che dorme;
 sì l'agevolerò per la sua via'.
Sordel rimase e l'altre gentil forme:

Ganymede's companions were abandoned by him
   when he was abducted and borne to the most lofty council.[7]
I thought to myself: "Perhaps this bird pounces
   only here, out of habit, and perhaps from any other place
   it disdains to carry people skyward in its talons."
Then I dreamed that, after it had wheeled a few times,
   it descended, terrible as a lightning bolt,
   and snatched me upward all the way to the fire.[8]
There I dreamed that both it and I were burning;
   and the blaze in my dream scorched me so much
   that my slumber was forced to break off.
Not otherwise did Achilles rouse himself,
   turning his awakened eyes in every direction,
   ignorant of his whereabouts,
when his mother stole him away asleep
   in her arms from Chiron[9] to Scyros,
   whence the Greeks later removed him;[10]
than I started up, so that slumber
   fled from my face and I turned pale,
   like a man who freezes up from fright.
Beside me there was only my encourager,
   and the sun had already been in the sky over two hours,
   and my face was turned toward the seacoast.
"Have no fear," my lord said;
   "be reassured, for we are in a good situation:
   do not diminish, but expand, all your vigor.
You have now arrived at Purgatory:
   see, over there, the ledge that encloses it all around;
   see the entrance where the ledge seems breached.
Early, at the dawn that precedes the day,
   when your soul was asleep within you
   and you were lying on the flowers which adorn that spot,
a lady came, and said: 'I am Lucy:
   let me take the man who is sleeping;
   thus I shall make his journey easy for him.'
Sordello remained behind, as did the other noble souls:

---

7. The eagle of Jupiter (Zeus) abducted the handsome youth Ganymede to be a servant of the gods.   8. The sphere of fire, located between the earth's atmosphere and
the heaven of the moon.   9. Achilles' centaur tutor.   10. For this story, see *Hell*,
Canto XXVI, note 9.

ella ti tolse, e come il dì fu chiaro,
    sen venne suso; e io per le sue orme.
Qui ti posò, ma pria mi dimostraro
    li occhi suoi belli quella intrata aperta;
    poi ella e 'l sonno ad una se n'andaro.»
A guisa d'uom che 'n dubbio si raccerta,
    e che muta in conforto sua paura,
    poi che la verità li è discoperta,
mi cambia' io; e come sanza cura
    vide me 'l duca mio, su per lo balzo
    si mosse, ed io di retro inver l'altura.
Lettor, tu vedi ben com'io innalzo
    la mia matera, e però con più arte
    non ti maravigliar s'io la rincalzo.
Noi ci appressammo, ed eravamo in parte,
    che là dove pareami prima rotto,
    pur come un fesso che muro diparte,
vidi una porta, e tre gradi di sotto
    per gire ad essa, di color diversi,
    e un portier ch'ancor non facea motto.
E come l'occhio più e più v'apersi,
    vidil seder sovra 'l grado soprano,
    tal nella faccia ch'io non lo soffersi;
e una spada nuda avea in mano,
    che reflettea i raggi sì ver noi,
    ch'io dirizzava spesso il viso in vano.
«Dite costinci: che volete voi?»
    cominciò elli a dire: «ov'è la scorta?
    guardate che 'l venir su non vi noi.»
«Donna del ciel, di queste cose accorta,»
    rispuose il mio maestro a lui, «pur dianzi
    ne disse: 'Andate là: quivi è la porta'.»
«Ed ella i passi vostri in bene avanzi»
    ricominciò il cortese portinaio:
    «venite dunque a' nostri gradi innanzi.»
Là ne venimmo; e lo scaglion primaio
    bianco marmo era sì pulito e terso,
    ch'io mi specchiai in esso qual io paio.
Era il secondo tinto più che perso,
    d'una petrina ruvida ed arsiccia,
    crepata per lo lungo e per traverso.

she picked you up, and when the day was bright,
    came up here; and I followed her trail.
She set you down here, but first her lovely eyes
    showed me that open entrance;
    then she and your slumber departed at the same time."
Like a man whose doubts are dispelled,
    and who turns his fear into consolation
    once the truth is revealed to him,
so did I change; and when my guide
    saw I was no longer worried, he moved
    up along the ledge, and I behind him, toward the heights.
Reader, you clearly see how I am raising the level
    of my subject matter, and therefore do not be surprised
    if I reinforce it with greater art.
We drew near, and were at a point
    where, in the place that earlier seemed to be broken,
    like a crack that splits apart a wall,
I now saw a gate, with three steps below
    for reaching it, steps of different colors,
    and a gatekeeper who as yet spoke not a word.
And, as I opened my eyes more and more,
    I saw him sitting above the topmost step,
    his face so bright I could not bear to behold it;
and he had in his hand a naked sword,
    which reflected its rays toward us in such a manner
    that I often tried to look that way, but in vain.
"Tell me, from the spot where you stand: what do you two want?"
    he started to say. "Where is your escort?
    Take care lest your coming up here be harmful to you."
"A lady from heaven, experienced in such matters,"
    my master replied to him, "just a while ago
    said to us: 'Go there: here is the gate.'"
"And may she speed your journey for your good!"
    resumed the courteous gatekeeper:
    "Come before our steps, then."
We came there; and the first tread
    was of white marble so polished and smooth
    that I saw my image in it distinctly.
The second one was extremely dark purple in color,
    of a rough, scorched kind of stone,
    with a crack running lengthwise and another crosswise.

Lo terzo, che di sopra s'ammassicia,
  porfido mi parea sì fiammeggiante,
  come sangue che fuor di vena spiccia.
Sovra questo tenea ambo le piante
  l'angel di Dio, sedendo in su la soglia,
  che mi sembiava pietra di diamante.
Per li tre gradi su di buona voglia
  mi trasse il duca mio, dicendo: «Chiedi
  umilemente che 'l serrame scioglia.»
Divoto mi gittai a' santi piedi:
  misericordia chiesi che m'aprisse,
  ma pria nel petto tre fiate mi diedi.
Sette *P* nella fronte mi descrisse
  col punton della spada, e «Fa che lavi,
  quando se' dentro, queste piaghe» disse.
Cenere o terra che secca si cavi
  d'un color fora col suo vestimento;
  e di sotto da quel trasse due chiavi.
L'una era d'oro e l'altra era d'argento:
  pria con la bianca e poscia con la gialla
  fece alla porta sì, ch'i' fu' contento.
«Quandunque l'una d'este chiavi falla,
  che non si volga dritta per la toppa»
  diss'elli a noi, «non s'apre questa calla.
Più cara è l'una; ma l'altra vuol troppa
  d'arte e d'ingegno avanti che diserri,
  perch'ella è quella che nodo digroppa.
Da Pier le tegno; e dissemi ch'i' erri
  anzi ad aprir ch'a tenerla serrata,
  pur che la gente a' piedi mi s'atterri.»
Poi pinse l'uscio alla porta sacrata,
  dicendo: «Intrate; ma facciovi accorti
  che di fuor torna chi 'n dietro si guata.»
E quando fuor ne' cardini distorti
  li spigoli di quella regge sacra,
  che di metallo son sonanti e forti,

The third step, whose hardened mass lies uppermost,
    seemed to me to be of porphyry as bright red
    as blood that gushes from a vein.[11]
On this one the angel of God
    rested both his feet, while he sat on the threshold,
    which seemed to me a stone of adamant.
Up the three steps, gladly
    my guide brought me, saying: "Ask him
    humbly to open the lock."
Piously I threw myself at his holy feet:
    I asked him to open the gate for me mercifully,
    but first I struck three blows on my breast.
He drew seven P's[12] on my brow
    with the point of his sword, and said:
    "See that you wash away these wounds when you are inside."
Ashes, or dug-out dry earth,
    would be of one color with his robe,
    from beneath which he drew two keys.
One was of gold and the other was of silver:[13]
    first with the white one and then with the yellow
    he manipulated the gate in such a way as to satisfy me.
"Whenever one of these keys fails,
    so that it does not turn properly in the lock,"
    he told us, "this path does not lie open.
One of the keys is more precious; but the other one requires extreme
    skill and wisdom before it unlocks,
    because that is the key which unties the knot.
I was given them by Peter, who told me I ought to err
    on the side of indulgence in opening the gate rather than keeping it locked,
    always provided that those applying fall to the ground at my feet."
Then he pushed open the door of the blessed portal,
    saying: "Enter; but I warn you
    that whoever looks back is cast out again."
And when the pivots of that sacred gate,
    which are of strong, resonant metal,
    turned in their hinges,

---

11. Most commentators interpret these three steps as contrition, confession, and repentance; they also have been regarded as innocence, sin, and atonement. 12. Standing for *peccatum* ("sin"). 13. The gold key represents the confessor's divine authorization; the silver one, the human discernment he requires.

non rugghiò sì nè si mostrò sì acra
  Tarpea, come tolto le fu il buono
  Metello, per che poi rimase macra.
Io mi rivolsi attento al primo tuono,
  e 'Te Deum laudamus' mi parea
  udire in voce mista al dolce suono.
Tale imagine a punto mi rendea
  ciò ch'io udiva, qual prender si sòle
  quando a cantar con organi si stea;
ch'or sì, or non s'intendon le parole.

[SUMMARY OF CANTO X: As the gate clangs shut behind them, Dante and Vergil climb up a tortuous path until they reach a flat marble terrace, the inner bank of which is adorned with sculptured scenes exemplifying humility: the angel Gabriel announcing the Conception to Mary; the Ark of the Covenant on its oxcart, with King David dancing before it; and the Roman

Canto XI

«O Padre nostro, che ne' cieli stai,
  non circunscritto, ma per più amore
  ch'ai primi effetti di là su tu hai,
laudato sia 'l tuo nome e 'l tuo valore
  da ogni creatura, com'è degno
  di render grazie al tuo dolce vapore.
Vegna ver noi la pace del tuo regno,
  chè noi ad essa non potem da noi,
  s'ella non vien, con tutto nostro ingegno.
Come del suo voler li angeli tuoi
  fan sacrificio a te, cantando osanna,
  così facciano li uomini de' suoi.
Dà oggi a noi la cotidiana manna,
  sanza la qual per questo aspro diserto
  a retro va chi più di gir s'affanna.
E come noi lo mal ch'avem sofferto
  perdoniamo a ciascuno, e tu perdona

the Tarpeian rock[14] did not roar so loud, or show itself
  so unyielding, when it was deprived of honest
  Metellus, so that it later remained emptied of its contents.
I turned attentively at the first tone,
  and I seemed to hear *Te Deum laudamus*[15]
  sung by a mixed choir to[16] sweet music.
What I heard gave me exactly
  that impression which we are accustomed to receive
  when we are singing to an organ accompaniment,
when the words are understood clearly at some moments but not at others.

emperor Trajan granting a poor widow's request (as a reward for which
he was later brought out of Hell). Dante now sees approaching a group of
people bowed down under the heavy stones they carry; they are here being
purged of their pridefulness.]

Canto XI

"O our father, You that are in heaven,
  not because You are restricted to it, but for the greater love
  You bear toward Your first creations,[1] which are up there,
praised be Your name and Your power
  by every creature, since it is fitting
  to give thanks to Your sweet spirit.
May the peace of Your kingdom come upon us,
  for on our own we are powerless to attain it,
  if it does not come freely, despite all our intellect.
Just as Your angels voluntarily
  make sacrifice to You, singing hosanna,
  thus let men also do voluntarily.
Give us today our daily manna,
  without which, in this rugged desert,
  the man who strives most to advance goes backward.
And just as, for the evil we have suffered,
  we forgive each man, You too forgive us

14. Site of the treasury in Rome, which the tribune Metellus failed to keep from falling into Julius Caesar's hands during the civil wars.   15. Famous hymn of thanksgiving to God.   16. Or: "a voice mingled with."   1. The heavens and the angels.

benigno, e non guardar lo nostro merto.
    Nostra virtù che di leggier s'adona,
        non spermentar con l'antico avversaro,
        ma libera da lui che sì la sprona.
    Quest'ultima preghiera, signor caro,
        già non si fa per noi, chè non bisogna,
        ma per color che dietro a noi restaro.»
Così a sè e noi buona ramogna
        quell'ombre orando, andavan sotto il pondo,
        simile a quel che tal volta si sogna,
disparmente angosciate tutte a tondo
        e lasse su per la prima cornice,
        purgando la caligine del mondo.
Se di là sempre ben per noi si dice,
        di qua che dire e far per lor si puote
        da quei ch'hanno al voler buona radice?
Ben si de' loro atar lavar le note
        che portar quinci, sì che, mondi e lievi,
        possano uscire alle stellate rote.
«Deh, se giustizia e pietà vi disgrievi
        tosto, sì che possiate muover l'ala,
        che secondo il disio vostro vi lievi,
mostrate da qual mano inver la scala
        si va più corto; e se c'è più d'un varco,
        quel ne 'nsegnate che men erto cala;
chè questi che vien meco, per lo 'ncarco
        della carne d'Adamo onde si veste,
        al montar su, contra sua voglia, è parco.»
Le lor parole, che rendero a queste
        che dette avea colui cu' io seguiva,
        non fur da cui venisser manifeste;
ma fu detto: «A man destra per la riva
        con noi venite, e troverete il passo
        possibile a salir persona viva.
E s'io non fossi impedito dal sasso
        che la cervice mia superba doma,
        onde portar convienmi il viso basso,
cotesti, ch'ancor vive e non si noma,

in Your kindness, without regard to what we deserve.
Do not tempt our virtue, which is easily
    subdued, with our ancient Adversary,
    but free us from him who spurs it to such evil courses.
That last prayer, dear Lord,
    is no longer made on our account, for we do not need it,
    but for those who have remained behind us."[2]
Thus those souls, praying for a good journey[3]
    for themselves and for us, walked beneath their weights,
    which were such as are sometimes seen in nightmares,
all anguished in varying degrees, round and round
    the first terrace, wearily,
    purging away their earthly soot.
If in the next world people always pray for us,
    what should not be said and done for them
    by those of us who have a will rooted in goodness?
Truly, we should help them wash away the stains
    they bore here below, so that, cleansed and light,
    they can ascend to the starry spheres.
"Please—so may justice and compassion unburden you
    soon, so that you can spread your wings
    and they can lift you up as you desire!—
show us in which direction we can most quickly arrive
    at a place of ascent; and, if there is more than one passage,
    indicate to us the one that drops least steeply;
for the man who comes with me, because of the burden
    of Adam's flesh that he wears,
    despite his wishes is slow at climbing."
Their words, with which they replied to those
    spoken by the one I was following,
    did not clearly indicate the individual speaker;
but this is what was said: "Come with us
    along the bank to the right, and you will find a passage
    suitable for a living person to climb.
And, if I were not hindered by the rock
    that tames my haughty neck
    and forces me to keep my face down,
I would look at this man, who still lives

---

2. Those already in Purgatory cannot be led into evil.   3. The very rare Italian word
may mean "augury" or "fortune" instead.

guardere' io, per veder s'i' 'l conosco,
e per farlo pietoso a questa soma.
Io fui latino e nato d'un gran tosco:
Guiglielmo Aldobrandesco fu mio padre;
non so se 'l nome suo già mai fu vosco.
L'antico sangue e l'opere leggiadre
di miei maggior mi fer sì arrogante,
che, non pensando alla comune madre,
ogn'uomo ebbi in despetto tanto avante,
ch'io ne mori'; come, i Sanesi sanno
e sallo in Campagnatico ogni fante.
Io sono Omberto; e non pur a me danno
superbia fè, chè tutt'i miei consorti
ha ella tratti seco nel malanno.
E qui convien ch'io questo peso porti
per lei, tanto che a Dio si sodisfaccia,
poi ch'io nol fe' tra' vivi, qui tra' morti.»
Ascoltando chinai in giù la faccia;
e un di lor, non questi che parlava,
si torse sotto il peso che li 'mpaccia,
e videmi e conobbemi e chiamava,
tenendo li occhi con fatica fisi
a me che tutto chin con loro andava.
«Oh!» diss'io lui, «non se' tu Oderisi,
l'onor d'Agobbio e l'onor di quell'arte
ch'alluminar chiamata è in Parisi?»
«Frate,» diss'elli «più ridon le carte
che pennelleggia Franco bolognese:
l'onore è tutto or suo, e mio in parte.
Ben non sare' io stato sì cortese
mentre ch'io vissi, per lo gran disio
dell'eccellenza ove mio core intese.
Di tal superbia qui si paga il fio;
e ancor non sarei qui, se non fosse
che, possendo peccar, mi volsi a Dio.
Oh vana gloria dell'umane posse!

but does not state his name, to see if I know him,
and to make him pity this load of mine.
I was an Italian, the son of a great Tuscan:
    Guglielmo Aldobrandeschi[4] was my father;
    I do not know whether you were ever familiar with his name.
My ancient lineage and the noble deeds
    of my forebears made me so arrogant
    that, disregarding the common mother of us all,[5]
I held every man in such great contempt
    that it caused my death—in what way, the Sienese know
    and every child in Campagnatico[6] knows.
I am Omberto; and not to me only did pride
    do harm, for it drew all my relatives
    to ruin along with it.
And here I must carry this weight
    because of pride until satisfaction is made to God,
    here among the dead, because I did not do so among the living."
As I listened, I bowed my face down;
    and one of them, not the one who was speaking,
    twisted around beneath the weight that impeded him,
saw me, recognized me, and started to call me,
    keeping his eyes laboriously fixed
    on me as I walked along with them, all stooped over.
"Oh," I said to him, "are you not Oderisi,[7]
    the glory of Gubbio and the glory of that art
    which is called illumination in Paris?"
"Brother," he said, "the leaves painted by
    Franco[8] of Bologna are brighter and fairer:
    the glory is all his now, and only partly mine.
I would surely not have been so courteous
    while I lived, because of the great desire
    for preeminence that my heart was set on.
For such pride the fee is paid here;
    and I would not even be here, except that,
    while still able to sin, I turned to God.
Oh, the vanity of human powers!

---

4. The count of Santafiora, a region mentioned in Canto VI.   5. The earth.   6. The
Aldobrandeschi castle; there are different stories about how the speaker died.   7. An
innovative 13th-century painter of manuscript miniatures.   8. His works and career
are no longer known.

com poco verde in su la cima dura,
    se non è giunta dall'etati grosse!
Credette Cimabue nella pintura
    tener lo campo, e ora ha Giotto il grido,
    sì che la fama di colui è scura:
così ha tolto l'uno all'altro Guido
    la gloria della lingua; e forse è nato
    chi l'uno e l'altro caccerà del nido.
Non è il mondan romore altro ch'un fiato
    di vento, ch'or vien quinci e or vien quindi,
    e muta nome perchè muta lato.
Che voce avrai tu più, se vecchia scindi
    da te la carne, che se fossi morto
    anzi che tu lasciassi il 'pappo' e 'l 'dindi',
pria che passin mill'anni? ch'è più corto
    spazio all'etterno, ch'un muover di ciglia
    al cerchio che più tardi in cielo è torto.
Colui che del cammin sì poco piglia
    dinanzi a me, Toscana sonò tutta;
    e ora a pena in Siena sen pispiglia,
ond'era sire quando fu distrutta
    la rabbia fiorentina, che superba
    fu a quel tempo sì com'ora è putta.
La vostra nominanza è color d'erba,
    che viene e va, e quei la discolora
    per cui ella esce della terra acerba.»
E io a lui: «Tuo vero dir m'incora
    bona umiltà, e gran tumor m'appiani:
    ma chi è quei di cui tu parlavi ora?»
«Quelli è» rispuose «Provenzan Salvani;
    ed è qui perchè fu presuntüoso
    a recar Siena tutta alle sue mani.
Ito è così e va, sanza riposo,

How briefly the green lasts at the top of the tree,
   unless a generation of inferior people follows!
Cimabue[9] thought that in painting
   he was master of the field, and now Giotto[10] is all the cry,
   so that the earlier man's reputation is dimmed:
similarly, one Guido has taken from another
   the glory of poetry;[11] and perhaps someone is already born
   who will chase both of them out of the nest.
Worldly fame is nothing but a puff
   of wind that blows now here, now there,
   changing its name as it changes direction.
What greater reputation will you have, if your flesh is old
   when you cast it off, than if you had died
   before you left off speaking baby talk,[12]
once a thousand years have passed?—a time span that is shorter,
   compared with eternity, than the blinking of an eye is, compared
   with the time it takes the slowest heavenly circle to revolve.[13]
The man in front of me, whose strides
   cover so little ground, was famed all over Tuscany;
   and now he is hardly whispered about in Siena,
where he was lord when the rage of the Florentines
   was quashed,[14] which at that time
   was as haughty as it now is prostituted.
Reputation among you is like the color of grass,
   which comes and goes, and is faded by the same power
   that makes it spring freshly from the earth."
I said to him: "Your true words instill in my heart
   worthy humility, and you reduce my great swelling:
   but who is the man you were just speaking of?"
"He," he replied, "is Provenzano Salvani;[15]
   and he is here because he had the presumptuous desire
   to take all of Siena into his hands.
Thus has he gone, and thus does he go, without repose,

9. The greatest Italian painter of the generation before Dante's.   10. The greatest painter of Dante's generation, an innovator in perspective and three-dimensionality.   11. Dante's friend Guido Cavalcanti (died 1300) was considered superior to the founder of their poetic school, Guido Guinizelli (died 1276).   12. The Italian specifically gives the childish words for *pane* ("bread") and *denaro* ("money").   13. The sphere of the fixed stars was thought to take 360 centuries to revolve.   14. At the battle of Montaperti (1260), which Dante mentions so often.   15. Lord of Siena, killed by the Florentines in 1269.

poi che morì: cotal moneta rende
a sodisfar chi è di là troppo oso.»
E io: «Se quello spirito ch'attende,
pria che si penta, l'orlo della vita,
qua giù dimora e qua su non ascende,
se buona orazïon lui non aita,
prima che passi tempo quanto visse,
come fu la venuta a lui largita?»
«Quando vivea più glorïoso» disse,
«liberamente nel Campo di Siena,
ogni vergogna diposta, s'affisse;
e lì, per trar l'amico suo di pena
che sostenea nella prigion di Carlo,
si condusse a tremar per ogni vena.
Più non dirò, e scuro so che parlo;
ma poco tempo andrà, che' tuoi vicini
faranno sì che tu potrai chiosarlo.
Quest'opera li tolse quei confini.»

[SUMMARY OF CANTO XII: As Dante proceeds with Vergil, he sees underfoot further sculptured scenes, these exemplifying pridefulness: a long series of figures from the Bible and Greek mythology. Circling the terrace, around noon they meet an angel robed in white who shows them the next, more easily climbed, flight of stairs. The angel touches Dante's forehead with his wings, erasing the first P, representing pride. Voices sing "Blessed are the poor in spirit." The travelers ascend; Dante feels less weighed down, now that one P has been removed.

SUMMARY OF CANTO XIII: Dante and Vergil reach the second terrace, where the sin of envy is purged away. Those seated along the rim, huddled against one another, are dressed in haircloth, and their eyes are sewn shut with wire like those of an untrained hunting falcon. Dante asks whether anyone there is from Italy. A Sienese woman named Sapia tells how she had exulted at a bloody defeat of her own townspeople. Dante prophesies that, when his time comes, he will not remain long on this terrace, because he is much less subject to envy than to pride.

SUMMARY OF CANTO XIV: Two other Italian spirits engage Dante in

since he died; such coin is paid
   in satisfaction by the man who was too daring on earth."
I said: "If the spirit who has awaited
   the brink of life before repenting
   dwells down below and does not ascend up here—
unless a worthy prayer assists him—
   until as much time as he lived goes by,
   how is it that he was allowed to come here?"
"While he was living in the greatest honors," he said,
   "of his own free will in the main square of Siena
   he took his stand, setting aside all feelings of shame;
and there, in order to rescue a friend from the pain
   he was suffering in Charles's prison,
   he brought himself to tremble to the depths of his heart.[16]
I shall say no more, and I know that my last phrase is obscure;
   but not much time will pass before your townspeople
   will make you able to interpret it.[17]
That deed liberated him from those confines."

---

conversation. The poet hints that his home is on the Arno. One spirit, Guido del Duca, inveighs against those who dwell along that river's course, prophesies further trouble, and berates the degenerate inhabitants of the Romagnola region. The voices of Cain and another envious soul rend the air.

SUMMARY OF CANTO XV: At 3 P.M., Dante and Vergil meet the next angelic stairkeeper and begin an easier ascent as voices sing "Blessed are the merciful." Interpreting some of Guido del Duca's words for Dante, Vergil explains that envy springs from a desire for material goods, which can only be owned in exclusivity, whereas spiritual goods (such as love) exist to be shared with others, and are thus to be preferred; Beatrice will explain further when Dante reaches her. Now on the third terrace, that of the wrathful, the poet sees visions, including one of Mary finding the young Jesus expounding the Law in the Temple, and another of the protomartyr Stephen being stoned: examples of meekness. It is evening, and dark smoke envelops the travelers.

SUMMARY OF CANTO XVI: Voices sing the *Agnus Dei*. The spirit of Marco Lombardo, when asked by Dante whether the current degeneracy on earth is due to astrological or human causes, explains that man has free will, and so

---

16. Salvani humbled his pride, through a great mental and physical effort, by begging in the square for money with which to ransom a friend held captive by Charles of Anjou.   17. A prophecy of Dante's exile; the poet will know what it means to mortify himself painfully.

human error is to be blamed. Man is inherently good, but must have a caring ruler to guide him away from evil. The chief cause of the present troubles is the Church, which, no longer recognizing its parity and partnership with the Holy Roman Emperors (the "two suns" theory), yearns for temporal goods and lets everything go to ruin; only three old men, whom Marco names, are as just as those of the past. Now the light emanating from another angel is visible through the murk.

SUMMARY OF CANTO XVII: As the smoky mist clears, Dante has visions of famous wrathful people from the Bible and Greek myth. At the next staircase, another angel's wingstroke erases another P from Dante's forehead as a voice calls, "Blessed are the peacemakers." The stars are out by the time Dante and Vergil reach the top of the stairs, and there they must stay for that night. The fourth terrace is reserved for those who were slothful in doing good; that is, lukewarm in their love. Vergil explains that love directs the entire universe (in the nonhuman realm, it takes the form of attractions or affinities). Evil in man is love turned awry, and changed to hate. Since no one can hate himself or God, evil is the hatred of one's fellow man. The residents on the first three terraces—the prideful, envious, and wrathful—all exemplify such a deviation from love. Those on the fifth, sixth, and seventh terraces went astray by being too keen in their love.

SUMMARY OF CANTO XVIII: Vergil, continuing to discuss love, describes how a first pleasant impression engenders desire, which demands fruition; but not every individual instance of love is necessarily good. Dante asks wherein human merit lies if love is imposed upon us by an external power. Vergil replies that man has an innate love for God and the good, to which no merit attaches. His merit derives from his ability, via his free will, to make his individual loves conform to the same high standard. It is nearly midnight when Dante sees the once slothful residents of the fourth terrace dashing around it at a mad pace to make up for their former negligence; among them is a former Veronese abbot. Dante drops off to sleep, and has a dream.

SUMMARY OF CANTO XIX: An hour before dawn, Dante dreams of an ugly woman who turns into a beautiful siren and tempts the poet until Vergil exposes her real loathsomeness. Dante awakens; it is day; they proceed and find the next staircase; the angel calls: "Blessed are they that mourn." Dante recounts his dream to Vergil, who encourages him to be holy. On the fifth terrace people are lying on the ground face downward; they are misers and spendthrifts, unable to behold higher things. Dante converses with Pope Hadrian V, who reigned for just one month in 1276, at which time he forswore his earlier avarice. Hadrian does not allow Dante to kneel to him, because earthly distinctions are here abolished.

SUMMARY OF CANTO XX: Dante, cursing avarice, hears a spirit praising exemplars of a plain but pious life. It is Hugh Capet, founder in 987 of the dynasty that still rules France in Dante's day. He inveighs against his recent and current descendants, who have caused much harm at home and abroad, including Charles of Anjou; Charles of Valois, who reinstalled the Black faction in power in Florence in 1302; and the then king, Philip IV, who destroyed the order of the Templars—all from greed. At night the souls on the fifth terrace constantly recall examples of avarice in the Bible and ancient history. Now an earthquake shakes the mountain, while everyone around calls: "Glory to God in the highest."

SUMMARY OF CANTO XXI: Dante, consumed with curiosity, proceeds with Vergil. They meet a spirit who greets them amicably and asks who they are. Vergil explains their situation without naming names. The spirit tells them that the mountain quakes when a soul finishes its purgation and is free to ascend toward Paradise; he himself has just been liberated after five hundred years. He is the ancient Latin poet Statius (1st century A.D.), who claims to have been inspired by the supreme poet Vergil. Vergil signals to Dante to be silent, but Dante cannot suppress a smile, and their identities are revealed. Statius is so overcome by awe that, forgetting the rules, he tries to embrace Vergil's feet.

SUMMARY OF CANTO XXII: An angel directs Dante, Vergil, and Statius to the sixth terrace, effacing yet another P, and saying: "Blessed are those who thirst after righteousness." Vergil asks Statius how, being so wise, he could have yielded to avarice. Statius replies that his long sojourn on the fifth terrace was due to his prodigality, which was cured by a quotation from Vergil's writings. Vergil asks how Statius came to be a Christian (historically, this is nonsense). Statius says that he was converted by another Vergilian passage often taken (erroneously) to be a prophecy of Christ's coming; because he was only a lukewarm Christian at first, he spent more than four hundred years on the fourth terrace. He asks Vergil about other Roman authors, and Vergil describes their life in Limbo. It is now past ten A.M. They find a fruit tree with branches growing smaller from top to bottom, so that it cannot be climbed; a waterfall moistens it. A voice from the foliage praises biblical and Roman figures who were abstemious in eating and drinking.

SUMMARY OF CANTO XXIII: The travelers move on and hear the words "Lord, open my lips" (recited at the beginning of sacred offices). They are overtaken and left behind by a troop of emaciated spirits purging themselves of the sin of gluttony; they suffer from the presence of the fruit and water, which instill an unfulfillable desire to partake of them. Dante recognizes one spirit—by his voice only—as his old friend Forese Donati, a cousin of the poet's wife. Dante expected this reprobate, who failed to repent until the last moment, to be down in Ante-Purgatory; the explanation for his presence here is that his loving wife Nella prayed for him. Her piety contrasts with the general looseness of modern Florentine women. Dante regrets his past rowdy days with Forese, from which Vergil saved him (at the beginning of the whole poem).]

Canto XXIV

Nè 'l dir l'andar, nè l'andar lui più lento
   facea; ma, ragionando, andavam forte,
   sì come nave pinta da buon vento;
e l'ombre, che parean cose rimorte,
   per le fosse delli occhi ammirazione
   traean di me, di mio vivere accorte.
E io, continüando al mio sermone,
   dissi: «Ella sen va su forse più tarda
   che non farebbe, per altrui cagione.
Ma dimmi, se tu sai, dov'è Piccarda;
   dimmi s'io veggio da notar persona
   tra questa gente che sì mi riguarda.»
«La mia sorella, che tra bella e bona
   non so qual fosse più, triunfa lieta
   nell'alto Olimpo già di sua corona.»
Sì disse prima; e poi: «Qui non si vieta
   di nominar ciascun, da ch'è sì munta
   nostra sembianza via per la dïeta.
Questi» e mostrò col dito «è Bonagiunta,
   Bonagiunta da Lucca; e quella faccia
   di là da lui più che l'altre trapunta
ebbe la Santa Chiesa in le sue braccia:
   dal Torso fu, e purga per digiuno
   l'anguille di Bolsena e la vernaccia.»
Molti altri mi nomò ad uno ad uno;
   e del nomar parean tutti contenti,
   sì ch'io però non vidi un atto bruno.
Vidi per fame a voto usar li denti
   Ubaldin dalla Pila e Bonifazio
   che pasturò col rocco molte genti.

Canto XXIV

Neither did our speaking make our walking slower, nor our walking
    our speaking; but, conversing, we were making good time,
    like a ship propelled by a favorable wind;
and the shades, who seemed like things twice dead,[1]
    from the cavities of their eyes shot amazement
    at me when they became aware I was alive.
And I, continuing my speech,
    said: "It[2] is perhaps proceeding more slowly
    than it otherwise would, for the sake of another.[3]
But tell me, if you know, where Piccarda[4] is;
    tell me whether I see any person of note
    among these people who are looking at me that way."
"My sister, of whom I cannot say whether she excelled more
    in beauty than in goodness, is already triumphing
    joyfully in her crown on lofty Olympus."[5]
That is what he said first; and then: "Here it is not forbidden
    to name each person, since our appearance
    is so wasted away by our fasting.
This man," and he pointed with his finger, "is Bonagiunta,
    Bonagiunta from Lucca;[6] and that face
    beyond him, which is more stitched through by hunger than the rest,
belongs to one that held the Holy Church in his arms:[7]
    he came from Tours, and by fasting is atoning for
    the eels from Lake Bolsena cooked in Ligurian white wine."
He named many others for me individually;
    and they all seemed pleased at being named,
    so that I did not see one gesture of displeasure because of it.
I saw Ubaldino of La Pila[8] clamping his teeth
    on thin air in his hunger, and that Bonifacio[9]
    who pastured[10] many people with his crozier.

---

1. Because they are so emaciated. 2. The shade of Statius, which was the last thing mentioned in the preceding canto. 3. In order to linger with Vergil. 4. Forese's sister (Dante is addressing Forese). 5. In Paradise. 6. Bonagiunta Orbicciani, a poet of Dante's time who still imitated the old style of the Provençal troubadours. 7. Martin IV, pope from 1281 to 1285. 8. Ubaldino degli Ubaldini; La Pila was a stronghold of his; he was the father of Archbishop Ruggieri, whom Ugolino gnaws in Cantos XXXII and XXXIII of *Hell*. 9. A prelate variously identified. 10. Meaning either that he was their spiritual guide, or that he fed them; if the latter, he might have fed the poor during a famine, or supported hangers-on.

Vidi messer Marchese, ch'ebbe spazio
    già di bere a Forlì con men secchezza,
    e sì fu tal, che non si sentì sazio.
Ma come fa chi guarda e poi si prezza
    più d'un che d'altro, fei a quel da Lucca,
    che più parea di me voler contezza.
El mormorava; e non so che 'Gentucca'
    sentiv'io là, ov'el sentìa la piaga
    della giustizia che sì li pilucca.
«O anima» diss'io «che par sì vaga
    di parlar meco, fa sì ch'io t'intenda,
    e te e me col tuo parlare appaga.»
«Femmina è nata, e non porta ancor benda»
    cominciò el, «che ti farà piacere
    la mia città, come ch'uom la riprenda.
Tu te n'andrai con questo antivedere:
    se nel mio mormorar prendesti errore,
    dichiareranti ancor le cose vere.
Ma dì s'i' veggio qui colui che fore
    trasse le nove rime, cominciando
    'Donne ch'avete intelletto d'amore'.»
E io a lui: «I' mi son un, che quando
    Amor mi spira, noto, e a quel modo
    ch'e' ditta dentro vo significando.»
«O frate, issa vegg'io» diss'elli «il nodo
    che 'l Notaro e Guittone e me ritenne
    di qua dal dolce stil novo ch'i' odo!
Io veggio ben come le vostre penne
    di retro al dittator sen vanno strette,
    che delle nostre certo non avvenne;
e qual più a riguardare oltre si mette,
    non vede più dall'uno all'altro stilo»;
    e, quasi contentato, si tacette.

I saw Sir Marchese,[11] who formerly had the leisure
   to drink at Forlì with less aridity,
   and yet whose nature was such that he never felt sated.
But, like one who looks and then thinks better
   of one man than of another, so did I single out the Luccan,
   who seemed most desirous of acquaintance with me.
He was murmuring, and I heard something like "Gentucca"[12]
   coming from the place[13] where he felt the torment
   of that justice which plucks away at them so strongly.
"O soul," I said, "you that appear so eager
   to speak with me, allow me to understand you,
   and satisfy both yourself and me with your speech."
"A woman has been born, but does not yet wear a married woman's veil,"
   he began, "who will make you delight
   in my city, no matter how it may be reproached.
You will now depart with this prediction:
   if my murmuring created confusion in your mind,
   the reality of things will make everything plain in the future.
But tell me whether I see here the man who
   invented the new style of poetry, beginning with
   'You ladies who have an understanding of love.'"[14]
And I replied: "I am such a man that, what
   Love inspires in me, I write down, and in the fashion
   in which he dictates it within me, I express it."
"O brother," he said, "now[15] I see the obstacle
   that kept the notary,[16] Guittone,[17] and me
   outside the sweet new style[18] that I hear!
I see clearly that your pens
   follow closely behind the one who dictates to you,
   which certainly was not the case with ours;
and anyone who takes the trouble to investigate further
   will see no other difference between one style and the other";
   and, as if satisfied, he fell silent.

---

11. Marchese degli Orgogliosi, a bibulous politician.   12. The reference is obscure, but the following passage hints that this was a hostess of Dante's in Lucca.   13. From his mouth.   14. One of Dante's major lyric poems, a manifesto of the new trend. 15. The Italian word used here for "now," *issa,* is characteristic of Lucca.   16. Jacopo da Lentini, a major poet of the Sicilian school earlier in the 13th century.   17. Guittone d'Arezzo, the major Tuscan follower of the troubadours.   18. It is from this line that literary historians derived the name *dolce stil novo* for the poetic style that Dante perfected.

Come li augei che vernan lungo 'l Nilo,
  alcuna volta in aere fanno schiera,
  poi volan più a fretta e vanno in filo;
così tutta la gente che lì era,
  volgendo 'l viso, raffrettò suo passo,
  e per magrezza e per voler leggera.
E come l'om che di trottare è lasso,
  lascia andar li compagni, e sì passeggia
  fin che si sfoghi l'affollar del casso,
sì lasciò trapassar la santa greggia
  Forese, e dietro meco sen veniva,
  dicendo: «Quando fia ch'io ti riveggia?»
«Non so» rispuos'io lui «quant'io mi viva;
  ma già non fia 'l tornar mio tanto tosto,
  ch'io non sia col voler prima alla riva;
però che 'l loco u' fui a viver posto,
  di giorno in giorno più di ben si spolpa,
  e a trista ruina par disposto.»
«Or va» diss'el; «che quei che più n'ha colpa,
  vegg'io a coda d'una bestia tratto
  inver la valle ove mai non si scolpa.
La bestia ad ogni passo va più ratto,
  crescendo sempre, fin ch'ella il percuote,
  e lascia il corpo vilmente disfatto.
Non hanno molto a volger quelle rote»,
  e drizzò li occhi al ciel, «che ti fia chiaro
  ciò che 'l mio dir più dichiarar non pote.
Tu ti rimani omai; chè 'l tempo è caro
  in questo regno, sì ch'io perdo troppo
  venendo teco sì a paro a paro.»
Qual esce alcuna volta di gualoppo
  lo cavalier di schiera che cavalchi,
  e va per farsi onor del primo intoppo,
tal si partì da noi con maggior valchi;
  e io rimasi in via con esso i due
  che fuor del mondo sì gran marescalchi.
E quando innanzi a noi intrato fue,

Just as the birds that winter along the Nile
  sometimes assemble in the sky,
    then fly more swiftly, forming a line;
in the same way all the people who were there
  turned their faces and quickened their steps,
    light in weight because of both their thinness and their eagerness.
And, just as a man who is weary from walking briskly
  lets his companions pass him, and walks at a normal pace
    until he recovers from the heaving of his chest,
in the same way Forese let the holy throng
  go by, and walked behind with me,
    saying: "When shall I see you again?"
"I do not know," I replied, "how long I shall live;
  but my return will not be so soon
    that I shall not have come back earlier in my wishes;
because the place where I have been assigned to live
  is being stripped of goodness more and more daily,
    and seems destined for an unhappy downfall."
"Go now," he said, "for the man who is most to blame for that[19]
  I see being dragged from a horse's tail
    toward the valley where crimes can never be atoned for.
At every step the horse goes faster,
  constantly speeding up until it kicks him,
    leaving his body vilely mangled.
Those spheres," and here he raised his eyes to heaven,
  "do not have long to revolve before you see clearly
    that which my words cannot make plainer for you.
Now stay here, because time is dear
  in this realm, and so I am spending too much of it
    by walking side by side with you this way."
Just as sometimes, at a gallop,
  a cavalryman will leave his mounted troop behind
    and sally out for the honor of the first encounter,
in the same way he departed from us with longer strides;
  and I remained on the path with those two
    who were such great marshals of the world.[20]
And when he was so far ahead of us

---

19. Forese's brother, Corso Donati, head of the Black faction of the Florentine
Guelfs, and virtual dictator of the city from 1302 until his death (described exagger-
atedly here) in 1308.   20. Vergil and Statius.

che li occhi miei si fero a lui seguaci,
    come la mente alle parole sue,
    parvermi i rami gravidi e vivaci
d'un altro pomo, e non molto lontani
    per esser pur allora volto in laci.
Vidi gente sott'esso alzar le mani
    e gridar non so che verso le fronde
    quasi bramosi fantolini e vani,
che pregano e 'l pregato non risponde,
    ma, per fare esser ben la voglia acuta,
    tien alto lor disio e nol nasconde.
Poi si partì sì come ricreduta;
    e noi venimmo al grande arbore adesso,
    che tanti prieghi e lagrime rifiuta.
«Trapassate oltre sanza farvi presso:
    legno è più su che fu morso da Eva,
    e questa pianta si levò da esso.»
Sì tra le frasche non so chi diceva;
    per che Virgilio e Stazio e io, ristretti,
    oltre andavam dal lato che si leva.
«Ricordivi» dicea «de' maladetti
    nei nuvoli formati, che, satolli,
    Teseo combatter co' doppi petti;
e delli Ebrei ch'al ber si mostrar molli,
    per che no i volle Gedeon compagni,
    quando ver Madïan discese i colli.»
Sì accostati all'un de' due vivagni
    passammo, udendo colpe della gola
    seguite già da miseri guadagni.
Poi, rallargati per la strada sola,
    ben mille passi e più ci portar oltre,
    contemplando ciascun sanza parola.
«Che andate pensando sì voi sol tre?»
    subita voce disse; ond'io mi scossi
    come fan bestie spaventate e poltre.
Drizzai la testa per veder chi fossi;
    e già mai non si videro in fornace

that my eyes could only follow him at a distance,
    just as my mind could only follow his words that way,
I caught sight of the heavily laden, verdant boughs
    of another fruit tree; it was at no great distance,
    but it was only then that I turned in that direction.
I saw people beneath it raising their hands
    toward its leaves, as they shouted something or other,
    like greedy, silly children
when they ask for something, and the one asked makes no reply
    but, to whet their longing further,
    holds what they want up in the air without concealing it.
Then they departed as if they had changed their mind;
    and we arrived now at the tall tree
    that is deaf to such great entreaties and tears.
"Pass by without drawing near:
    there is a tree higher up that was bitten by Eve,
    and this plant was a slip taken from that one."
Thus spoke someone from among the branches;
    and so Vergil, Statius, and I, huddled together,
    passed by along the side of the path next to the rising slope.
The voice said: "Recall that accursed crew
    created in the clouds,[21] who, when drunk,
    fought against Theseus with their twofold fronts.
and recall the Hebrews who showed their weakness when drinking,[22]
    so that Gideon did not want them as companions
    when he descended from the hills toward Midian."
Thus we passed very close to one of the two
    edges of the path, hearing of sins of the gullet
    that were now being followed by their sad rewards.
Then, spreading out again on the unencumbered road,
    we proceeded a good thousand paces or more,
    each of us lost in thought and silent.
"What are you three thinking of as you walk by yourselves?"
    said a sudden voice; so that I started
    the way unbroken colts do[23] when they are frightened.
I turned my head to see who it was;
    and there never was seen in a furnace

---

21. The centaurs, who got out of hand at Pirithous's wedding banquet.   22. Gideon
considered this group unfit for warfare because they knelt to drink at a spring instead
of scooping up the water while standing.   23. Or: "the way sluggish animals do."

vetri o metalli sì lucenti e rossi,
com'io vidi un che dicea: «S'a voi piace
montare in su, qui si conven dar volta;
quinci si va chi vuole andar per pace.»
L'aspetto suo m'avea la vista tolta;
per ch'io mi volsi dietro a'miei dottori,
com'uom che va secondo ch'elli ascolta.
E quale, annunziatrice delli albori,
l'aura di maggio movesi ed olezza,
tutta impregnata dall'erba e da' fiori;
tal mi senti' un vento dar per mezza
la fronte, e ben senti' mover la piuma,
che fè sentir d'ambrosïa l'orezza.
E senti' dir: «Beati cui alluma
tanto di grazia, che l'amor del gusto
nel petto lor troppo disir non fuma,
esurïendo sempre quanto è giusto!»

Canto XXV

Ora era onde 'l salir non volea storpio;
chè 'l sole avea il cerchio di merigge
lasciato al Tauro e la notte allo Scorpio:
per che, come fa l'uom che non s'affigge
ma vassi alla via sua, che che li appaia,
se di bisogno stimolo il trafigge,
così entrammo noi per la callaia,
uno innanzi altro prendendo la scala
che per artezza i salitor dispaia.
E quale il cicognin che leva l'ala
per voglia di volare, e non s'attenta
d'abbandonar lo nido, e giù la cala;
tal era io con voglia accesa e spenta
di dimandar, venendo infino all'atto
che fa colui ch'a dicer s'argomenta.
Non lasciò, per l'andar che fosse ratto,
lo dolce padre mio, ma disse: «Scocca

glass or metal so glowing and red
as the one I saw there, who was saying: "If you want
    to ascend, here is where you must turn;
    this is the route for those who wish to go in search of peace."
His appearance had deprived me of my sight;
    so that I fell in behind my professors,
    like a man who depends on his hearing alone.
And, just as a springtime breeze, herald
    of the dawn, bestirs itself fragrantly,
    fully permeated with the aroma of the grass and the flowers;
in the same way I felt a gust strike me in the middle
    of my forehead, and I clearly felt the motion of the angel's wing
    making the breeze smell of ambrosia.
And I heard his voice say: "Blessed are those illumined
    with so much grace that the pleasures of the palate
    do not inspire excessive desire in their breast,
so that they never hunger for more than the proper amount!"

Canto XXV

It was an hour when no delay in ascending could be countenanced;
    for the sun had abandoned its meridian
    to Taurus, and the night had left its own to Scorpio:[1]
so that, just like a man who does not stop short
    but goes his way, no matter what he may see,
    if the goad of necessity spurs him,
in like manner we entered the passage,[2]
    one in front of the other climbing the staircase
    whose narrowness separates those who ascend it.
And, like the young stork that raises its wings
    from a desire to fly, but lacks the confidence
    to leave the nest, and lowers them again,
so did I continue with a desire to ask a question, a desire
    now ignited, now extinguished, until I finally made the gesture
    that those do who prepare to speak.[3]
Even though our pace was rapid, my sweet father
    did not desert me, but said: "Release

---

1. Thus, it was about 2 P.M.   2. The ascent from the sixth to the seventh, and last,
terrace.   3. I opened my mouth.

l'arco del dir, che 'nfino al ferro hai tratto.»
Allor sicuramente aprì' la bocca
   e cominciai: «Come si può far magro
   là dove l'uopo di nodrir non tocca?»
«Se t'ammentassi come Meleagro
   si consumò al consumar d'un stizzo,
   non fora» disse «a te questo sì agro;
e se pensassi come, al vostro guizzo,
   guizza dentro allo specchio vostra image,
   ciò che par duro ti parrebbe vizzo.
Ma perchè dentro a tuo voler t'adage,
   ecco qui Stazio; e io lui chiamo e prego
   che sia or sanator delle tue piage.»
«Se la veduta etterna li dislego»
   rispuose Stazio «là dove tu sie,
   discolpi me non potert'io far nego.»
Poi cominciò: «Se le parole mie,
   figlio, la mente tua guarda e riceve,
   lume ti fiero al come che tu die.
Sangue perfetto, che mai non si beve
   dell'assetate vene, e si rimane
   quasi alimento che di mensa leve,
prende nel core a tutte membra umane
   virtute informative, come quello
   ch'a farsi quelle per le vene vane.
Ancor digesto, scende ov'è più bello
   tacer che dire; e quindi poscia geme
   sovr'altrui sangue in natural vasello.
Ivi s'accoglie l'uno e l'altro inseme,
   l'un disposto a patire, e l'altro a fare
   per lo perfetto loco onde si preme;
e, giunto lui, comincia ad operare
   coagulando prima, e poi avviva
   ciò che per sua matera fè constare.
Anima fatta la virtute attiva
   qual d'una pianta, in tanto differente,

the bow of speech, which you have drawn up to the arrowhead."
Then I opened my mouth confidently
    and began: "How can a person grow thin
    in a place where the need for nourishment does not apply?"
"If you recalled how Meleager[4]
    was consumed when a firebrand was consumed,"
    he said, "this would not create such a difficulty for you;
and if you thought of how, whenever you move,
    your image in the mirror moves,
    that which seems hard would seem easy to you.
But, in order that you may feel at ease to your heart's content,
    here is Statius: and I call on him and ask him
    to be the healer of your wounds now."
"If I reveal the eternal vision to him,"
    Statius replied, "while a man like you is present,
    may I be excused by my powerlessness to refuse you."
Then he began: "If, my son, your mind
    receives and stores up my words,
    they will shed light on the question you raise.
The perfect blood, which is never drunk up
    by the thirsty veins, but is left over
    like food you remove from the table,
takes on, in the heart, a formative power
    for all human members, since it is the same blood
    that courses through the veins to create those members.
Retransformed, it descends to a place which it is more seemly
    not to name than to name;[5] and from here it later trickles
    onto other blood in a natural container.[6]
There both bloods are gathered together,
    one of them disposed to undergo, and the other to act,
    because of the perfect place from which it was pumped;[7]
and, when this male blood has come,[8] it begins to act;
    first it condenses, and then it lends life
    to that which it made consistent with its substance.[9]
This lifegiving power, having become a soul
    like that of a plant—but with this difference:

---

4. An ancient Greek hero whose life was magically tied to the intact existence of a firebrand. 5. The male genitals. 6. The womb. 7. The heart. 8. Or: "when this male blood has been mingled with the female." 9. Or: "to that which it has made consistent, so it may serve as its material."

che questa è in via e quella è già a riva,
tanto ovra poi, che già si move e sente,
  come fungo marino; e indi imprende
  ad organar le posse ond'è semente.
Or si spiega, figliuolo, or si distende
  la virtù ch'è dal cor del generante,
  dove natura a tutte membra intende.
Ma come d'animal divenga fante,
  non vedi tu ancor: quest'è tal punto,
  che più savio di te fè già errante,
sì che per sua dottrina fè disgiunto
  dall'anima il possibile intelletto,
  perchè da lui non vide organo assunto.
Apri alla verità che viene il petto;
  e sappi che, sì tosto come al feto
  l'articular del cerebro è perfetto,
lo motor primo a lui si volge lieto
  sovra tant'arte di natura, e spira
  spirito novo, di vertù repleto,
che ciò che trova attivo quivi, tira
  in sua sustanzia, e fassi un'alma sola,
  che vive e sente e sè in sè rigira.
E perchè meno ammiri la parola,
  guarda il calor del sol che si fa vino,
  giunto all'omor che della vite cola.
Quando Lachèsis non ha più del lino,
  solvesi dalla carne, ed in virtute
  ne porta seco e l'umano e 'l divino:
l'altre potenze tutte quante mute;
  memoria, intelligenza e volontade
  in atto molto più che prima agute.
Sanza restarsi, per sè stessa cade
  mirabilmente all'una delle rive:
  quivi conosce prima le sue strade.

that this soul is still developing, whereas the plant's has reached its limit—
continues to operate until it achieves motion and sensation,
    like a sponge;[10] and from that point it proceeds
    to organize the faculties of which it is the seed.
Now, my son, the power that came from the heart of the begetter
    unfolds, and now it spreads
    where nature provides for every part of the body.
But how, from a lower animal, it becomes a human child,[11]
    you do not yet see; this is such a difficult point
    that it has already made a wiser man than you go astray,
so that in his teachings he proclaimed
    that the potential intellect[12] was something separate from the soul,
    because he saw no organ that it occupied.
Open your bosom to the truth that is coming;
    and know that, as soon as the articulation
    of the embryo's brain is complete,
the Prime Mover[13] turns to it, happy
    over such skill of nature's, and breathes into it
    a new spirit, replete with power.
which takes the life forces that it finds there, and draws
    them into its own substance, making a single soul
    that lives and senses and revolves around itself.[14]
And, so that you may be less astounded by my words,
    look at the sun's heat, which becomes wine
    when joined to the liquid that flows from the vine.
When Lachesis[15] has no more flax,
    this soul is released from the flesh, and through its power
    bears off with it its specifically human and divine elements:
all its other faculties are mute,
    but its memory, intelligence, and will
    are much livelier in their actions than they were before.
Without delay, of its own accord, the soul lands
    miraculously on one of the two shores:[16]
    here it first learns which path it is to take.

---

10. Representative of a low form of animal life, not yet capable of reason.   11. Or: "it becomes a person capable of speech."   12. Dante seems to be using an Aristotelian term without adopting Aristotle's specific reason for introducing it; here it just means "the rational mind."   13. God.   14. That is, it can contemplate its own identity.   15. The Greek Fate who spun the thread of human existence; when she "has no more flax," the individual dies.   16. The bank of the Acheron for those destined to Hell, the mouth of the Tiber for those destined to Purgatory.

Tosto che loco lì la circunscrive,
  la virtù informativa raggia intorno
  così e quanto nelle membra vive:
e come l'aere, quand'è ben pïorno,
  per l'altrui raggio che 'n sè si reflette,
  di diversi color diventa adorno;
così l'aere vicin quivi si mette
  in quella forma che in lui suggella
  virtüalmente l'alma che ristette;
e simigliante poi alla fiammella
  che segue il foco là 'vunque si muta,
  segue lo spirto sua forma novella.
Però che quindi ha poscia sua paruta,
  è chiamata ombra; e quindi organa poi
  ciascun sentire infino alla veduta.
Quindi parliamo e quindi ridiam noi;
  quindi facciam le lacrime e' sospiri
  che per lo monte aver sentiti puoi.
Secondo che ci affiggono i disiri
  e li altri affetti, l'ombra si figura;
  e quest'è la cagion di che tu miri.»
E già venuto all'ultima tortura
  s'era per noi, e volto alla man destra,
  ed eravamo attenti ad altra cura.
Quivi la ripa fiamma in fuor balestra,
  e la cornice spira fiato in suso
  che la reflette e via da lei sequestra;
ond'ir ne convenìa dal lato schiuso
  ad uno ad uno; e io temea il foco
  quinci, e quindi temea cader giuso.
Lo duca mio dicea: «Per questo loco
  si vuol tenere alli occhi stretto il freno,
  però ch'errar potrebbesi per poco.»
'Summae Deus clementïae' nel seno
  al grande ardore allore udi' cantando,
  che di volger mi fè caler non meno;
e vidi spirti per la fiamma andando;
  per ch'io guardava a loro e a'miei passi

As soon as it is confined within a given place in the afterlife,
    its formative power radiates all around,
    in the same way and to the same extent as in its living body:
and, just as the air, when it is very humid,
    becomes adorned with various colors
    by the external rays reflected in it;
in like manner, here, the adjacent air assumes
    the shape that is imprinted on it
    by the power of the soul that has been stationed there;
then, similar to the flame
    that follows the fire wherever it moves,
    this new shape follows the spirit.
Because it has derived its appearance from it,
    it is called a shade; and from it it then develops
    every sense, up to and including sight.
Therefore we speak and therefore we smile;
    therefore we shed the tears and emit the sighs
    that you may have heard throughout the mountain.
Accordingly as desires and other emotions
    affect us, our shade takes its shape;
    and that is the cause of the matter you marvel at."
And we had already arrived
    at the final turning of the road, and were facing right,
    prepared to see another form of torment.
Here the mountainside shoots forth flames,
    and the brink blows a wind upward
    that deflects them and moves them to a distance;
so that we were compelled to walk along the precipice
    in single file; and I was afraid of the fire
    on one side, and on the other, afraid of falling down.
My guide repeated: "In this spot
    you must keep your eyes tightly bridled,
    because it would be so easy to make a mistake."
"Summae Deus clementiae,"[17] I then heard being sung
    in the heart of the great conflagration,
    and this made me want to turn nonetheless;
and I saw spirits walking through the flames;
    so that I was looking both at them and at where I was walking,

17. "God of supreme clemency": a hymn that deals with lust, the vice that is purged
on the seventh terrace.

compartendo la vista a quando a quando.
Appresso il fine ch'a quell'inno fassi,
    gridavano alto: '*Virum non cognosco*';
    indi ricominciavan l'inno bassi.
Finitolo anco, gridavano: «Al bosco
    si tenne Diana, ed Elice caccionne
    che di Venere avea sentito il tosco.»
Indi al cantar tornavano; indi donne
    gridavano e mariti che fuor casti
    come virtute e matrimonio imponne.
E questo modo credo che lor basti
    per tutto il tempo che 'l foco li abbrucia:
    con tal cura conviene e con tai pasti
che la piaga da sezzo si ricucia.

[SUMMARY OF CANTO XXVI: The sufferers in the fire become aware that
Dante is alive, and begin to address him, when another company of souls arrives from the opposite direction, but still in the fire. The newcomers exchange affectionate greetings with the first group, but do not tarry, moving
on rapidly. They are homosexuals, whereas the first group are heterosexuals
whose passion overstepped the proper bounds. Dante's chief informant

---

Canto XXVII

Sì come quando i primi raggi vibra
    là dove il suo fattor lo sangue sparse,
    cadendo Ibero sotto l'alta Libra,
e l'onde in Gange da nona rïarse,
    sì stava il sole; onde 'l giorno sen giva,
    come l'angel di Dio lieto ci apparse.
Fuor della fiamma stava in su la riva,
    e cantava '*Beati mundo corde!*'
    in voce assai più che la nostra viva.

distributing my gazes from moment to moment.
After the end of that hymn
   they shouted out loud: "*Virum non cognosco*";[18]
   then they recommenced the hymn in a low voice.
When it was finished again, they shouted: "Diana
   remained in the forest, chasing out of it Helice,
   who had tasted the poison of Venus."[19]
Then they returned to the chant; then they called the names
   of wives and husbands who were chaste,
   as virtue and matrimony enjoins upon us.
And I believe that this procedure endures for them
   for all the period in which the fire burns them:
   with such a cure and with such nourishment
their wound must finally be healed up again.

---

proves to be the Bolognese poet Guido Guinizelli, spiritual father of the *dolce stil novo* school (see *Purgatory*, Canto XI, note 11). After he and Dante exchange compliments, Guido points out the soul of the late-12th-century French troubadour Arnaut Daniel, who—in Provençal!—introduces himself and asks Dante to remember him.]

Canto XXVII

As when it darts its earliest beams
   on the place where its Maker shed His blood,
   while the Ebro falls beneath lofty Libra
and the waters of the Ganges are burning hot at noon:
   thus did the sun stand;[1] and so day was departing
   when God's angel appeared happily before us.
He was standing outside the flame, on the bank,
   and singing: "*Beati mundo corde!*"[2]
   in a voice much more stirring than ours.

---

18. "I know not a man": spoken by Mary at the Annunciation; this is the first of the many examples of chastity that the sufferers from lust call to mind. 19. Diana (Artemis), the chaste goddess, drove away the nymph Helice, who had had intercourse. 1. It is daybreak in Jerusalem, midnight in Spain (the western limit of Dante's world), noon in India (the eastern limit), and sunset in Purgatory. 2. "Blessed are the pure in heart."

Poscia «Più non si va, se pria non morde,
   anime sante, il foco: intrate in esso,
   ed al cantar di là non siate sorde»
ci disse come noi li fummo presso;
   per ch'io divenni tal, quando lo 'ntesi,
   qual è colui che nella fossa è messo.
In su le man commesse mi protesi,
   guardando il foco e imaginando forte
   umani corpi già veduti accesi.
Volsersi verso me le buone scorte;
   e Virgilio mi disse: «Figliuol mio,
   qui può esser tormento, ma non morte.
Ricorditi, ricorditi! E se io
   sovresso Gerïon ti guidai salvo,
   che farò ora presso più a Dio?
Credi per certo che se dentro all'alvo
   di questa fiamma stessi ben mille anni,
   non ti potrebbe far d'un capel calvo.
E se tu forse credi ch'io t'inganni,
   fatti ver lei, e fatti far credenza
   con le tue mani al lembo de' tuoi panni.
Pon giù omai, pon giù ogni temenza:
   volgiti in qua; vieni ed entra sicuro!»
   E io pur fermo e contra coscïenza.
Quando mi vide star pur fermo e duro
   turbato un poco, disse: «Or vedi, figlio:
   tra Beatrice e te è questo muro».
Come al nome di Tisbe aperse il ciglio
   Piramo in su la morte, e riguardolla,
   allor che 'l gelso diventò vermiglio;
così, la mia durezza fatta solla,
   mi volsi al savio duca, udendo il nome
   che nella mente sempre mi rampolla.
Ond'ei crollò la fronte e disse: «Come!
   volenci star di qua?»; indi sorrise
   come al fanciul si fa ch'è vinto al pome.
Poi dentro al foco innanzi mi si mise,

Then, "Holy souls, it is impossible to advance
    unless the fire bites you first: enter it,
    and do not be deaf to the singing on the other side,"
he said when we were close to him;
    at which, when I understood it, I became
    like a man who is placed in the grave.
I leaned forward over my clasped hands,
    looking at the fire and bringing vividly to mind
    human bodies I had already seen ignited.
My kind escorts turned toward me;
    and Vergil said to me: "My son,
    here there can be torment, but not death.
Remember, remember! If I
    guided you safely on Geryon's back,
    what will I do now that we are closer to God?
Believe for a certainty that if you stood inside
    the heart of these flames for a good thousand years,
    they could not make you bald by a single hair.
And if you perhaps believe I am deceiving you,
    approach them, and give yourself confidence
    with your own hands by exposing the hem of your robe.
Now set aside, set aside all fear:
    turn in this direction; come and enter without worry!"
    But I remained stock still, fighting my conscience.
When he saw me standing still and obdurate,
    he was somewhat vexed, and said: "Look here, my son:
    this is a wall between Beatrice and you."
Just as, at the name of Thisbe, Pyramus opened
    his eyes at the point of death and looked at her,
    at the time when the mulberry turned vermilion;[3]
in like manner, my obduracy becoming soft,
    I turned toward my wise guide when I heard the name
    that always sprouts anew in my mind.
Whereupon he shook his brow and said: "What!
    Do we want to stay on this side?" Then he smiled
    as one smiles at a child that has been won over by an apple.
Next, he entered the fire in front of me,

---

3. Pyramus and Thisbe, the two lovers in ancient Babylon who killed themselves through a tragic misunderstanding, used to meet by a mulberry tree, whose fruits were turned red by their blood.

pregando Stazio che venisse retro,
che pria per lunga strada ci divise.
Sì com fui dentro, in un bogliente vetro
gittato mi sarei per rinfrescarmi,
tant'era ivi lo 'ncendio sanza metro.
Lo dolce padre mio, per confortarmi,
pur di Beatrice ragionando andava,
dicendo: «Li occhi suoi già veder parmi».
Guidavaci una voce che cantava
di là; e noi, attenti pur a lei,
venimmo fuor là ove si montava.
'Venite, benedicti Patris mei,'
sonò dentro a un lume che lì era,
tal, che mi vinse e guardar nol potei.
«Lo sol sen va» soggiunse, «e vien la sera:
non v'arrestate, ma studiate il passo,
mentre che l'occidente non si annera».
Dritta salìa la via per entro 'l sasso
verso tal parte ch'io togliea i raggi
dinanzi a me del sol ch'era già basso.
E di poche scaglion levammo i saggi,
che 'l sol corcar, per l'ombra che si spense,
sentimmo dietro e io e li miei saggi.
E pria che 'n tutte le sue parti immense
fosse orizzonte fatto d'uno aspetto,
e notte avesse tutte sue dispense,
ciascun di noi d'un grado fece letto;
chè la natura del monte ci affranse
la possa del salir più e 'l diletto.
Quali si stanno ruminando manse
le capre, state rapide e proterve
sovra le cime avante che sien pranse,
tacite all'ombra, mentre che 'l sol ferve,
guardate dal pastor, che 'n su la verga
poggiato s'è e lor poggiato serve;
e quale il mandrïan che fori alberga,
lungo il peculio suo queto pernotta,
guardando perchè fiera non lo sperga;

asking Statius to come after him,
   Statius who earlier had walked between us on our long path.
As soon as I was inside, I would have hurled myself
   into molten glass to cool off,
   so immeasurable was the blaze there.
My sweet father, to comfort me,
   kept on talking about Beatrice,
   saying: "I think I can already see her eyes."
We were guided by a voice that was singing
   on the far side; and we, attentive to it alone,
   emerged at a place of further ascent.
"Venite, benedicti Patris mei,"[4]
   we heard from within a light that was there,
   so strong that I was overcome and could not look at it.
"The sun is going down," it added, "and evening is coming:
   do not halt, but speed up your steps,
   as long as the western sky is not yet blackened."
The path climbed straight up among the rocks,
   leading in such a direction that, in front of me,
   I was intercepting the beams of the already low sun.
And we had made experiment of only a few steps of the stair
   when my sages and I sensed that the sun was setting
   behind us, because my shadow was extinguished.
And, before the horizon, in all its immense extent,
   acquired one and the same appearance,
   and before night occupied all its due territory,
each of us made his bed on a step;
   for the nature of the mountain deprived us
   of the power and the delight of ascending further.
Just as she-goats stand quietly chewing the cud,
   although they had skipped, headstrong and swift,
   over the peaks before being fed,
now silent in the shade while the sun bakes down,
   guarded by the goatherd who is leaning
   on his staff and, leaning thus, looks after them;
and just as the shepherd who spends the night outdoors
   keeps vigil calmly alongside his flock,
   taking care that no wild animal disperses them;

---

4. "Come, you blessed of my Father," the words Christ will address to the elect on Judgment Day.

tali eravam noi tutti e tre allotta,
   io come capra, ed ei come pastori,
   fasciati quinci e quindi d'alta grotta.
Poco parer potea lì del di fori;
   ma, per quel poco, vedea io le stelle
   di lor solere e più chiare e maggiori.
Sì ruminando e sì mirando in quelle,
   mi prese il sonno; il sonno che sovente,
   anzi che 'l fatto sia, sa le novelle.
Nell'ora, credo, che dell'orïente,
   prima raggiò nel monte Citerea,
   che di foco d'amor par sempre ardente,
giovane e bella in sogno mi parea
   donna vedere andar per una landa
   cogliendo fiori; e cantando dicea:
«Sappia qualunque il mio nome dimanda
   ch'i' son Lia, e vo movendo intorno
   le belle mani a farmi una ghirlanda.
Per piacermi allo specchio, qui m'adorno;
   ma mia suora Rachel mai non si smaga
   dal suo miraglio, e siede tutto giorno.
Ell'è de' suoi belli occhi veder vaga
   com'io dell'adornarmi con le mani;
   lei lo vedere, e me l'ovrare appaga.»
E già per li splendori antelucani,
   che tanto a' pellegrin surgon più grati,
   quanto, tornando, albergan men lontani,
le tenebre fuggìan da tutti lati,
   e 'l sonno mio con esse; ond'io leva'mi,
   veggendo i gran maestri già levati.
«Quel dolce pome che per tanti rami
   cercando va la cura de' mortali,
   oggi porrà in pace le tue fami.»
Virgilio inverso me queste cotali
   parole usò; e mai non furo strenne
   che fosser di piacere a queste iguali.
Tanto voler sopra voler mi venne
   dell'esser su, ch'ad ogni passo poi

in a like situation were all three of us at that time,
  I like a she-goat, and they like goatherds,
  all of us hemmed in by high rocks on either side.
Little could be seen there of the world outside;
  but, through that little space, I saw the stars
  both brighter and larger than they are accustomed to be.
As I was thus ruminating and thus looking at them,
  I was overcome by sleep, that sleep which frequently
  knows what is to come before the reality arrives.
At the hour, I believe, when in the east
  Venus first shed her rays on the mountain,
  Venus who seems ever aglow with the fire of love,
I thought I saw in a dream a beautiful
  young lady walking through a plain
  and picking flowers; and she said in song:
"Let anyone who asks my name know
  that I am Leah, and that I am moving my beautiful
  hands all about in order to make myself a garland.
Here I adorn myself so I can please myself with my reflection;
  my sister Rachel, however, never turns away
  from her mirror, but sits there all day.
She is desirous of seeing her beautiful eyes,
  as I am of adorning myself with my hands;
  she delights in seeing, I in doing."[5]
And by this time, in the face of the pre-dawn splendors,
  which, when they rise, are all the more pleasing to wanderers
  the less far they lodge from home, on their return journey,
the darkness was fleeing on all sides,
  and my slumber with it; so that I arose,
  seeing my great masters already arisen.
"That sweet fruit which on so many boughs
  is sought for by the solicitude of mortals
  will set your hunger at rest today."
Vergil addressed such words
  to me; and there were never gifts
  equal to these in giving pleasure.
So much did desire upon desire to be up above
  come over me, that at every step thereafter

5. Of the two biblical matriarchs, wives of Jacob, Leah here symbolizes the active
life, and Rachel the contemplative life.

al volo mi sentìa crescer le penne.
Come la scala tutta sotto noi
    fu corsa e fummo in su 'l grado superno,
    in me ficcò Virgilio li occhi suoi,
e disse: «Il temporal foco e l'etterno
    veduto hai, figlio; e se' venuto in parte
    dov'io per me più oltre non discerno.
Tratto t'ho qui con ingegno e con arte;
    lo tuo piacere omai prendi per duce:
    fuor se' dell'erte vie, fuor se' dell'arte.
Vedi lo sol che in fronte ti riluce;
    vedi l'erbetta, i fiori e li arbuscelli
    che qui la terra sol da sè produce.
Mentre che vegnan lieti li occhi belli
    che, lacrimando, a te venir mi fenno,
    seder ti puoi e puoi andar tra elli.
Non aspettar mio dir più nè mio cenno:
    libero, dritto e sano è tuo arbitrio,
    e fallo fora non fare a suo senno;
per ch'io te sovra te corono e mitrio.»

Canto XXVIII

Vago già di cercar dentro e dintorno
    la divina foresta spessa e viva,
    ch'alli occhi temperava il novo giorno,
sanza più aspettar, lasciai la riva,
    prendendo la campagna lento lento
    su per lo suol che d'ogni parte auliva.
Un'aura dolce, sanza mutamento
    avere in sè, mi ferìa per la fronte
    non di più colpo che soave vento;
per cui le fronde, tremolando, pronte
    tutte quante piegavano alla parte
    u'la prim'ombra gitta il santo monte;
non però dal loro esser dritto sparte
    tanto, che li augelletti per le cime

I felt my feathers growing for the flight.
When the entire staircase below us
    was climbed and we stood on the topmost step,
    Vergil fixed his eyes on me
and said: "Both the temporary and the eternal fires[6]
    you have seen, my son; and you have come to a place
    where I can make out nothing further by my own powers.
I have brought you here with wisdom and with skill;
    from here on, take your pleasure as a guide:
    you have emerged from the steep paths, you have emerged from the narrow.
See the sun shining on your brow:
    see the fresh grass, the flowers, and the shrubs
    which the earth produces spontaneously here.
Until the beautiful eyes come here in happiness,
    those same eyes which, in tears, made me come to you,
    you can sit down or you can walk around among them.
No longer await either words or signs from me;
    your will is free, upright, and sound,
    and it would be an error not to act as it directs:
so that I crown you emperor and pope over yourself."[7]

Canto XXVIII

Eager to explore, within and round about,
    the dense and verdant divine forest
    that the temperate morning light revealed to my eyes,
waiting no longer, I left the bank,
    walking very slowly into the countryside
    upon the ground that was fragrant on all sides.
A gentle breeze, that did not vary
    in velocity, touched me on the brow
    with force no stronger than that of a soft wind;
responding readily to it, the trembling leaves,
    one and all, were bending in the direction
    toward which the holy mountain casts its first shadow;
but they were not deflected from their normal position
    so much that the songbirds in the treetops

---

6. That is, the fires of Purgatory and Hell, respectively.   7. Dante is now so puri-
fied that he is master of both his body and his soul.

lasciasser d'operare ogni lor arte;
ma con piena letizia l'ore prime,
     cantando, ricevìeno intra le foglie,
     che tenevan bordone alle sue rime,
tal qual di ramo in ramo si raccoglie
     per la pineta in su 'l lito di Chiassi,
     quand'Eolo Scirocco fuor discioglie.
Già m'avean trasportato i lenti passi
     dentro alla selva antica tanto, ch'io
     non potea rivedere ond'io mi 'ntrassi;
ed ecco più andar mi tolse un rio,
     che 'nver sinistra con sue picciole onde
     piegava l'erba che 'n sua ripa uscìo.
Tutte l'acque che son di qua più monde,
     parrìeno avere in sè mistura alcuna,
     verso di quella, che nulla nasconde,
avvegna che si mova bruna bruna
     sotto l'ombra perpetua, che mai
     raggiar non lascia sole ivi nè luna.
Coi piè ristetti e con li occhi passai
     di là dal fiumicello, per mirare
     la gran varïazion di freschi mai;
e là m'apparve, sì com'elli appare
     subitamente cosa che disvia
     per maraviglia tutto altro pensare,
una donna soletta che si gìa
     cantando e scegliendo fior da fiore
     ond'era pinta tutta la sua via.
«Deh, bella donna, che a' raggi d'amore
     ti scaldi, s'i' vo' credere a' sembianti
     che soglion esser testimon del core,
vegnati in voglia di trarreti avanti»
     diss'io a lei «verso questa rivera,
     tanto ch'io possa intender che tu canti.
Tu mi fai rimembrar dove e qual era
     Proserpina nel tempo che perdette

ceased to exercise all their art;
rather, in full happiness they were welcoming
   the morning hours[1] with song amid the leaves,
   which murmured a deep accompaniment to their verses,
like the one generated from bough to bough
   in the pine grove on the shore at Classe[2]
   when Aeolus[3] sets the scirocco free.
My slow steps had already transported me
   so far inside the ancient forest that I
   could not relocate the place where I had entered;
and behold, my advance was barred by a river
   that with its little waves was bending
   toward the left the grass that sprang up on its banks.
All the waters that are cleanest here on earth
   would seem to have some impurity in them
   compared with that one, which conceals nothing
even though it flows quite darkly
   beneath the perpetual shade, which never
   allows either sun or moon to shine upon it.
With my feet I halted, but with my eyes I crossed
   over the stream, to gaze at
   the great variety of freshly flowering branches;
and there appeared to me there, just as, suddenly,
   a thing will appear that diverts
   all other thoughts by its wondrousness,
a solitary lady, who, as she walked,
   was singing and selecting flowers to pick
   from among those which adorned her entire path.
"Please, lovely lady, you that are warming yourself
   in the rays of love, if I may believe so from your features,
   which are usually a witness to the heart,
may you consent to come forward,"
   I said to her, "toward this river,
   close enough for me to understand what you are singing.
You bring to mind the person of Proserpina[4]
   and the place she was in when her mother

---

1. In some editions, *ore* ("hours") appears as *ôre* ("breezes").   2. The port of
Ravenna.   3. In Greek mythology, the ruler of the winds, who keeps them confined
until he wishes to release them.   4. Proserpina (Persephone), daughter of Ceres
(Demeter), was abducted by the god of the underworld while picking flowers in Sicily.

la madre lei, ed ella primavera.»
Come si volge con le piante strette
  a terra ed intra sè donna che balli,
  e piede innanzi piede a pena mette,
volsesi in su i vermigli ed in su i gialli
  fioretti verso me non altrimenti
  che vergine che li occhi onesti avvalli;
e fece i prieghi miei esser contenti,
  sì appressando sè, che 'l dolce sono
  veniva a me co' suoi intendimenti.
Tosto che fu là dove l'erbe sono
  bagnate già dall'onde del bel fiume,
  di levar li occhi suoi mi fece dono:
non credo che splendesse tanto lume
  sotto le ciglia a Venere, trafitta
  dal figlio fuor di tutto suo costume.
Ella ridea dall'altra riva dritta,
  trattando più color con le sue mani,
  che l'alta terra sanza seme gitta.
Tre passi ci facea il fiume lontani;
  ma Ellesponto, là 've passò Serse,
  ancora freno a tutti orgogli umani,
più odio da Leandro non sofferse
  per mareggiare intra Sesto ed Abido,
  che quel da me perch'allor non s'aperse.
«Voi siete nuovi, e forse perch'io rido»
  cominciò ella «in questo luogo eletto
  all'umana natura per suo nido,
maravigliando tienvi alcun sospetto;
  ma la luce rende il salmo *Delectasti,*
  che puote disnebbiar vostro intelletto.
E tu che se' dinanzi e mi pregasti,
  dì s'altro vuoli udir; ch'i' venni presta
  ad ogni tua question tanto che basti.»

lost her and *she* lost the springtime."[5]
Just as a woman dancing makes a turn
    with her feet close together and close to the ground,
    scarcely placing one foot in front of the other,
she turned toward me, above the vermilion
    and the yellow flowers, exactly like
    a maiden lowering her modest eyes;
and she gave satisfaction to my entreaties,
    approaching so close that her sweet music
    came to my ears along with its meaningful words.
As soon as she had arrived where the grass is
    already moistened by the water of the lovely river,
    she made me the gift of raising her eyes:
I do not believe that such a great light shone
    beneath Venus's eyebrows when she was pierced
    by her son, contrary to his usual practice.[6]
She was smiling from the other straight bank,
    trailing in her hands a multitude of colors,
    which that lofty soil produces without seeds.
The river was separating us by three paces;
    but the Hellespont, where Xerxes crossed it,[7]
    still a check to all human pride,
did not endure more hatred from Leander[8]
    for surging between Sestus and Abydus,
    than that river did from me for not parting its waters.
"You are newcomers, and perhaps because I laugh,"
    she began, "in this place chosen
    for human nature to be its nest,
you are amazed and have some misgivings;
    but light is shed on this by the psalm *Delectasti*,[9]
    which is able to dispel the fog from your mind.
And you that are walking ahead of the others, you that entreated me,
    tell me if you want to hear more; for I have come prepared
    for all your questions to give you satisfaction."

---

5. Or: "*she* lost the flowers she had gathered."   6. Cupid (Amor, Eros), who usually shot his arrows intentionally, once accidentally wounded his mother Venus (Aphrodite), who then fell in love with Adonis.   7. Xerxes, king of Persia, was retreating from his abortive invasion of Greece when he found his pontoon bridge over the Hellespont had been wrecked by a storm.   8. The youth Leander used to swim the Hellespont to keep trysts with his sweetheart Hero.   9. Psalm 92, concerned with man's delight in God's creation.

«L'acqua»diss'io, «e 'l suon della foresta
  impugnan dentro a me novella fede
  di cosa ch'io udi' contraria a questa.»
Ond'ella: «Io dicerò come procede
  per sua cagion ciò ch'ammirar ti face,
  e purgherò la nebbia che ti fiede.
Lo sommo ben, che solo esso a sè piace,
  fece l'uom buono a bene, e questo loco
  diede per arra a lui d'etterna pace.
Per sua difalta qui dimorò poco;
  per sua difalta in pianto ed in affanno
  cambiò onesto riso e dolce gioco.
Perchè 'l turbar che sotto da sè fanno
  l'essalazion dell'acqua e della terra,
  che quanto posson dietro al calor vanno,
all'uomo non facesse alcuna guerra,
  questo monte salìo verso 'l ciel tanto,
  e libero n'è d'indi ove si serra.
Or perchè in circuito tutto quanto
  l'aere si volge con la prima volta,
  se non li è rotto il cerchio d'alcun canto,
in questa altezza ch'è tutta disciolta
  nell'aere vivo, tal moto percuote,
  e fa sonar la selva perch'è folta;
e la percossa pianta tanto puote,
  che della sua virtute l'aura impregna,
  e quella poi, girando, intorno scuote;
e l'altra terra, secondo ch'è degna
  per sè e per suo ciel, concepe e figlia
  di diverse virtù diverse legna.
Non parrebbe di là poi maraviglia,
  udito questo, quando alcuna pianta
  sanza seme palese vi s'appiglia.
E saper dèi che la campagna santa

"The water," I said, "and the rustling of the forest
  contradict in my mind my newly acquired trust
  in something that I heard to the contrary."[10]
She replied: "I shall tell you how that which amazes you
  proceeds from an intrinsic cause,
  and I shall dissipate the fog that assails you.
The Highest Good,[11] who is alone capable of delighting Himself,
  made man good for good purposes, and gave him
  this place as a pledge of eternal peace.
Through his own shortcoming he remained here only briefly,
  through his own shortcoming he converted to tears and distress
  his honest laughter and his gentle pleasures.
In order that the perturbations caused down below
  by the exhalations of water and earth,
  which adapt themselves to temperature as much as possible,
might not cause any inconvenience to man,
  this mountain rose as high into the sky as it does,
  and is free from them, beginning with the locked gateway.
Now, because the air in its entirety
  turns in a circle along with the Prime Mover,
  unless its round is broken in some quarter,
this lofty region, which is entirely exposed
  to the moving air, is affected by that motion,
  which makes the forest rustle because it is dense;
and the trees, once struck, have such inner power
  that the breeze is permeated with their vital force,
  which then circulates and stirs everything round about it;
and the other land,[12] accordingly as it is worthy
  in its soil and in its climate, conceives and bears
  various trees of various qualities.
Then, it should not seem like a miracle there on earth,
  on the basis of what you are hearing, if some tree
  takes root there without an apparent seed.
And you ought to know that the holy countryside

---

10. In Canto XXI, Statius, discussing the earthquake attendant on his liberation from Purgatory, tells Dante that no atmospheric perturbation from external causes ever affects Purgatory; here, Dante does not yet realize that, although he is still on (now at the top of) the same mountain as before, he has passed beyond Purgatory proper and is in the terrestrial paradise, which has atmospheric conditions of its own (flowing water, wind-blown trees, etc.).   11. God.   12. Our own earth.

dove tu se', d'ogni semenza è piena,
e frutto ha in sè che di là non si schianta.
L'acqua che vedi non surge di vena
che ristori vapor che gel converta,
come fiume ch'acquista e perde lena;
ma esce di fontana salda e certa,
che tanto dal voler di Dio riprende,
quant'ella versa da due parti aperta.
Da questa parte con virtù discende
che toglie altrui memoria del peccato;
dall'altra d'ogni ben fatto la rende.
Quinci Letè; così dall'altro lato
Eünoè si chiama; e non adopra
se quinci e quindi pria non è gustato:
a tutti altri sapori esto è di sopra.
E avvegna ch'assai possa esser sazia
la sete tua perch'io più non ti scopra,
darotti un corollario ancor per grazia;
nè credo che 'l mio dir ti sia men caro,
se oltre promission teco si spazia.
Quelli ch'anticamente poetaro
l'età dell'oro e suo stato felice,
forse in Parnaso esto loco sognaro.
Qui fu innocente l'umana radice;
qui primavera sempre ed ogni frutto;
nettare è questo di che ciascun dice.»
Io mi rivolsi 'n dietro allora tutto
a'miei poeti, e vidi che con riso
udito avean l'ultimo costrutto;
poi alla bella donna torna' il viso.

[SUMMARY OF CANTO XXIX: The lady sings: "Blessed is he whose sin is covered." She and Dante walk along the stream, abreast but on opposite sides.
Dante hears a beautiful chant and sees a great light in the distance, but it
takes a while for him to make out the details of the procession now before
him. Even Vergil cannot explain it. People dressed in white approach. Seven
candlesticks leave trails of colored light behind them, like the seven bands of

where you now stand is filled with every kind of seed,
and bears fruits that are not plucked there on earth.
The water that you see does not rise from a spring
fed by vapors that condense into rain from the cold,
like a river that gains and loses volume and force;
rather, it issues from a firm and sure fountain,
which is replenished through the will of God
by the same amount that it pours forth through its double outlet.
On one side the descending water has the power
to take away one's remembrance of sin;
on the other, it restores one's remembrance of every good deed.
There it is called Lethe; and so, on the other side,
it is called Eunoe; and it does not take effect
until it is first tasted on both sides:
its flavor is superior to any other.
And, even though your thirst may be
so fully slaked that I need not reveal more to you,
I shall give one more additional fact as a free favor;
and I do not think my words will be less dear to you
if I expatiate further than I promised you.
Those poets who in ancient times described
the age of gold and its blissful circumstances,
were perhaps dreaming of this place while on Parnassus.[13]
Here the root of humanity[14] was innocent;
here it is eternally springtime and every sort of fruit grows;
this is the nectar that they were all speaking of."
Then I turned completely around to face
my poets, and I saw that they had heard
the final explanation with a warm smile;
next, I turned my face toward the beautiful lady.

---

a rainbow. Twenty-four elders crowned with lilies chant a hymn to the Virgin.
The four animals of the Evangelists enclose a two-wheeled triumphal chariot drawn by a griffin. Three ladies dance near the left wheel, four near the
right. Next come Saints Luke and Paul; the authors of the non-Pauline New
Testament epistles; and Saint John, author of Revelation.]

---

13. The mountain of Apollo and the Muses.   14. Adam and Eve.

Canto XXX

Quando il settentrïon del primo cielo,
  che nè occaso mai seppe nè orto
  nè d'altra nebbia che di colpa velo,
e che faceva lì ciascuno accorto
  di suo dover, come 'l più basso face
  qual temon gira per venire a porto,
fermo s'affisse, la gente verace
  venuta prima tra 'l grifone ed esso,
  al carro volse sè come a sua pace;
e un di loro, quasi da ciel messo,
  'Veni, sponsa, de Libano' cantando
  gridò tre volte, e tutti li altri appresso.
Quali i beati al novissimo bando
  surgeran presti ognun di sua caverna,
  la revestita carne alleluiando;
cotali in su la divina basterna
  si levar cento, ad vocem tanti senis,
  ministri e messagier di vita etterna.
Tutti dicean: «Benedictus qui venis!»,
  e fior gittando di sopra e dintorno,
  «Manibus, oh, date lilïa plenis!»
Io vidi già nel cominciar del giorno
  la parte orïental tutta rosata,
  e l'altro ciel di bel sereno adorno;
e la faccia del sol nascere ombrata,
  sì che, per temperanza di vapori,
  l'occhio la sostenea lunga fïata:
così dentro una nuvola di fiori
  che dalle mani angeliche saliva
  e ricadeva in giù dentro e di fori,
sovra candido vel cinta d'uliva

Canto XXX

When the Little Dipper of the highest heaven[1]—
  which has never known setting or rising
  nor obscuration by any fog other than sin,
and which was making everyone there alert
  to his duty, just as the lower one[2] alerts
  the man who turns the helm to arrive in port—
came to a halt, the truthful people[3]
  who had earlier come between it and the griffin,
  turned toward the chariot as if toward the source of peace;
and one of them,[4] as if sent from heaven,
  chanted "*Veni, sponsa, de Libano*"[5] in a loud voice
  three times, and all the rest repeated it.
Just as the blessed at the last summons
  will each arise quickly from the tomb,
  singing hallelujah for the flesh that once more clothes them,
thus, upon the divine carriage,
  at the voice of such a great old man, there arose a hundred
  ministers and messengers of eternal life.[6]
All were saying "*Benedictus qui venis!*"[7]
  and, as they scattered flowers from above and all around,
  "*Manibus, oh, date lilia plenis!*"[8]
In the past I have seen, at daybreak,
  the eastern part of the sky all pink
  and the rest of the sky adorned with a beautiful blue,
while the face of the sun rose behind a cloud,
  so that, because vapor was mitigating its force,
  the eye could endure it for a long time:
in like manner, within the cloud of flowers
  that was issuing from the angels' hands
  and falling down, within and without,
a lady appeared to me, wreathed with olive

---

1. The seven candlesticks of the preceding canto (symbolizing the sevenfold gifts of the spirit), which, in the Empyrean, are like the seven stars of the Little Dipper (which includes the North Star).   2. The real Little Dipper, which is lower than the Empyrean, being in the eighth heaven.   3. The 24 elders of the preceding canto, who symbolize the books of the Old Testament.   4. The one symbolizing the Song of Songs.   5. "Come, my bride, from Lebanon."   6. Angels.   7. "Blessed are you that come."   8. "Oh, scatter lilies from full hands"; this quotation is not from the Bible, like all the others in this canto, but from the *Aeneid*.

donna m'apparve, sotto verde manto
vestita di color di fiamma viva.
E lo spirito mio, che già cotanto
tempo era stato che alla sua presenza
non era di stupor, tremando, affranto,
sanza delli occhi aver più conoscenza,
per occulta virtù che da lei mosse,
d'antico amor sentì la gran potenza.
Tosto che nella vista mi percosse
l'alta virtù che già m'avea trafitto
prima ch'io fuor di puerizia fosse,
volsimi alla sinistra col rispitto
col quale il fantolin corre alla mamma
quando ha paura o quando elli è afflitto,
per dicere a Virgilio: «Men che dramma
di sangue m'è rimaso che non tremi:
conosco i segni dell'antica fiamma»;
ma Virgilio n'avea lasciati scemi
di sè, Virgilio dolcissimo patre,
Virgilio a cui per mia salute die'mi;
nè quantunque perdeo l'antica matre,
valse alle guance nette di rugiada,
che, lacrimando, non tornasser atre.
«Dante, perchè Virgilio se ne vada,
non pianger anco, non piangere ancora;
chè pianger ti convien per altra spada.»
Quasi ammiraglio che in poppa ed in prora
viene a veder la gente che ministra
per li altri legni, e a ben far l'incora;
in su la sponda del carro sinistra,
quando mi volsi al suon del nome mio,
che di necessità qui si registra,
vidi la donna che pria m'apparìo
velata sotto l'angelica festa,
drizzar li occhi ver me di qua dal rio.
Tutto che 'l vel che le scendea di testa,

over a white veil, and, beneath her green cloak,
clad in the color of living flame.[9]
And my spirit—which, for so long a time
   already, had not trembled,
   overcome with stupor, in her presence—
gaining no further visual recognition of her,
   but touched by a hidden power emanating from her,
   felt the great force of its earlier love.
As soon as my eyes were smitten
   by the lofty power that had already pierced me
   before I was out of my childhood,
I turned to the left, with the same expectation[10]
   with which a little child runs to its mother
   when afraid or in distress,
to say to Vergil: "Less than a dram
   of blood is left in me that is not trembling:
   I recognize the signs of my previous flame";
but Vergil had left us bereft
   of himself, Vergil, that most gentle father,
   Vergil, to whom I had entrusted myself for safekeeping;
not even all that our original mother lost[11]
   had the power to keep my dew-cleansed cheeks
   from turning dark again with tears.[12]
"Dante, even though Vergil is departing,
   do not weep yet, do not weep yet;
   for it behooves you to weep for another sword of affliction."
Like an admiral, who at stern and bow
   comes to inspect the crew serving
   on the rest of the fleet, inciting them to brave deeds;
just so did I see standing on the left sideboard of the chariot,
   when I turned at the sound of my name,
   which is recorded here out of necessity,
the lady who had earlier appeared to me
   veiled beneath the angels' festivity,
   and who was now looking at me on this side of the stream.[13]
Although the veil that hung from her head,

---

9. Beatrice wears the colors of faith, hope, and charity.   10. Or: "confidence."   11. Presence in the earthly paradise (lost by Eve).   12. This refers to the cleaning of Dante's cheeks from the soot of Hell before his entry into Purgatory.   13. Lethe.

cerchiato delle fronde di Minerva,
non la lasciasse parer manifesta,
regalmente nell'atto ancor proterva
continüò come colui che dice
e 'l più caldo parlar dietro reserva:
«Guardaci ben! Ben son, ben son Beatrice.
Come degnasti d'accedere al monte?
non sapei tu che qui è l'uom felice?»
Li occhi mi cadder giù nel chiaro fonte;
ma veggendomi in esso, i trassi all'erba,
tanta vergogna mi gravò la fronte.
Così la madre al figlio par superba,
com'ella parve a me; perchè d'amaro
sent'il sapor della pietade acerba.
Ella si tacque; e li angeli cantaro
di subito '*In te, Domine, speravi*';
ma oltre '*pedes meos*' non passaro.
Sì come neve tra le vive travi
per lo dosso d'Italia si congela,
soffiata e stretta dalli venti schiavi,
poi, liquefatta, in sè stessa trapela,
pur che la terra che perde ombra spiri,
sì che par foco fonder la candela;
così fui sanza lacrime e sospiri
anzi 'l cantar di quei che notan sempre
dietro alle note delli etterni giri;
ma poi ch'i' 'ntesi nelle dolci tempre
lor compatire a me, più che se detto
avesser: «Donna, perchè sì lo stempre?»,
lo gel che m'era intorno al cor ristretto,
spirito e acqua fessi, e con angoscia
della bocca e delli occhi uscì del petto.
Ella, pur ferma in su la detta coscia
del carro stando, alle sustanze pie
volse le sue parole così poscia:
«Voi vigilate nell'etterno dìe,

circled with Minerva's leaves,[14]
did not permit her to be seen distinctly,
regally, and still impetuous in gesture,
   she continued, like a speaker
   saving his most scathing words for the last:
"Take a good look at me! I really am, I really am Beatrice.
   How did you deign to approach the mountain?
   Were you unaware that those here are in a state of bliss?"
I lowered my eyes to the clear fountain;
   but seeing my reflection there, I turned them to the grass,
   such great shame weighed down my brow.
Just as a mother appears disdainful to her son,
   so did she appear to me; because the taste
   of reproachful affection is bitter.
She fell silent; and the angels suddenly
   sang *"In te, Domine, speravi"*;
   but they did not go beyond *"pedes meos."*[15]
Just as the snow congeals amid the living rafters[16]
   along the spine of Italy,[17]
   blown and compacted by the winds from Slavonia,
and later, melting, drips onto itself,
   provided that the wind blows from the shadow-losing land,[18]
   so that a fire seems to be melting a candle;
just so did I remain tearless and sighless
   until the singing of those[19] who in their chant
   always follow the music of the eternal spheres;
but after I discerned in their sweet airs
   their compassion for me, more clearly than if
   they had said: "Lady, why do you enfeeble him so?,"
the frost that had locked itself around my heart
   became breath and water, and in anguish
   issued from my breast through my mouth and eyes.
She, still standing motionless on the aforesaid flank
   of the chariot, then addressed her words
   to these compassionate beings, as follows:
"You keep vigil in the eternal day,

---

14. Olive leaves, sacred to Minerva (Athene).   15. They sang: "In you, O Lord, I have my hope" (Psalm 31), down to the words "my feet"; that part of the psalm is concerned with the forgiveness of sin.   16. The trees.   17. The Apennines.   18. Africa, where the high vertical sun eliminates shadows.   19. The angels.

sì che notte nè sonno a voi non fura
passo che faccia il secol per sue vie;
onde la mia risposta è con più cura
    che m'intenda colui che di là piagne,
    perchè sia colpa e duol d'una misura.
Non pur per ovra delle rote magne,
    che drizzan ciascun seme ad alcun fine
    secondo che le stelle son compagne,
ma per larghezza di grazie divine,
    che sì alti vapori hanno a lor piova,
    che nostre viste là non van vicine,
questi fu tal nella sua vita nova
    virtüalmente, ch'ogni abito destro
    fatto averebbe in lui mirabil prova.
Ma tanto più maligno e più silvestro
    si fa 'l terren col mal seme e non colto,
    quant'elli ha più di buon vigor terrestro.
Alcun tempo il sostenni col mio volto:
    mostrando li occhi giovanetti a lui,
    meco il menava in dritta parte volto.
Sì tosto come in su la soglia fui
    di mia seconda etade e mutai vita,
    questi si tolse a me, e diessi altrui.
Quando di carne a spirto era salita
    e bellezza e virtù cresciuta m'era,
    fu'io a lui men cara e men gradita;
e volse i passi suoi per via non vera,
    imagini di ben seguendo false,
    che nulla promission rendono intera.
Nè l'impetrare inspirazion mi valse,
    con le quali ed in sogno e altrimenti
    lo rivocai; sì poco a lui ne calse!
Tanto giù cadde, che tutti argomenti
    alla salute sua eran già corti,
    fuor che mostrarli le perdute genti.
Per questo visitai l'uscio de' morti,
    e a colui che l'ha qua su condotto,
    li preghi miei, piangendo, furon porti.

so that neither night nor sleep robs from your sight
a single step taken by human beings along their paths;
therefore, my reply is more especially framed
to make myself understood by the man weeping yonder,
in order that his sin and his penalty may be commensurate.
Not merely through the workings of the great wheels[20]
which direct each seed to some fulfillment
in accordance with the stars that accompany it,[21]
but also through the generosity of divine grace,
whose rain is of vapors so lofty
that our sight cannot approach it,
this man had such great potential
in his youth that any proper disposition
would have led him to wonderful success.
But a soil becomes all the more infertile and wild
when poorly sowed and uncultivated,
the more natural vigor it starts out with.
For a time I sustained him with my face:
showing him my girlish eyes,
I led him with me, facing in the right direction.
As soon as I was on the threshold
of my young womanhood, and passed from life to death,
this man detached himself from me and gave himself to another.
When I had ascended from the flesh into spirit,
and my beauty and virtue had increased,
I was less dear and less pleasing to him;
and he turned his steps onto a path that was not true,
following false images of happiness
which never keep all their promises.
Nor did it do me any good when I was granted the power to inspire him,
with which, both in dreams and in other ways,
I tried to call him back; so little was he concerned with that!
He fell so low that all means
for saving him were already running out,
except for showing him the damned.
To do that, I visited the door of the dead,
and to the one who led him up here
my tearful entreaties were carried.

---

20. The heavens.   21. Its guardian planet.

Alto fato di Dio sarebbe rotto,
  se Letè si passasse e tal vivanda
  fosse gustata sanza alcuno scotto
di pentimento che lagrime spanda.»

[SUMMARY OF CANTO XXXI: When Dante tearfully confesses that he did
indeed go astray after Beatrice's death, she retorts that he should have been
restrained by the memory of her unusual qualities, especially since he was already mature. Dante, repentant, is led through Lethe by the lady from Canto
XXVIII, and he drinks of its waters while voices sing "Purge me with hyssop."
Now on the far side, he dances with the nymphs who symbolize the four cardinal virtues. Approaching Beatrice, who is standing near the griffin, which
symbolizes the dual nature of Christ, he sees the two natures—human and
divine—alternately reflected in her eyes. The three theological virtues
dance, too.

SUMMARY OF CANTO XXXII: The procession now moves on, following the
sun, with Dante, Statius, and the lady of Canto XXVIII walking alongside the
chariot. They come to a bare tree, which bursts into leaf and flower after the
griffin shows it marks of respect. (The chariot symbolizes the Church, and
the tree is the tree of the knowledge of good and evil, symbolizing the Holy
Roman Empire.) Dante sleeps, and is awakened by that lady. Beatrice has

A lofty decree of God would be infringed
   if Lethe were crossed and such noble food
   were tasted without some payment
of penitence and shedding of tears."

---

now descended from the chariot and is surrounded by the seven nymphs, who now hold the seven candlesticks. Everyone except them, that lady, and the two poets, is gone. Dante now sees visions portraying attacks on the chariot (persecutions, heresies, schisms, and improper relations with secular authorities).

SUMMARY OF CANTO XXXIII: The nymphs sing "The heathen have come into Your inheritance," and Beatrice sings "A little while, and you shall not see me." Beatrice now explains the latest visions in deeply enigmatic terms, although she does evidently promise that a deliverer will come to save Church and state. Dante, having drunk of Lethe, which obliterates remembrance of sin, no longer recalls that he was ever estranged from Beatrice. She promises to speak more clearly in the future. The group now comes to the stream of Eunoe, where it is revealed that the lady of Canto XXVIII is named Matelda. Now Dante and Statius drink of the waters, which restore the remembrance of all good impressions, and our poet is born again and ready to ascend to the stars.]

PARADISO

[SUMMARY OF CANTO I: Dante calls upon Apollo for aid in describing Paradise. It is now noon on the mountain of Purgatory. Beatrice stares at the sun; when Dante follows suit, he sees a second sun. Dante is now more than human, perceiving new sights and sounds. With Beatrice he soars through the sphere of fire that encloses the earth's atmosphere. When he wonders how this is possible for him, Beatrice explains that the fundamental force of "gravity" in the universe is the movement of things seeking their true place; thus, it is only natural for man to ascend toward God, once he is rid of gross impediments.

SUMMARY OF CANTO II: Dante warns the reader that he is now sailing into difficult waters. He and Beatrice enter the moon (which governs the first heaven) miraculously, without cleaving it. Dante believes that the dark spots

Canto III

Quel sol che pria d'amor mi scaldò 'l petto,
   di bella verità m'avea scoverto,
   provando e riprovando, il dolce aspetto;
e io, per confessar corretto e certo
   me stesso, tanto quanto si convenne
   leva' il capo a proferer più erto;
ma visïon apparve che ritenne
   a sè me tanto stretto, per vedersi,
   che di mia confession non mi sovvenne.
Quali per vetri trasparenti e tersi,
   o ver per acque nitide e tranquille,
   non sì profonde che i fondi sien persi,

PARADISE

on the moon are evidence of variations in its density. Beatrice sets him right: if the moon were porous through and through in places, that would be revealed by light shining right through it during eclipses of the sun; if the lack of density extended only part of the way inward, the light reflected from the dense parts of the surface, and the light reflected from the denser interior parts backing up the hollows, would be equal in brightness. This can be proved by an experiment with a lamp and three mirrors, of which one is placed farther away than the others. The power from the Prime Mover is differentiated, as it permeates the universe, by the individual qualities of the heavenly bodies, just as the soul is variously manifested in the various parts of the body. It is not a question of variation of density, but a variation of light.]

Canto III

That sun which first warmed my breast with love[1]
    had revealed the sweet appearance
    of lovely truth to me by proofs and refutations;
and I, to confess that I stood corrected
    and now possessed certainty, raised my head higher
    to a seemly extent in order to speak out;
but a vision appeared that held me
    so closely glued to it, so I could gaze on it,
    that I no longer recalled my confession.
Just as, through transparent and smooth panes of glass,
    or else through limpid and calm waters
    that are not so deep that the bottom is lost to sight,

---

1. Beatrice.

tornan di nostri visi le postille
   debili sì, che perla in bianca fronte
   non vien men tosto alle nostre pupille;
tali vid'io più facce a parlar pronte;
   per ch'io dentro all'error contrario corsi
   a quel ch'accese amor tra l'omo e 'l fonte.
Subito sì com'io di lor m'accorsi,
   quelle stimando specchiati sembianti,
   per veder di cui fosser, li occhi torsi;
e nulla vidi, e ritorsili avanti
   dritti nel lume della dolce guida,
   che, sorridendo, ardea nelli occhi santi.
«Non ti maravigliar perch'io sorrida»
   mi disse «appresso il tuo pueril coto,
   poi sopra 'l vero ancor lo piè non fida,
ma te rivolve, come suole, a vòto:
   vere sustanze son ciò che tu vedi,
   qui rilegate per manco di vóto.
Però parla con esse e odi e credi;
   chè la verace luce che li appaga
   da sè non lascia lor torcer li piedi.»
Ed io all'ombra che parea più vaga
   di ragionar drizza'mi, e cominciai,
   quasi com'uom cui troppa voglia smaga:
«O ben creato spirito, che a' rai
   di vita etterna la dolcezza senti
   che, non gustata, non s'intende mai,
grazïoso mi fia se mi contenti
   del nome tuo e della vostra sorte.»
   Ond'ella, pronta e con occhi ridenti:
«La nostra carità non serra porte
   a giusta voglia, se non come quella
   che vuol simile a sè tutta sua corte.
I' fui nel mondo vergine sorella;
   e se la mente tua ben sè riguarda,
   non mi ti celerà l'esser più bella,
ma riconoscerai ch'i' son Piccarda,

the images of our faces are reflected
    so feebly that a pearl on a white forehead
    is not perceived by our eyes with less difficulty,
in like manner I saw several faces on the point of speaking;
    so that I fell into an error opposite
    to the one that kindled love between the man and the fountain.[2]
As soon as I became aware of them,
    believing them to be mirror images,
    I turned my eyes to see whose faces they were;
but I saw nothing, and turned my eyes back ahead of me
    straight at the luminous face of my sweet guide,
    who, smiling, blazed at me from her holy eyes.
"Do not be surprised if I smile,"
    she said, "at your childish reasoning,
    since your foot does not yet have a trusty hold on truth,
but, as usual, is spinning you around in the void;
    these that you see are true substances,
    relegated to this heaven because they did not fulfill a vow.
Speak to them, then, hear them out and believe them;
    for the light of truth that makes them contented
    does not allow them to swerve away from itself."
And I turned toward the shade that seemed
    most eager to converse, and I began,
    almost like a man bewildered by an excess of longing:
"O well-created spirit, you that in the rays
    of eternal life experience the sweetness
    that can never be understood unless it is tasted,
I will be grateful if you are pleased to tell me
    your name and the condition of you and your fellows."
    Whereupon, readily and with smiling eyes, it replied:
"Our charitable love does not lock the door
    to a proper desire, any more than that Love does
    which wants Its entire court to be like Itself.
In the world I was a nun;
    and if your memory scrutinizes itself well,
    my being more beautiful now will not hide me from you,
but you will recognize that I am Piccarda,[3]

---

2. Narcissus fell in love with his image, which he took for reality; Dante is doing the opposite, taking a real substance for an image.   3. Sister of Forese and Corso Donati (see *Purgatory*, Cantos XXIII and XXIV).

che, posta qui con questi altri beati,
   beata sono in la spera più tarda.
Li nostri affetti che solo infiammati
   son nel piacer dello Spirito Santo,
   letizian del suo ordine formati.
E questa sorte che par giù cotanto,
   però n'è data, perchè fuor negletti
   li nostri vóti, e vòti in alcun canto.»
Ond'io a lei: «Ne' mirabili aspetti
   vostri risplende non so che divino
   che vi trasmuta da' primi concetti:
però non fui a rimembrar festino;
   ma or m'aiuta ciò che tu mi dici,
   sì che raffigurar m'è più latino.
Ma dimmi: voi che siete qui felici,
   disiderate voi più alto loco
   per più vedere e per più farvi amici?»
Con quelle altr'ombre pria sorrise un poco;
   da indi mi rispuose tanto lieta,
   ch'arder parea d'amor nel primo foco:
«Frate, la nostra volontà quïeta
   virtù di carità, che far volerne
   sol quel ch'avemo, e d'altro non ci asseta.
Se disïassimo esser più superne,
   foran discordi li nostri disiri
   dal voler di colui che qui ne cerne;
che vedrai non capere in questi giri,
   s'essere in carità è qui necesse,
   e se la sua natura ben rimiri.
Anzi è formale ad esto beato esse
   tenersi dentro alla divina voglia,
   per ch'una fansi nostre voglie stesse;
sì che, come noi sem di soglia in soglia
   per questo regno, a tutto il regno piace
   com'allo re ch'a sua voler ne invoglia.
E 'n la sua volontade è nostra pace:
   ell'è quel mare al qual tutto si move
   ciò ch'ella cria e che natura face.»

who, placed here with these other blessed souls,
   am blessed within the slowest-moving sphere.[4]
Our emotions, which are inflamed solely
   by the will of the Holy Spirit,
   take joy in conforming to His established order.
And our lot, which is seen to be so lowly,
   was assigned to us because our vows
   were forgotten or else broken to some extent."
Then I replied: "In the wondrous appearance
   of you and your fellows there shines something divine
   that transforms you from one's earlier impressions of you:
that is why I was not swift to recall you;
   but now I am aided by what you tell me,
   so that it is easier for me to picture you.
But tell me: your group that is so happy here,
   do you yearn for a loftier position
   to see more of God and become closer friends of His?"
Along with those other shades she first smiled a little;
   then she answered me so joyfully
   that she seemed ablaze with love in the foremost fire:
"Brother, our wishes are stilled
   by the power of charitable love, which makes us desire
   solely what we have, and gives us no thirst for other things.
If we longed to be up higher,
   our desires would clash
   with the will of Him who assigns us here;
you will see that such discord has no place in these spheres
   if dwelling in charity is a necessity here,
   and if you examine the nature of charity closely.
On the contrary, it is essential to this state of blessedness
   to remain within the limits of the divine will,
   through which our own wills become as one;
so that our organization by various thresholds
   throughout this realm is pleasing to the entire realm,
   as it is to the King who bends our will to His own wishes.
And in His will is our peace:
   it is the sea to which flows everything
   that it creates directly or that nature has a hand in forming."

---

4. The heaven of the moon, which has the longest orbit.

Chiaro mi fu allor come ogni dove
   in cielo è paradiso, etsi la grazia
   del sommo ben d'un modo non vi piove.
Ma sì com'elli avvien, s'un cibo sazia
   e d'un altro rimane ancor la gola,
   che quel si chere e di quel si ringrazia,
così fec'io con atto e con parola,
   per apprender da lei qual fu la tela
   onde non trasse infino a co la spola.
«Perfetta vita e alto merto inciela
   donna più su» mi disse «alla cui norma
   nel vostro mondo giù si veste e vela,
perchè fino al morir si vegghi e dorma
   con quello sposo ch'ogni voto accetta
   che caritate a suo piacer conforma.
Dal mondo, per seguirla, giovinetta
   fuggi'mi, e nel suo abito mi chiusi,
   e promisi la via della sua setta.
Uomini poi, a mal più ch'a bene usi,
   fuor mi rapiron della dolce chiostra:
   Iddio si sa qual poi mia vita fusi.
E quest'altro splendor che ti si mostra
   dalla mia destra parte e che s'accende
   di tutto il lume della spera nostra,
ciò ch'io dico di me, di sè intende:
   sorella fu, e così le fu tolta
   di capo l'ombra delle sacre bende.
Ma poi che pur al mondo fu rivolta
   contra suo grado e contra buona usanza,
   non fu dal vel del cor già mai disciolta.
Quest'è la luce della gran Costanza
   che del secondo vento di Soave
   generò il terzo e l'ultima possanza.»
Così parlommi, e poi cominciò 'Ave,
   Maria' cantando, e cantando vanìo

Then it was clear to me that every part
   of heaven is Paradise, even if the grace
   of the Highest Good does not rain down in one and the same way.
But, just as it occurs that one food satisfies you
   while another still leaves you with a craving for more,
   so that you ask for more of one and say "no, thanks" to the other,
in like manner did I react with gesture and with words,
   to learn from her what the woven web was like
   through which she had not drawn the shuttle to the end.
"Her perfect life and lofty merit have placed higher up
   in heaven a lady,"[5] she said, "following whose rule
   women in your world below take the robe and veil,
so that until death they may wake and sleep
   with that Bridegroom who accepts every vow
   that charity makes conformable to His will.
To follow her, as a young woman I fled
   the world and dressed myself in her habit,
   promising to follow the path of her order.
Later on, men who were more accustomed to evil than to good
   abducted me from that sweet convent:[6]
   God knows what my life was like after that.
And this other shining spirit that you can see
   at my right, which is ignited
   with all the light of our sphere,
applies to herself everything I say about myself:
   she was a nun, and in the same way the shadow
   of the holy veil was snatched from her head.
But even after she returned to secular life
   against her will and contrary to proper custom,
   she was never separated from the veil in her heart.
This is the light of great Constance,
   who by the second stormwind from Swabia
   became mother of the third, the last great power."[7]
Thus she spoke to me, and then began to sing
   "*Ave Maria*," and as she sang she vanished

---

5. Saint Clare of Assisi.   6. Piccarda was abducted by Corso to be married to one
of his political allies.   7. This Constance was the wife of Holy Roman Emperor Henry
VI of the Swabian line and mother of Holy Roman Emperor Frederick II (called by
Dante the "last great power," though he died in 1250, because he was the last emperor
before 1300, the date of Dante's journey in the otherworld, to be crowned in Italy).
Constance was never really a nun.

come per acqua cupa cosa grave.
La vista mia, che tanto la seguìo
    quanto possibil fu, poi che la perse,
    volsesi al segno di maggior disio,
e a Beatrice tutta si converse;
    ma quella folgorò nel mïo sguardo
    sì che da prima il viso non sofferse;
e ciò mi fece a dimandar più tardo.

[SUMMARY OF CANTO IV: Beatrice intuits the nature of Dante's further questions and answers them before he can articulate them: (1) All souls are really located in the highest heaven, the Empyrean, but appear symbolically as if they were distributed among the various heavens according to their merit. Plato was wrong in saying that the souls of the dead return to particular planets, though he was partially correct if he meant that the planets influence our lives—the concept that, misunderstood, led the world into its original idolatry. (2) Piccarda and her fellows are not undeserving of their low position in Paradise, because even though they broke their vows against their will, they consented under pressure. Dante realizes that the human mind cannot rest until it is illumined by divine truth. He now asks whether satisfaction for broken vows can ever be made.

SUMMARY OF CANTO V: The answer is: basically, no, because a vow entails a partial sacrifice of one's free will, which is sacred, being God's finest gift to man. The Church does, however, allow some dispensations, wherein the "content" of the vow—the thing vowed—may be exchanged for something else (this does not apply to monastic vows). Men should never make foolish or evil vows. Dante and Beatrice now ascend to the second heaven, that of Mercury, where more than a thousand residents greet them happily. One of them prepares to tell Dante about himself and this heaven.

SUMMARY OF CANTO VI: The speaker is the 6th-century Byzantine emperor Justinian, who promulgated just laws after he was converted to pure orthodoxy from a heretical belief. He reviews Roman history for Dante from the days of the Trojan founders through the monarchy, republic, Julius Caesar's civil wars, the death of Christ under Tiberius, the vengeance taken on the Jews by Titus, and the advent of the Holy Roman Empire under Charlemagne. Those who combat or misuse the Empire through party strife are evil. The souls on Mercury desired fame in life, but were somewhat too ambitious or too jealous of their reputation. Another resident is the 12th-century statesman Romeo of Villeneuve.

SUMMARY OF CANTO VII: Justinian and his fellows depart. Out of Love, as

like a heavy object in dark waters.
My eyes, which followed her
    as far as possible, after they lost sight of her
    turned toward the target of their greatest longing,
and were completely trained on Beatrice;
    but she flashed such a lightning bolt in my face
    that at first my eyes could not endure it;
and that made me more hesitant to ask questions.

Beatrice now tells Dante, Christ joined His divine nature to sinful human nature to atone for Adam's sin. On the Cross, human nature was justly "executed," but Christ's divine nature was outraged, and vengeance on the Jews
was necessary. Man on his own could never have redeemed himself because
his humility was limited; God had to do it, and the way He chose was preferable, because more just, to a simple decree of forgiveness. Heaven and the
angels are made directly by God, but the angels created the four elements
and their compounds, including plant and animal life. Human beings before
Adam's fall were direct, immortal creations of God, and so will all redeemed
humanity be.

SUMMARY OF CANTO VIII: Dante and Beatrice imperceptibly rise to the
third heaven, that of Venus, once falsely worshipped as the goddess of love.
There, spirits leave their eternal round dance to welcome the newcomers.
One of them quotes an appropriate lyric poem of Dante's, and identifies himself as Dante's friend Charles Martel, heir to Provence and the Kingdom of
Naples. Charles bewails the inferiority of his brother, Robert of Naples, to
their noble father Charles II. Questioned by Dante, Charles explains that
heredity is not as important in determining a man's character as the planetary influences that insure the necessary diversity among beings. People are
wrong in demanding that a man follow his father's profession; instead, he
should be given one in conformity with his individual gifts.

SUMMARY OF CANTO IX: The souls on Venus erred on earth by an overly
great emphasis on romantic love. The next one to address Dante is Cunizza
da Romano, a sister of the notorious tyrant Ezzolino; she predicts a chain of
disasters that are to befall her native northeast Italy. Next, the early 13th-
century troubadour Foulques of Marseilles discusses his present blissful
state, and tells Dante that the soul next to him is that of the biblical harlot
Rahab, who saved the lives of Joshua's spies in Jericho; she was brought here
from Limbo by Christ as a trophy of the victory of Christianity. Now the
clergy forget the Holy Land, where she lived, and think only about the florins
coined in Dante's native city.]

Canto X

Guardando nel suo Figlio con l'Amore
   che l'uno e l'altro etternalmente spira,
   lo primo ed ineffabile Valore,
quanto per mente e per loco si gira
   con tant'ordine fè, ch'esser non puote
   sanza gustar di lui chi ciò rimira.
Leva dunque, lettore, all'alte ruote
   meco la vista, dritto a quella parte
   dove l'un moto e l'altro si percuote;
e lì comincia a vagheggiar nell'arte
   di quel maestro che dentro a sè l'ama,
   tanto che mai da lei occhio non parte.
Vedi come da indi si dirama
   l'oblico cerchio che i pianeti porta,
   per sodisfare al mondo che li chiama.
E se la strada lor non fosse torta,
   molta virtù nel ciel sarebbe in vano,
   e quasi ogni potenza qua giù morta;
e se dal dritto più o men lontano
   fosse 'l partire, assai sarebbe manco
   e giù e su dell'ordine mondano.
Or ti riman, lettor, sovra 'l tuo banco,
   dietro pensando a ciò che si preliba,
   s'esser vuoi lieto assai prima che stanco.
Messo t'ho innanzi: omai per te ti ciba;
   chè a sè torce tutta la mia cura
   quella materia ond'io son fatto scriba.
Lo ministro maggior della natura
   che del valor del ciel lo mondo imprenta
   e col suo lume il tempo ne misura,
con quella parte che su si rammenta
   congiunto, si girava per le spire

Canto X

Looking upon His Son with that Love
   which eternally emanates from both of Them,
   the foremost, inexpressible Power
created all that exists, either intellectively or in a material location,
   with such great order that the man who has regard for this
   cannot help delighting in Him.
Therefore, reader, raise your eyes along with me
   to the lofty wheels of heaven, directly toward the place
   where one motion comes in contact with the other;[1]
and there begin to contemplate lovingly the art
   of that Master who loves that art within Himself
   to such an extent that He never takes His eyes off it.
See how, from that point, there branches off
   the oblique circle that bears the planets,
   to give contentment to the world that clamors for them.[2]
And if their path were not set at a slant,
   many heavenly forces would operate in vain,
   and almost every life force here on earth would be dead;
and if its deflection from a straight line
   were greater or smaller, there would be a great defect
   in the world's order both below and above.[3]
Now, reader, remain seated on your bench of study
   thinking over that which is merely hinted at here,
   if you wish to be happy much sooner than you are weary.[4]
I have set it before you: now consume it on your own;
   for the subject of which I have become the scribe
   calls all my attention to itself.
The greatest servant of nature,[5]
   which imprints the power of heaven on our world
   and measures time for us with its light,
was in conjunction with the above-mentioned place,[6]
   and was moving through the spirals

---

1. At the equinoctial point where the celestial equator (path of the sun's daily rotation) crosses the ecliptic (path of its annual revolution), the point from which the sun's path through the zodiac branches off obliquely (that is, at Aries, where the ecliptic slants across the equator). 2. Because the earth needs the planetary influences. 3. Meaning either: "on both sides of the equator" or "both on earth and in heaven." 4. Weary with further intense study. 5. The sun. 6. It was in Aries.

in che più tosto ognora s'appresenta;
e io era con lui; ma del salire
non m'accors'io, se non com'uom s'accorge,
anzi 'l primo pensier, del suo venire.
È Beatrice quella che sì scorge
di bene in meglio sì subitamente
che l'atto suo per tempo non si sporge.
Quant'esser convenia da sè lucente
quel ch'era dentro al sol dov'io entra'mi,
non per color, ma per lume parvente!
Perch'io lo 'ngegno e l'arte e l'uso chiami
sì nol direi, che mai s'imaginasse;
ma creder puossi e di veder si brami.
E se le fantasie nostre son basse
a tanta altezza, non è maraviglia;
chè sopra 'l sol non fu occhio ch'andasse.
Tal era quivi la quarta famiglia
dell'alto Padre, che sempre la sazia,
mostrando come spira e come figlia.
E Beatrice cominciò: «Ringrazia,
ringrazia il sol delli angeli, ch'a questo
sensibil t'ha levato per sua grazia.»
Cor di mortal non fu mai sì digesto
a divozione ed a rendersi a Dio
con tutto il suo gradir cotanto presto,
come a quelle parole mi fec'io;
e sì tutto 'l mio amore in lui si mise,
che Beatrice eclissò nell'oblio.
Non le dispiacque; ma sì se ne rise,
che lo splendor delli occhi suoi ridenti
mia mente unita in più cose divise.
Io vidi più fulgor vivi e vincenti
far di noi centro e di sè far corona,
più dolci in voce che in vista lucenti:
così cinger la figlia di Latona
vedem tal volta, quando l'aere è pregno,

in which it shows itself to us earlier every day;[7]
and I was with it; but I did not become aware
    of my ascent to it, any more than a man is aware
    of the coming of a thought before it is already in his mind.
Beatrice is the one who conducts me
    from good to better[8] so suddenly
    that her action has no temporal extension.
How luminous in themselves they had to be,
    those who were within the sun, which I entered,
    since they were visible not as colored bodies but as intenser light!
Even though I were to call upon my intellect, skill, and experience,
    I could not narrate this so that it could ever be pictured;
    but it *can* be believed, and people should yearn to see it.
And if our imaginations are too low
    for such heights, it is not surprising;
    for no eye has gone to the sun and beyond.
Of such a nature, there, was the fourth family[9]
    of the exalted Father, who constantly sates them,
    showing them the emanation of the Spirit and the engendering of the Son.
And Beatrice began: "Give thanks,
    give thanks to the Sun of the angels[10] for raising you
    to this visible one through His grace."
Never was the heart of a mortal so disposed
    toward devotion or so ready to surrender itself
    to God with its every inclination,
as I became at those words;
    and all my love was so centered in Him
    that He eclipsed Beatrice, making me forget her.
She was not vexed, but smiled at this so sweetly
    that the glow of her smiling eyes
    turned my singlemindedness back into various directions.
I saw several vivid, overpowering flashes
    make a ring, with us in the center,
    the sweetness of their voices surpassing the luminosity of their faces:
in the same way we sometimes see a ring around
    the daughter of Latona,[11] when the air is heavy with moisture,

---

7. The sun, which, in the Ptolemaic system, moved in spirals, rises earlier every day after the spring equinox.   8. From each heaven to the next higher one.   9. The residents of the fourth heaven, that of the sun.   10. God.   11. The moon (Diana, Artemis).

sì che ritenga il fil che fa la zona.
Nella corte del cielo, ond'io rivegno,
  si trovan molte gioie care e belle
  tanto che non si possono trar del regno;
e 'l canto di quei lumi era di quelle;
  chi non s'impenna sì che là su voli,
  dal muto aspetti quindi le novelle.
Poi, sì cantando, quelli ardenti soli
  si fuor girati intorno a noi tre volte,
  come stelle vicine a' fermi poli,
donne mi parver non da ballo sciolte,
  ma che s'arrestin tacite, ascoltando
  fin che le nove note hanno ricolte;
e dentro all'un senti' cominciar: «Quando
  lo raggio della grazia, onde s'accende
  verace amore e che poi cresce amando,
multiplicato in te tanto resplende,
  che ti conduce su per quella scala
  u' sanza risalir nessun discende;
qual ti negasse il vin della sua fiala
  per la tua sete, in libertà non fora
  se non com'acqua ch'al mar non si cala.
Tu vuo' saper di quai piante s'infiora
  questa ghirlanda che 'ntorno vagheggia
  la bella donna ch'al ciel t'avvalora.
Io fui delli agni della santa greggia
  che Domenico mena per cammino
  u' ben s'impingua se non si vaneggia.
Questi che m'è a destra più vicino,
  frate e maestro fummi, ed esso Alberta
  è di Cologna, e io Thomàs d'Aquino.
Se sì di tutti li altri esser vuo' certo,
  di retro al mio parlar ten vien col viso
  girando su per lo beato serto.
Quell'altro fiammeggiare esce del riso
  di Grazïan, che l'uno e l'altro foro

so that her beams are held back and form a halo.
In the court of heaven, from which I am returning,
    there exist many jewels so precious and beautiful
    that they cannot be exported from the kingdom;
and the singing of those glowing figures was one of those;
    whoever does not grow wings so he can fly up there—
    let him wait to hear news of it from a mute!
After those blazing suns, singing in that way,
    had circled us three times
    like stars that are close to the fixed poles,[12]
they seemed to me like women who have not left their dance formation
    but are pausing in silence, listening
    until they have heard the continuation of the music;
from within one of them I heard the words: "Since
    the ray of grace, with which is kindled
    that true love which increases as it loves,
shines on you with such intensity
    that it is leading you up that staircase
    which no one descends unless he is to climb back up;
anyone who denied you the wine from his bottle,
    to slake your thirst, would be under constraint
    no less than water that is kept from running down to the sea.
You wish to know what plants lend their flowers
    to this garland which encircles and lovingly contemplates
    the beautiful lady who empowers you to see heaven.
I was one of the lambs of the holy flock
    that Dominic leads along a path
    where they grow good and fat if they do not go astray after vanity.[13]
This man who is nearest to me on the right
    was my brother and teacher; he is Albert
    of Cologne,[14] and I am Thomas Aquinas.[15]
If you wish to be equally acquainted with all the rest,
    follow my words with your eyes
    as we make the circle of the blessed garland.
That next blaze issues from the face
    of Gratian,[16] who aided both jurisdictions

---

12. And thus move slowly.   13. This line should be kept in mind, because it furnishes Dante with thematic material for the next canto.   14. The great theologian
Albertus Magnus (died 1280).   15. The celebrated author of the *Summa theologiae*
(died 1274).   16. A 12th-century father of canon law; he "aided both jurisdictions" by
making clear distinctions between civil and ecclesiastical law.

aiutò sì che piace in paradiso.
L'altro ch'appresso adorna il nostro coro,
   quel Pietro fu che con la poverella
   offerse a Santa Chiesa suo tesoro.
La quinta luce, ch'è tra noi più bella,
   spira di tale amor, che tutto 'l mondo
   là giù ne gola di saper novella:
entro v'è l'alta mente u' sì profondo
   saver fu messo, che se 'l vero è vero
   a veder tanto non surse il secondo.
Appresso vedi il lume di quel cero
   che giù, in carne, più a dentro vide
   l'angelica natura e 'l ministero.
Nell'altra piccioletta luce ride
   quello avvocato de' tempi cristiani
   del cui latino Augustin si provide.
Or se tu l'occhio della mente trani
   di luce in luce dietro alle mie lode,
   già dell'ottava con sete rimani.
Per vedere ogni ben dentro vi gode
   l'anima santa che 'l mondo fallace
   fa manifesto a chi di lei ben ode:
lo corpo ond'ella fu cacciata giace
   giuso in Cieldauro; ed essa da martiro
   e da essilio venne a questa pace.
Vedi oltre fiammeggiar l'ardente spiro
   d'Isidoro, di Beda e di Riccardo,
   che a considerar fu più che viro.

in a way pleasing to Paradise
The one who adorns our choir after him
    was that Peter who, along with the poor widow,
    offered his treasure to Holy Church.[17]
The fifth light, which is the most beautiful one among us,
    is inspired by such love that the whole world
    below craves to hear news of him:
within the light is the lofty mind in which such deep
    knowledge was placed that, if the truth is true,
    no second man rose so high as to see that much.[18]
After him, you see the light of that taper
    which on earth, in the flesh, looked most deeply into
    the nature and ministry of the angels.[19]
In the next, very small, light there smiles
    that advocate[20] of Christian times
    of whose Latin Saint Augustine laid in provisions.
Now if you draw the eye of your mind
    from light to light, following me as I praise them,
    you remain by now thirsting for the eighth one.
Through seeing all good things, within it there rejoices
    the holy soul that reveals the deceitfulness
    of the world to the man who listens to its words carefully:
the body from which it was expelled lies
    down below in Cielo d'Oro;[21] and from its martyrdom
    and its exile it arrived at this peace.
In addition, see flaming there the ardent spirits
    of Isidore,[22] Bede,[23] and Richard,[24]
    who, in contemplating, was more than mere man.

---

17. Peter Lombard, a 12th-century theologian who compared his own scholarly contributions to the widow's mite.   18. The fifth light is Solomon. He is said to be "inspired by . . . love" because the Song of Songs was attributed to him; the world "craves to hear news of him" because it was hotly disputed whether he went to heaven or not; "if the truth is true" means "if the Bible can be believed." This last line furnishes thematic material for Canto XIII.   19. Dionysius the Areopagite, a disciple of Saint Paul credited with writing the (actually much later) standard work on the hierarchy of the angels.   20. Most editors take this to be the 5th-century apologist Paulus Orosius, but a number of other early Christian writers have been suggested. *Tempi* ("times") has also been read as the plural of *tempio* ("temples").   21. The man buried in San Pietro in Cielo d'Oro, in Pavia, is the 6th-century philosopher Boethius, who was put to death by the Ostrogoth Theodoric.   22. The Christian encyclopedist Isidore of Seville (died 636).   23. The English ecclesiastical historian (died 735).   24. The theologian Richard of Saint Victor (died 1173).

Questi onde a me ritorna il tuo riguardo,
 è 'l lume d'uno spirto che 'n pensieri
 gravi a morir li parve venir tardo:
essa è la luce etterna di Sigieri,
 che, leggendo nel vico delli strami,
 sillogizzò invidïosi veri.»
Indi, come orologio che ne chiami
 nell'ora che la sposa di Dio surge
 a mattinar lo sposo perchè l'ami,
che l'una parte l'altra tira e urge,
 tin tin sonando con sì dolce nota,
 che 'l ben disposto spirto d'amor turge;
così vid'io la glorïosa rota
 muoversi e render voce a voce in tempra
 ed in dolcezza ch'esser non pò nota
se non colà dove gioir s'insempra.

Canto XI

O insensata cura de' mortali,
 quanto son difettivi sillogismi
 quei che ti fanno in basso batter l'ali!
Chi dietro a iura, e chi ad aforismi
 sen giva, e chi seguendo sacerdozio,
 e chi regnar per forza o per sofismi,
e chi rubare, e chi civil negozio;
 chi nel diletto della carne involto
 s'affaticava, e chi si dava all'ozio,
quando, da tutte queste cose sciolto,
 con Beatrice m'era suso in cielo
 cotanto glorïosa-mente accolto.
Poi che ciascuno fu tornato ne lo
 punto del cerchio in che avanti s'era,
 fermossi, come a candellier candelo.

This one, from whom your gaze will then return to me,
   is the light of a spirit whose serious
   thoughts made death seem to come too slowly for him:[25]
it is the eternal light of Sigier,[26]
   who, lecturing in the street of straw,[27]
   syllogized enviable truths."[28]
Then, just like a clock that calls us
   at the hour when the bride of God[29] arises
   to sing matins to her Bridegroom so He will love her,
one part of its mechanism pulling or pressing another,
   ringing "ding, ding" with such a sweet sound
   that the well-disposed spirit swells with love;
in the same guise I saw the glorious circle of souls
   in motion, blending voices in a harmony
   of such sweetness that it can only be known
there, where joy is eternalized.

Canto XI

O foolish preoccupations of mortals,
   how imperfect is the reasoning
   that makes you beat your wings at such a low level!
One man was pursuing the law; another, medical aphorisms;[1]
   another was pursuing the priesthood;
   and others, power through force or through sophistry;[2]
one man was out for theft; another, out for business;
   one was wearying himself wrapped in the pleasures
   of the flesh, and another was indulging in leisure,
all the time that I, freed from all these things,
   was up in heaven with Beatrice,
   being welcomed so gloriously.
After each spirit was back at the
   point of the circle that he had previously occupied,
   they halted, erect as a candle in its stick.

---

25. He was impatient to learn the whole truth in Paradise.   26. Sigier of Brabant
(13th century).   27. The Rue du Fouarre in the Latin Quarter in Paris. Scholars who
believe that Dante visited Paris depend partially on this line; how else, they ask, could
he have known this street?   28. Or: "truths hostile to one another"; or: "truths that
made him hated."   29. The Church.   1. The reference is to the *Aphorisms* of
Hippocrates.   2. Or: "through politics or through scholarly endeavors."

E io senti' dentro a quella lumera
   che pria m'avea parlato, sorridendo
   incominciar, faccendosi più mera:
«Così com'io del suo raggio resplendo,
   sì, riguardando nella luce etterna,
   li tuoi pensieri onde cagioni apprendo.
Tu dubbi, e hai voler che si ricerna
   in sì aperta e 'n sì distesa lingua
   lo dicer mio, ch'al tuo sentir si sterna,
ove dinanzi, dissi 'U' ben s'impingua',
   e là u' dissi 'Non surse il secondo';
   e qui è uopo che ben si distingua.
La provedenza, che governa il mondo
   con quel consiglio nel quale ogni aspetto
   creato è vinto pria che vada al fondo,
però che andasse ver lo suo diletto
   la sposa di colui ch'ad alte grida,
   disposò lei col sangue benedetto,
in sè sicura e anche a lui più fida,
   due principi ordinò in suo favore,
   che quinci e quindi le fosser per guida.
L'un fu tutto serafico in ardore;
   l'altro per sapïenza in terra fue
   di cherubica luce uno splendore.
Dell'un dirò, però che d'amendue
   si dice l'un pregiando, quale uom prende,
   perch'ad un fine fuor l'opere sue.
Intra Tupino e l'acqua che discende
   del colle eletto dal beato Ubaldo,
   fertile costa d'alto monte pende,
onde Perugia sente freddo e caldo
   da Porta Sole; e di retro le piange
   per grave giogo Nocera con Gualdo.
Di questa costa, là dov'ella frange
   più sua rattezza, nacque al mondo un sole,
   come fa questo tal volta di Gange.

And from within that light which had first
  addressed me,[3] I heard the smiling
  words, as it grew more luminous:
"Just as I shine by its rays,
  thus, by gazing into the eternal light,
  I can tell from where your thoughts are derived.
You are in doubt, and you want my sayings
  to be explained again in language so lucid
  and plain that they become level with your perception—that is,
why I said earlier, 'where they grow good and fat,'
  and why I said, 'no second man rose so high';
  and now clear distinctions must be made.
Providence, which rules the world
  with that wisdom by which the sight of all
  created things is overcome before it can plumb its depths,
in order that the bride[4] of the One who, crying loudly,
  wed her with His blessed blood
  might journey toward her Darling
feeling self-confident and also more faithful to Him,
  ordained two princes[5] in her behalf
  to guide her on this side and that.
One of them was completely seraphic in his glowing love;
  the other, through his wisdom, was on earth
  a splendor of cherubic light.
I shall speak about one of them,[6] because both
  are spoken of when one is praised, no matter which,
  as they both worked toward a single end.
Between the Tupino and the river[7] that runs down
  from the hill[8] chosen by the blessed Ubaldo[9]
  a fertile slope descends the high mountain[10]
from which Perugia feels the cold and the heat
  through its Sun Gate; and, behind the mountain,
  Nocera and Gualdo[11] weep because of the weighty yoke.[12]
From this slope, where it most fully
  leaves off its steepness, a sun was born to the world,
  just as this sun, where we are, is sometimes born from the Ganges.[13]

---

3. Saint Thomas Aquinas. 4. The Church. 5. Saint Francis of Assisi and Saint Dominic. 6. Saint Francis (1182–1226). 7. The Chiascio. 8. The hill of Gubbio. 9. For his hermitage. 10. Mount Subiaso. 11. Towns. 12. The yoke of the mountains or of political oppression. 13. The sun rises from the easternmost part of the world at the spring equinox.

Però chi d'esso loco fa parole,
   non dica Ascesi, chè direbbe corto,
   ma Orïente, se proprio dir vole.
Non era ancor molto lontan dall'orto,
   ch'el cominciò a far sentir la terra
   della sua gran virtute alcun conforto;
chè per tal donna, giovinetto, in guerra
   del padre corse, a cui, come alla morte,
   la porta del piacer nessun diserra;
e dinanzi alla sua spirital corte
   et coram patre le si fece unito;
   poscia di dì in dì l'amò più forte.
Questa, privata del primo marito,
   millecent'anni e più dispetta e scura
   fino a costui si stette sanza invito;
nè valse udir che la trovò sicura
   con Amiclate, al suon della sua voce,
   colui ch'a tutto 'l mondo fè paura;
nè valse esser costante nè feroce,
   sì che, dove Maria rimase giuso,
   ella con Cristo pianse in su la croce.
Ma perch'io non proceda troppo chiuso,
   Francesco e Povertà per questi amanti
   prendi oramai nel mio parlar diffuso.
La lor concordia e i lor lieti sembianti,
   amore e maraviglia e dolce sguardo
   facìeno esser cagion di pensier santi;
tanto che 'l venerabile Bernardo
   si scalzò prima, e dietro a tanta pace
   corse e, correndo, li parve esser tardo.
Oh ignota ricchezza! oh ben ferace!
   Scalzasi Egidio, scalzasi Silvestro
   dietro allo sposo, sì la sposa piace.
Indi sen va quel padre e quel maestro
   con la sua donna e con quella famiglia
   che già legava l'umile capestro.

Therefore, whoever speaks about that place
  should call it not 'Ascesi,'[14] for he would be saying too little,
  but 'Dayspring,' if he wishes to give it its right name.
He was not yet far distant from his rising
  when he began making the earth experience
  some consolation thanks to his great holy influence;
for, as a young man, he entered into hostilities with his father
  for the sake of a lady to whom no one opens
  the door of his pleasure, any more than to death itself;
and in the face of his local spiritual court,[15]
  and with his father as witness, he united himself to her;
  afterwards, from day to day he loved her more strongly.
She, widowed of her first Husband,
  rejected and obscured for eleven hundred years and more,
  had remained uninvited until he came along;
she derived no benefit from the report that
  the man who frightened the entire world
  found her fearless, along with Amyclas, at the sound of his voice;[16]
nor did it do her any good to be constant and unsubdued
  to the extent that, while Mary remained below at the foot,
  she wept along with Christ on the Cross itself.
But, in order that I do not continue speaking too obscurely,
  now, in my lengthy discourse, take
  Francis and Poverty to be these two lovers.
Their concord and their joyful looks,
  their love and admiration and tender glances,
  made them the cause of holy thoughts;
so much so that the venerable Bernard[17]
  was the first to go barefoot and run after
  such great peace; and, though running, he felt slow.
Oh, unsuspected wealth! Oh, productive property!
  Egidio does barefoot, Silvestro goes barefoot
  following the bridegroom, so pleasing is the bride.
From there that father and teacher departs
  with his lady and with those followers
  who were already girding themselves with the humble rope.

---

14. An old form of Assisi that can be read as "I have ascended." 15. The court of
the bishop of Assisi. 16. The poor fisherman Amyclas was totally unconcerned when
Julius Caesar launched the civil wars. 17. An early disciple of the saint, like the two
mentioned four lines later.

Nè li gravò viltà di cor le ciglia
　　per esser fi' di Pietro Bernardone,
　　nè per parer dispetto a maraviglia;
ma regalmente sua dura intenzione
　　ad Innocenzio aperse, e da lui ebbe
　　primo sigillo a sua religïone.
Poi che la gente poverella crebbe
　　dietro a costui, la cui mirabil vita
　　meglio in gloria del ciel si canterebbe,
di seconda corona redimita
　　fu per Onorio dall'Etterno Spiro
　　la santa voglia d'esto archimandrita.
E poi che, per la sete del martiro,
　　nella presenza del Soldan superba
　　predicò Cristo e li altri che 'l seguiro,
e per trovare a conversione acerba
　　troppo la gente, per non stare indarno,
　　reddissi al frutto dell'italica erba,
nel crudo sasso intra Tevero e Arno
　　da Cristo prese l'ultimo sigillo,
　　che le sue membra due anni portarno.
Quando a colui ch'a tanto ben sortillo
　　piacque di trarlo suso alla mercede
　　ch'el meritò nel suo farsi pusillo,
a' frati suoi, sì com'a giuste rede,
　　raccomandò la donna sua più cara,
　　e comandò che l'amassero a fede;
e del suo grembo l'anima preclara
　　mover si volse, tornando al suo regno,
　　e al suo corpo non volse altra bara.
Pensa oramai qual fu colui che degno
　　collega fu a mantener la barca
　　di Pietro in alto mar per dritto segno;
e questo fu il nostro patrïarca;
　　per che, qual segue lui com'el comanda,
　　discerner puoi che buone merce carca.

Abjectness of heart never weighed down his brows
    either because he was the son of Pietro Bernardone,[18]
    or because he saw himself wondrously despised;
but regally he proclaimed his difficult intentions
    to Innocent,[19] and obtained from him
    the first seal of approval for his order.
After the folk dedicated to poverty grew in numbers
    as they followed that man, whose marvelous life
    it would be better to sing in the glory of heaven,[20]
the holy wishes of this arch-shepherd
    were crowned a second time
    by the Holy Spirit, acting through Honorius.[21]
And after he had felt a thirst for martyrdom
    and had preached in the haughty presence of the Sultan
    about Christ and those others who followed His steps,
and, finding those people too
    unripe for conversion, so as not to remain there for nothing,
    had returned to the fruitful field of Italy,
on the rugged crag[22] between the Tiber and the Arno
    he received from Christ the ultimate seal,
    which his body bore for his last two years.
When He who destined him for such great good
    was pleased to raise him upward for the reward
    he had earned by making himself lowly,
to his brothers, as to rightful heirs,
    he commended the lady who was dearest to him,
    commanding them to love her faithfully;
and from his bosom his illustrious soul
    decided to depart and return to its realm,
    and desired no further coffin for its body.
Just think now how great that man[23] was who was his worthy
    colleague in guiding Saint Peter's
    boat on the high seas with the proper goal in view;
and this last-mentioned man was our founder;
    so that whoever follows the rule he established—
    you can tell what good merchandise is in his cargo.

---

18. His father was a merchant.   19. Pope Innocent III gave the saint permission to found his order.   20. Meaning either "in the highest heaven" or "for the glory of heaven"; there are other interpretations.   21. Pope Honorius III issued a bull granting the order further privileges.   22. Mount Alvernia.   23. Saint Dominic.

Ma 'l suo peculio di nova vivanda
    è fatto ghiotto, sì ch'esser non puote
    che per diversi salti non si spanda;
e quanto le sue pecore remote
    e vagabunde più da esso vanno,
    più tornano all'ovil di latte vote.
Ben son di quelle che temono 'l danno
    e stringonsi al pastor; ma son sì poche,
    che le cappe fornisce poco panno.
Or se le mie parole non son fioche
    e se la tua audienza è stata attenta,
    se ciò ch'è detto alla mente rivoche,
in parte fia la tua voglia contenta,
    perchè vedrai la pianta onde si scheggia,
    e vedra' il corregger che argomenta
'U' ben s'impingua, se non si vaneggia'.»

[SUMMARY OF CANTO XII: A second ring of dancing and singing bright spirits surrounds the first one. One of the newcomers undertakes to tell the life of Saint Dominic. Born in Spain, he was marked out as a great spiritual leader from his infancy. A great teacher, he combated heresy. The Franciscan order is now facing the same perils as the Dominican. The speaker identifies himself as Saint Bonaventure, and introduces Dante to a number of other Franciscans and theologians of earlier centuries.

SUMMARY OF CANTO XIII: The two rings of bright spirits sing about the Trinity. Then Saint Thomas Aquinas picks up where he left off at the end of Canto XI, and answers Dante's unspoken question about Solomon: why he should be considered wiser than Adam or Christ, at whose creation the universe was in a perfect condition to form the most excellent beings (God's power pervades the entire universe, but the qualities of individual creatures depend on various natural circumstances as well). Dante is right when it comes to Adam and Christ, but the statement about Solomon referred solely to the wisdom that a king needs in order to rule his realm; Thomas's exact words about Solomon included the verb "rose"—Solomon had to *rise* to his height, unlike Adam and Christ. Dante is warned never to make hasty

But his flock has become greedy
   for new kinds of nourishment, so that it is unavoidable
   for them to be scattered over various precipitous heights;[24]
and the farther his straying, vagabond
   sheep grow distant from him,
   the more do they return to the fold empty of milk.
Yes, there are some who fear this harm
   and remain close to their shepherd; but they are so few
   that only a little cloth is needed to supply their robes.
Now, if my words are not feeble
   and if you have listened attentively,
   if you call to mind what has been said,
your wishes will be partially[25] satisfied,
   because you will see where the tree has been splintered,[26]
   and you will understand the meaning of my proviso in saying[27]
'where they grow good and fat *if they do not go astray.*'"

---

judgments on the basis of an insufficient examination of all factors involved—a dangerous procedure.

SUMMARY OF CANTO XIV: Dante has a flash of thought that is perceived
and enunciated by Beatrice: When reunited with their bodies at the Last
Judgment, will these heavenly souls be more encumbered than they now
are? Solomon himself replies: When reunited with their bodies, they will be
more complete and perfect; they will enjoy greater bliss, and their sensory
organs will be able to endure their even greater brightness. Now Dante
catches a glimpse of yet a third outer circle of spirits, and Beatrice raises him
to the fifth heaven, that of Mars. Against the red background of the planet a
white cross is outlined. First Dante sees the image of Christ flashing on it;
then he sees that the cross is covered with moving bright spirits.

SUMMARY OF CANTO XV: These spirits on Mars are warriors of God. One
of them descends from the white cross like a shooting star and welcomes
Dante as a descendant of his, whose coming he had been led to expect.
Asked by Dante to identify himself, the spirit says he is his great-great-grand-
father, whose son was the Alighieri that gave the family its surname. He describes the simple, pure life of Florence in those good old days. His name is

---

24. Or: "various wild pastures."   25. Because so far Saint Thomas has addressed
only one of the two questions he read in Dante's mind.   26. "Where the bad
Dominicans have broken from the good," or "where the rottenness of the Dominicans
is located," or "where I have broken off the splinters of my rebuke."   27. This line has
been interpreted differently, but the other versions are much more far-fetched.

Cacciaguida and he was knighted by the Holy Roman Emperor Conrad III
while serving in the Second Crusade (ca. 1147), in which he was killed.

SUMMARY OF CANTO XVI: Dante, at whose family pride Beatrice smiles, asks
to hear more about old Florence. The number of men able to bear arms was

Canto XVII

Qual venne a Climenè, per accertarsi
   di ciò ch'avea incontro a sè udito,
   quei ch'ancor fa li padri ai figli scarsi;
tal era io, e tal era sentito
   e da Beatrice e dalla santa lampa
   che pria per me avea mutato sito.
Per che mia donna «Manda fuor la vampa
   del tuo disio» mi disse, «sì ch'ella esca
   segnata bene della interna stampa;
non perchè nostra conoscenza cresca
   per tuo parlare, ma perchè t'ausi
   a dir la sete, sì che l'uom ti mesca.»
«O cara piota mia che sì t'insusi,
   che come veggion le terrene menti
   con capere in trïangol due ottusi,
così vedi le cose contingenti
   anzi che sieno in sè, mirando il punto
   a cui tutti li tempi son presenti;
mentre ch'io era a Virgilio congiunto
   su per lo monte che l'anime cura
   e discendendo nel mondo defunto,
dette mi fuor di mia vita futura
   parole gravi, avvegna ch'io mi senta
   ben tetragono ai colpi di ventura.
Per che la voglia mia saría contenta
   d'intender qual fortuna mi s'appressa;
   chè saetta prevista vien più lenta.»
Così diss'io a quella luce stessa

only a fifth of what it now is (in 1300), but the city's blood lines were still un-
contaminated with outsiders, and there was no civil strife. Cacciaguida alludes
to the fortunes of an extremely large number of Florentine families (this is the
canto with the most exclusively "local interest" in the entire work).]

Canto XVII

Just as the man who still makes fathers cautious of their sons
    came to Clymene to learn the truth
    about what he had heard said against him;[1]
in such a state was I, and so I was felt to be
    both by Beatrice and by the holy light
    that had earlier changed its place for my sake.[2]
Therefore my lady said to me: "Send forth
    the flame of your desire, so that it issues
    well marked with your inner stamp;
not that our knowledge will increase
    by your speaking, but in order that you grow accustomed
    to express your thirst, so that people will offer you drink."
"O my dear ancestor, you that dwell so high in heaven
    that, just as earthly minds see
    that a triangle cannot contain two obtuse angles,
you can see contingent, casual occurrences
    before they come to be, by gazing at the Point
    to which all times are as the present;
while I was together with Vergil
    upon the mountain that heals souls
    and down in the dead world,
weighty words were spoken to me
    about my future life,[3] although I feel that I am
    foursquare and solid in the face of chance's blows.
Therefore, my desire would be satisfied
    if I could hear what kind of fortune is drawing near me;
    for an arrow foreseen arrives more slowly."
Thus I spoke to that very same light

---

1. Phaethon asked his mother Clymene whether he was really the son of the sun
god. When he insisted on driving the sun's chariot, he came to grief.   2. Cacciaguida,
who had left his place on the white cross to converse with Dante.   3. Various predic-
tions of exile.

che pria m'avea parlato; e come volle
Beatrice, fu la mia voglia confessa.
Nè per ambage, in che la gente folle
già s'inviscava pria che fosse anciso
l'Agnel di Dio che le peccata tolle,
ma per chiare parole e con preciso
latin rispuose quello amor paterno,
chiuso e parvente del suo proprio riso:
«La contingenza, che fuor del quaderno
della vostra matera non si stende,
tutta è dipinta nel cospetto etterno:
necessità però quindi non prende
se non come dal viso in che si specchia
nave che per corrente giù discende.
Da indi sì come viene ad orecchia
dolce armonia da organo, mi vene
a vista il tempo che ti s'apparecchia.
Qual si partìo Ippolito d'Atene
per la spietata e perfida noverca,
tal di Fiorenza partir ti convene.
Questo si vuole e questo già si cerca,
e tosto verrà fatto a chi ciò pensa
là dove Cristo tutto dì si merca.
La colpa seguirà la parte offensa
in grido, come suol; ma la vendetta
fia testimonio al ver che la dispensa.
Tu lascerai ogni casa diletta
più caramente; e questo è quello strale
che l'arco dello essilio pria saetta.
Tu proverai sì come sa di sale
lo pane altrui, e come è duro calle
lo scendere e 'l salir per l'altrui scale.
E quel che più ti graverà le spalle,
sarà la compagnia malvagia e scempia
con la qual tu cadrai in questa valle;
che tutta ingrata, tutta matta ed empia
si farà contra te; ma, poco appresso,
ella, non tu, n'avrà rossa la tempia.

which had earlier spoken to me; and, as Beatrice
  wished, my desire was expressed.
Not in those ambiguous terms in which foolish folk
  were once ensnared before the killing of
  the Lamb of God who takes away our sins,
but in clear words and precise
  speech that loving father replied,
  who was both enclosed and visible in his own smiling flame:
"Contingency, which does not extend
  beyond the volume of your material world,
  is entirely depicted in the gaze of the Eternal:
but contingent things do not thereby become necessarily existent,
  any more than a boat descending a stream
  derives its reality from the eyes in which it is mirrored.
Therefore, just as sweet harmony reaches
  the ear from an organ, I see
  before me the times that are readying themselves for you.
Just as Hippolytus left Athens
  because of his pitiless, treacherous stepmother,[4]
  in the same way you must leave Florence.
This is desired and this is already being planned,
  and it will soon be accomplished by the man[5] who has it in mind
  in the place where Christ is daily bought and sold.[6]
The blame will attach to the injured party
  in the common report, as usual; but the vindication
  will bear witness to the truth that dispenses it.
You will leave behind everything you cherish
  most dearly; this is the arrow
  that the bow of exile shoots first.
You will learn what a salty flavor
  other people's bread has, and what a hard path it is
  to climb up and down other people's stairs.
But what will place the heaviest burden on your back
  will be the malevolent and foolish company
  with which you will fall into this low estate;
for they will become totally ungrateful to you,
  wild and godless; but, soon afterward,
  they, and not you, will have their temples flushed with shame.

---

4. Phaedra, whose amorous advances were rebuffed by her stepson, slandered him
and had him exiled.   5. Pope Boniface VIII.   6. The Vatican.

Di sua bestialità il suo processo
  farà la prova; sì ch'a te fia bello
  averti fatta parte per te stesso.
Lo primo tuo refugio, il primo ostello
  sarà la cortesia del gran Lombardo
  che 'n su la scala porta il santo uccello;
ch'in te avrà sì benigno riguardo,
  che del fare e del chieder, tra voi due,
  fia primo quel che, tra gli altri, è più tardo.
Con lui vedrai colui che 'mpresso fue,
  nascendo, sì da questa stella forte,
  che notabili fien l'opere sue.
Non se ne son le genti ancora accorte
  per la novella età, chè pur nove anni
  son queste rote intorno di lui torte;
ma pria che 'l Guasco l'alto Arrigo inganni,
  parran faville della sua virtute
  in non curar d'argento nè d'affanni.
Le sue magnificenze conosciute
  saranno ancora, sì che' suoi nemici
  non ne potran tener le lingue mute.
A lui t'aspetta ed a' suoi benefici;
  per lui fia trasmutata molta gente,
  cambiando condizion ricchi e mendici.
E portera'ne scritto nella mente
  di lui, e nol dirai»; e disse cose
  incredibili a quei che fien presente.
Poi giunse: «Figlio, queste son le chiose
  di quel che ti fu detto; ecco le 'nsidie
  che dietro a pochi giri son nascose.
Non vo' però ch'a' tuoi vicini invidie,
  poscia che s'infutura la tua vita
  vie più là che 'l punir di lor perfidie.»
Poi che, tacendo, si mostrò spedita
  l'anima santa di metter la trama

Their own proceedings will furnish the proof
   of their bestial nature; so that it will be a fine thing for you
   that you became a party of one.[7]
Your first refuge, your first lodging
   will be due to the courtesy of the great North Italian
   whose armorial bearing is the sacred bird on the ladder;[8]
for he will have such benevolent regard for you
   that, between you two, when it comes to granting and requesting,
   that will precede which, among others, follows.
With him you will see the man[9] who was so influenced
   at birth by this powerful planet[10]
   that his deeds will be noteworthy.
People have not yet become aware of this
   because he is so young, since for only nine years
   these spheres have revolved around him;
but before the Gascon[11] deceives noble Henry,[12]
   sparks of his virtue will become apparent
   through his indifference to money and labors.
His magnificent ways will be known
   in the future, so that even his enemies
   will be unable to keep their tongues silent about it.
Entrust yourself to him and to his benevolence;
   because of him many people will be transformed,
   rich men and beggars exchanging their status.
And you will bear this written in your mind
   about him, but will not speak it"; and he told me things
   unbelievable even to those who will witness them.
Then he added: "My son, these are the explanations
   of what you were told; this is the ambush
   that is hidden behind merely a few revolutions of the sun.
But I do not want you to hate your neighbors,
   because your life will extend
   far beyond the punishment of their treachery."
After his silence showed that the holy soul
   had finished adding the woof

---

7. The Whites with whom Dante went into exile in 1302 failed in their attack on Florence two years later.   8. Bartolommeo della Scala, lord of Verona.   9. Bartolommeo's brother, Cangrande della Scala (see also *Hell*, Canto I, note 9).   10. Mars, where this conversation is taking place.   11. Pope Clement V.   12. Holy Roman Emperor Henry VII, invited to Italy by Clement, who then turned against him.

in quella tela ch'io le porsi ordita,
io cominciai, come colui che brama,
 dubitando, consiglio da persona
 che vede e vuol dirittamente e ama:
«Ben veggio, padre mio, sì come sprona
 lo tempo verso me, per colpo darmi
 tal, ch'è più grave a chi più s'abbandona;
per che di provedenza è buon ch'io m'armi,
 sì che, se 'l loco m'è tolto più caro,
 io non perdessi li altri per miei carmi.
Giù per lo mondo sanza fine amaro,
 e per lo monte del cui bel cacume
 li occhi della mia donna mi levaro,
e poscia per lo ciel di lume in lume,
 ho io appreso quel che s'io ridico,
 a molti fia sapor di forte agrume;
e s'io al vero son timido amico,
 temo di perder viver tra coloro
 che questo tempo chiameranno antico.»
La luce in che rideva il mio tesoro
 ch'io trovai lì, si fè prima corusca,
 quale a raggio di sole specchio d'oro;
indi rispuose: «Coscïenza fusca
 o della propria o dell'altrui vergogna
 pur sentirà la tua parola brusca.
Ma nondimen, rimossa ogni menzogna,
 tutta tua visïon fa manifesta;
 e lascia pur grattar dov'è la rogna.
Chè se la voce tua sarà molesta
 nel primo gusto, vital nutrimento
 lascerà poi, quando sarà digesta.
Questo tuo grido farà come vento,
 che le più alte cime più percuote;
 e ciò non fa d'onor poco argomento.
Però ti son mostrate in queste rote,
 nel monte e nella valle dolorosa
 pur l'anime che son di fama note,
che l'animo di quel ch'ode, non posa
 nè ferma fede per essemplo ch'aia
 la sua radice incognita ed ascosa,
nè per altro argomento che non paia.»

to the web whose warp I had set up for him,
I began, like a man in doubt
   and eager for counsel from a person
   who has foresight, a proper mind-set, and love:
"I see clearly, father, how time
   is spurring toward me to give me a blow
   of the type that is weightier for whoever is more heedless;
therefore it behooves me to arm myself with foresight
   so that, if the city dearest to me is taken from me,
   I do not destroy my chances in the rest because of my poems.
Down in the realm that is eternally bitter,
   and on the mountain from whose beautiful peak
   my lady's eyes raised me,
and afterwards in heaven, from one light to the next,
   I have learned things which, if I report them,
   will leave many people with a very sour taste;
but, if I am a timid friend of the truth,
   I fear losing my chance to live among those
   who will call these days the old days."
The light within which that treasure of mine I had found there
   was smiling, first began to scintillate
   like a golden mirror struck by a sunbeam,
then replied: "Only a conscience darkened
   by its own shame or that of another
   will find your words tart.
But, just the same, with all lies set aside,
   proclaim everything that you have seen;
   and just let them scratch where they itch.
For, if your words will be bothersome
   at first taste, they will leave behind
   vital nourishment when fully digested.
This outcry of yours will be like a wind
   that strikes hardest at the summits that are highest;
   and that is no small proof of honor.
That is why you are being shown, in these spheres,
   on the mountain, and in the valley of sorrow,
   only the souls that have a great reputation,
because the listener's soul does not establish
   or strengthen its belief on the basis of an example that has
   an unknown, hidden root,
or on any other line of reasoning that is not immediately apparent."

[SUMMARY OF CANTO XVIII: Beatrice points out other warriors for the faith who have their places on the white cross: Joshua, Judah Maccabee, Charlemagne, Roland, and others. Seeing Beatrice more beautiful than ever, Dante realizes he has arrived in the sixth heaven, that of Jupiter, which has a white glow. Here, a number of souls form the letters of the Latin text of "Love righteousness, you that judge the earth." Then the final M of the Latin phrase is transformed into the head and neck of a Roman imperial eagle. Dante makes the fervent wish that similar justice may prevail on earth.

SUMMARY OF CANTO XIX: The righteous rulers who form the eagle speak with a single voice. Intuiting the nature of a question Dante wishes to raise, they explain that the reason for the exclusion of the virtuous heathen from Paradise is hidden within God's eternal plan and is inaccessible to mortals. On the other hand, at the Last Judgment, many who now proclaim their faith in Christ will be thrust farther from Him than some of the heathen. There follows a list of recent Christian rulers to whom that statement applies.

SUMMARY OF CANTO XX: Between two bursts of multivoiced song, the eagle tells Dante, in a single voice, that the six noblest lights in it are those forming its pupil (King David) and eyebrow (Trajan—for whom see the summary of Canto X of *Purgatory*—Hezekiah, Constantine, William the Good of the Two Sicilies, and the Trojan Ripheus mentioned in the *Aeneid*). Trajan and Ripheus are there, surprisingly to Dante, because they actually died in the true faith. Predestination is naturally a mystery to us on earth, but even the souls already in Paradise do not know exactly whom God will save. This makes them glad, because they are bowing to His will.

SUMMARY OF CANTO XXI: Beatrice now raises Dante to the seventh heaven,

---

Canto XXIII

Come l'augello, intra l'amate fronde,
    posato al nido de' suoi dolci nati
    la notte che le cose ci nasconde,
che, per veder li aspetti disïati
    e per trovar lo cibo onde li pasca,
    in che gravi labor li sono aggrati,
previene il tempo in su aperta frasca,
    e con ardente affetto il sole aspetta,
    fiso guardando pur che l'alba nasca;
così la donna mia stava eretta
    e attenta, rivolta inver la plaga
    sotto la quale il sol mostra men fretta:

that of Saturn, but this time does not smile at him because he would be unable to stand the radiance. Dante sees a golden ladder, on which numerous bright lights are descending from above. One of them approaches and, asked by Dante why the poet no longer hears music, says that he is not yet strong enough to hear the now more rarefied music. Dante asks this spirit why it was particularly assigned to welcome him. The reply: only God knows. The spirit identifies himself as Peter Damian, an 11th-century writer on Church discipline who became a cardinal shortly before his death; he laments current Church affairs. Dante now hears a loud, but unintelligible, cry from the spirits on the ladder.

SUMMARY OF CANTO XXII: Beatrice explains that the cry was one calling for divine vengeance. Dante now is addressed by Saint Benedict, the 6th-century founder of the Benedictine order, who is accompanied by many souls of contemplative Christians. Dante asks to see him in his absolutely uncloaked form; this will be possible in the highest heaven, where everything attains perfection. That is where the top of the ladder is, but the Church is now so degenerate that no one is any longer ascending that ladder. All the lights are now wafted back upward, as by a whirlwind. Beatrice thrusts Dante up the ladder into the constellation of Gemini, his natal sign. He is now in the eighth heaven, that of the fixed stars. Beatrice says that Dante is so near his goal that, before continuing, he should purify his eyes by looking back down at the path they have traveled. He sees the seven heavens he has passed, and, below them, the earth, no bigger than a threshing floor, with the course of every river fully visible.]

Canto XXIII

Just as a bird amid the foliage it loves,
   resting on the nest of its sweet offspring
   during the night, which hides all objects from us,
wishing to see their longed-for appearance
   and to find the food wherewith to nourish them,
   in doing which it finds even heavy toil a pleasure,
anticipates the hour at the open treetop
   and with ardent love awaits the sun,
   staring in hopes that the dawn will break;
in like manner my lady was standing erect
   and attentive, looking toward the quarter of the sky
   beneath which the sun shows least haste:[1]

---

1. Toward the meridian, directly overhead; or: "toward the south."

sì che, veggendola io sospesa e vaga,
   fecimi qual è quei che disïando
   altro vorrìa, e sperando s'appaga.
Ma poco fu tra uno e altro quando,
   del mio attender, dico, e del vedere
   lo ciel venir più e più rischiarando.
E Beatrice disse: «Ecco le schiere
   del triunfo di Cristo e tutto il frutto
   ricolto del girar di queste spere!»
Parìemi che 'l suo viso ardesse tutto,
   e li occhi avea di letizia sì pieni,
   che passar men convien sanza costrutto.
Quale ne' plenilunii sereni
   Trivïa ride tra le ninfe etterne
   che dipingon lo ciel per tutti i seni,
vidi sopra migliaia di lucerne
   un sol che tutte quante l'accendea,
   come fa il nostro le viste superne;
e per la viva luce trasparea
   la lucente sustanza tanto chiara
   nel viso mio, che non la sostenea.
Oh Beatrice dolce guida e cara!
   Ella mi disse: «Quel che ti sobranza
   è virtù da cui nulla si ripara.
Quivi è la sapïenza e la possanza
   ch'aprì le strade tra 'l cielo e la terra,
   onde fu già sì lunga disïanza.»
Come foco di nube si diserra
   per dilatarsi sì che non vi cape,
   e fuor di sua natura in giù s'atterra,
la mente mia così, tra quelle dape
   fatta più grande, di sè stessa uscìo,
   e che si fesse rimembrar non sape.
«Apri li occhi e riguarda qual son io:
   tu hai vedute cose, che possente
   se' fatto a sostener lo riso mio.»
Io era come quei che si risente
   di visïone oblita e che s'ingegna

so that, seeing her in suspense and eager,
    I myself became like a man who, in his yearning,
        would like something new and comforts himself with hopes.
But only a little time passed between one moment and the other—
    I mean, between my waiting and my seeing
        the sky grow brighter and brighter.
And Beatrice said: "Here are the companies
    of Christ's triumph and all the fruit
        harvested from the turning of these spheres!"[2]
It seemed to me as if her face were all ablaze,
    and her eyes were so full of joy
        that I must pass over this without further comment.
Just as, on clear nights of full moon,
    Trivia smiles among the eternal nymphs
        that ornament the sky on all sides,[3]
I saw, above thousands of lights,
    a Sun that was igniting them all,
        just as ours illuminates the higher apparitions;[4]
and through the vivid light the glowing Substance
    shone so brightly
        onto my face that I was unable to endure it.
Oh, Beatrice, my sweet, dear guide!
    She said to me: "That which overcomes you
        is a force against which there is no defense.
Here is the Wisdom and the Power
    that opened the roads between heaven and earth,
        and that was once longed after for such a long time."
Just as fiery lightning is loosed from a cloud
    because its vapors have so expanded that they cannot be contained in it,
        and, contrary to its nature,[5] heads down toward the earth,
in like manner my mind, having expanded
    amid that feast, became beside itself,
        and cannot remember what happened to it.
"Open your eyes and see what I look like now:
    you have seen things that have made you
        able to withstand my smiling face."
I was like a man returning to his senses
    out of a dream he has forgotten, and striving

2. All the saints and elect.   3. The moon shines among the stars.   4. The stars.
5. Fire should theoretically head upward toward the sphere of fire.

indarno di ridurlasi alla mente,
quand'io udi' questa proferta, degna
   di tanto grato, che mai non si stingue
   del libro che 'l preterito rassegna.
Se mo sonasser tutte quelle lingue
   che Polimnìa con le suore fero
   del latte lor dolcissimo più pingue,
per aiutarmi, al millesmo del vero
   non si verrìa, cantando il santo riso
   e quanto il santo aspetto facea mero;
e così, figurando il paradiso,
   convien saltar lo sacrato poema,
   come chi trova suo cammin riciso.
Ma chi pensasse il ponderoso tema
   e l'omero mortal che se ne carca,
   nol biasmerebbe se sott'esso trema:
non è pileggio da picciola barca
   quel che fendendo va l'ardita prora,
   nè da nocchier ch'a sè medesmo parca.
«Perchè la faccia mia sì t'innamora,
   che tu non ti rivolgi al bel giardino
   che sotto i raggi di Cristo s'infiora?
Quivi è la rosa in che il verbo divino
   carne si fece; quivi son li gigli
   al cui odor si prese il buon cammino.»
Così Beatrice; e io, che a' suoi consigli
   tutto era pronto, ancora mi rendei
   alla battaglia de' debili cigli.
Come a raggio di sol che puro mei
   per fratta nube già prato di fiori
   vider, coverti d'ombra, li occhi miei;
vid'io così più turbe di splendori,
   fulgorate di su da raggi ardenti,
   sanza veder principio di fulgori.
O benigna vertù che sì li 'mprenti,
   su t'essaltasti, per largirmi loco
   alli occhi lì che non t'eran possenti.

in vain to bring it back to mind,
when I heard that utterance, which was deserving
    of such great gratitude that it will never be erased
    from the book that records the past.
If all those tongues which Polyhymnia[6]
    and her sisters made fatter
    with their very sweet milk were now to speak out
in my aid, they would not arrive at
    a thousandth part of the truth while singing of that holy smile
    and how resplendent it made her[7] holy face;
and so, in describing Paradise,
    the sacred poem must skip over this,
    like a man who finds his path interrupted by gaps.
But any one who took into consideration the weighty theme,
    and the mortal shoulder that is laden with it,
    would not blame it for trembling beneath it:
it is no route for a tiny boat
    that my bold prow is now cleaving through,
    nor one for a steersman who spares himself.
"Why does my face so enamor you
    that you do not turn toward the beautiful garden
    that is blossoming beneath the rays of Christ?
Here is the Rose in which the divine Word
    made Itself flesh; here are the lilies[8]
    following whose fragrance man took the proper road."
Thus spoke Beatrice; and I, fully obedient
    to her instructions, once again returned
    to the warfare of my weak eyes.
Just as, in a pure sunbeam issuing
    from a rent cloud, my eyes,
    covered with shade, once saw a flowery meadow;
in like manner I now saw troops of splendors
    illuminated in flashes from above by burning rays,
    although I could not see the source of the flashing.
O benevolent Power that imprints them thus,
    You rose aloft to grant me a place there
    for my eyes, which were not strong enough for You.[9]

---

6. The muse of lyric poetry; those whom she and her sisters nourished are the poets.
7. Beatrice's.   8. The Apostles.   9. Christ has returned to the Empyrean; Dante can now look at those who came with Him.

Il nome del bel fior ch'io sempre invoco
    e mane e sera, tutto mi ristrinse
    l'animo ad avvisar lo maggior foco.
E come ambo le luci mi dipinse
    il quale e il quanto della viva stella
    che là su vince, come qua giù vinse,
per entro il cielo scese una facella,
    formata in cerchio a guisa di corona,
    e cinsela e girossi intorno ad ella.
Qualunque melodia più dolce sona
    qua giù e più a sè l'anima tira,
    parrebbe nube che squarciata tona,
comparata al sonar di quella lira
    onde si coronava il bel zaffiro
    del quale il ciel più chiaro s'inzaffira.
«Io sono amore angelico, che giro
    l'alta letizia che spira del ventre
    che fu albergo del nostro disiro;
e girerommi, donna del ciel, mentre
    che seguirai tuo figlio, e farai dia
    più la spera suprema perchè li entre.»
Così la circulata melodia
    si sigillava, e tutti li altri lumi
    facean sonar lo nome di Maria.
Lo real manto di tutti i volumi
    del mondo, che più ferve e più s'avviva
    nell'alito di Dio e nei costumi,
avea sopra di noi l'interna riva
    tanto distante, che la sua parvenza,
    là dov'io era, ancor non appariva:
però non ebber li occhi miei potenza
    di seguitar la coronata fiamma
    che si levò appresso sua semenza.
E come fantolin che 'nver la mamma
    tende le braccia, poi che 'l latte prese,
    per l'animo che 'nfin di fuor s'infiamma;
ciascun di quei candori in su si stese

The naming of the beautiful flower[10] that I always invoke,
   morning and evening, compelled my entire
   mind to look at the greatest among the lights.
And when both my eyes received the image
   of the quality and magnitude of the vivid star
   that is victorious in heaven, as it was on earth,
from amid the sky there descended a torch[11]
   shaped like a circle in the guise of a crown,
   and placed itself around her head, revolving all about her.
Whatever melody sounds sweetest
   here on earth, and most attracts our soul,
   would resemble thunder from a riven cloud
when compared with the playing of the lyre[12]
   that wreathed the beautiful sapphire
   with which heaven is more brightly ensapphired.
"I am angelic love, and I encircle
   the lofty joy that emanates from the womb
   that once lodged the object of our desire;
and I shall go on encircling you, lady of heaven, until
   you follow your Son and make more divine
   the highest sphere by entering it."
Thus did the revolving melody
   come to a close, and all the other lights
   made the name of Mary resound.
The royal mantle[13] of all the spheres
   of the universe, which is most fervent and is most enlivened
   by the breath of God and by His activity,
had its inner edge[14] so far
   above us that its appearance,
   from where I stood, was not yet visible:
thus, my eyes did not have the power
   to follow the crowned flame
   that rose aloft after her Seed.
And like a little child who stretches out his arms
   toward his mother after drinking her milk,
   in a blaze of love that is visible even externally;
each one of those white lights extended

---

10. The rose: the Virgin Mary.   11. The archangel Gabriel.   12. Again, Gabriel.
13. The sphere of the Prime Mover.   14. The surface nearest to the eighth heaven,
where Dante is located.

con la sua fiamma, sì che l'alto affetto
  ch'elli avìeno a Maria mi fu palese.
Indi rimaser lì nel mio cospetto,
  'Regina coeli' cantando sì dolce,
  che mai da me non si partì 'l diletto.
Oh quanta è l'ubertà che si soffolce
  in quelle arche ricchissime che foro
  a seminar qua giù buone bobolce!
Quivi si vive e gode del tesoro
  che s'acquistò piangendo nello essilio
  di Babilon, ove si lasciò l'oro.
Quivi triunfa, sotto l'alto filio
  di Dio e di Maria, di sua vittoria,
  e con l'antico e col novo concilio,
colui che tien le chiavi di tal gloria.

[SUMMARY OF CANTO XXIV: Beatrice asks the souls in the eighth heaven to be indulgent to Dante. Saint Peter responds to the appeal, and prepares to examine Dante concerning Faith, as a professor examines a student. Basing himself on Saint Paul, Dante defines Faith as the substance of things hoped for and the argument for things unseen. Asked about the source of his faith, the poet says it was the Bible, further bolstered by Christ's miracles; indeed, if Christianity had conquered without them, that would have been the greatest miracle of all. Asked about the exact content of his faith, Dante says it is belief in one God in three Persons. The poet has passed with flying colors, and Saint Peter blesses him.

SUMMARY OF CANTO XXV: Now Saint James, the patron saint of Spain, examines Dante concerning Hope. Beatrice answers for him, asserting that Dante is particularly well endowed with Hope. Then the poet himself defines Hope as the expectation of future glory; he bases his hope on biblical statements; its specific content is the resurrection of the body and the

---

Canto XXVII

«Al Padre, al Figlio, allo Spirito Santo»
  cominciò «gloria!» tutto il paradiso,
  sì che m'inebriava il dolce canto.

its flame upwards, so that the deep affection
    they had for Mary was evident to me.
Then they remained there in my sight,
    singing the *Regina coeli*[15] so sweetly
    that the pleasure of it has never left me.
Oh, how great is the abundance stored
    in those most rich granaries who were
    good husbandmen while they sowed on earth!
Up here they live and enjoy the treasure
    that was acquired while weeping in exile
    in Babylon, where gold was spurned.
Here, triumphing in his victory,
    beneath the lofty Son of God and Mary,
    and alongside the old and the new council,[16]
is the man who keeps the keys to such great glory.[17]

---

immortality of the soul. Now the group is joined by the apostle John, who
tells Dante that only Jesus and Mary ascended to heaven in the body. Dante
has been blinded by John's radiance.

SUMMARY OF CANTO XXVI: Saint John, assuring Dante that Beatrice will
restore his sight, examines him concerning Love (Charity). Dante states that
his great love, which was kindled by Beatrice, is love for God, which is only
natural, because to know God's supreme goodness is to love Him.
Questioned further, he lists some of the many favors God has done for
mankind. Beatrice heals Dante, who now sees better than ever before, and
catches sight of a newcomer to the group: Adam, who, in response to as-yet-
unspoken questions, tells the poet that he lost Eden specifically because he
disobeyed God, that he lived on earth 930 years, remained in Limbo for
4,302 years, originally spoke a now extinct language—human language
evolves perpetually—and remained in Eden somewhat over six hours.]

Canto XXVII

"To the Father, to the Son, to the Holy Spirit—
    glory!" all of Paradise began to chant
    in such a way that the sacred song intoxicated me.

---

15. "Queen of heaven," a hymn to Mary.   16. Blessed souls from the Old and New
Testaments.   17. Saint Peter.

Ciò ch'io vedeva mi sembiava un riso
dell'universo; per che mia ebbrezza
intrava per l'udire e per lo viso.
Oh gioia! oh ineffabile allegrezza!
oh vita integra d'amore e di pace!
oh sanza brama sicura ricchezza!
Dinanzi alli occhi miei le quattro face
stavano accese, e quella che pria venne
incominciò a farsi più vivace,
e tal nella sembianza sua divenne,
qual diverrebbe Giove, s'elli e Marte
fossero augelli e cambiassersi penne.
La provedenza, che quivi comparte
vice ed officio, nel beato coro
silenzio posto avea da ogni parte,
quand'io udi': «Se io mi trascoloro,
non ti maravigliar; chè, dicend'io,
vedrai trascolorar tutti costoro.
Quelli ch'usurpa in terra il luogo mio,
il luogo mio, il luogo mio, che vaca
nella presenza del Figliuol di Dio,
fatt'ha del cimiterio mio cloaca
del sangue e della puzza; onde 'l perverso
che cadde di qua su, là giù si placa.»
Di quel color che per lo sole avverso
nube dipigne da sera e da mane,
vid'io allora tutto il ciel cosperso.
E come donna onesta che permane
di sè sicura, e per l'altrui fallanza,
pur ascoltando, timida si fane,
così Beatrice trasmutò sembianza;
e tale eclissi credo che 'n ciel fue,
quando patì la suprema possanza.
Poi procedetter le parole sue
con voce tanto da sè trasmutata,
che la sembianza non si mutò piùe;
«Non fu la sposa di Cristo allevata

That which I was beholding seemed to me a smile
   of the universe; and so my intoxication
   was entering through my hearing and my sight.
Oh, joy! Oh, inexpressible happiness!
   Oh, that life made up fully of love and peace!
   Oh, secure wealth unaffected by greed!
Before my eyes the four torches[1]
   were ablaze, and the one that had first approached me[2]
   started to grow brighter,
and in its appearance became the same
   as Jupiter would become if he and Mars
   were birds and exchanged plumage.[3]
Providence, which here distributes
   each task in its proper turn, had imposed silence
   on all sides upon the blessed choir,
when I heard: "If I change color,
   do not be surprised; for, while I speak,
   you will see all the rest change color.
The man who is usurping my place on earth,[4]
   my place, my place, which is vacant
   in the sight of the Son of God,
has turned my burial site into a sewer
   of blood and stench; so that the rebellious angel
   who fell from up here is satisfied down below."
In that color which, the sun being opposite,
   paints the clouds at sunset and daybreak
   I then saw the entire sky bathed.
And, like a modest woman who remains
   sure of her own morals, but becomes fearful
   because of other people's wrongdoing, if she merely hears about it,
thus Beatrice changed her appearance;
   and I believe there was a similar eclipse in heaven
   when the Supreme Power suffered on the Cross.
Then his words were uttered
   in a voice so altered from itself
   that the alteration in his appearance was no greater:
"The bride of Christ[5] was not nurtured

---

1. Adam, and Saints Peter, James, and John. 2. Saint Peter. 3. In his anger, Saint
Peter's glow changes from white to red. 4. Pope Boniface VIII. 5. The Church.

del sangue mio, di Lin, di quel di Cleto,
  per essere ad acquisto d'oro usata;
ma, per acquisto d'esto viver lieto,
  e Sisto e Pio e Calisto e Urbano
  sparser lo sangue dopo molto fleto.
Non fu nostra intenzion ch'a destra mano
  de' nostri successor parte sedesse,
  parte dall'altra del popol cristiano;
nè che le chiavi che mi fuor concesse
  divenisser signaculo in vessillo
  che contra battezzati combattesse;
nè ch'io fossi figura di sigillo
  a privilegi venduti e mendaci,
  ond'io sovente arrosso e disfavillo.
In vesta di pastor lupi rapaci
  si veggion di qua su per tutti i paschi:
  o difesa di Dio, perchè pur giaci?
Del sangue nostro Caorsini e Guaschi
  s'apparecchian di bere: o buon principio,
  a che vil fine convien che tu caschi!
Ma l'alta provedenza che con Scipio
  difese a Roma la gloria del mondo,
  soccorrà tosto, sì com'io concipio.
E tu, figliuol, che per lo mortal pondo
  ancor giù tornerai, apri la bocca,
  e non asconder quel ch'io non ascondo.»
Sì come di vapor gelati fiocca
  in giuso l'aere nostro, quando il corno
  della capra del ciel col sol si tocca,
in su vid'io così l'etera adorno
  farsi e fioccar di vapor triunfanti
  che fatto avean con noi quivi soggiorno.
Lo viso mio seguiva i suoi sembianti,
  e seguì fin che 'l mezzo, per lo molto,
  li tolse il trapassar del più avanti.
Onde la donna, che mi vide assolto

by my blood, or by that of Linus and Cletus,[6]
in order to become a means to acquire gold;
rather, it was to acquire this blissful life
that Sixtus, Pius, Calixtus, and Urban
shed their blood after great torments.
It was not our intention that one part
of Christianity should sit at the right hand
of our successors, and another part at the left;
nor that the keys which were granted to me
should become an emblem on a battle standard
for making war on baptized people;
nor that I should be an image on a seal
to be affixed to bartered, false charters,
so that I often blush and emit flames.
In shepherd's garb ravening wolves
are seen from up here in every pasture:
O protection of God, why, oh why do you lie inactive?
Men from Cahors and Gascons[7] prepare to drink
our blood: O good beginnings,
to what a base end you must fall!
But the lofty providence that through Scipio[8]
secured the glory of the world for Rome
will soon come to our aid, as I see it.
And you, my son, you that, because of your mortal weight,
will return down there again, open your mouth,
and do not conceal that which I do not conceal."
Just as our atmosphere flakes
frozen vapors downward when the horn
of the heavenly Goat is in conjunction with the sun,
in like manner I saw the ether become adorned
and flake upward with the triumphant vapors
who had tarried with us there.
My eyes kept following their images,
and followed until the intervening air, by its extent,
prevented them from piercing any farther.
Whereupon my lady, who saw me free

6. These two and the next four named were martyred bishops of Rome (popes) of the first three centuries A.D. 7. The successors of Boniface VIII to the papacy: Clement V (a Gascon) and John XXII (from the city of Cahors in southwestern France, ill-famed as a den of usury). 8. Scipio Africanus, victor over Hannibal.

dell'attendere in su, mi disse: «Adima
   il viso, e guarda come tu se' volto.»
Dall'ora ch'io avea guardato prima
   i' vidi mosso me per tutto l'arco
   che fa dal mezzo al fine il primo clima;
sì ch'io vedea di là da Gade il varco
   folle d'Ulisse, e di qua presso il lito
   nel qual si fece Europa dolce carco.
E più mi fora discoverto il sito
   di questa aiuola; ma 'l sol procedea
   sotto i mie' piedi un segno e più partito.
La mente innamorata, che donnea
   con la mia donna sempre, di ridure
   ad esse li occhi più che mai ardea:
e se natura o arte fè pasture
   da pigliare occhi, per aver la mente,
   in carne umana o nelle sue pitture,
tutte adunate, parrebber nïente
   ver lo piacer divin che mi refulse,
   quando mi volsi al suo viso ridente.
E la virtù che lo sguardo m'indulse,
   del bel nido di Leda mi divelse,
   e nel ciel velocissimo m'impulse.
Le parti sue vicinissime e eccelse
   sì uniformi son, ch'i' non so dire
   qual Beatrice per loco mi scelse.
Ma ella, che vedea il mio disire,
   incominciò, ridendo tanto lieta,
   che Dio parea nel suo volto gioire:
«La natura del mondo, che quïeta
   il mezzo e tutto l'altro intorno move,
   quinci comincia come da sua meta;
e questo cielo non ha altro dove

from turning my attention upward, said to me: "Lower
    your eyes, and see what a turn you have made."
Since the time when I had first looked down[9]
    I now saw that I had moved through the entire arc
    that the first climate[10] of earth makes from its center to its end;[11]
so that I saw, beyond Cadiz, the mad
    passage of Ulysses,[12] and, on this side, I nearly saw the shore
    on which Europa made herself so sweet a burden.[13]
And the extent of that threshing floor[14] would have been
    further revealed to me; but the sun was proceeding
    beneath my feet, having traversed more than a full constellation.
My enamored mind, which constantly
    pays court to my lady, was more than ever
    desirous of turning its eyes back to her:
and if nature or art ever created baits,
    in human flesh or depictions of it,
    to catch the eye in order to possess the mind,
all of them combined would seem as nothing
    compared with the divine pleasure that beamed on me
    when I turned toward her smiling face.
And the power that her glance bestowed upon me
    tore me away from Leda's beautiful nest[15]
    and thrust me into the swiftest heaven.[16]
Its nearest and its loftiest parts
    are so uniform that I cannot say
    what part of it Beatrice chose for me.
But she, seeing my desire for knowledge,
    began, smiling so joyously
    that God seemed to be rejoicing in her face:
"The nature of the world, which stills
    its center[17] and makes everything else circle around it,
    takes its start here, as if from its source;
and this heaven has no other spatial extension

---

9. In Canto XXII.   10. One of the strips into which the surface of the earth was theoretically divided.   11. Dante has moved through 90 degrees, which takes six hours.   12. Referring to *Hell*, Canto XXVI.   13. Europa was carried off by Jupiter (Zeus), who had changed himself into a bull, in Phoenicia.   14. The image Dante had already used for the tiny earth in Canto XXII.   15. The constellation Gemini; the Twins are Castor and Pollux, who emerged from the egg Leda laid after Jupiter (Zeus) had seduced her in the form of a swan.   16. The ninth, the Primum Mobile (First Mover).   17. The earth, thought of as motionless at the center of the universe.

che la mente divina, in che s'accende
l'amor che il volge e la virtù ch'ei piove.
Luce ed amor d'un cerchio lui comprende,
   sì come questo li altri; e quel precinto
   colui che 'l cinge solamente intende.
Non è suo moto per altro distinto;
   ma li altri son misurati da questo,
   sì come diece da mezzo e da quinto.
E come il tempo tegna in cotal testo
   le sue radici e ne li altri le fronde,
   omai a te può esser manifesto.
Oh cupidigia che i mortali affonde
   sì sotto te, che nessuno ha podere
   di trarre li occhi fuor delle tue onde!
Ben fiorisce nelli uomini il volere;
   ma la pioggia continüa converte
   in bozzacchioni le susine vere.
Fede ed innocenzia son reperte
   solo ne' parvoletti; poi ciascuna
   pria fugge che le guance sian coperte.
Tale, balbuzïendo ancor, digiuna,
   che poi divora, con la lingua sciolta,
   qualunque cibo per qualunque luna;
e tal, balbuzïendo, ama e ascolta
   la madre sua, che, con loquela intera,
   disïa poi di vederla sepolta.
Così si fa la pelle bianca nera
   nel primo aspetto della bella figlia
   di quel ch'apporta mane e lascia sera.
Tu, perchè non ti facci maraviglia,
   pensa che 'n terra non è chi governi;
   onde sì svia l'umana famiglia.
Ma prima che gennaio tutto si sverni

than the mind of God, in which is kindled
  the love that turns it and the influence that it showers down.
Light and love[18] envelop it in a ring,
  just as it envelops the others, and that highest region
  is understood only by the One who girds it around.
The motion of this heaven is not determined by that of any other;
  rather, all the rest are measured by this one,
  just as ten is measured by its half multiplied by its fifth.
And the way in which Time has its roots
  in *this* flowerpot, and its leaves in the others,
  can now be clear to you.
Oh, greed, you that sink mortals
  so far under you that no one has the power
  to raise his eyes above your waters!
Yes, the will to do so thrives among men,
  but the unending rain turns
  the good plums into ones that spoil on the tree.
Faith and innocence are to be found
  in small children only; later they both
  flee before the youth's cheeks are covered with down.
Many a man who, while still stammering in childhood, observes fast days
  will later, when his tongue is nimble, devour
  any kind of food during any month;
and many a man who, while still stammering, loves and obeys
  his mother will later, when his speech becomes perfected,
  wish to see her in her grave.
Thus the white skin of the beautiful daughter
  of the one that brings us the morning and leaves us the evening
  is darkened in the primal sight.[19]
So that this does not amaze you,
  keep in mind that on earth there is no one that governs;
  and so the human family goes so far astray.
But before all of January ceases to be a winter month

---

18. "Light and love" stands for the Empyrean, site of God's throne.   19. This is one of the most obscure passages in the entire poem. The "one that brings us the morning" clearly is the sun, but who is his "beautiful daughter"? If it is the Church, or humanity in general, then "in the primal sight" means "in the eyes of God." If, as other commentators claim, she is the ancient sorceress Circe, who transformed people, the passage becomes: "Thus white skin is darkened immediately on being viewed by the beautiful daughter of [the sun]."

per la centesma ch'è là giù negletta,
   raggeran sì questi cerchi superni,
che la fortuna che tanto s'aspetta,
   le poppe volgerà u' son le prore,
   sì che la classe correrà diretta;
e vero frutto verrà dopo 'l fiore.»

[SUMMARY OF CANTO XXVIII: Dante sees, reflected in Beatrice's eyes, a point of intense light encompassed by nine concentric circles. These are the orders of angels connected with the nine heavens, all encircling the Empyrean and set in motion by it. The angelic rings are brighter and swifter in proportion to their proximity to the central point, and Dante asks why the reverse should not be the case (like the heavenly spheres encompassing the earth). Beatrice replies that, in this instance, the organization is by excellence, not by size. God may be regarded not only as the sphere that most widely embraces the universe, but also as its center. The circles now shoot sparks and sing hosanna. They comprise: Seraphs, Cherubs, and Thrones; Dominations, Virtues, and Powers; and Principalities, Archangels, and just plain Angels. This sequence was established by (the pseudo-) Dionysius the Areopagite (see *Paradise*, Canto X, note 19); Pope Gregory the Great (died 604), who had differed from him, saw the light when he himself arrived in Paradise.

Canto XXX

Forse semilia miglia di lontano
   ci ferve l'ora sesta, e questo mondo
   china già l'ombra quasi al letto piano,
quando il mezzo del cielo, a noi profondo,
   comincia a farsi tal, ch'alcuna stella
   perde il parere infino a questo fondo;
e come vien la chiarissima ancella
   del sol più oltre, così 'l ciel si chiude
   di vista in vista infino alla più bella.
Non altrimenti il triunfo che lude

because of the hundredth of a day that is overlooked on earth,[20]
  these heavenly circles will so radiate[21]
that the storm that has been so long awaited
  will turn the sterns around to where the bows are now,
    so that the fleet will sail in the right direction;
and proper fruit will develop from the flower."

SUMMARY OF CANTO XXIX: Answering unspoken questions, Beatrice continues: merely so that His light might enjoy a state of existence, God instilled
Himself in his creatures, the angels, as love. There is no such thing as a time
before Creation, because time itself was created then. Form (the angels),
brute matter, and their combination (the heavens) arose simultaneously.
Saint Jerome erred in his belief that the angels preceded the heavens. Some
of the angels fell almost at once, because of Lucifer's pride, but most of them
acknowledged their debt to God. Angels have neither memory nor lapses of
memory because they perpetually have their eyes on God. Clergymen ought
to hew to the Bible, which confirms all this, instead of preaching trifling
things and selling indulgences. The number of the angels is uncountable, but
they differ in individual nature in proportion to the amount of divine love
that fuels them.]

Canto XXX

Some six thousand miles away
  from us it is hot noon, and our earth
    is already inclining its shadow almost to the flat bed of the horizon,[1]
when the atmosphere in the sky, deep above us,
  begins to become such that an occasional star
    loses its power to be seen all the way down to our low level;
and as that most bright servant of the sun[2]
  advances farther, the heavens close up
    from star to star until even the most beautiful one is gone.
In like manner, the triumphant dance that sports

---

20. The Julian calendar failed to take into account $\frac{1}{100}$ of each day, so that eventually the months would no longer correspond with the seasons associated with them.
21. Some Italian editions have *ruggeran* instead of *raggeran:* "roar" instead of "radiate."   1. Stripped of Dante's complicated medieval astronomy, this means it is an
hour before dawn.   2. Dawn.

sempre dintorno al punto che mi vinse,
  parendo inchiuso da quel ch'elli 'nchiude,
a poco a poco al mio veder si stinse;
  per che tornar con li occhi a Beatrice
  nulla vedere ed amor mi costrinse.
Se quanto infino a qui di lei si dice
  fosse conchiuso tutto in una loda,
  poco sarebbe a fornir questa vice.
La bellezza ch'io vidi si trasmoda
  non pur di là da noi, ma certo io credo
  che solo il suo fattor tutta la goda.
Da questo passo vinto mi concedo
  più che già mai da punto di suo tema
  soprato fosse comico o tragedo;
chè, come sole in viso che più trema,
  così lo rimembrar del dolce riso
  la mente mia da me medesmo scema.
Dal primo giorno ch'i' vidi il suo viso
  in questa vita, infino a questa vista,
  non m'è il seguire al mio cantar preciso;
ma or convien che mio seguir desista
  più dietro a sua bellezza, poetando,
  come all'ultimo suo ciascuno artista.
Cotal qual io la lascio a maggior bando
  che quel della mia tuba, che deduce
  l'ardüa sua matera terminando,
con atto e voce di spedito duce
  ricominciò: «Noi siamo usciti fore
  del maggior corpo al ciel ch'è pura luce:
luce intellettüal, piena d'amore;
  amor di vero ben, pien di letizia;
  letizia che trascende ogni dolzore.
Qui vederai l'una e l'altra milizia
  di paradiso, e l'una in quelli aspetti
  che tu vedrai all'ultima giustizia.»
Come subito lampo che discetti

eternally around the luminous point that dazzled me,
seemingly enclosed by that which it encloses,[3]
gradually faded before my eyes;
so that the lack of anything to see, and also my love for her,
compelled me to turn my eyes toward Beatrice.
If everything said about her up to now
were summed up in a single hymn of praise,
it would be inadequate to accomplish the present purpose.
The beauty I then saw not merely surpasses
any measure of ours, but I firmly believe
that only its Creator can enjoy it in its entirety.
I confess myself inferior to this particular subject,
more so than any author in the comic or tragic style
has ever been unequal to an incident in his work;
for, like the sun shining on the weakest eyes,
the recollection of her sweet smile
deprives my mind of myself.
From the first day I saw her face
in this life, until that sight of her,
continuity in my song has not been cut off from me;
but now I am forced to desist from pursuing
her beauty further in my verses,
like every artist who has reached his limit.
Looking the way she did at the point where I leave her to a greater heralding
than that of my trumpet, which is drawing
its difficult subject matter to a close,
with the gestures and voice of a ready leader[4]
she resumed: "We have emerged from
the largest material body[5] into the heaven that is pure light:[6]
light of the intellect, filled with love;
love of the true good, filled with joy;
joy that transcends every sweetness.
Here you will see both armies[7]
of Paradise, and one of them in the guise
you will see them have at the Last Judgment."[8]
Just as a sudden lightning flash disconcerts

---

3. This refers to the spatial paradox expounded in Canto XXVIII.   4. Or: "a leader who has fulfilled his mission."   5. The ninth heaven, or Primum Mobile, is the last one to be made up of matter.   6. The Empyrean.   7. The angels and the blessed human souls.   8. The blessed souls will appear to be clothed in their bodies.

li spiriti visivi, sì che priva
   dall'atto l'occhio di più forti obietti,
così mi circunfulse luce viva;
   e lasciommi fasciato di tal velo
   del suo fulgor, che nulla m'appariva.
«Sempre l'amor che queta questo cielo
   accoglie in sè con sì fatta salute,
   per far disposto a sua fiamma il candelo.»
Non fur più tosto dentro a me venute
   queste parole brievi, ch'io compresi
   me sormontar di sopr'a mia virtute;
e di novella vista mi raccesi
   tale, che nulla luce è tanto mera,
   che li occhi miei non si fosser difesi.
E vidi lume in forma di rivera
   fluvido di fulgore, intra due rive
   dipinte di mirabil primavera.
Di tal fiumana uscìan faville vive,
   e d'ogni parte si mettìen ne' fiori,
   quasi rubin che oro circunscrive.
Poi, come inebriate dalli odori,
   riprofondavan sè nel miro gurge;
   e s'una intrava, un'altra n'uscìa fori.
«L'alto disio che mo t'infiamma e urge,
   d'aver notizia di ciò che tu vei,
   tanto mi piace più quanto più turge;
ma di quest'acqua convien che tu bei
   prima che tanta sete in te si sazii»:
   così mi disse il sol delli occhi miei.
Anche soggiunse: «Il fiume e li topazii
   ch'entrano ed escono e 'l rider dell'erbe
   son di lor vero umbriferi prefazii.
Non che da sè sian queste cose acerbe;
   ma è difetto dalla parte tua,
   che non hai viste ancor tanto superbe.»
Non è fantin che sì subito rua
   col volto verso il latte, se si svegli
   molto tardato dall'usanza sua,
come fec'io, per far migliori spegli

the powers of vision, so that it deprives
the eye of the effect of even the brightest objects,
in like manner I was enveloped in vivid light;
and it left me swathed in such a veil
of effulgence that I could see nothing at all.
"The Love that stills this heaven always
welcomes one to Itself with a greeting of this sort
in order to make the candle ready for its flame."
As soon as those brief words
penetrated me, I realized
that I was rising beyond my normal powers;
and I rekindled myself with new sight
of such a kind that there is no light so unalloyed
that my eyes could not withstand it.
And I saw light in the form of a river
flowing and glowing between two banks
adorned with miraculous spring flowers.
From that stream living sparks issued,
settling on the flowers on all sides
like rubies set in gold.[9]
Then, as if intoxicated with the fragrance,
they plunged again into the wondrous flood;
whenever one of them entered, another one came out.
"That lofty desire to learn about
what you are seeing which now inflames and drives you
pleases me all the more, the more it swells within you;
but you must drink of this water
before such great thirst as you now have is slaked":
thus did the sun of my eyes address me.
Then she added: "The river and the topazes
that enter and leave it, and the smiling of the plants,
are only foreshadowing preambles of their true nature.
Not that these things are unripe as they stand;
but the shortcoming is on your side
because your vision is not yet so elevated."
No infant darts so suddenly
with its face toward its mother's milk after awakening
much later than it is used to,
than I rushed in order to make even better

---

9. The flowers are the human souls, the sparks are the angels.

ancor delli occhi, chinandomi all'onda
che si deriva perchè vi s'immegli;
e sì come di lei bevve la gronda
delle palpebre mie, così mi parve
di sua lunghezza divenuta tonda.
Poi come gente stata sotto larve
che pare altro che prima, se si sveste
la sembianza non sua in che disparve,
così mi si cambiaro in maggior feste
li fiori e le faville, sì ch'io vidi
ambo le corti del ciel manifeste.
O isplendor di Dio, per cu' io vidi
l'alto triunfo del regno verace,
dammi virtù a dir com'io il vidi!
Lume è là su che visibile face
lo creatore a quella creatura
che solo in lui vedere ha la sua pace.
E' si distende in circular figura,
in tanto che la sua circunferenza
sarebbe al sol troppo larga cintura.
Fassi di raggio tutta sua parvenza
reflesso al sommo del mobile primo,
che prende quindi vivere e potenza.
E come clivo in acqua di suo imo
si specchia, quasi per vedersi adorno,
quando è nel verde e ne' fioretti opimo,
sì soprastando, al lume intorno intorno,
vidi specchiarsi in più di mille soglie
quanto di noi là su fatto ha ritorno.
E se l'infimo grado in sè raccoglie
sì grande lume, quanta è la larghezza
di questa rosa nell'estreme foglie!
La vista mia nell'ampio e nell'altezza
non si smarriva, ma tutto prendeva
il quanto e 'l quale di quella allegrezza.
Presso e lontano, lì, nè pon nè leva;
chè dove Dio sanza mezzo governa,
la legge natural nulla rileva.
Nel giallo della rosa sempiterna,

mirrors of my eyes, stooping down to the water
   that flows so that a man may improve himself in it;
and, as soon as the eaves of my eyelids[10]
   drank of it, it appeared to me
   no longer extended in length, but circular.
Then, just as people who have gone about masked
   appear different from the way they did, once they remove
   the face not really theirs under which they had vanished,
in like manner the flowers and sparks were transformed
   into a more festive appearance, so that I saw
   distinctly the two courts of heaven.
O splendor of God, by means of which I saw
   the lofty triumph of the truthful kingdom,
   give me the power to tell the form in which I saw it!
There is a light up there which makes the Creator
   visible to that created being
   which finds peace only in seeing Him.
It extends in the form of a circle
   so large that its circumference
   would be a belt too wide for the sun.
Its entire appearance is made up of a ray
   reflected from the surface of the Primum Mobile,
   which derives its own life and force from it.
And, just as a hill mirrors itself
   in the water at its foot, as if wishing to see how it is adorned
   when it is rich with greenery and flowers,
in like manner I saw, all around that light and standing above it,
   all the souls that have returned up there from our world
   mirroring themselves in it in over a thousand tiers.
And if the lowest tier encloses within itself
   so large a light, what must be the extent
   of that rose at the level of its most distant petals!
My eyes did not lose themselves
   in the width and height of it, but took in
   all the extent and quality of that joyousness.
There, nearness and distance neither add nor subtract;
   for in a place where God governs without an intermediary,
   the laws of nature do not apply.
Into the yellow center of that eternal rose

---

10. Or: "as soon as my knit brows."

che si dilata ed ingrada e redole
odor di lode al sol che sempre verna
qual è colui che tace e dicer vole,
    mi trasse Beatrice, e disse: «Mira
    quanto è 'l convento delle bianche stole!
Vedi nostra città quant'ella gira:
    vedi li nostri scanni sì ripieni,
    che poca gente più ci si disira.
E 'n quel gran seggio a che tu li occhi tieni
    per la corona che già v'è su posta,
    prima che tu a queste nozze ceni,
sederà l'alma, che fia giù agosta,
    dell'alto Arrigo, ch'a drizzare Italia
    verrà in prima ch'ella sia disposta.
La cieca cupidigia che v'ammalia
    simili fatti v'ha al fantolino
    che muor per fame e caccia via la balia.
E fia prefetto nel foro divino
    allora tal, che palese e coverto
    non anderà con lui per un cammino.
Ma poco poi sarà da Dio sofferto
    nel santo officio; ch'el sarà detruso
    là dove Simon mago è per suo merto,
e farà quel d'Alagna intrar più giuso.»

Canto XXXI

In forma dunque di candida rosa
    mi si mostrava la milizia santa
    che nel suo sangue Cristo fece sposa;
ma l'altra, che volando vede e canta
    la gloria di colui che la innamora
    e la bontà che la fece cotanta,

which expands, forms tiers, and emits
  a fragrance of praise to the Sun that is always in Its springtime,
Beatrice drew me—I was like a man who is silent
  but wishes to speak—saying: "See
  how great is the white-robed assembly!
See how wide the circumference of our city is:
  see our seats, which are already so filled
  that only a few more people are still lacking.[11]
And on that great chair you are gazing at
  because of the crown that is already placed on it,
  before you dine at this wedding feast
that soul will sit which will be an emperor's on earth,
  that of lofty Henry,[12] who will come
  to set Italy to rights before she is ready for it.
The blind greed that holds your people spellbound
  has made all of you like the infant
  who is dying of hunger but drives away his wetnurse.
And at that time the president of the spiritual court[13]
  will be of such a kind that, between his public and his secret actions,
  he will not deal with Henry in a uniform manner.[14]
But, after that, God will not allow him to retain
  the holy office very long; for he will be thrust down
  where Simon Magus is receiving his just deserts,
and he will make the man from Anagni[15] sink lower into the pit."[16]

Canto XXXI

And so, in the shape of a white rose
  there was being shown to me the sacred soldiery
  that Christ made His bride in His blood;[1]
but that other army,[2] which, as it flies, sees and hymns
  the glory of the One who enamors it
  and the goodness that made it so great—

11. This indicates that (1) very few people still living will be saved, and (2) the end of the world is approaching. 12. Holy Roman Emperor Henry VII. 13. The pope—at the time of Henry's visit to Italy, Clement V, who invited Henry but later plotted against him. 14. Or: "he will not travel the same road that Henry does." 15. Pope Boniface VIII. 16. The last three lines refer to the mode of punishment of evil popes described in Canto XIX of *Hell*. 1. The "army" of blessed human souls. 2. The angels.

sì come schiera d'ape, che s'infiora
  una fïata e una si ritorna
  là dove suo laboro s'insapora,
nel gran fior discendeva che s'adorna
  di tante foglie, e quindi risaliva
  là dove 'l suo amor sempre soggiorna.
Le facce tutte avean di fiamma viva,
  e l'ali d'oro, e l'altro tanto bianco,
  che nulla neve a quel termine arriva.
Quando scendean nel fior, di banco in banco
  porgevan della pace e dell'ardore
  ch'elli acquistavan ventilando il fianco.
Nè l'interporsi tra 'l disopra e 'l fiore
  di tanta plenitudine volante
  impediva la vista e lo splendore;
chè la luce divina è penetrante
  per l'universo secondo ch'è degno,
  sì che nulla le puote essere ostante.
Questo sicuro e gaudïoso regno,
  frequente in gente antica ed in novella,
  viso e amore avea tutto ad un segno.
Oh trina luce che 'n unica stella
  scintillando a lor vista, sì li appaga!
  Guarda qua giuso alla nostra procella!
Se i barbari, venendo da tal plaga
  che ciascun giorno d'Elice si copra,
  rotante col suo figlio ond'ella è vaga,
veggendo Roma e l'ardüa sua opra,
  stupefacìensi, quando Laterano
  alle cose mortali andò di sopra;
ïo, che al divino dall'umano,
  all'etterno dal tempo era venuto,
  e di Fiorenza in popol giusto e sano,
di che stupor dovea esser compiuto!
  Certo tra esso e 'l gaudio mi facea
  libito non udire e starmi muto.

like a swarm of bees that settles on flowers
   at one time and, at another, returns
   to the place where its labors are turned into sweetness—
was descending into the great flower that is adorned
   with so many leaves, and from it was reascending
   to the place where its Love always sojourns.
Their faces were all of living flame,
   and their wings of gold, and all the rest so white
   that no snow attains to that degree.
When they descended into the flower, from tier to tier
   they offered a portion of the peace and ardor
   that they acquired as they fanned their sides.[3]
Nor did the interposition, between the upper region and the flower,
   of such a great flying multitude
   impede the view or its splendor;
for the light of God penetrates
   every part of the universe in proportion to its merit,
   so that nothing can block it.
This secure and joyful realm,
   abounding in people of old times and new,
   kept its eyes and its love directed at a single mark.
Oh, triune light which, gleaming in their eyes
   from a single star, contents them so thoroughly!
   Gaze down here on earth at our storm!
If the barbarians, arriving from a region
   that is daily covered by Helice,
   who revolves along with the son she is so fond of,[4]
and seeing Rome and its bold architecture,
   were lost in amazement, at the time when the Lateran[5]
   surpassed all other works of mortals;
I, who had ascended into the divine, coming from the human,
   into eternity, coming from temporality,
   and among a righteous and healthy people, coming from Florence—
with what amazement must I have been filled!
   Certainly, what with that and my joy, it became
   only natural that I could hear nothing and say nothing.

---

3. By flapping their wings to fly up to God.   4. Helice, the nymph banished by Diana (see *Purgatory*, Canto XXV, note 19), was transformed into the constellation Ursa Major; her son, Arcas, or Boötes, became a nearby constellation; the region they cover is northern Europe.   5. The papal palace in early Christian centuries.

E quasi peregrin che si ricrea
   nel tempio del suo voto riguardando,
   e spera già ridir com'ello stea,
su per la viva luce passeggiando,
   menava ïo li occhi per li gradi,
   mo su, mo giù, e mo recirculando.
Vedea visi a carità süadi,
   d'altrui lume fregiati e di suo riso,
   e atti ornati di tutte onestadi.
La forma general di paradiso
   già tutta mïo sguardo avea compresa,
   in nulla parte ancor fermato fiso;
e volgeami con voglia rïaccesa
   per domandar la mia donna di cose
   di che la mente mia era sospesa.
Uno intendea, e altro mi rispose:
   credea veder Beatrice, e vidi un sene
   vestito con le genti glorïose.
Diffuso era per li occhi e per le gene
   di benigna letizia, in atto pio
   quale a tenero padre si convene.
E «Ov'è ella?» subito diss'io.
   Ond'elli: «A terminar lo tuo disiro
   mosse Beatrice me del loco mio;
e se riguardi su nel terzo giro
   dal sommo grado, tu la rivedrai
   nel trono che suoi merti le sortiro.»
Sanza risponder, li occhi su levai,
   e vidi lei che si facea corona
   reflettendo da sè li etterni rai.
Da quella regïon che più su tona
   occhio mortale alcun tanto non dista,
   qualunque in mare più giù s'abbandona,
quanto lì da Beatrice la mia vista;
   ma nulla mi facea, chè sua effige
   non discendea a me per mezzo mista.
«O donna in cui la mia speranza vige,
   e che soffristi per la mia salute
   in inferno lasciar le tue vestige,
di tante cose quant'i' ho vedute,
   dal tuo podere e dalla tua bontate

And, just like a pilgrim who refreshes himself
   by looking around the church to which he has vowed to journey,
   and who already hopes he will be able to report what it was like,
roaming through the vivid light
   I moved my eyes along the tiers,
   now up, now down, now all around.
I saw faces that persuaded you to be charitable,
   decorated with the light of Another and with their own smiles,
   and gestures adorned by every form of dignity.
The general form of Paradise
   my eyes had already entirely encompassed,
   still remaining fixed on no one place;
and I was turning with rekindled desire
   to ask my lady about things
   that were keeping my mind in suspense.
I had one thing in mind, but another thing responded:
   I thought I would see Beatrice, but I saw an old man
   dressed like the other glorious people.
His eyes and cheeks were suffused
   with benevolent joy, and his attitude was pious,
   as befitting a tender father.
And "Where is she?" I suddenly asked.
   And he replied: "To give you your final answers
   Beatrice stirred me from my place;
and if you look up at the third row
   down from the highest tier, you will see her again
   on the throne that her merits allotted to her."
Without replying, I raised my eyes
   and saw her making a crown for herself
   out of the eternal rays that reflected from her.
When it is plunged most deeply in the sea,
   the eye of man is not as distant
   from that region of sky which thunders highest
than my eyes were from Beatrice in that place;
   but that meant nothing to me, because her image
   was not descending to me blurred by any atmosphere.
"O lady in whom my hope thrives,
   you that, for my salvation, deigned
   to leave your footprints in Hell,
I owe the grace and power
   of all the things I have seen

riconosco la grazia e la virtute.
Tu m'hai di servo tratto a libertate
    per tutte quelle vie, per tutt'i modi
    che di ciò fare avei la potestate.
La tua magnificenza in me custodi,
    sì che l'anima mia, che fatt'hai sana,
    piacente a te dal corpo si disnodi.»
Così orai; e quella, sì lontana
    come parea, sorrise e riguardommi;
    poi si tornò all'etterna fontana.
E 'l santo sene «Acciò che tu assommi
    perfettamente» disse «il tuo cammino,
    a che priego e amor santo mandommi,
vola con li occhi per questo guardino;
    chè veder lui t'acconcerà lo sguardo
    più al montar per lo raggio divino.
E la regina del cielo, ond'io ardo
    tutto d'amor, ne farà ogni grazia,
    però ch'i' sono il suo fedel Bernardo.»
Qual è colui che forse di Croazia
    viene a veder la Veronica nostra,
    che per l'antica fame non sen sazia,
ma dice nel pensier, fin che si mostra:
    «Signor mio Gesù Cristo, Dio verace,
    or fu sì fatta la sembianza vostra?»;
tal era io mirando la vivace
    carità di colui che 'n questo mondo,
    contemplando, gustò di quella pace.
«Figliuol di grazia, quest'esser giocondo»
    cominciò elli «non ti sarà noto,
    tenendo li occhi pur qua giù al fondo;
ma guarda i cerchi infino al più remoto,
    tanto che veggi seder la regina
    cui questo regno è suddito e devoto.»
Io levai li occhi; e come da mattina
    la parte orïental dell'orizzonte
    soverchia quella dove 'l sol declina,
così, quasi di valle andando a monte

to your might and your goodness.
You have brought me from servitude to freedom
    along all those roads, by all those means
    which were in your power, in order to do this.
Preserve your magnanimity in my behalf,
    so that my soul, which you have made whole,
    is pleasing to you when it is untied from my body."
Thus I prayed; and she, far away
    as she appeared, smiled and looked at me;
    then she turned back to the eternal fountain.
And the holy old man said: "In order that you accomplish
    your journey perfectly,
    for which purpose her entreaty and sacred love sent me,
fly through this garden with your eyes;
    for seeing it will adapt your vision
    for further ascent along the divine ray.
And the Queen of Heaven, for whom I am completely
    consumed with love, will grant us every grace,
    because I am her devotee Bernard."[6]
Just as a man coming, perhaps, from Croatia
    to see our Veronica's Veil,
    cannot see enough of it because of his long-standing craving,
but says in his mind, all the while it is on display,
    "My Lord Jesus Christ, God of truth,
    was this, then, what Your face was like?"—
such was I as I beheld the intense
    charity of the man who, even in this world,
    tasted that peace through his contemplation.
"Son of grace, this happy existence,"
    he began, "will not be known to you
    if you merely keep your eyes down here at the bottom;
rather, look at the tiers all the way to the most distant,
    until you see, where she sits, the Queen
    to whom this realm is subject and devoted."
I raised my eyes; and just as, in the morning,
    the eastern side of the horizon
    is brighter than the one where the sun sets,
in like manner, as if climbing from valley to mountain

---

6. Saint Bernard of Clairvaux (1091–1153), a contemplative mystic and a fervent
devotee of the Virgin.

con li occhi, vidi parte nello stremo
  vincer di lume tutta l'altra fronte.
E come quivi ove s'aspetta il temo
  che mal guidò Fetonte, più s'infiamma,
  e quinci e quindi il lume si fa scemo,
così quella pacifica oriafiamma
  nel mezzo s'avvivava, e d'ogni parte
  per igual modo allentava la fiamma.
E a quel mezzo, con le penne sparte,
  vid'io più di mille angeli festanti,
  ciascun distinto di fulgore e d'arte.
Vidi a' lor giochi quivi ed a' lor canti
  ridere una bellezza, che letizia
  era nelli occhi a tutti li altri santi.
E s'io avessi in dir tanta divizia
  quanta ad imaginar, non ardirei
  lo minimo tentar di sua delizia.
Bernardo, come vide li occhi miei
  nel caldo suo calor fissi e attenti,
  li suoi con tanto affetto volse a lei,
che i miei di rimirar fè più ardenti.

Canto XXXII

Affetto al suo piacer, quel contemplante
  libero officio di dottore assunse,
  e cominciò queste parole sante:
«La piaga che Maria richiuse e unse,
  quella ch'è tanto bella da' suoi piedi
  è colei che l'aperse e che la punse.
Nell'ordine che fanno i terzi sedi,
  siede Rachel di sotto da costei
  con Beatrice, sì come tu vedi.
Sara e Rebecca, Iudìt e colei
  che fu bisava al cantor che per doglia

with my eyes, I saw a section of the highest tier
   surpass in brightness all the rest of the rim.
And, just as the spot where people expect to see the chariot-pole
   that Phaethon guided badly[7] is more greatly inflamed,
   while the light is diminished on either side of it,
in like manner that oriflamme of peace
   was brightest in the center, and on each side
   the flame was uniformly slackened.
And in that center, their wings spread,
   I saw more than a thousand jubilant angels,
   each one different in brightness and behavior.
There I saw, smiling at their dances and songs,
   a beauty that was joy
   to the eyes of all the other saints.
And, even if I had speech as rich
   as my imagination, I would not dare
   to attempt the least description of the delight she gave.
When Bernard saw my eyes
   attentively fixed on the warm object of his ardor,
   he turned his own toward her with such affection
that he made mine more ardent to gaze.

Canto XXXII

Intent on his delight, that contemplative man
   freely assumed the duty of a professor,
   and began to speak these holy words:
"The wound[1] that Mary healed, applying salve to it—
   that woman[2] at her feet[3] who is so beautiful
   is the one who made it, tearing it open.
In the tier made up of the third-row seats
   Rachel sits below her
   together with Beatrice, as you see.
Sarah, Rebecca, Judith, and the woman[4]
   who was great-grandmother to the singer[5] who, grieving

---

7. This is the fourth reference in the *Commedia* to Phaethon, son of the sun god, who was killed when driving the solar chariot; the "spot where people expect . . ." is the point of sunrise.   1. Original sin.   2. Eve.   3. In the row below her.   4. Ruth. 5. David.

del fallo disse *'Miserere mei'*,
puoi tu veder così di soglia in soglia
   giù digradar, com'io ch'a proprio nome
   vo per la rosa giù di foglia in foglia.
E dal settimo grado in giù, sì come
   infino ad esso, succedono Ebree,
   dirimendo del fior tutte le chiome;
perchè, secondo lo sguardo che fee
   la fede in Cristo, queste sono il muro
   a che si parton le sacre scalee.
Da questa parte onde 'l fiore è maturo
   di tutte le sue foglie, sono assisi
   quei che credettero in Cristo venturo;
dall'altra parte onde sono intercisi
   di voti i semicirculi, si stanno
   quei ch'a Cristo venuto ebber li visi.
E come quinci il glorïoso scanno
   della donna del cielo e li altri scanni
   di sotto lui cotanta cerna fanno,
così di contra quel del gran Giovanni,
   che sempre santo 'l diserto e 'l martiro
   sofferse, e poi l'inferno da due anni;
e sotto lui così cerner sortiro
   Francesco, Benedetto e Augustino
   e altri fin qua giù di giro in giro.
Or mira l'alto proveder divino;
   chè l'uno e l'altro aspetto della fede
   igualmente empierà questo giardino.
E sappi che dal grado in giù che fiede
   a mezzo il tratto le due discrezioni,
   per nullo proprio merito si siede,
ma per l'altrui, con certe condizioni;
   chè tutti questi son spiriti assolti
   prima ch'avesser vere elezïoni.

at his sin, said '*Miserere mei*'[6]
you can see there from tier to tier
    as the rows descend, just as I name them individually
    while going through the rose petal by petal.
And from the seventh row down, just as
    in the rows leading to that one, the succession of Hebrew women continues,
    dividing vertically all the petals of the flower;
because, in correspondence to the direction of the gaze
    which faith cast on Christ, those women form the wall
    that partitions the sacred amphitheater.[7]
On this side, where the flower is complete
    with all its petals, are seated
    those who believed in Christ before His coming;
on the other side, where the semicircles
    are interrupted by gaps, are those
    who turned their eyes to Christ after He had come.
And, just as, over here, the glorious seat
    of the Lady of Heaven and the other seats
    below that one make such a great partition,
the same is true, opposite us, of the seat of that great John[8]
    who, a saint at all times, suffered life in the wilderness
    and martyrdom, and then Hell for two years;[9]
and, likewise, below him, chosen to form a vertical partition,
    are Francis, Benedict, and Augustine,
    and others from tier to tier down to this level.
Now consider the heights of God's providence;
    for both aspects of the faith[10]
    will one day fill this garden in equal measure.
And know that, below the tier that horizontally cuts
    through the two divisions halfway down,
    no one is seated because of any personal merit,
but because of that of others,[11] subject to fixed conditions;
    for all of these are spirits released from the body
    before they were old enough to make a true choice on their own.

---

6. "Have mercy on me."   7. Depending on whether they believed in Christ before or after His coming, the souls are seated on one side or the other of the "partition" formed by the vertical line of the matriarchs.   8. Saint John the Baptist.   9. Until Christ harrowed Hell.   10. The group of those who believed in Christ before His coming, and the group who were already Christians when they died.   11. Because of their parents' merit; they were too young to have acquired any of their own.

Ben te ne puoi accorger per li volti
   e anche per le voci puerili,
   se tu li guardi bene e se li ascolti.
Or dubbi tu, e dubitando sili;
   ma io dissolverò 'l forte legame
   in che ti stringon li pensier sottili.
Dentro all'ampiezza di questo reame
   casüal punto non puote aver sito,
   se non come tristizia o sete o fame;
chè per etterna legge è stabilito
   quantunque vedi, sì che giustamente
   ci si risponde dall'anello al dito.
E però questa festinata gente
   a vera vita non è sine causa
   intra sè qui più e meno eccellente.
Lo rege per cui questo regno pausa
   in tanto amore ed in tanto diletto,
   che nulla volontà è di più ausa,
le menti tutte nel suo lieto aspetto
   creando, a suo piacer di grazia dota
   diversamente; e qui basti l'effetto.
E ciò espresso e chiaro vi si nota
   nella Scrittura santa in quei gemelli
   che nella madre ebber l'ira commota.
Però, secondo il color de' capelli
   di cotal grazia, l'altissimo lume
   degnamente convien che s'incappelli.
Dunque, sanza merzè di lor costume,
   locati son per gradi differenti,
   sol differendo nel primiero acume.
Bastavasi ne' secoli recenti
   con l'innocenza, per aver salute,
   solamente la fede de' parenti.
Poi che le prime etadi fuor compiute,
   convenne ai maschi all'innocenti penne

You can clearly perceive this from their faces
    and also from their childish voices,
    if you look at them and listen to them carefully.
Now you are puzzled, and in your puzzlement you keep silent;
    but I shall untie the strong knot
    in which your subtle thoughts bind you.
Within all the amplitude of this realm
    there is no place for a single accidental occurrence,
    any more than for sadness, thirst, or hunger;
because everything you see is established
    by an eternal law, so that here there is an exact
    correspondence between the ring and the finger.
And therefore these children who arrived so hastily
    at the true life do not differ among themselves
    in excellence here without a good reason.
The King through whom this kingdom reposes
    in such great love and in such great pleasure
    that no one's desire could possibly be ambitious for more,
when He creates all minds in His gratified sight,
    endows them, as He sees fit, with varying measures
    of grace; and now just let this fact satisfy you.
This is recorded for you expressly and clearly
    in the Holy Scriptures in the case of those twins[12]
    who, while still in the womb, had their anger aroused.
Therefore it must be in accordance with the hair color[13]
    of such grace that this most lofty light of bliss
    worthily forms a halo on their heads.[14]
In short, without regard to the merit of their behavior,
    they are placed in different tiers
    differing only in the keenness of spiritual sight received at birth.
In the earliest centuries of the world,[15] all that was needed
    to obtain salvation, besides innocence,
    was merely one's parents' belief.
After those first ages were past,
    males had to acquire power

---

12. Jacob and Esau.   13. That is, the particular nature; Dante probably used this image because Jacob and Esau had hair of different colors.   14. That is, their degree of blessedness is due solely to their potential natural endowments from God. 15. Down to the time of Abraham.

per circuncidere acquistar virtute.
Ma poi che 'l tempo della grazia venne,
    sanza battesmo perfetto di Cristo,
    tale innocenza là giù si ritenne.
Riguarda omai nella faccia che a Cristo
    più si somiglia, chè la sua chiarezza
    sola ti può disporre a veder Cristo.»
Io vidi sopra lei tanta allegrezza
    piover, portata nelle menti sante
    create a trasvolar per quella altezza,
che quantunque io avea visto davante
    di tanta ammirazion non mi sospese,
    nè mi mostrò di Dio tanto sembiante;
e quello amor che primo lì discese,
    cantando 'Ave, Maria, gratïa plena',
    dinanzi a lei le sue ali distese.
Rispuose alla divina cantilena
    da tutte parti la beata corte,
    sì ch'ogni vista sen fè più serena.
«O santo padre, che per me comporte
    l'esser qua giù, lasciando il dolce loco
    nel quale tu siedi per etterna sorte,
qual è quell'angel che con tanto gioco
    guarda nelli occhi la nostra regina,
    innamorato sì che par di foco?»
Così ricorsi ancora alla dottrina
    di colui ch'abbelliva di Maria
    come del sole stella mattutina.
Ed elli a me: «Baldezza e leggiadria
    quant'esser puote in angelo ed in alma,
    tutta è in lui; e sì volem che sia,
perch'elli è quelli che portò la palma
    giuso a Maria, quando 'l Figliuol di Dio
    carcar si volse della nostra salma.
Ma vieni omai con li occhi sì com'io
    andrò parlando, e nota i gran patrici
    di questo imperio giustissimo e pio.

for their innocent wings[16] through circumcision.
But ever since the time of grace arrived,
   without Christ's perfect form of baptism
   such innocents have been kept down below.[17]
Now gaze upon the face[18] that most resembles
   Christ's, for only its brightness
   can prepare you to see Christ."
I saw such joy rain down
   upon her, borne by the sacred intelligences[19]
   who were created to fly back and forth at those heights,
that nothing I had previously seen
   held me rapt in such great amazement
   or showed me anything so closely resembling God;
and that love[20] which once descended to her
   singing "*Ave Maria, gratia plena*"[21]
   spread its wings before her.
The court of the blessed responded
   to that godlike song on all sides
   in such a way that all faces became more serene thereby.
"O holy father, you that for my sake deign
   to be down here, leaving the sweet place
   in which it is your lot to sit eternally,
who is that angel who with such joy
   is looking into the eyes of our Queen,
   so much in love that he seems to be made of fire?"
With these words I again had recourse to the teachings
   of the man who was acquiring beauty from Mary
   as the morning star does from the sun.
And he replied: "As much daring and gallantry
   as an angel or a soul can contain
   is all in him; and we want it to be so,
because he is the one who bore the palm of victory
   down to Mary when the Son of God
   deigned to load Himself with our burden.
But now follow along with your eyes as I
   continue speaking, and observe the great patricians
   of this most righteous and pious empire.

---

16. After Abraham's covenant, male children dying in infancy could only "fly" to heaven if they were circumcised. 17. In Limbo. 18. The Virgin's. 19. The angels. 20. Gabriel. 21. "Hail Mary, full of grace."

Quei due che seggon là su più felici
   per esser propinquissimi ad Augusta,
   son d'esta rosa quasi due radici:
colui che da sinistra le s'aggiusta
   è il padre per lo cui ardito gusto
   l'umana specie tanto amaro gusta;
dal destro vedi quel padre vetusto
   di Santa Chiesa a cui Cristo le chiavi
   raccomandò di questo fior venusto.
E quei che vide tutti i tempi gravi,
   pria che morisse, della bella sposa
   che s'acquistò con la lancia e coi chiavi,
siede lungh'esso, e lungo l'altro posa
   quel duca sotto cui visse di manna
   la gente ingrata, mobile e retrosa.
Di contr'a Pietro vedi sedere Anna
   tanto contenta di mirar sua figlia,
   che non move occhio per cantare osanna;
e contro al maggior padre di famiglia
   siede Lucia, che mosse la tua donna,
   quando chinavi, a ruinar, le ciglia.
Ma perchè 'l tempo fugge che t'assonna,
   qui farem punto, come buon sartore
   che com'elli ha del panno fa la gonna;
e dirizzerem li occhi al primo amore,
   sì che, guardando verso lui, penetri
   quant'è possibil per lo suo fulgore.
Veramente, ne forse tu t'arretri
   movendo l'ali tue, credendo oltrarti,
   orando grazia conven che s'impetri;
grazia da quella che puote aiutarti;
   e tu mi seguirai con l'affezione,
   sì che dal dicer mio lo cor non parti.»
E cominciò questa santa orazïone:

Those two who, sitting up there, are most blissful
    because they are closest to the Empress
    are, as it were, two roots of this rose:
the one next to her on the left
    is the father[22] through whose audacious palate
    the human race tastes so much bitterness;
on the right you see that ancient father[23]
    of the Holy Church to whom Christ entrusted
    the keys to this lovely flower.
And the man[24] who, before he died, foresaw
    all the hard times to be suffered by the beautiful bride[25]
    who was won by means of the lance and the nails,
sits beside him, while beside that other man[26] rests
    the commander[27] under whose rule the ungrateful,
    fickle, and recalcitrant nation lived on manna.
Seated opposite Peter you see Anne,
    so contented with gazing at her daughter
    that she does not tear her eyes away, although she, too, sings hosanna;
and opposite the greatest father of a family[28]
    sits Lucy, who bestirred your lady
    when you were lowering your brows to plunge into ruin.
But, because the time that makes you sleep[29] is fleeing,
    we shall stop here,[30] like a good tailor
    who makes the garment to match the amount of cloth he has;
and we shall direct our eyes at the Primal Love,
    so that, gazing in His direction, you may penetrate
    His effulgence as far as possible.
Nevertheless, lest you should perchance go backward
    as you beat your wings, expecting to go forward,
    you must first pray to obtain grace;
grace from the Lady who is able to aid you;
    and you will follow me with your affections,
    so closely that you do not turn your heart away from my words."
And he began this holy prayer:

---

22. Adam. 23. Saint Peter. 24. Saint John the Evangelist, here regarded as the author of Revelation. 25. The Church. 26. Adam. 27. Moses. 28. Adam. 29. This may be the only strong indication that Dante's entire journey is a dream. Some commentators take the phrase to mean "time, which makes mortals sleep (though sleep is unknown here in heaven)," but then one would expect the Italian to have v'assonna rather than t'assonna.   30. There may very well be a pun here, based on the image of the tailor: fare un punto can also mean "to take a stitch."

Canto XXXIII

«Vergine madre, figlia del tuo figlio,
    umile e alta più che creatura,
    termine fisso d'etterno consiglio,
tu se' colei che l'umana natura
    nobilitasti sì, che 'l suo fattore
    non disdegnò di farsi sua fattura.
Nel ventre tuo si raccese l'amore
    per lo cui caldo nell'etterna pace
    così è germinato questo fiore.
Qui se' a noi meridïana face
    di caritate, e giuso, intra i mortali,
    se' di speranza fontana vivace.
Donna, se' tanto grande e tanto vali,
    che qual vuol grazia ed a te non ricorre,
    sua disïanza vuol volar sanz'ali.
La tua benignità non pur soccorre
    a chi domanda, ma molte fïate
    liberamente al dimandar precorre.
In te misericordia, in te pietate,
    in te magnificenza, in te s'aduna
    quantunque in creatura è di bontate.
Or questi, che dall'infima lacuna
    dell'universo infin qui ha vedute
    le vite spiritali ad una ad una,
supplica a te, per grazia, di virtute
    tanto, che possa con li occhi levarsi
    più alto verso l'ultima salute.
E io, che mai per mio veder non arsi
    più ch'i' fo per lo suo, tutti miei preghi
    ti porgo, e priego che non sieno scarsi,
perchè tu ogni nube li disleghi
    di sua mortalità co' prieghi tuoi,
    sì che 'l sommo piacer li si dispieghi.
Ancor ti priego, regina, che puoi
    ciò che tu vuoli, che conservi sani,
    dopo tanto veder, li affetti suoi.
Vinca tua guardia i movimenti umani:

Canto XXXIII

"Virgin mother, daughter of your Son,
  humbler and more exalted than any other created being,
  established beginning of the eternal plan,[1]
you are the woman who so ennobled
  human nature that its Maker
  did not think it beneath Him to make Himself a thing made.
In your womb was kindled the love
  through whose warmth this flower[2]
  has thus sprouted here in eternal peace.
Here you are to us a noonday blaze
  of charity, and below, among mortals,
  you are a living wellspring of hope.
Lady, you are so great and your power is so great
  that whoever wishes grace and does not resort to you
  wishes his desire to fly without wings.
Your benevolence not only comes to the aid
  of those who request it, but many times
  generously anticipates the request.
In you mercy, in you pity,
  in you magnificence, in you is joined together
  all the goodness to be found in a created being.
Now this man who, from the lowest cavity
  in the universe all the way up here, has beheld
  the souls of men, one by one,
implores you to grant him, as a gracious favor, sufficient
  power so that he can raise his eyes
  higher, toward the ultimate source of salvation.
And I, who have never been more eager for my own sake to see this
  than I am for his sake, offer you
  all my prayers, and I pray that they may not be inadequate,
so that you may dispel from him every cloud
  of his mortality with your prayers,
  in order that the highest delight may be unfurled for him.
I also beg you, Queen, you who can do
  anything you wish, to preserve his affections
  in a sound condition after such a mighty vision.
Let your protection surmount his human inclinations:

---

1. The plan of redemption.   2. The "rose" of saints.

vedi Beatrice con quanti beati
per li miei preghi ti chiudon le mani!»
Li occhi da Dio diletti e venerati,
   fissi nell'orator, ne dimostraro
   quanto i devoti prieghi le son grati;
indi all'etterno lume si drizzaro,
   nel qual non si dee creder che s'invii
   per creatura l'occhio tanto chiaro.
E io ch'al fine di tutt'i disii
   appropinquava, sì com'io dovea,
   l'ardor del desiderio in me finii.
Bernardo m'accennava e sorridea
   perch'io guardassi suso; ma io era
   già per me stesso tal qual ei volea;
chè la mia vista, venendo sincera,
   e più e più intrava per lo raggio
   dell'alta luce che da sè è vera.
Da quinci innanzi il mio veder fu maggio
   che 'l parlar nostro, ch'a tal vista cede,
   e cede la memoria a tanto oltraggio.
Qual è colui che somnïando vede,
   che dopo il sogno la passione impressa
   rimane, e l'altro alla mente non riede,
cotal son io, chè quasi tutta cessa
   mia visïone, ed ancor mi distilla
   nel core il dolce che nacque da essa.
Così la neve al sol si disigilla;
   così al vento nelle foglie levi
   si perdea la sentenza di Sibilla.
O somma luce che tanto ti levi
   da' concetti mortali, alla mia mente
   ripresta un poco di quel che parevi,
e fa la lingua mia tanto possente,
   ch'una favilla sol della tua gloria
   possa lasciare alla futura gente;
chè, per tornare alquanto a mia memoria
   e per sonare un poco in questi versi,
   più si conceperà di tua vittoria.

see how Beatrice and all those saints
are clasping their hands in unison with my prayers to you!"
The eyes that are cherished and venerated by God,
fixed on the speaker, demonstrated to us
how pleasing devout prayers are to her;
then they were directed to the eternal light,
into which it must not be thought that the eyes
of any other created being can enter with equal clarity.
And approaching the final moment
of all my desires, as was proper for me to do,
I raised the ardor of my longing to its height.[3]
Bernard was indicating to me by signs and smiles
to look upward; but I was
already spontaneously acting as he wished;
for my sight, becoming pure,
penetrated more and more deeply into the ray
of exalted light that is intrinsically true.
From then on, my sight was superior
to human language, which succumbs to so great a sight,
just as our memory succumbs to a similar onslaught.
Like a man seeing things in a dream,
for whom, after the dream, the imprinted emotion
remains, while the rest does not return to his mind,
such am I now, because the details of my vision
are almost all gone, while the sweetness born of it
is distilled in my heart to this day.
In the same way, snow is unsealed in the sunshine;
in the same way the Sibyl's oracular response,
written on light leaves, used to be lost in the wind.[4]
O highest light, which is raised so far above
human concepts, lend again to my mind
a little of the form in which you appeared,
and make my tongue so powerful
that it can bequeath to posterity
even a single spark of your glory;
for, if it can return partially to my memory
and be recorded to some extent in these verses,
the greater will be man's conception of your victory.

---

3. Or (less preferable): "I brought the ardor of my longing to a termination."
4. The Cumaean Sibyl used to write her responses on tree leaves.

Io credo, per l'acume ch'io soffersi
   del vivo raggio, ch'i' sarei smarrito,
   se li occhi miei da lui fossero aversi.
E' mi ricorda ch'io fui più ardito
   per questo a sostener, tanto ch'i' giunsi
   l'aspetto mio col valore infinito.
Oh abbondante grazia ond'io presunsi
   ficcar lo viso per la luce etterna,
   tanto che la veduta vi consunsi!
Nel suo profondo vidi che s'interna
   legato con amore in un volume,
   ciò che per l'universo si squaderna;
sustanze e accidenti e lor costume,
   quasi conflati insieme, per tal modo
   che ciò ch'i' dico è un semplice lume.
La forma universal di questo nodo
   credo ch'i' vidi, perchè più di largo,
   dicendo questo, mi sento ch'i' godo.
Un punto solo m'è maggior letargo
   che venticinque secoli alla 'mpresa,
   che fè Nettuno ammirar l'ombra d'Argo.
Così la mente mia, tutta sospesa,
   mirava fissa, immobile e attenta,
   e sempre di mirar facìesi accesa.
A quella luce cotal si diventa,
   che volgersi da lei per altro aspetto
   è impossibil che mai si consenta;
però che 'l ben, ch'è del volere obietto,
   tutto s'accoglie in lei, e fuor di quella
   è defettivo ciò ch'è lì perfetto.
Omai sarà più corta mia favella,
   pur a quel ch'io ricordo, che d'un fante
   che bagni ancor la lingua alla mammella.
Non perchè più ch'un semplice sembiante

I believe that, because of the sharpness of the living ray
    that I endured, I would have been totally dazzled
    if my eyes had turned away from it.
I recall that, with this in mind, I became
    more emboldened to withstand it, until I linked up
    my sight to that infinite power.
Oh, grace abounding, thanks to which I presumed
    to fix my eyes on the eternal light
    until my power of sight reached its maximum![5]
In the depths of it I saw that it contains,
    bound by love into a single volume,
    that which exists in the universe as loose signatures:
essential substances, their contingent combinations, and their mode of combining,
    as if fused together, in such a fashion
    that what I speak of is a single light.[6]
I believe that I beheld the universal form
    of this combination, because, as I report this,
    I feel more amply joyful.
A single moment brought me greater loss of memory[7]
    than twenty-five centuries have done since the enterprise
    that made Neptune marvel at the shadow of the *Argo*.[8]
Just as he marveled, my mind, all in suspense,
    gazed fixedly, motionlessly, and attentively,
    growing more and more desirous of gazing.
In that light, one arrives at such a state
    that it is impossible one would ever consent
    to turn away from it to look at anything else;
because the good, which is the object of volition,
    is all gathered within it, and outside of it
    that which is perfect within it is defective.
From this point on, my words—to the extent I can recall things—
    will be fewer than those of a child
    that is still wetting its tongue at the breast.
Not because there was more than a single image

---

5. Or: "until my power of sight was spent."   6. Many commentators suggest the meaning: "that what I speak of is a mere hint (of what I saw)."   7. Either the vision made Dante forget everything else, or the moment of awakening from it (or a moment spent looking away from it) made him forget the vision.   8. The ship sailed by the Argonauts was said to be the first ship, so that Neptune (Poseidon) had never seen anything like it.

fosse nel vivo lume ch'io mirava,
  che tal è sempre qual s'era davante;
ma per la vista che s'avvalorava
  in me guardando, una sola parvenza,
  mutandom'io, a me si travagliava.
Nella profonda e chiara sussistenza
  dell'alto lume parvermi tre giri
  di tre colori e d'una contenenza;
e l'un dall'altro come iri da iri
  parea reflesso, e 'l terzo parea foco
  che quinci e quindi igualmente si spiri.
Oh quanto è corto il dire e come fioco
  al mio concetto! e questo, a quel ch'i' vidi,
  è tanto, che non basta a dicer 'poco'.
O luce etterna che sola in te sidi,
  sola t'intendi, e da te intelletta
  e intendente te ami e arridi!
Quella circulazion che sì concetta
  pareva in te come lume reflesso,
  dalli occhi miei alquanto circunspetta,
dentro da sè, del suo colore stesso,
  mi parve pinta della nostra effige;
  per che 'l mio viso in lei tutto era messo.
Qual è 'l geomètra che tutto s'affige
  per misurar lo cerchio, e non ritrova,
  pensando, quel principio ond'elli indige,
tal era io a quella vista nova:
  veder volea come si convenne
  l'imago al cerchio e come vi s'indova;
ma non eran da ciò le proprie penne:
  se non che la mia mente fu percossa
  da un fulgore in che sua voglia venne.
All'alta fantasia qui mancò possa;
  ma già volgeva il mio disio e 'l velle,
  si come rota ch'igualmente è mossa,
l'amor che move il sole e l'altre stelle.

within the living light I was gazing at,
for it remains always what it was before;
but because the power of sight was growing stronger
in me as I gazed, that single apparition
was being transformed for me[9] while I myself was changing.
Within the deep, clear substance
there appeared to me three circles of exalted light
with three colors and one amplitude;
and one of them seemed to be reflected from another
like one arch of a double rainbow from the other, while the third
seemed like fire emanating equally from the other two.[10]
Oh, how inadequate are my words and how inferior
to my conception! And even the latter, compared to what I saw,
falls so far short that to say "too little" is not enough.
O eternal light, you that reside solely in yourself,
are the only one to understand yourself, and, understood by yourself
and understanding yourself, you smile on us lovingly!
That circle which, in that conception of mine,
seemed like a reflected light within you,
when studied a little longer by my eyes
seemed to me to be painted with our human image
within itself and in its own color;
so that my eyes were completely fixed on it.
Just like a geometer who is totally absorbed
in squaring the circle but, in his chain of thought,
does not find the principle he is in need of,
just so was I at that new vision:
I wanted to see how the image
conformed to the circle and how it is situated within it;
but my own wings were not up to it:
except that my mind was struck
by a lightning flash in which its wish was granted.
At this point, power failed my high-soaring imagination;
but my desire and my volition were already being turned,
like a wheel that is uniformly set in motion,
by the love that moves the sun and the other stars.

---

9. This translation seems preferable to: "was causing me to make a greater effort."
10. God the Father is beaming light on the Son, while the Holy Spirit issues from both
of them.

A CATALOG OF SELECTED
DOVER BOOKS
IN ALL FIELDS OF INTEREST

A CATALOG OF SELECTED DOVER
BOOKS IN ALL FIELDS OF INTEREST

CONCERNING THE SPIRITUAL IN ART, Wassily Kandinsky. Pioneering work by father of abstract art. Thoughts on color theory, nature of art. Analysis of earlier masters. 12 illustrations. 80pp. of text. 5⅜ x 8½.   23411-8 Pa. $4.95

ANIMALS: 1,419 Copyright-Free Illustrations of Mammals, Birds, Fish, Insects, etc., Jim Harter (ed.). Clear wood engravings present, in extremely lifelike poses, over 1,000 species of animals. One of the most extensive pictorial sourcebooks of its kind. Captions. Index. 284pp. 9 x 12.   23766-4 Pa. $14.95

CELTIC ART: The Methods of Construction, George Bain. Simple geometric techniques for making Celtic interlacements, spirals, Kells-type initials, animals, humans, etc. Over 500 illustrations. 160pp. 9 x 12. (USO)   22923-8 Pa. $9.95

AN ATLAS OF ANATOMY FOR ARTISTS, Fritz Schider. Most thorough reference work on art anatomy in the world. Hundreds of illustrations, including selections from works by Vesalius, Leonardo, Goya, Ingres, Michelangelo, others. 593 illustrations. 192pp. 7⅛ x 10¼.   20241-0 Pa. $9.95

CELTIC HAND STROKE-BY-STROKE (Irish Half-Uncial from "The Book of Kells"): An Arthur Baker Calligraphy Manual, Arthur Baker. Complete guide to creating each letter of the alphabet in distinctive Celtic manner. Covers hand position, strokes, pens, inks, paper, more. Illustrated. 48pp. 8¼ x 11.   24336-2 Pa. $3.95

EASY ORIGAMI, John Montroll. Charming collection of 32 projects (hat, cup, pelican, piano, swan, many more) specially designed for the novice origami hobbyist. Clearly illustrated easy-to-follow instructions insure that even beginning papercrafters will achieve successful results. 48pp. 8¼ x 11.   27298-2 Pa. $3.50

THE COMPLETE BOOK OF BIRDHOUSE CONSTRUCTION FOR WOOD-WORKERS, Scott D. Campbell. Detailed instructions, illustrations, tables. Also data on bird habitat and instinct patterns. Bibliography. 3 tables. 63 illustrations in 15 figures. 48pp. 5¼ x 8½.   24407-5 Pa. $2.50

BLOOMINGDALE'S ILLUSTRATED 1886 CATALOG: Fashions, Dry Goods and Housewares, Bloomingdale Brothers. Famed merchants' extremely rare catalog depicting about 1,700 products: clothing, housewares, firearms, dry goods, jewelry, more. Invaluable for dating, identifying vintage items. Also, copyright-free graphics for artists, designers. Co-published with Henry Ford Museum & Greenfield Village. 160pp. 8¼ x 11.   25780-0 Pa. $10.95

HISTORIC COSTUME IN PICTURES, Braun & Schneider. Over 1,450 costumed figures in clearly detailed engravings–from dawn of civilization to end of 19th century. Captions. Many folk costumes. 256pp. 8⅜ x 11¾.   23150-X Pa. $12.95

CATALOG OF DOVER BOOKS

STICKLEY CRAFTSMAN FURNITURE CATALOGS, Gustav Stickley and L. & J. G. Stickley. Beautiful, functional furniture in two authentic catalogs from 1910. 594 illustrations, including 277 photos, show settles, rockers, armchairs, reclining chairs, bookcases, desks, tables. 183pp. 6½ x 9¼. 23838-5 Pa. $11.95

AMERICAN LOCOMOTIVES IN HISTORIC PHOTOGRAPHS: 1858 to 1949, Ron Ziel (ed.). A rare collection of 126 meticulously detailed official photographs, called "builder portraits," of American locomotives that majestically chronicle the rise of steam locomotive power in America. Introduction. Detailed captions. xi + 129pp. 9 x 12. 27393-8 Pa. $13.95

AMERICA'S LIGHTHOUSES: An Illustrated History, Francis Ross Holland, Jr. Delightfully written, profusely illustrated fact-filled survey of over 200 American lighthouses since 1716. History, anecdotes, technological advances, more. 240pp. 8 x 10¾. 25576-X Pa. $12.95

TOWARDS A NEW ARCHITECTURE, Le Corbusier. Pioneering manifesto by founder of "International School." Technical and aesthetic theories, views of industry, economics, relation of form to function, "mass-production split" and much more. Profusely illustrated. 320pp. 6⅛ x 9¼. (USO) 25023-7 Pa. $9.95

HOW THE OTHER HALF LIVES, Jacob Riis. Famous journalistic record, exposing poverty and degradation of New York slums around 1900, by major social reformer. 100 striking and influential photographs. 233pp. 10 x 7⅞. 22012-5 Pa. $11.95

FRUIT KEY AND TWIG KEY TO TREES AND SHRUBS, William M. Harlow. One of the handiest and most widely used identification aids. Fruit key covers 120 deciduous and evergreen species; twig key 160 deciduous species. Easily used. Over 300 photographs. 126pp. 5⅜ x 8½. 20511-8 Pa. $3.95

COMMON BIRD SONGS, Dr. Donald J. Borror. Songs of 60 most common U.S. birds: robins, sparrows, cardinals, bluejays, finches, more—arranged in order of increasing complexity. Up to 9 variations of songs of each species.
Cassette and manual 99911-4 $8.95

ORCHIDS AS HOUSE PLANTS, Rebecca Tyson Northen. Grow cattleyas and many other kinds of orchids—in a window, in a case, or under artificial light. 63 illustrations. 148pp. 5⅜ x 8½. 23261-1 Pa. $5.95

MONSTER MAZES, Dave Phillips. Masterful mazes at four levels of difficulty. Avoid deadly perils and evil creatures to find magical treasures. Solutions for all 32 exciting illustrated puzzles. 48pp. 8¼ x 11. 26005-4 Pa. $2.95

MOZART'S DON GIOVANNI (DOVER OPERA LIBRETTO SERIES), Wolfgang Amadeus Mozart. Introduced and translated by Ellen H. Bleiler. Standard Italian libretto, with complete English translation. Convenient and thoroughly portable—an ideal companion for reading along with a recording or the performance itself. Introduction. List of characters. Plot summary. 121pp. 5¼ x 8½. 24944-1 Pa. $3.95

TECHNICAL MANUAL AND DICTIONARY OF CLASSICAL BALLET, Gail Grant. Defines, explains, comments on steps, movements, poses and concepts. 15-page pictorial section. Basic book for student, viewer. 127pp. 5⅜ x 8½. 21843-0 Pa. $4.95

BRASS INSTRUMENTS: Their History and Development, Anthony Baines. Authoritative, updated survey of the evolution of trumpets, trombones, bugles, cornets, French horns, tubas and other brass wind instruments. Over 140 illustrations and 48 music examples. Corrected and updated by author. New preface. Bibliography. 320pp. 5⅜ x 8½. 27574-4 Pa. $9.95

HOLLYWOOD GLAMOR PORTRAITS, John Kobal (ed.). 145 photos from 1926-49. Harlow, Gable, Bogart, Bacall; 94 stars in all. Full background on photographers, technical aspects. 160pp. 8⅜ x 11¼. 23352-9 Pa. $12.95

MAX AND MORITZ, Wilhelm Busch. Great humor classic in both German and English. Also 10 other works: "Cat and Mouse," "Plisch and Plumm," etc. 216pp. 5⅜ x 8½. 20181-3 Pa. $6.95

THE RAVEN AND OTHER FAVORITE POEMS, Edgar Allan Poe. Over 40 of the author's most memorable poems: "The Bells," "Ulalume," "Israfel," "To Helen," "The Conqueror Worm," "Eldorado," "Annabel Lee," many more. Alphabetic lists of titles and first lines. 64pp. 5 3/16 x 8¼. 26685-0 Pa. $1.00

PERSONAL MEMOIRS OF U. S. GRANT, Ulysses Simpson Grant. Intelligent, deeply moving firsthand account of Civil War campaigns, considered by many the finest military memoirs ever written. Includes letters, historic photographs, maps and more. 528pp. 6⅛ x 9¼. 28587-1 Pa. $12.95

AMULETS AND SUPERSTITIONS, E. A. Wallis Budge. Comprehensive discourse on origin, powers of amulets in many ancient cultures: Arab, Persian Babylonian, Assyrian, Egyptian, Gnostic, Hebrew, Phoenician, Syriac, etc. Covers cross, swastika, crucifix, seals, rings, stones, etc. 584pp. 5⅜ x 8½. 23573-4 Pa. $15.95

RUSSIAN STORIES/PYCCKNE PACCKA3bl: A Dual-Language Book, edited by Gleb Struve. Twelve tales by such masters as Chekhov, Tolstoy, Dostoevsky, Pushkin, others. Excellent word-for-word English translations on facing pages, plus teaching and study aids, Russian/English vocabulary, biographical/critical introductions, more. 416pp. 5⅜ x 8½. 26244-8 Pa. $9.95

PHILADELPHIA THEN AND NOW: 60 Sites Photographed in the Past and Present, Kenneth Finkel and Susan Oyama. Rare photographs of City Hall, Logan Square, Independence Hall, Betsy Ross House, other landmarks juxtaposed with contemporary views. Captures changing face of historic city. Introduction. Captions. 128pp. 8¼ x 11. 25790-8 Pa. $9.95

AIA ARCHITECTURAL GUIDE TO NASSAU AND SUFFOLK COUNTIES, LONG ISLAND, The American Institute of Architects, Long Island Chapter, and the Society for the Preservation of Long Island Antiquities. Comprehensive, well-researched and generously illustrated volume brings to life over three centuries of Long Island's great architectural heritage. More than 240 photographs with authoritative, extensively detailed captions. 176pp. 8¼ x 11. 26946-9 Pa. $14.95

NORTH AMERICAN INDIAN LIFE: Customs and Traditions of 23 Tribes, Elsie Clews Parsons (ed.). 27 fictionalized essays by noted anthropologists examine religion, customs, government, additional facets of life among the Winnebago, Crow, Zuni, Eskimo, other tribes. 480pp. 6⅛ x 9¼. 27377-6 Pa. $10.95

FRANK LLOYD WRIGHT'S HOLLYHOCK HOUSE, Donald Hoffmann. Lavishly illustrated, carefully documented study of one of Wright's most controversial residential designs. Over 120 photographs, floor plans, elevations, etc. Detailed perceptive text by noted Wright scholar. Index. 128pp. 9¼ x 10¾. 27133-1 Pa. $11.95

THE MALE AND FEMALE FIGURE IN MOTION: 60 Classic Photographic Sequences, Eadweard Muybridge. 60 true-action photographs of men and women walking, running, climbing, bending, turning, etc., reproduced from rare 19th-century masterpiece. vi + 121pp. 9 x 12. 24745-7 Pa. $10.95

1001 QUESTIONS ANSWERED ABOUT THE SEASHORE, N. J. Berrill and Jacquelyn Berrill. Queries answered about dolphins, sea snails, sponges, starfish, fishes, shore birds, many others. Covers appearance, breeding, growth, feeding, much more. 305pp. 5¼ x 8¼. 23366-9 Pa. $9.95

GUIDE TO OWL WATCHING IN NORTH AMERICA, Donald S. Heintzelman. Superb guide offers complete data and descriptions of 19 species: barn owl, screech owl, snowy owl, many more. Expert coverage of owl-watching equipment, conservation, migrations and invasions, etc. Guide to observing sites. 84 illustrations. xiii + 193pp. 5⅜ x 8½. 27344-X Pa. $8.95

MEDICINAL AND OTHER USES OF NORTH AMERICAN PLANTS: A Historical Survey with Special Reference to the Eastern Indian Tribes, Charlotte Erichsen-Brown. Chronological historical citations document 500 years of usage of plants, trees, shrubs native to eastern Canada, northeastern U.S. Also complete identifying information. 343 illustrations. 544pp. 6½ x 9¼. 25951-X Pa. $12.95

STORYBOOK MAZES, Dave Phillips. 23 stories and mazes on two-page spreads: Wizard of Oz, Treasure Island, Robin Hood, etc. Solutions. 64pp. 8¼ x 11. 23628-5 Pa. $2.95

NEGRO FOLK MUSIC, U.S.A., Harold Courlander. Noted folklorist's scholarly yet readable analysis of rich and varied musical tradition. Includes authentic versions of over 40 folk songs. Valuable bibliography and discography. xi + 324pp. 5⅜ x 8½. 27350-4 Pa. $9.95

MOVIE-STAR PORTRAITS OF THE FORTIES, John Kobal (ed.). 163 glamor, studio photos of 106 stars of the 1940s: Rita Hayworth, Ava Gardner, Marlon Brando, Clark Gable, many more. 176pp. 8⅜ x 11¼. 23546-7 Pa. $14.95

BENCHLEY LOST AND FOUND, Robert Benchley. Finest humor from early 30s, about pet peeves, child psychologists, post office and others. Mostly unavailable elsewhere. 73 illustrations by Peter Arno and others. 183pp. 5⅜ x 8½. 22410-4 Pa. $6.95

YEKL and THE IMPORTED BRIDEGROOM AND OTHER STORIES OF YIDDISH NEW YORK, Abraham Cahan. Film Hester Street based on Yekl (1896). Novel, other stories among first about Jewish immigrants on N.Y.'s East Side. 240pp. 5⅜ x 8½. 22427-9 Pa. $6.95

SELECTED POEMS, Walt Whitman. Generous sampling from *Leaves of Grass*. Twenty-four poems include "I Hear America Singing," "Song of the Open Road," "I Sing the Body Electric," "When Lilacs Last in the Dooryard Bloom'd," "O Captain! My Captain!"–all reprinted from an authoritative edition. Lists of titles and first lines. 128pp. 5$\frac{3}{16}$ x 8¼. 26878-0 Pa. $1.00

THE BEST TALES OF HOFFMANN, E. T. A. Hoffmann. 10 of Hoffmann's most important stories: "Nutcracker and the King of Mice," "The Golden Flowerpot," etc. 458pp. 5⅜ x 8½. 21793-0 Pa. $9.95

FROM FETISH TO GOD IN ANCIENT EGYPT, E. A. Wallis Budge. Rich detailed survey of Egyptian conception of "God" and gods, magic, cult of animals, Osiris, more. Also, superb English translations of hymns and legends. 240 illustrations. 545pp. 5⅜ x 8½. 25803-3 Pa. $13.95

FRENCH STORIES/CONTES FRANÇAIS: A Dual-Language Book, Wallace Fowlie. Ten stories by French masters, Voltaire to Camus: "Micromegas" by Voltaire; "The Atheist's Mass" by Balzac; "Minuet" by de Maupassant; "The Guest" by Camus, six more. Excellent English translations on facing pages. Also French-English vocabulary list, exercises, more. 352pp. 5⅜ x 8½. 26443-2 Pa. $9.95

CHICAGO AT THE TURN OF THE CENTURY IN PHOTOGRAPHS: 122 Historic Views from the Collections of the Chicago Historical Society, Larry A. Viskochil. Rare large-format prints offer detailed views of City Hall, State Street, the Loop, Hull House, Union Station, many other landmarks, circa 1904-1913. Introduction. Captions. Maps. 144pp. 9⅜ x 12¼. 24656-6 Pa. $12.95

OLD BROOKLYN IN EARLY PHOTOGRAPHS, 1865-1929, William Lee Younger. Luna Park, Gravesend race track, construction of Grand Army Plaza, moving of Hotel Brighton, etc. 157 previously unpublished photographs. 165pp. 8⅞ x 11¾. 23587-4 Pa. $13.95

THE MYTHS OF THE NORTH AMERICAN INDIANS, Lewis Spence. Rich anthology of the myths and legends of the Algonquins, Iroquois, Pawnees and Sioux, prefaced by an extensive historical and ethnological commentary. 36 illustrations. 480pp. 5⅜ x 8½. 25967-6 Pa. $10.95

AN ENCYCLOPEDIA OF BATTLES: Accounts of Over 1,560 Battles from 1479 B.C. to the Present, David Eggenberger. Essential details of every major battle in recorded history from the first battle of Megiddo in 1479 B.C. to Grenada in 1984. List of Battle Maps. New Appendix covering the years 1967-1984. Index. 99 illustrations. 544pp. 6½ x 9¼. 24913-1 Pa. $16.95

SAILING ALONE AROUND THE WORLD, Captain Joshua Slocum. First man to sail around the world, alone, in small boat. One of great feats of seamanship told in delightful manner. 67 illustrations. 294pp. 5⅜ x 8½. 20326-3 Pa. $6.95

ANARCHISM AND OTHER ESSAYS, Emma Goldman. Powerful, penetrating, prophetic essays on direct action, role of minorities, prison reform, puritan hypocrisy, violence, etc. 271pp. 5⅜ x 8½. 22484-8 Pa. $7.95

MYTHS OF THE HINDUS AND BUDDHISTS, Ananda K. Coomaraswamy and Sister Nivedita. Great stories of the epics; deeds of Krishna, Shiva, taken from puranas, Vedas, folk tales; etc. 32 illustrations. 400pp. 5⅜ x 8½. 21759-0 Pa. $12.95

BEYOND PSYCHOLOGY, Otto Rank. Fear of death, desire of immortality, nature of sexuality, social organization, creativity, according to Rankian system. 291pp. 5⅜ x 8½. 20485-5 Pa. $8.95

A THEOLOGICO-POLITICAL TREATISE, Benedict Spinoza. Also contains unfinished Political Treatise. Great classic on religious liberty, theory of government on common consent. R. Elwes translation. Total of 421pp. 5⅜ x 8½. 20249-6 Pa. $9.95

MY BONDAGE AND MY FREEDOM, Frederick Douglass. Born a slave, Douglass became outspoken force in antislavery movement. The best of Douglass' autobiographies. Graphic description of slave life. 464pp. 5⅜ x 8½. 22457-0 Pa. $8.95

FOLLOWING THE EQUATOR: A Journey Around the World, Mark Twain. Fascinating humorous account of 1897 voyage to Hawaii, Australia, India, New Zealand, etc. Ironic, bemused reports on peoples, customs, climate, flora and fauna, politics, much more. 197 illustrations. 720pp. 5⅜ x 8½. 26113-1 Pa. $15.95

THE PEOPLE CALLED SHAKERS, Edward D. Andrews. Definitive study of Shakers: origins, beliefs, practices, dances, social organization, furniture and crafts, etc. 33 illustrations. 351pp. 5⅜ x 8½. 21081-2 Pa. $8.95

THE MYTHS OF GREECE AND ROME, H. A. Guerber. A classic of mythology, generously illustrated, long prized for its simple, graphic, accurate retelling of the principal myths of Greece and Rome, and for its commentary on their origins and significance. With 64 illustrations by Michelangelo, Raphael, Titian, Rubens, Canova, Bernini and others. 480pp. 5⅜ x 8½. 27584-1 Pa. $9.95

PSYCHOLOGY OF MUSIC, Carl E. Seashore. Classic work discusses music as a medium from psychological viewpoint. Clear treatment of physical acoustics, auditory apparatus, sound perception, development of musical skills, nature of musical feeling, host of other topics. 88 figures. 408pp. 5⅜ x 8½. 21851-1 Pa. $11.95

THE PHILOSOPHY OF HISTORY, Georg W. Hegel. Great classic of Western thought develops concept that history is not chance but rational process, the evolution of freedom. 457pp. 5⅜ x 8½. 20112-0 Pa. $9.95

THE BOOK OF TEA, Kakuzo Okakura. Minor classic of the Orient: entertaining, charming explanation, interpretation of traditional Japanese culture in terms of tea ceremony. 94pp. 5⅜ x 8½. 20070-1 Pa. $3.95

LIFE IN ANCIENT EGYPT, Adolf Erman. Fullest, most thorough, detailed older account with much not in more recent books, domestic life, religion, magic, medicine, commerce, much more. Many illustrations reproduce tomb paintings, carvings, hieroglyphs, etc. 597pp. 5⅜ x 8½. 22632-8 Pa. $12.95

SUNDIALS, Their Theory and Construction, Albert Waugh. Far and away the best, most thorough coverage of ideas, mathematics concerned, types, construction, adjusting anywhere. Simple, nontechnical treatment allows even children to build several of these dials. Over 100 illustrations. 230pp. 5⅜ x 8½. 22947-5 Pa. $8.95

DYNAMICS OF FLUIDS IN POROUS MEDIA, Jacob Bear. For advanced students of ground water hydrology, soil mechanics and physics, drainage and irrigation engineering, and more. 335 illustrations. Exercises, with answers. 784pp. 6⅛ x 9¼. 65675-6 Pa. $19.95

SONGS OF EXPERIENCE: Facsimile Reproduction with 26 Plates in Full Color, William Blake. 26 full-color plates from a rare 1826 edition. Includes "The Tyger," "London," "Holy Thursday," and other poems. Printed text of poems. 48pp. 5¼ x 7. 24636-1 Pa. $4.95

OLD-TIME VIGNETTES IN FULL COLOR, Carol Belanger Grafton (ed.). Over 390 charming, often sentimental illustrations, selected from archives of Victorian graphics—pretty women posing, children playing, food, flowers, kittens and puppies, smiling cherubs, birds and butterflies, much more. All copyright-free. 48pp. 9¼ x 12¼. 27269-9 Pa. $7.95

PERSPECTIVE FOR ARTISTS, Rex Vicat Cole. Depth, perspective of sky and sea, shadows, much more, not usually covered. 391 diagrams, 81 reproductions of drawings and paintings. 279pp. 5⅜ x 8½. 22487-2 Pa. $7.95

DRAWING THE LIVING FIGURE, Joseph Sheppard. Innovative approach to artistic anatomy focuses on specifics of surface anatomy, rather than muscles and bones. Over 170 drawings of live models in front, back and side views, and in widely varying poses. Accompanying diagrams. 177 illustrations. Introduction. Index. 144pp. 8⅜ x11¼. 26723-7 Pa. $8.95

GOTHIC AND OLD ENGLISH ALPHABETS: 100 Complete Fonts, Dan X. Solo. Add power, elegance to posters, signs, other graphics with 100 stunning copyright-free alphabets: Blackstone, Dolbey, Germania, 97 more–including many lower-case, numerals, punctuation marks. 104pp. 8⅛ x 11. 24695-7 Pa. $8.95

HOW TO DO BEADWORK, Mary White. Fundamental book on craft from simple projects to five-bead chains and woven works. 106 illustrations. 142pp. 5⅜ x 8. 20697-1 Pa. $5.95

THE BOOK OF WOOD CARVING, Charles Marshall Sayers. Finest book for beginners discusses fundamentals and offers 34 designs. "Absolutely first rate . . . well thought out and well executed."–E. J. Tangerman. 118pp. 7¾ x 10⅝. 23654-4 Pa. $7.95

ILLUSTRATED CATALOG OF CIVIL WAR MILITARY GOODS: Union Army Weapons, Insignia, Uniform Accessories, and Other Equipment, Schuyler, Hartley, and Graham. Rare, profusely illustrated 1846 catalog includes Union Army uniform and dress regulations, arms and ammunition, coats, insignia, flags, swords, rifles, etc. 226 illustrations. 160pp. 9 x 12. 24939-5 Pa. $10.95

WOMEN'S FASHIONS OF THE EARLY 1900s: An Unabridged Republication of "New York Fashions, 1909," National Cloak & Suit Co. Rare catalog of mail-order fashions documents women's and children's clothing styles shortly after the turn of the century. Captions offer full descriptions, prices. Invaluable resource for fashion, costume historians. Approximately 725 illustrations. 128pp. 8⅜ x 11¼. 27276-1 Pa. $11.95

THE 1912 AND 1915 GUSTAV STICKLEY FURNITURE CATALOGS, Gustav Stickley. With over 200 detailed illustrations and descriptions, these two catalogs are essential reading and reference materials and identification guides for Stickley furniture. Captions cite materials, dimensions and prices. 112pp. 6½ x 9¼. 26676-1 Pa. $9.95

EARLY AMERICAN LOCOMOTIVES, John H. White, Jr. Finest locomotive engravings from early 19th century: historical (1804–74), main-line (after 1870), special, foreign, etc. 147 plates. 142pp. 11⅜ x 8¼. 22772-3 Pa. $10.95

THE TALL SHIPS OF TODAY IN PHOTOGRAPHS, Frank O. Braynard. Lavishly illustrated tribute to nearly 100 majestic contemporary sailing vessels: Amerigo Vespucci, Clearwater, Constitution, Eagle, Mayflower, Sea Cloud, Victory, many more. Authoritative captions provide statistics, background on each ship. 190 black-and-white photographs and illustrations. Introduction. 128pp. 8⅞ x 11¾. 27163-3 Pa. $14.95

THE INFLUENCE OF SEA POWER UPON HISTORY, 1660–1783, A. T. Mahan. Influential classic of naval history and tactics still used as text in war colleges. First paperback edition. 4 maps. 24 battle plans. 640pp. 5⅜ x 8½. 25509-3 Pa. $14.95

THE STORY OF THE TITANIC AS TOLD BY ITS SURVIVORS, Jack Winocour (ed.). What it was really like. Panic, despair, shocking inefficiency, and a little heroism. More thrilling than any fictional account. 26 illustrations. 320pp. 5⅜ x 8½. 20610-6 Pa. $8.95

FAIRY AND FOLK TALES OF THE IRISH PEASANTRY, William Butler Yeats (ed.). Treasury of 64 tales from the twilight world of Celtic myth and legend: "The Soul Cages," "The Kildare Pooka," "King O'Toole and his Goose," many more. Introduction and Notes by W. B. Yeats. 352pp. 5⅜ x 8½. 26941-8 Pa. $8.95

BUDDHIST MAHAYANA TEXTS, E. B. Cowell and Others (eds.). Superb, accurate translations of basic documents in Mahayana Buddhism, highly important in history of religions. The Buddha-karita of Asvaghosha, Larger Sukhavativyuha, more. 448pp. 5⅜ x 8½. 25552-2 Pa. $12.95

ONE TWO THREE . . . INFINITY: Facts and Speculations of Science, George Gamow. Great physicist's fascinating, readable overview of contemporary science: number theory, relativity, fourth dimension, entropy, genes, atomic structure, much more. 128 illustrations. Index. 352pp. 5⅜ x 8½. 25664-2 Pa. $8.95

ENGINEERING IN HISTORY, Richard Shelton Kirby, et al. Broad, nontechnical survey of history's major technological advances: birth of Greek science, industrial revolution, electricity and applied science, 20th-century automation, much more. 181 illustrations. ". . . excellent . . ."–*Isis*. Bibliography. vii + 530pp. 5⅜ x 8¼. 26412-2 Pa. $14.95

DALÍ ON MODERN ART: The Cuckolds of Antiquated Modern Art, Salvador Dalí. Influential painter skewers modern art and its practitioners. Outrageous evaluations of Picasso, Cézanne, Turner, more. 15 renderings of paintings discussed. 44 calligraphic decorations by Dalí. 96pp. 5⅜ x 8½. (USO) 29220-7 Pa. $4.95

ANTIQUE PLAYING CARDS: A Pictorial History, Henry René D'Allemagne. Over 900 elaborate, decorative images from rare playing cards (14th–20th centuries): Bacchus, death, dancing dogs, hunting scenes, royal coats of arms, players cheating, much more. 96pp. 9¼ x 12¼. 29265-7 Pa. $12.95

MAKING FURNITURE MASTERPIECES: 30 Projects with Measured Drawings, Franklin H. Gottshall. Step-by-step instructions, illustrations for constructing handsome, useful pieces, among them a Sheraton desk, Chippendale chair, Spanish desk, Queen Anne table and a William and Mary dressing mirror. 224pp. 8⅛ x 11¼. 29338-6 Pa. $13.95

THE FOSSIL BOOK: A Record of Prehistoric Life, Patricia V. Rich et al. Profusely illustrated definitive guide covers everything from single-celled organisms and dinosaurs to birds and mammals and the interplay between climate and man. Over 1,500 illustrations. 760pp. 7½ x 10⅛. 29371-8 Pa. $29.95

Prices subject to change without notice.

Available at your book dealer or write for free catalog to Dept. GI, Dover Publications, Inc., 31 East 2nd St., Mineola, N.Y. 11501. Dover publishes more than 500 books each year on science, elementary and advanced mathematics, biology, music, art, literary history, social sciences and other areas.